Jealous God

To Chris,

with many thanks for

all your help

Mary x

ISBN-13: 978-1518786570

To John,
in the hope that one day,
things may be different.

Thank you, Roger, for your encouragement and love; Gordon Snr for your help with editing; Gordon Jnr and Rachel for your enthusiasm; my writing group – Chris, John, John and Muriel – for your invaluable feedback; and the staff of my local library for finding me all those books...

CHAPTER 1

July 1199
Fontevraud Abbey; on the border of the three provinces of Anjou, Touraine and Poitou

The second funeral of the Countess of Toulouse, the first having taken place in Rouen, was nearing its closing stages and Matthieu smothered his irritation. If only it had been Catharine, demurely veiled and with eyes downcast who diverted his attention. That would at least be forgivable for they were betrothed to be married soon; but unfortunately it was her younger sister, Joana, who captivated him every time he looked in their direction.

Matthieu put a finger into the collar of his robe and felt sweat soaking into the velvet. Even the thick stone walls of Fontevraud Abbey could not keep out the heat of this hot summer day. In the south, where he now lived, fashions were much less formal and he wasn't used to having to wear such ostentatious garments – even at funerals. He sighed and tried to turn his attention back to the altar, but...

What was it about the girl that attracted him? True, her beauty was hinted at, rather than full-blown. Today her thick black hair had been hidden beneath a netted caul, and her gown was plain, as befitted the younger daughter of an impoverished noble; but it was the little things that entranced him – the nape of her neck where her hair disappeared into the net, the laughter in her eyes as she watched everywhere the spectacle unfolding about her, and the generous smile that lit up not only her face but the faces of those around her.

This would not do. Matthieu forced his eyes back towards the altar, but whichever way he looked there was distraction. On the front seats, nobles loyal to the Plantagenet kings jostled to outdo each other, and their jewelled belts and caps sparkled in the light that streamed through the high stained-glass windows. The Countess' bier stood in the centre of the nave, draped in a purple velvet pall, and about it burned five red candles, one for each of the wounds of Christ. On the altar Matthieu counted seven silver candlesticks, one for each gift of the Holy Spirit, and seven silver chalices, one for each of the priests who stood with their arms raised heavenward, golden vestments shining like the sun.

When the Bishop elevated the slim white Host before the congregation, Matthieu knelt down and clasped his hands. *Please God, forgive me – a poor sinner. Forgive the treacherous thoughts of my heart.* The altar servers swung their silver thuribles, releasing clouds of fragrant incense and everyone bowed their heads. Finally, blessedly, Matthieu managed to still his wayward thoughts long enough to pray for the Countess' soul, and to pray that when they were married, he would become a loving and loyal husband to Catharine.

At the close of the service, the newly-crowned Plantagenet king, John of England, escorted his sister's coffin from the Abbey. He was closely followed by his mother, the dowager Queen Aliénor, Duchess of Aquitaine. The Queen had lost two of her children in the previous three months, the other being her favourite, Richard 'the Lion Hearted'. Matthieu thought it unlikely that she would be in the mood for the letter he carried at his breast.

*

'Matthieu.'

As he came out of the Abbey church, into the full glare of the sun, Matthieu heard the Queen calling to him from the shade of cloister, and his heart stuttered in his chest. This was the moment he had been dreading, for he carried a letter from the Count of Toulouse.

Although Aliénor was now well into her seventh decade, her figure was still slender and starkly accentuated by the white silk mourning robe she wore. Her eyes had lost none of the fire of her youth – but the skin of her hand felt papery as Matthieu brought it to his lips.

'Your Grace,' he said, dropping to his knees and bowing his head low. 'May I offer you my deepest condolences.'

He took the scroll from inside his robe and held it out to her, and with the faintest wiggle of her fingers, Aliénor indicated that he should rise.

'This is from Count Raimon, I take it?' she said, accepting but not opening the scroll.

Matthieu saw her eyes narrow, and knew that the Count's lavishly expressed regrets could not in any way be considered sincere, as he had never forgiven his wife for deserting him.

He nodded. 'He is inconsolable, and might I add that I wish I had died myself, instead of our beloved Countess.'

'You could not have prevented her death,' Aliénor said. 'Even God did not see fit to do that.' He watched light and pain alternating on her face as the altar servers filed past, carrying candles. 'She was badly burned and she was pregnant... did you know? The babe didn't survive either. You'd better tell Count Raimon that.'

Matthieu nodded and watched the Queen nip in her lower lip to stop it from trembling.

'He's in there with her,' she said, gesturing as the coffin passed by them. 'We named him Richard...' Aliénor closed her eyes briefly and then seemed to collect herself. 'How is my grandson, Raimondet?'

Matthieu took a breath. This was a less contentious subject, and one he knew quite a lot about. 'Strong and fearless – as you might expect, given his lineage,' he said. 'My lady mother dotes on him, and I'm to be his tutor as soon as he's old enough.'

The Queen's eyes narrowed again and tension began to rise in Matthieu's neck; but it was with relief that he realised she was looking beyond his shoulder.

'John!'

Matthieu turned to see John of England, talking to Catharine and Joana, as they waited outside the church with the other women. He heard Joana's laugh ring out and felt a throb of alarm and jealousy. There was danger in her encouraging a man as unprincipled as John. At least Catharine's eyes were properly lowered. They would need to take a firm hand with the girl, once he and Catharine were married.

'Did you want something, Maman?' John asked, coming towards them, one eyebrow quizzically raised.

Matthieu saw bright spots appearing on Joana's face as she suddenly realised to whom she'd been talking. Queen Aliénor took hold of John's arm and steered him away, and left Matthieu unsure what to do. Should he greet Catharine? She was looking at him with a pleasure rarely seen on her normally sombre face, but his business with the Queen wasn't over, yet.

'Lady Catharine,' he said, sweeping her a bow.

'Sir Matthieu,' Catharine murmured. 'Such sad news about the Countess. Her husband must be distraught.'

'Yes,' Matthieu said, recalling the Count had barely managed to drag himself out of the arms of his latest mistress, in order to dictate the letter to Queen Aliénor.

'Hello, Matthieu,' Joana said, coming forwards. 'It's an unexpected pleasure to see you here today, even though it is such a sad occasion.'

'Lady Joana.' Matthieu kept his expression neutral but inside he was cursing. Didn't the girl know how to behave around men when she was in public? Whatever was their mother thinking of? Joana was nearly thirteen now – almost a woman, and her skin was as fresh and white as the may blossom. There was an eagerness about her that stirred not only his heart but less worthy parts of Matthieu's body. Dear God.

'Please forgive me,' he said, backing away. 'I must return to the Queen.'

Joana's face fell, but Catharine merely returned to looking at the ground. At least one of them had been schooled in how to behave, pity it hadn't extended to Joana.

Matthieu found John and Queen Aliénor standing at the far side of the cloister. The Queen was looking up at the bleached walls of the Abbey as if she never wanted to leave them again. John's voice had risen a notch.

'I'd like to see you safely in England this winter,' he said. 'Don't you realise what's going to happen here now Richard is dead?'

'Of course I do,' Aliénor sighed, 'but I feel the need to stay, for now.

Eighteen years in England, as your father's prisoner, was quite long enough for me. I never want to pass another winter there, if I can help it.'

John's lip pouted. 'As you wish.'

'I shall be in Castile in the new year...'

'Are you absolutely sure you wish to travel over the Pyrenees, in winter?' John said.

'There's no one else who *can* go now, is there?' the Queen said. 'Hardly any of us left, in case you hadn't noticed.'

John flushed and dragged his toe across the ground. Matthieu was amused. Even a king could be reduced to a boy by his mother.

'May I congratulate you, Maman.' John said. 'No one else could have persuaded the King of France to marry his son into our family.'

Matthieu decided that he couldn't eavesdrop much longer without being caught, and coughed to attract their attention. He he was anxious to be away because the Count had demanded that he return to Toulouse as soon as possible.

'Ah, Matthieu,' the Queen said, turning towards him. 'I need to talk to you about my daughter's will. I'd like you to take the terms of it back with you to Toulouse.'

'Your Grace,' he said, already dreading what those terms might be.

'Are we to be introduced?' John said, peevishly. He obviously resented being interrupted before he had got his way.

'Of course,' Aliénor said. 'This is Sir Matthieu of Poitiers. His mother was in my service, before your father saw fit to imprison me, and he is now at the court of Count Raimon in Toulouse. Matthieu is betrothed to Catharine of Tours. You were talking to her sister earlier.'

'Catharine of Tours?' John's eyes danced. 'Ah, yes. Pity you're not marrying the younger one, Matthieu.'

'John-' The Queen checked herself. 'Joana is but a child and Catharine a lovely young woman. Your father, Matthieu, God rest his soul, is to be congratulated on making such a fine match for you.'

'Well, she might be a child now,' John persisted, 'but I'd vouch she's very soon to be a woman.'

Aliénor looked away and Matthieu saw her jaw clench. When the Queen's seneschal arrived, he was relieved to be able to take his leave; but once he was safely out of sight beyond the Abbey's many chimneyed kitchen, he drew an unsteady breath and slammed his fist into the wall. If only Joana *were* the older sister! His heart twisted in his breast. Why could he not just accept his fate? His father had betrothed him to Catharine, a good and virtuous woman who would make him an excellent, well-connected wife. But Joana she was not.

CHAPTER 2

March 1538
Glastonbury Abbey, England

'Matthew, my son, I have a task for you,' Abbot Whiting said, leading Matthew into the darkened crypt beneath Glastonbury Abbey.

The tall, white haired Abbot walked sure-footedly before Matthew towards the altar and lit a candle. To Matthew's surprise, there was stranger kneeling there, dressed in travelling clothes. He was not tonsured like the monks at the Abbey, and his face bore a moustache that pointed downwards over his mouth, like the hands of a clock.

'We shall pray to the Blessed Lord, for your safety,' the Abbot said, kneeling before the altar, but not giving any explanation of the stranger.

'What is it you would have me do, my lord?' Matthew said, looking about himself with trepidation. He was only a pupil at the Abbey, not even a novice. Why should the Abbot have chosen him?

'Shh,' Abbot Whiting said, but not unkindly, 'prayers first.' He bent his head and prayed a decade of the Rosary out-loud, contemplating the Sorrowful Mystery of The Carrying of the Cross. Then he looked up to the altar and said: 'Dear Lord, look kindly upon Matthew, your servant, make straight his path and bring him safely back into our arms.'

The Abbot reached deep into sleeve of his robe. 'I have a message for Father Peter here,' he said. 'You will need to take it to Canterbury, and this is very important, Matthew, speak to no one if you can help it, neither on the road nor in Canterbury. Father Peter will meet you in the cathedral and give you a package.' The Abbot took a deep breath and Matthew glanced out of the corner of his eye at the man who still knelt to his right, in front the altar. Why was he there?

'You must guard the package with your life, Matthew,' the Abbot said, grimly, and a chill shook its way down Matthew's spine. 'Do you understand? This is God's work. If anyone presses you, say only that you are visiting your choir master to undertake voice training and must keep silent.'

The blood buzzed madly in Matthew's ears as he struggled to understand. Not only was he being chosen for an important task, but he was to go to Canterbury, the burial place of blessed Saint Thomas Becket! Many were the miracles he'd heard about that had been performed by the Saint, and there was a matter very close to Matthew's heart right now that needed a miracle.

'When do I leave, my lord?' he asked, getting to his feet.

'As soon as we've finished praying,' the Abbot said, pulling him back down again.

*

Matthew knew how to travel. His father had been a woodcutter and a messenger for the Abbot, and had taught Matthew well. At his belt he carried a long knife, its handle worn smooth by generations of his family and its blade ground down by constant sharpening – but it was keen, no doubt about that. He'd hesitated to bring it, for the Abbot had stressed that this was God's work; but if God needed him to use a knife then he would have one to hand – and if not? So much the better.

He was allowed one of the fastest horses in the Abbey's stables and travelled mainly in the quietest hours, keeping out of sight when the road was busy. But even on a horse with a gait so smooth it felt like he were barely riding at all, it still took Matthew the best part of a week to reach the outskirts of Canterbury.

When the cathedral spire first came into view, reaching way, way up beyond earthly corruption, Matthew was still a long way from reaching the city walls. He watched the spire grow taller and taller, until it dominated the sky, before he allowed himself to join with the press of pilgrims waiting to pass through the great West Gate. The Spring rains and relentless feet had churned the road there to mud, but even so Matthew's horse had to pick its way around those who choose to shuffle along on their knees – the greater penance to perform. A whiff of putrid flesh sent Matthew's hand hurrying to his nose and he averted his eyes from the sight of the pathetic figure being carried between two struggling men. They had kerchiefs tied about their faces, no doubt stuffed with herbs to keep away the smell. Would such a person live long enough to reach the shrine? Unsettled, he offered up a prayer and would have fingered the amulet he usually wore about his neck, had not he been told to put it off. These days, the Abbot said, the King was not so fond of saints and their relics.

Matthew wound his way through the narrow streets of Canterbury. One hand was on the horse's rein, the other guarded the money the Abbot had given him. The looming spire guided him towards the outer entrance of the cathedral and there Matthew gave up his horse's reins to an ostler, jingling some of his precious coins into the man's palm.

The vast columns lining the interior of the cathedral overawed and dizzied Matthew as he followed their course upwards towards a vault so lofty it was surely in Heaven itself; and the windows that glittered with stained glass, were of a size to challenge the walls. Who could have built a marvel like this, save those helped and guided by God?

The queue of pilgrims shuffled forwards along the side of the nave and down to the place where Saint Thomas had been martyred. Matthew fell to his knees on the stone slabs, overcome with emotion. How could anyone have countenanced such evil in this holy place? A tonsured monk stood by, selling wooden crosses and pieces of material that had touched the tomb of the Saint, and Matthew looked at them longingly, but alas, he had no money of his own to spend. Too soon he was swept along by the other pilgrims, all eager to mount the stairs and see the Saint's shrine in the Trinity Chapel. There he found a place to kneel on icy, smooth marble, and joined his hands together. Would Father Peter have someone looking out for him? As the coldness seeped into his knees, Matthew looked nervously from side to side. The Saint's casket was hid behind a plain wooden casing, but when it was lifted, he expected to see marvels of gold and fabulous jewels, all of which had been donated by grateful pilgrims.

But even though Matthew waited patiently, the casket remained covered, and no monks appeared. Murmurs grew up. Was this another of the King's reforms – no viewing of the casket? What about those poor souls who had suffered so much on the road?

A scuffle broke out. Someone tumbled from a litter and a woman screamed. The stink of rotting flesh grew unbearable and Matthew pulled his cloak across his face. It was the poor man he'd seen on the road who fell, and to all intents now lay dead. Matthew groaned softly. How on Earth would he find enough peace to pray to the Saint with all this commotion? He bent his head again and tried to concentrate. This is what he had come for himself, to ask God and Saint Thomas to take care of his mother who was dying of the wasting disease and terribly thin. Even though Abbot Whiting had assured him there'd be someone to watch over her whilst he was away, Matthew still fretted about how she would feel if she called for him in the night.

A hand touched his shoulder and he looked round in time to see the portly form of Father Peter walking towards the door in the southern transept. Matthew hurried to catch him and saw the priest go through a door in a terrace of low, red-roofed buildings.

'Father-' he said, as the priest opened the door to him, but Father Peter put a finger to his lips and pulled Matthew inside.

He entered a sparsely, but elegantly, furnished room. Father Peter neither asked Matthew to sit beside the bright fire in the hearth nor offered any refreshment – which would have been customary – but simply held out his hand. Matthew fumbled for the letter the Abbot had given him and handed it over. It was written on fine white parchment and sealed with the Abbot's own seal, but after reading, Father Peter threw it straight away onto the fire. He then went over to a wooden cot in the corner and from beneath the brown woollen blankets removed an object wrapped in sacking cloth.

When Father Peter handed it to him, Matthew could feel right away that the object inside was heavy and hard – perhaps a hand span in width, slightly more than that in height, but narrow – maybe only half a hand across. He found it hard to contain his curiousity, but the Abbot had not said *what* he was to carry – only that he must bring it safely.

Matthew pushed the package into his waist belt and pulled his cloak tightly across. No one would take it from him now without a fight. Father Peter now scrawled on a scrap of paper that lay on his desk and held it out for Matthew to read. '*You must wait for a travelling companion by the West Gate of the city. I will give you something so that you may be recognised.*'

He watched the priest throw that note into the fire too, and then pull a wooden crucifix from around his neck. It was a beautiful thing, fashioned of a wood that had dark brown swirls in the grain. Father Peter motioned him to put it on and to leave it visible outside his cloak. How anyone would recognise him from that alone, Matthew had no idea. Most of the pilgrims he'd seen on the road were wearing a crucifix of one sort or another.

Father Peter made the Sign of the Cross and then ushered Matthew out of the door.

'Go with God', the priest mouthed.

The courtyard was empty and Matthew crossed it swiftly, retracing his steps until he had joined with the mass of pilgrims leaving the cathedral. As he retrieved his mount from the ostler, he could hardly believe how quickly everything had happened. With luck he would soon be back in Glastonbury – that is if whoever he was to meet at the West Gate didn't hold him up too much. Matthew raised his head. If the Abbot was pleased with him, he might even pass over Matthew's impoverished state and allow him to become a novice at the Abbey. How he longed for that to happen!

CHAPTER 3

June
Station View, Wesley Village, Yorkshire

Jo opened the door and found Blanche's nephew, Mat, standing just inside the hallway of her neighbour's house. He was looking through a pile of unopened post on the dresser.

'How is she?' she said, hanging her denim jacket on the coat stand.

'Sleeping,' Mat said, checking his watch. 'I wish I was.'

Even though she was tall, Jo still had to tilt her head to look up into his tired grey eyes.

'Did you get any sleep at all?' she asked.

'Not much. She was rambling on about all sorts. At one point I wondered about ringing the district nurses, but she settled down.'

'You must be exhausted,' Jo said, thinking she didn't feel much better herself. It had been a really tough night-shift at the hospice. 'How if I take over, so you can get to bed?'

Mat hesitated. 'I ought to sort these out. There could be bills that need paying.'

'Can't they wait a bit longer?'

She watched the shadows lengthen around his face as he looked at the pile.

'OK,' he said, giving her an appreciative smile. 'You're a great help, Jo.'

'That's all right,' she said, brightening in response to his smile. 'Blanche is more than just a neighbour, you know, and I'm glad you're able to be here now. Was it hard to get away?'

Mat grimaced and ran a hand through his sandy hair. 'Yes, but nearly all the students have gone home now and the Bishop has given me leave to stay here until...'

She knew he had stopped short of saying, 'until Blanche dies', and found it odd that a priest could have difficulty talking about someone dying; but then it was different when that dying person was someone you loved.

'If you really don't mind,' he said, 'I'd love to get a couple of hours. I can't see straight at the moment.'

Jo watched Mat take the steps two at a time. For a man who probably sat around drinking tea and listening sympathetically to old ladies, he seemed pretty fit. How old was he? It was hard to tell because he dressed in a rather old-fashioned way – smart black trousers and shiny shoes, but she would be surprised if he was much older than thirty. In fact, he was probably not much older than she was herself.

As she passed the hall mirror, Jo prodded at her hair. She'd added copper highlights last week, and a style that framed her face. Until then, she'd simply pulled whatever length of hair she had into a ponytail; but the girls at work had talked her into trying something different, and this *was* different. Even Simon, the hospice treasurer, had commented on it. Hm. Jo wasn't too sure what she thought about that. He'd been over friendly recently, asking her opinion of various restaurants and talking about the films he'd seen. She couldn't figure out why he'd picked on her but she had no objections to being chatted up – except it would have been better if it wasn't someone at work.

In the kitchen, Blanche's elderly range filled the chimney recess beating out heat, summer and winter alike. Beside it stood two chintzy armchairs – one a rocker – and both well worn and comfortable. Jo put the kettle on to boil and went through into Blanche's makeshift bedroom. Stale, tired air met her as she pushed open the door and the tiny figure lying in the hospital bed was only dimly visible because the curtains were still closed. The room had once been Blanche's work room and her sewing machine sat on the table near her bed. The waste bin underneath still held snippets of cloth and thread that Jo hadn't had the heart to empty out. When the hospital bed had arrived, several weeks ago, they'd moved the rest of the furniture out into the hallway and now, when she sat up, Blanche could see the birds as they thronged her many feeders.

In front of the sewing machine, Blanche had insisted they place her 'essentials': an olive-wood crucifix bought on pilgrimage to Jerusalem, Rosary beads bought from a South American missionary, and a leather bound prayer book dedicated to '*Blanche, on the occasion of your Confirmation*', from Father Patrick McReady, Mat's spiritual mentor and the only man Blanche had ever loved.

Not being a Catholic herself, Jo found it almost impossible to understand how men like Mat and Patrick could accept being celibate, especially when priests of other faiths had wives.

'Blanche, are you awake?' Jo asked, softly, so as not to wake her if she was asleep.

Blanche's face creased and her top lip drew back so that it looked as if she was snarling. Jo slid her arm beneath the frail body and helped Blanche to move onto her side.

'Is that better?'

One eye opened in its cavernous socket. 'Where's Patrick gone? Hadn't finished talking to him.'

'He's saying Mass,' Jo said, hoping to pacify Blanche.

'When'll be back?' Blanche said, slurring the words that seemed to stick in her throat.

Not for a long time, Jo thought, remembering how they had been at Patrick's funeral only last year. 'I'm not sure. Can I get you anything in the meantime?'

Blanche's other eye opened now, and a dry, fissured tongue made it's appearance between cracked lips. Jo smeared gel onto a sponge and wiped it carefully around Blanche's mouth. Her tongue licked at it and, with a sigh, disappeared.

'I'll have a cup of tea, ple...'

By the time Jo brought it back into the room, Blanche was fast asleep.

CHAPTER 4

July 1202
The Château Narbonnais, Toulouse

Matthieu looked fondly at Raimondet. Now six years old, the young Count-to-be was a sturdy, ruddy-haired boy, already long of limb and showing all the drive and fearlessness of his ancestors. After a wistful look out of the schoolroom window, Raimondet suddenly declared that today was not a day to spend inside, and demanded to go swimming.

Matthieu was more than happy to agree with his young charge, especially since shimmers of heat were already rising from the tiled roofs below the school room. In the courtyard, Raimondet refused help from the squires who rushed to him and climbed alone onto his pony. Matthieu sat astride his own splendid chestnut mare, a recent gift from the Count, and waited for the entourage to assemble. As the Count's only legitimate son and heir, Raimondet was escorted by a party of heavily armed men whenever he went outside the walls of the Narbonnais.

Under his chain mail, Matthieu sweated profusely and chose a path keeping the shade of the woods as much as possible, moving upstream of the city to where the wide river had a shady beach. Raimondet jumped from his mount, threw off his clothing and waded into the water wearing only his linen braies. Matthieu's squire, Bernard, followed the boy into the water whilst the Count's men mounted guard on the bank.

Watching Raimondet splashing happily in the water, Matthieu reflected that a similar scene could be repeated when – if – he and Catharine had a son of their own. He pursed his lips. Therein lay the thought that of late had given him no ease. Catharine had not been well these last few months, and her fleshless ribs could be counted in rows above her narrow belly. Three years they had been wed, and still no child. It was a pain he could barely admit to himself. Oh, there had been no difficulty getting her pregnant to begin with. He had been a young knight then, of only twenty two summers and knew his duty to God. When Catharine's belly began to swell, he thought his joy could know no bounds – until all their hopes were carried away on a river of blood.

Matthieu brushed away the tears that always threatened when he thought about his tiny, dead son. The next time the babe had not even been properly formed; and though Catharine now prayed daily to the Virgin Mary, her courses had come with crushing regularity ever since.

A whoop came from the river and Matthieu held his breath as

Raimondet splashed his first few strokes alone; but almost immediately the current swept him towards the middle of the river. Bernard swam frantically after him and Matthieu tore off his hauberk and waded in. As Raimondet's head disappeared beneath the churning water, Bernard dived under too, but came up gasping for breath and shook his head. Matthieu's quilted gambeson dragged him down in the water but he struggled on. There wasn't time to unlace it.

'Try further down!' he shouted to the Count's men, but they were already stinging out along the bank and preparing to jump in.

Matthieu cast about feverishly, terror gripping his heart. The boy would not have the lungs to hold his breath for so long – he must be trapped somewhere. Dear God! Only a miracle could save him now. Matthieu dived below the water. Churning sand and mud made it impossible to see and he groped around for anything that might have been the boy; but soon his lungs were screaming and he had to come up for air. Straight away he went down again, and after what seemed like an age, stumbled on something soft, tangled in the river weeds. Matthieu tugged hard, praying it was Raimondet.

'Help me!' he gasped, having to come to the surface again.

Two of the soldiers swam towards him and together they heaved the lifeless boy out onto the bank. Matthieu shook Raimondet roughly, bellowing his name into his ear and then held him upside down to drain the water from his lungs. He offered every prayer he could think of, but still there was no response from the boy.

Dear God! He is the flower of our land, the hope of our future. Take me instead. I am nothing compared to him.

Matthieu wrenched his amulet from his neck and placed it across Raimondet's chest. All the soldiers made the Sign of the Cross and those who carried amulets, took them off and gravely placed them about the boy's body, knowing that Matthieu wouldn't be the only one to experience the Count's wrath if the boy did not survive. Matthieu himself prayed so hard that he forgot to breathe, and would gladly have plunged his dagger into his own heart if he'd thought it would help. But then, when all seemed lost, Raimondet's chest heaved and river water poured from his mouth. Matthieu rolled the lad onto his side, thinking that he, personally, would never experience such sweet relief again, even if he lived until the end of time.

'The saints be praised,' he said, wiping Raimondet's face on his wet chemise and cradling his head in his arms.

What else did they need to assure them of this child's place in history, when God had chosen to return him to them?

All were silent as they rode back to the Château Narbonnais. Matthieu put Raimondet before him on the mare, and grasped the boy tightly whilst he rehearsed what he would say to the Count; but his wits were scattered and he feared that Raimondet would never again be allowed out of his father's sight if he said too much.

As the Château came into sight, rising massively above the city walls, Matthieu's prayers renewed. Once inside, he took Raimondet straight away to the infirmary and left him in the care of the Count's physician. Then Matthieu squared his shoulders and made his way to the Count's private solar.

'Have you heard the news?' the Count demanded, coming over as soon as he saw Matthieu. He wasn't even allowed time to complete his bow.

The Count was unusually well-dressed, wearing a robe of fine blue silk embroidered all over with the Cross of Toulouse. His long black hair had been oiled and brushed back, and in his deep green eyes sparkled the glint of mischief. Matthieu suddenly remembered that today was the feast day of the great Saint Raimon of Toulouse – a well-revered local saint.

'I – er no,' Matthieu replied, aware of how terrible he must look in his wet and bedraggled clothes. 'I merely came to report the safe return of your son.'

The Count's eyes narrowed. 'What's happened to him?'

'I – er.' Matthieu's mouth ran dry but his palms were wet with sweat, and he could smell the river water as it evaporated from his body. 'You may remember that Raimondet has been learning to swim?'

A few of the courtiers, who had until this time been playing dice, started to drift nearer. Jealous eyes triumphed in his discomfort, and even the falcon on the perch in the corner of the room screeched and flapped its wings.

'Today he excelled himself beyond all previous attempts, my lord, however, the current was stronger than we realised and for a time he was lost-'

'Lost?' the Count said, paling remarkably. 'Where is he now?'

'Safe, my lord,' Matthieu said. 'I've taken the precaution of letting your physician see to him.'

'Show me,' Raimon said, already on his way out of the solar. 'I want to see with my own eyes.'

A tall, grey-haired man followed them and Matthieu frowned to himself. He did not like Arnald of Fanjeaux, a man from one of noble houses, but well known for his strong links with heretics. Rumour even had it that he was one of their so-called 'perfected ones' – as if anyone could call themselves *perfect* when they had taken leave of their senses, and believed that there were two gods, one good, one evil, and that the evil one had made the Earth. That the Count tolerated them in his court troubled Matthieu, for in his opinion, they were truly insane. They couldn't wait to escape this life and go to Heaven – a place, he knew, they were most unlikely to ever see. The only place *they* were heading was the fires of Hell, in which he hoped they would roast for a long, long time.

'Keep saying your prayers,' the Count said, looking back over his shoulder. 'If Raimondet's hurt, you'll wish your life ended long ago, Matthieu. I told you his safety was more important to me than anything else, your life included. How could you be such a fool?' He stopped and stabbed a finger into Matthieu's chest. 'Never put him in danger again. Do you hear me? My father would have had you strung up by your ear lobes and don't think I won't, if he's harmed in any way...'

'Yes, sire. Of course, sire,' Matthieu said. As if his prayers needed any encouragement!

They entered the infirmary and found Raimondet playing on the floor with poupee dolls. He was attempting to run them through with a wooden sword. Apart from a slight pallor and puffiness about his face, the lad looked none the worse for his adventure and Matthieu let his pent up breath go with a sigh.

'Papa!' Raimondet caught sight of his father and came running over. 'Did you hear? I swam and then nearly drowned, but I'm safe. God looked after me. Isn't it wonderful?'

The Count took his son in his arms, his eyes bright with tears, and the physician quickly reassured them that he could find nothing wrong. Raimondet must rest for while, he said, but otherwise there was nothing to worry about. Matthieu offered up so many prayers of gratitude that he thought Heaven might be deafened, but felt genuine regret when he heard the Count forbid Raimondet to ever go swimming again, at least until he was older.

'But, Papa,' Raimondet protested. 'I thought you wanted me to learn to swim?' He twisted in his father's arms. 'You told me what a fool my cousin the King of France made of himself, by falling into a river and not being able to swim when my Uncle Richard was chasing him!'

'Shhh!' the Count laughed. 'Your Uncle Richard is dead now, and we might have to turn to your Cousin Philippe in future – so I won't have you mocking him.'

'I'm sorry, Papa,' the boy said, pouting a little. 'Will I ever learn what to say and what not?'

'Of course you will, chicken,' the Count said, putting him down on a chair and taking a seat beside him. He nodded to Arnald of Fanjeaux who smiled and then left. Matthieu ground his teeth. The heretics reminded him of vultures, ever circling when disaster or death approached, hoping to be able to administer *their* 'sacrament' – as if that would do anyone anything but ill.

‘But you’re too young to worry about politics yet,’ the Count was saying, ‘but let me tell you what I’ve just heard about the antics of another cousin of yours, Arthur of Brittany.’ He looked up. ‘You’ll want to hear this, Matthieu, I don’t doubt. Better sit down too.’

Matthieu drew up a chair and waited.

‘Arthur has just made the greatest mistake of his young life,’ the Count began. ‘He was besieging your lady grandmother, Queen Aliénor, at Mirebeau and she was none too pleased, by all accounts. In any case she refused all terms of surrender. Arthur was having breakfast when John of England, appeared ‘out of nowhere’ so they say, and took him captive- ’

‘My uncle of England can appear out of nowhere?’ Raimondet exclaimed, wriggling out of his father’s arms. Matthieu could not believe what he was hearing. Arthur of Brittany besieging his own grandmother?

‘And did he rescue my lady grandmother?’ Raimondet said, picking up the wooden sword again.

‘He did,’ the Count said, smirking at Matthieu. ‘And now Arthur and his knights are paying for their misdeeds at Corfe Castle in England – with half of the Luisignan clan thrown in for good measure. I shall not miss them one whit!’

‘Whoopee!’ The dolls were impaled one by one and thrown high into the air.

Matthieu frowned. Arthur must have been badly advised to attempt something so rash, and the most likely culprit sat on the throne of France. Now ’Coeur de Lion’ was dead, Philippe of France was gobbling up the Plantagenet empire by pitting the remaining family members against each other.

Count Raimon’s face grew suddenly serious. ‘Philippe has abandoned Arthur now, but I’m sorry to tell you, Matthieu, that he razed Tours in revenge before he left.’

Matthieu shut his eyes, imagining the devastation that lay behind those few words. Catharine’s family held their lands there. ‘I’ll send a messenger to find out how matters lie,’ he said. ‘Thank you for telling me, my lord.’

‘Arthur and John have been at it like dogs after a bone,’ the Count sighed. He got to his feet. ‘I think we need a little celebration, don’t you? My son safe and well, and a few less Lusignans raiding our borders for a while.’ He slung his arm around Matthieu’s shoulders. ‘You most certainly don’t deserve it, but I want you to join me in my chambers, Matthieu.’

Matthieu smothered his dismay. He never looked forward to an afternoon of drinking with the Count, and had hoped to spend some time recovering from his ordeal, but he knew he was very lucky to be having the offer.

'I'm honoured, my lord,' he said, 'but first may I be permitted to send a messenger?'

Count Raimon was already moving towards the door, but then he turned to wink at Matthieu as a middle-aged woman came panting into the Infirmary. She dropped a very quick curtsey when she saw the Count.

'My lord!' she exclaimed. 'How is he?'

'Well, good dame,' the Count said. 'It seems both of our sons have escaped with their lives today. May I leave them in your care, Blanche?'

Blanche of Poitiers pushed her escaped wisps of grey hair into her linen cap and stood with her hands on her hips to regain her breath. As soon as the Count departed, she dragged Matthieu into a quiet corner of the Infirmary.

'Whatever were you thinking of?' she hissed, her blue eyes flaming. 'Raimondet could have drowned! Do you want to destroy us?'

'Of course not,' Matthieu said, feeling sulky. Did his mother take him for a fool? 'He's fine. Just look at him.'

'Make sure nothing like this ever happens again,' Blanche said, squinting over to where Raimondet sat. 'The Count has been very generous to us. Never forget where our good fortune comes from, Matthieu, and keep that boy safe! Can't you just teach him his letters and numbers? There's not much danger in that, is there?'

'And not much fun either,' Matthieu said. 'Must Raimondet be cosseted all his life and miss out on being a boy? He descends from every noble house in Christendom, and carries some of the most valiant blood ever known in his veins. A boy like that wasn't born to sit at a desk!'

Just then they saw the person in question kicking dolls into the air, and the physician trying to save his precious bottles. Blanche clicked her tongue and hurried over.

'One day Ill be a great knight like my Uncle Richard!' Raimondet said, his pallor now completely gone.

'One day you're going to be a great knight and *alive*, I hope,' Blanche said, taking his arm and steering him out of the Infirmary. '*Unlike* your Uncle Richard.'

'Come on.' Matthieu heard her say. 'It's well past noon and after all that excitement, you must be starving.'

*

Being tutor to the Count's son, Matthieu mused, somewhat drunkenly, had its good and bad points. The Count rewarded him well, had given him the rooms in the Château for his personal use and a manor near Launaguet; enough rents and tithes to employ plenty of servants and have a comfortable living; oxen to plough his land, and many acres of vines; his barns were stocked with hay and grain; and if the men needed tools or the women needed kitchen utensils there was a smith living in one of the tied cottages in the village. All in all, if it were not for their lack of a child, he and Catharine should consider themselves the most fortunate of couples. So why did he feel like there was an axe hovering over his head?

'Catharine, dearest,' Matthieu said, finding his wife reclining in the solar of their apartment. 'How are you, my love?' He lifted her hand to his lips.

'A little better,' Catharine said, wrinkling her nose at the smell of his breath. She gave him a smile that barely lifted the corners of her eyes. 'How was your afternoon with the Count?'

'Long,' Matthieu said, 'and I'll have a headache tomorrow, but there wasn't much else I could do. Perhaps we could take a walk together?'

'A walk would be lovely,' Catharine said, surprising him with her eagerness. 'I must feel some air on my face soon, or I think I'll go mad – and I think it would do you good, too.'

Matthieu couldn't help noticing that the shadows underneath her once bright eyes grew ever darker and the hollows in her cheeks more pronounced every day. How he wished he could chase away those shadows, but unless Catharine bore a child, that was unlikely to happen. She swayed as she stood up and he called out for Ermessinda, who was never far from her mistress' side.

'Are you all right, my lady?' the maid said, hurrying in with a woollen cloak.

'Yes, I'm just a bit dizzy from sitting, that's all,' Catharine said.

Ermessinda deftly captured Catharine's dark hair in a broad ribbon, and then fixed a veil over it, framing her pale face.

'Are you sure you're all right?' Matthieu said, wondering at the frailty of women. How they ever managed to give birth to children he'd never know.

'Yes, I told you, I'm feeling better today,' Catharine said, pushing them both away. 'Don't fuss.'

With his wife clinging to his arm, they made their way through the corridors of the Château Narbonnais, nodding to those of their acquaintance and stopping for Catharine's sake to admire the view from the many windows. To the west, they could see the wide river Garonne and if one looked out far enough – that is past the stocks in the square and the whorehouses clustered around the docks – they could see the verdant marshes leading to L'Isle-Jourdain. To the south lay the valley of the Ariège, snaking from Pamiers up to Foix and thence to the rugged Pyrenees; whilst to the east lay the hospital and leper houses outside the Narbonnais gate. Beyond them the fields and vineyards of the Lauragais stretched in lazy profusion towards Castelnaudary, and many-turreted Carcassonne.

Matthieu knew exactly where to take Catharine once they reached the gardens. She loved to be by the fish pond, where huge carp swam in glittering shoals, and there was a sheltered bench under a rose arbour.

'Oh, Matthieu,' Catharine said, inhaling deeply, 'my soul has been aching for this. How long is it since I last ventured outside? The lavender wasn't even in flower then, and now it smells so wonderful, and these -' she cupped a downy rose in her hand and brought it to her nose. 'I'm sorry it's taken so long, my love, but I truly believe I'm getting better. Next time will be different, you'll see.'

Matthieu took a sharp breath. It was hard enough even thinking about the last pregnancy, let alone contemplating another.

'And now, you must tell me,' Catharine continued, seeming oblivious to his unease and pulling him down to sit with her on the bench, 'what happened to Raimondet this morning? Your mother came into the solar, threw up her hands, said a lot of not very complimentary things about you, and left. I didn't catch the details!'

Glad for some distraction and a tale that at least had a happy ending, Matthieu told Catharine all about the morning's events.

'Thanks be to God that I found him quickly, Catharine. The Count threatened to string me up by my ear lobes, even so, but the worst is, he won't let Raimondet go swimming again, not for a long time, and he's forbidden me to put him in danger ever again. How can I stop, 'Coeur de Lion's' nephew finding danger? It's in his blood.'

'By concentrating on his studies and leaving the physical things to the more physical knights?' Catharine said, arching an eyebrow at him.

Matthieu laughed. 'Are you calling me a flabby, useless knight? Only good for book work and keeping priests company? It has been said before.'

'Of course I'm not!'

His heart beat a little faster as he watched her mouth curve, and then she nestled into his side.

'Catharine, my love.'

How could he tell her about the sack of Tours, just when they had created this moment of happiness together? 'Um – nothing,' he said.

'What is it? You look so serious, Matthieu.'

'I only wanted to tell you that your eyes are the same colour as the sky.'

And I can tell her the rest later, when the messenger returns, he thought – when I know for sure.

CHAPTER 5

March 1538
Canterbury

Matthew was troubled as he made his way to the West Gate of the city. Why did he have to wait for a travelling companion? Why couldn't he go back to Glastonbury alone? Surely speed was of the utmost importance.

When he reached the gate, the throng of pilgrims was just as great as when he had arrived, and he could not imagine how anyone was going to recognise him by the crucifix he now wore.

'Matthew?'

The voice caught him off guard. It came from a heavily wrapped traveller that he had taken for a pilgrim.

'*Are* you Matthew?'

He said nothing, but peered curiously beneath the coarse woollen hood, and if Saint Thomas himself had been waiting in there, he could not have been more surprised. Startling green eyes and long fair lashes – how was he going to travel all that way with a *girl*?

'Father Peter told you about me, I hope?' she said, pulling her horse's head around. 'I'm to travel with you towards Glastonbury.'

Matthew tried to gather his wits, whilst guiding his horse through the shuffling pilgrims. She would never be able to sleep underneath hedges like he'd done on the way here. Whatever was Father Peter thinking of? She could stay at an inn for the night, but it would slow them down, and they'd have to travel by day – which would draw attention. He sweated under his robe, sure that every clop of hooves was someone coming to arrest them.

'Have you no speech?' the girl asked, and Matthew shook his head, stubbornly keeping to the Abbot's instructions.

'Oh.' That seemed to perplex her. 'I wasn't aware.' She shrugged. 'Never mind, I'm sure we'll manage.'

Matthew ground his teeth. In these uncertain days, everyone had to guard their tongues. Careless speech, overheard and then reported to the King's agents, could lead to a jail sentence – or worse.

'It's good of you to let me come with you,' the girl said, when the throng of pilgrims had thinned. She was looking around curiously, as if she hadn't seen the world for a long while.

'Have a care for what you say!' Matthew hissed. 'Anyone could be listening. Keep silent until I tell you it's safe, please.'

She looked at him in surprise, as though she'd really thought he couldn't speak, and then turned around slowly, searching for those who would be listening and, finding none, shrugged her shoulders again.

'Very well,' she said. 'As you wish.'

They rode until noon and the girl kept her word, speaking to no one, even those who greeted them. As soon as Matthew could, he steered them away from the road and on to the wilder pastures he had ridden on his way to Canterbury. When he was sure they were not being followed, he reined in his horse by a stream, near a copse of newly sprouting willow. The girl dismounted stiffly, and Matthew suppressed a sigh. How was she going to manage all the way to Glastonbury?

'Here,' he said, offering her some of his cheese and a crust of black bread, whilst still thinking how he could rid himself of her.

The girl seated herself on a patch of grass and gave the dried-up cheese and bread a puzzled look. 'Thank you. Are you sure you have enough for yourself?'

'Yes,' he said. 'But we'll have to get some more later on.'

'Oh,' the girl said, standing up again. 'Don't worry, I've brought food too. I'm sure there'll be enough for both of us.'

She rummaged in her saddle bags and brought out a packet tied in oiled paper. Inside were smaller packets of dried meat, wafers, figs and dates – costly goods he had rarely seen.

'Will that be enough?' she asked.

'Yes,' he said. He would have preferred more bread and cheese, but the meat was welcome.

They ate in silence, the girl chewing so long on the bread that he feared she might have no back teeth.

'What was that?' she asked, as she finally managed to swallow. 'It looks like bread but the taste is different.'

Matthew regarded her for a moment. There was no guile in her look. It seemed she had simply never seen that kind of bread before. For the first time he really studied her and saw that although she wore the garb of a traveller – coarse woollen cloak and leggings with leather boots – the collar of her chemise was finely embroidered, and the hands that she used to pick up his cheese were white and soft.

'Who are you?' he asked, thinking that no common woman could have escaped seeing black bread.

'My name is Johanna,' she said.

'Johanna...' He stopped, confused. 'You don't look like you've done anything like this before.'

'So?' She gave him a challenging look.

'Well, I can't... I mean, you can't-'

'What?' she said.

'Travel like this. It isn't proper for a woman anyway, but a lady...'

'Who said I'm a lady?' Johanna pushed her hood back to show that her hair was neatly secured under a plain linen cap. 'Do I look like a lady to you?'

He didn't know what to say. 'People might think so when they see your hands.'

'My hands?' She held them before her face. 'They look perfectly normal to me.'

In answer, he put one of his work roughened hands by hers.

'Ah, I see.' Johanna tucked them into the folds of her cloak. 'Then I'll just have to keep them hidden.'

'My lady,' Matthew said, trying to remain patient. 'I have to travel quickly and secretly to Glastonbury. Finding proper accommodation for you along the way will slow me down and make us visible to those I'd rather didn't see us. I think you should go back to your family, and put this journey out of your head because I simply cannot guarantee *your* safety and that of the package I carry.'

Johanna sighed. 'Please take me with you, Matthew. I'll do whatever it takes, sleep wherever I have to, but please don't make me go back – there's no safety for me there, whatever appearances may suggest to you.'

Matthew paused. Was she fleeing some tragedy, or perhaps an unhappy marriage alliance? Such things were common amongst the nobility – but that was even more reason to be rid of her as soon as possible.

'Where, exactly, are you going?' he asked.

'To Amesbury,' she said. 'And then you'll have no further cause for concern about me, because I'm to become a novice at the convent. It is my heart's greatest desire.'

Matthew felt a flood of relief. She was fleeing her fate in order to take the veil. No doubt Father Peter had been forced to give in to her demands due to her rank – or the rank of someone close to her.

'Forgive me, my lady,' he said, giving her a little bow, 'if I've been harsh with you. I see now that we're both hoping to do God's will in our own ways.' He paused. It was going to be extremely difficult to take her along, especially as the nights were still very cold; but if what she said was true, and she *really* was ready to face hardship...

'I'll help you as much as I can,' he said, 'but you'll have to be prepared to sleep roughly for a few nights. We'll attract too much attention otherwise.'

'Thank you, Matthew,' Johanna said, brightening up. 'I can't tell you how important this is to me.' She got to her feet. 'Let's be off, then.' She picked up her horse's rein.

'Not yet,' he said, taking it from her. 'This is when we rest, and then we travel at dusk – fewer people around then.' He fingered the knife at his belt. Fewer honest people anyway.

'But what shall we do until then?' she asked. 'I thought you were in a hurry.'

'I am,' he said, 'but this is when we rest. And if you can, try to sleep, my lady.'

He watched her spread out the blanket from her saddle roll, as though she were having a picnic, and then she lay down upon it and shuffled to and fro to find a comfortable spot.

'Let me,' he said, and she stood up whilst he folded the blanket in three and cleared the ground of stones and twigs. 'Do you have another one, to cover you?' he asked, but she shook her head.

Matthew gave her his, and rolled himself as best as he could in his cloak. He'd slept in worse conditions.

'Matthew,' Johanna said, just as he was dropping off to sleep.

'Mm?'

'You can call me Johanna instead of 'my lady', if you want. I no longer think of myself in that way, since I decided to devote myself to God.'

'It wouldn't seem right, my lady,' Matthew said, surprised. He'd never heard of a noble person willing to give up their title before.

'You can't address me like that when there are people around.'

Matthew thought for a minute. 'I'm not going to speak to you when there are people around. The Abbot was very clear about that. Speak to no one, he said.'

CHAPTER 6

June
Station View, Wesley Village, Yorkshire

Jo dozed in the rocking chair by the range. She could see Blanche through the open doorway and from time to time went to check on her, but there'd been little movement. At half past five, she heard Mat come down the stairs.

'How long have I been asleep?' he asked, looking around the kitchen and sniffing appreciatively. She'd tidied everything up and done some cleaning, so there was a faint smell of lemon bleach in the air.

'Couple of hours,' she said. 'Sure you wouldn't like a bit longer?'

He was dressed more casually now, in a rugby shirt and a pair of jeans. Seeing him like that, it was hard to imagine him being a priest.

'No. I'm OK. How is she?'

'Sleeping mostly. I had to move her once because she looked uncomfortable.'

'It's crazy,' Mat said. 'Asleep all day and awake most of the night.'

'Yes, it happens like that sometimes,' Jo said. 'She was rambling earlier. Thought she'd been with Patrick McReady again.'

'Oh, dear.' He smiled apologetically. 'And what did you tell her?'

'That he was saying Mass.' Mat seemed amazingly tolerant of his aunt's passion for his mentor. 'Seriously though,' Jo said, feeling her way, 'do you think we should ask the Macmillan nurses about her confusion?'

'Isn't it normal to be confused at this stage?' he said.

'Yes, but it could be related to her medication.' Jo bit her lip. Until Mat had arrived from Scotland, she'd been looking after Blanche on her own and she must try to remember that she wasn't a hospice nurse here, only a neighbour and a friend.

Mat made them both a mug of tea and then picked up the pile of post from the hallway and flopped down in the other armchair.

'OK,' he yawned. 'Sorry, Jo.' He took a slurp of his tea and relaxed back, his eyes half closed. 'Blanche isn't the only one who doesn't know whether it's day or night at the moment. Do you have the Macmillan nurse's number?'

'Yes. I could ring them if you like?'

'No, it's OK. I'll do it.' He pulled his mobile phone out of his jeans' pocket. 'You've done enough.'

She watched his long fingers moving quickly over the keys, and imagined him touching people, blessing them, comforting them. Whilst he talked to the Macmillan nurse, she found her eyes straying to the hairs that peeked out at the neck of his shirt. Somehow she'd assumed that priests would be kind of neutral underneath their clothes.

'Right, that's good,' he said, slipping the phone back into his pocket. 'They're coming later this afternoon. Do you want to get off now? I'm sure you must have a life to get back to.'

She couldn't help but blush. Apart from her work at the hospice, she had no real 'life' to speak of. She was only occasionally needed by her father who had recently met Cynthia on a singles holiday, and her sister, Catherine, lived in Canada with her three children. In the place next door that Jo called home, there wasn't even a dog or cat to welcome her.

'I'm all right for a bit longer if you want to get on with that,' she said, nodding at the post.

'Are you sure? If you *can* give me some more time, that would be wonderful.' He looked around. 'There's cold salmon and salad in the fridge. Do you fancy some? Why not stay and have lunch? It'd be lovely to have company.'

'That would be very nice,' she said, hoping to goodness he wasn't asking her because he felt sorry for her.

'It's a lovely afternoon. Why don't we eat outside? We could keep an eye on Blanche through the window. Or maybe even open it? Might do her good to get some air on her face. She always loved her garden so...'

Mat frowned and looked away.

'Mat...' Jo took a deep breath. 'She *is* quite unwell, you do know that, don't you?'

He nodded but didn't turn around and Jo fidgeted, feeling like she was intruding on his grief. Perhaps she should go after all.

'She's all I've got left,' he said, finally, his voice sounding strangled. 'It's going to hurt to lose her.'

The impulse to reach out to comfort him was strong. It was what she would have done to anyone else. Tentatively, Jo put a hand on his shoulder and felt a flow of grief and understanding pass between them.

'She thought of you as a daughter, really,' he said, putting his hand on hers. 'I guess it's going to be hard for you as well?'

Jo nodded, and great fat tears started rolling down her cheeks.

'Here.' Mat rooted around in his pocket and brought out a handkerchief. 'I know, Jo, I know. It's just that I don't want to have to face it. Oh, damn.'

She couldn't prevent a sob welling up inside her chest and before she knew it, he had taken her into his arms.

'Hey now,' he said, brushing at her hair. 'This is no good. Blanche has had a very full life and her faith is as strong as anyone I've ever met. Let's not be miserable.'

Jo wiped at her tears with the handkerchief and pulled back a little. Were priests supposed to do things like that?

'I know, she's lucky, really. It's just that...'

There were no words. She went over to the fridge and rummaged around in the chiller box for salad. Mat was right. Blanche wouldn't want either of them to be sad. 'I'm going to be with my beloved Patrick.' That's what she'd said. 'I couldn't be with him in life, but no one's going to keep me away from him when I'm dead!'

It didn't take Jo long to put together a salmon salad, whilst Mat sat at the kitchen table, working through the post.

'Water, Gas and an invitation to the Hospice garden party. I don't think she's going to make that, do you?' he said, with a strained laugh.

'No. I'd better tell fund-raising to stop sending post.'

Jo piled everything onto a tray ready to take out to the garden.

'Saturday 4th of July. Tombola, refreshment stall, plant sales... What would we do without garden parties? Blanche always used to love them.'

'I'd have thought you'd be fed up with them by now,' Jo said, going to fetch the embroidered cloth she knew Blanche kept in her dresser drawer. She wiped the little table on the terrace, before throwing it over.

'Ah, but they're important,' Mat said, coming standing in the doorway, 'for all sorts of reasons, not just for making money.'

She knew what he meant. Lots of people came to the hospice for the garden party. It seemed to galvanise those who found it hard to visit again after a death, and gave them a reason to come.'It's always nice to see how people are getting on.'

'And do you remember them all?'

She thought about this as she smoothed out the cloth. 'Mostly.'

A flower girl wearing a big bonnet was smiling up at her from the embroidered edge.

'Did my aunt do this, do you think?' Mat said, picking up the edge of the cloth.

'Probably,' Jo said. 'She's such a talented woman. I only wish she'd managed to teach me.' She went into the kitchen to fetch the tray, feeling unbearably sad. Blanche had been like a substitute mother, always there through the difficult times...

'Here, let me.' Mat came in and lifted the tray away from her. Their fingers touched and a frisson of electricity ran up Jo's arm.

'Thanks,' she said. He really was a very attractive man. Far too attractive for one who was strictly off limits. 'I'll bring the salad and the dressing.'

They sat opposite each other, cramped by the little table into being too close, their knees almost touching. The birds flew away from the feeders, chirping noisily, to find safer perches on trees that were full of new leaves. How ironic that Blanche should be dying, just as her garden was coming back to life. Jo tried to shuffle her chair backwards and made everything on the table rattle. The bottle of salad dressing tipped over and leaked all over the beautiful cloth. She leaped to her feet and Mat picked up his napkin. Only then did she notice that the dressing had soaked into her lap.

'It's OK,' Jo said, jumping up and wiping furiously at herself. The table rocked ominously. 'I'd better go and change,' she said.

What an idiot, she thought, as she rushed down the path towards her own cottage. What a fool. If he ever asks again, I'll say I'm too busy for lunch.

CHAPTER 7

August 1202
Launaguet, Languedoc

After the swimming incident, Count Raimon demanded strict rest for his son so Matthieu and Catharine took the opportunity to travel to their manor near Launaguet. Bernard and the two maids, Beatrice and Ermessinda accompanied them and as soon as they arrived, set about helping Walter, the steward who lived there, to spread rushes and matting about the floors. Catharine even managed to direct some of the proceedings herself, instructing Walter to open the best wine so that they could celebrate their return.

It was going to be all right, Matthieu thought, seeing her cheeks flushed with colour and her eyes shining once more. *They* were going to be all right. The news from Tours, when it came, didn't have to be *all* bad.

Despite his misgivings, Matthieu resumed sharing a bed with Catharine that night, although he hardly dared to touch her. She seemed less a thing of the Earth, so slight had she become, as a thing of spirit and he struggled to become intimate with her, as one would struggle to become intimate with a saint. But Catharine urged him on and he tried to respond. After all, was it not the purpose of a married couple – to continue God's creation?

Yet however much he tried, whatever he told himself, all of his efforts led to failure and, eventually, Matthieu fell into an exhausted, fitful sleep. In the morning, he woke to find Catharine had turned her back to him.

'Catharine, my love,' he said, reaching out to touch her bony shoulder. 'I'm sorry.'

'No, Matthieu,' Catharine said, her voice hoarse from crying, 'the fault is not yours. You should have a wife who can give you strong sons, not a pathetic creature like me.'

'But Catharine,' Mathieu said, pulling her round and into his arms, 'you *can* give me strong sons. Once you yourself are stronger, and I'm not so tired...'

'No, I can't,' she wept.

'Listen,' he said, angling her face up to him. It was streaked with tears and she looked so defeated that he thought his heart would break. 'You're not yet twenty summers old, there's plenty of time. The failure is mine, and mine alone. I won't let you say otherwise. Count Raimon has kept me so busy recently that it's made me tired, but I can rest now and all will be well, you'll see.'

Pity overwhelmed him as he wrapped his arms about her and held her as tightly as he dared. There and then he determined to donate a tenth of his income to the refurbishment of the cathedral in Toulouse, if only God would grant them a son.

Ermessinda's voice came to them from beyond the bed curtains.

'There's a messenger for you, my lord,' she said. 'He says it's urgent.'

'Oh, Matthieu,' Catharine said, looking stricken. 'I thought we were going to have some time together here.'

'And we will, never fear,' Matthieu said, kissing the top of her head.

He shrugged into his chemise and belted a robe about his waist, trying not to let Catharine see the worry in his face. That the messenger had returned so quickly, boded ill. How he wished he could spare his wife further tragedy, but it seemed it was not going to be.

'Send him into the solar, Ermessinda,' he said, and turned back to Catharine. 'I won't be long, my love.'

'Do you have any idea who it could it be?' Catharine said, now half out of bed.

Her nightgown had fallen open to reveal a apartment breast, with bluish discolouration around the nipple from where he had sought in vain to stimulate himself to what she so desired. Matthieu looked away, ashamed. How could he have hurt her like that?

'No,' he said. 'Perhaps it won't be a message from the Count. Try not to worry until we know there's something to worry about – promise?'

She nodded and he left, feeling uneasy.

The messenger and a woman traveller were waiting in the hall, standing awkwardly in their travel-stained clothes, with the smell of sweat and horses hanging heavily about them. Matthieu wished he'd asked Ermessinda to make them wait in the stables, but it was too late now. The woman traveller pushed back the hood of her cloak, and the sight of her sent shock reeling through Matthieu''s body.

'My lord,' the messenger bowed. 'Allow me to present the Lady Joana.'

Matthieu couldn't speak. She looked so very different from when he'd last seen her, which was the day he married Catharine.

'Don't you not know me, Matthieu?' Joana said, looking troubled.

'Barely,' he said. 'You look so changed.'

He turned to the messenger. 'Thank you, Peire.' Matthieu fumbled for his purse and brought out some coins. 'Walter will see you fed and give you a bed, if you need one.'

Peire left, and Matthieu returned his attention to his sister-in-law. She looked more beautiful than ever. Her cheeks were flushed with the embarrassment that he might not know her, and whatever trauma she had lived with had sharpened the angles of her face in a most becoming manner.

'What do you need?' he said, sounding stilted even to himself. 'Some food, a bath?' The truth of the matter was, his mind was racing so fast that he could hardly catch hold of his thoughts. 'Shall I send one of Catharine's ladies? What of your mother? I must tell Catharine you're here, she'll be delighted to see you.'

Joana shook her head and the corners of her mouth drooped. 'I doubt she will when she knows what news I bring. How is she?'

'Improving.'

'That's good,' Joana said, and gave him a bitter smile. 'What have you told her already?'

Matthieu hesitated. He could hardly admit that he'd told her nothing, out of sheer cowardice.

'Oh, Matthieu!' Joana came towards him, but Matthieu clenched his fists and stepped back, not daring to touch her, even in a brotherly fashion.

'Our mother's dead of the flux,' Joana said. 'Our land's been razed, our animals slaughtered and half of our farm hands killed. Is anyone well enough to hear that?'

No. No one was. Despite his misgivings, Matthieu finally took her in his arms and soothed her. He knew it was a risk, but how could he not comfort her? Sobbing and shaking, Joana clung to him, and he stroked her head, told her that he'd look after her. She was his sister, after all, and his home was hers for as long as she needed it; and all the while, he kept his eyes closed and begged God for the strength to resist the temptation he knew would inevitably come with her. Ever since the day of his marriage, he had tried to put her out of his mind. Only God knew how grateful he was that Arthur of Brittany and John of England's skirmishes in the north had kept the two families apart, and given him the time he needed to fall in love with Catharine. Their marriage was a good one, by any standards, filled with respect and affection – just as it ought to be. So why, oh why, had God seen fit to bring Joana back into his life, and why was he trembling?

'Joana,' he said, pushing her away. She looked up at him, her green eyes bright with tears. 'I need to find Catharine, and break your news to her, but I must do so gently.'

Joana's face crumpled. 'Of course. Poor little Catharine mustn't be upset, must she?' A kernel of spite had crept into her voice. 'Having to deal with this on my own has practically driven me into my grave, but Catharine is the the weak one and we must spare her. It's what our mother would have wanted.'

Matthieu didn't know what to say. She was right, of course; everyone had always treated Catharine as if she were fragile, despite being the older sister.

'I'll send Beatrice to you,' he said, desperate for a way to excuse himself. 'She'll attend to you. In the meantime, I must warn Catharine that you're here.'

CHAPTER 8

March 1538
Amesbury

When folk were putting their animals away and eating their evening meal, Matthew and Johanna travelled until it was almost too dark to see. Next morning, they rose whilst the dawn was still the faintest glimmer in the east, and in the afternoon took their rest and ate – keeping out of sight as far as possible. Matthew remembered the route, and had marked to himself places that would be good for sleeping on the way back, but had little realised that there would be two of them to accommodate.

Johanna hadn't told him much since the first day, but then he hadn't asked. She never complained, not even when, from the way she dismounted, he knew she was sore. Without comment, she slept or tried to sleep wherever he asked her, and once only, when they were almost at Amesbury, did she ask to go down to the river to wash. He even begrudged her this time, being afraid that she might attract attention, and kept watch from the bank, as discreetly as he could. After all, he told himself, he wasn't spying but looking out for her welfare.

He watched both banks of the river, alert to the slightest movement, his eyes darting anywhere but at the pale skin that dipped and splashed in the water, and to his utter amazement – swam. Where had she learned to do that? Matthieu felt himself grow hot and uncomfortable, and to his dismay – erect. Mother of God! Was that all it took for his body to sin? No wonder monastic men shunned women altogether.

Eventually, Johanna was ready to leave the water and he walked away to give her more privacy.

'Is something the matter?'

Matthew turned around to find Johanna clothed and ready to travel, but her hair hung damply about her shoulders. He found he could no longer look directly at her. It was as though he had developed some strange addition to his sight that no longer remained content with what reached his eyes, but *remembered* what he had seen, beneath.

'Pray don't worry,' he said, knowing he must move away for she was already beginning to affect him again. 'It's nothing.'

'All right.' She frowned and, to his relief, turned away to comb out her wet hair.

Now Matthew caught himself watching her body surreptitiously, and trembled inside his clothes.

'How long until we reach Amesbury?' Johanna asked.

'Another ten miles at most. We should be there by nightfall.'

And not a minute too soon, he thought, trying to ease his groin.

'That's good,' Johanna sighed. 'I can't wait to take my vows and leave this world behind,' she said, and started to coil her wet hair up under the linen cap. 'I can hardly believe I'm so near.'

*

They reached Amesbury Priory soon after dark and had to knock loudly until the gatekeeper arrived, grumbling and moaning, and pulling at the ties to his breeches. He grew more friendly when Johanna passed him a silver coin and after some anxious moments, returned with a nun carrying a lantern. The nun made no comment but bade Johanna follow her and indicated that Matthew should make his bed in the stables.

He was tired, but there was no one there to help feed and settle the horses. Just as he finished, and was looking forward to his warmest sleep for days, the gate keeper arrived with bread and cheese and a tankard of ale. Matthew downed the ale and the food, and then burrowed his way into the hay.

The bells of Lauds awoke him at dawn, but as he had not been invited to join the prayers, Matthew slept on until he heard the bells of Prime and knew it was morning. He saw Johanna briefly, whilst he was sluicing himself at the pump, and she only had time for the briefest of acknowledgments before running off towards the church. Soon she would be cloistered behind high walls and he would never see her again. Such was the monastic life, he though. Little time for idle thoughts or deeds. He could hardly wait.

Matthew ate a hearty breakfast in the guest house, sitting at a trestle table with a stout monk named Brother William. To his surprise he learned that Amesbury housed monks as well as nuns, as was usual in their mother house in France.

'I hear you're a novice at Glastonbury,' William said, slicing himself a chunk of fatty bacon.

Matthew shook his head as politely as he could and bit into a wedge of freshly baked bread. He was shocked at a monk eating bacon, *in Lent*, but sought to keep his expression neutral.

'So is it hunger or shyness keeping you so quiet?' William said, chewing noisily at the bacon with obvious relish.

Matthew shook his head again and hoped that the monk would get the message, but William was in a chatty mood.

'It can't have been easy not being able to talk and travelling with a woman like that. Turn your head, did she?'

Matthew looked away. The sin of his body was fresh in his mind and he hoped William would not guess; but there was to be no such luck.

'No need to blush, lad. That's why we monks have to lock ourselves away. Witches, the lot of them, if you ask me. Did anyone ever tell you what happened to Abelard?' William downed a draught of his ale and wiped at his mouth. 'Most learned man of his day he was, until he met Heloise. Lost his wits completely, they say. She was meant to be his pupil but he got her with child, and when she refused to marry him, her uncle sent someone to teach him a lesson. One that was hard to forget, I might add.' William picked up a wedge of bread and wiped it around his wooden trencher. 'They both had to take religious vows in the end, but I'd say if you're going to dedicate your life to God, it's better come with all your tackle intact...'

Matthew was wondering how soon he could escape from Brother William when Johanna arrived.

'I'm so glad you haven't left!' she said. 'I asked if I could come to say goodbye.'

Her hair was now tucked out of sight under a coarse brown veil and she was dressed in a robe of similar material, but her eyes shone and she looked more relaxed than at any time since their meeting.

'I hope everything goes well for you, Matthew. Will you walk with me?'

He nodded, and they walked out of the guest lodge and across the courtyard outside. Behind rose the octagonal spire of the church and the high walls of the convent.

'Johanna,' Matthew whispered. 'Are you sure I'm meant to be with you just now?'

'Of course,' she said. 'I'm not a novice yet – just a visitor until you leave here.' She clasped her hands to her chest. 'I know I shall be happy here, Matthew, but promise me one thing, if you may?'

Despite her joy, Johanna's eyes now shone a little too brightly if anything.

'What is it?' Matthew asked, gently.

'That you'll write and let me know that you're safely arrived at Glastonbury?'

Matthew swallowed and attempted to imagine what the Novice Master would say to such a request.

'I'll try,' he said.

'Goodbye then.'

She took his hand in hers, and grasped it tightly so that he could feel the tremor in her body. Impulsively, Matthew planted a kiss on top of her hand and she started to giggle, but stopped abruptly as a veiled nun opened the gate into the courtyard.

'Lady Johanna,' the nun said, the lines around her mouth folding sourly. 'My name is Mother Florence and I am the Prioress here. May I make it clear that this is absolutely the last time that you will be allowed to be so familiar with a man. Do you hear me?’

CHAPTER 9

July
Station View, Wesley Village, Yorkshire

Blanche was sitting up in bed with a cup of tea when Jo called round the following day. Typical, she thought, spell it out that someone's dying, and they perk up straight away.

'How are you, Blanche?' she asked.

'Tired,' Blanche said, 'but other than that...' Her bony shoulders rose in a shrug. 'How are you, Jo? Mat tells me you've been an angel.'

That was nice. 'I'm fine thanks, Blanche. Have you been watching the birds?'

A slow smile spread across Blanche's face. 'Yes, aren't they lovely?'

Jo went to the window. The bird table had half a dozen bags of seeds and nuts hanging from it, and two chaffinches pecked away at a coconut half, chirping happily.

'Mat tells me the nurses changed my medication yesterday,' Blanche said.

'Yes. You were pretty confused.'

'Was I?' Blanche said, looking wistful. 'Perhaps that's why I thought I wasn't alone.'

'Oh?' Jo turned around. 'Who were you with?'

'Never you mind. I'm neither too old nor too ill to still have my secrets.'

It was good to see Blanche smile again. Cancer was such a cruel illness, Jo thought, a series of non-stop losses; but Blanche would always be Mat's beloved aunt and her dear, dear friend.

'Will you sit with me?' Blanche said, pointing to the wicker chair by her bed. 'And tell me what you think of my nephew. He's wasted as a priest, don't you think?'

'Blanche!' Jo sat down quickly. 'How can you say that? I'm sure he's a wonderful priest.'

'But he'd make a good husband, don't you think?'

'Why on Earth are you asking me?' Jo said. 'Catholic priests aren't supposed to marry, are they?'

Blanche closed her eyes. 'No, but what's wrong with it? That's what I've always wondered.'

'I, er...' Jo floundered. 'Isn't it to do with dedication to God and being available for everyone?' How was Blanche managing this when she was so ill? There was even a twinkle in her eye.

'A priest can still be married and serve God,' Blanche said, squinting at her. 'The Anglicans manage it.'

'Yes, but wouldn't Catholic priests become Anglicans if they wanted to get married?'

'If only it were that simple.' Blanche shifted in the bed and grimaced. 'Can you fetch me another pillow, dear?'

'Does anyone fancy a cup of tea?' Mat's head appeared at the door and Jo felt her face burn. Had he heard what they were talking about?

'Please,' Blanche said. 'Two sugars.'

'You don't take sugar,' Mat said. 'I thought you were sweet enough?'

'Not now. Better make that three.'

'OK,' Mat laughed. 'Tea with three coming up, but don't blame me if it rots your teeth.'

'They''ll be safe enough in that glass over there...' Blanche managed a little laugh too, but then began to cough.

Jo helped her lean forwards until the spasm was over, and then slid the extra pillow behind her shoulders. Blanche leaned back with a sigh and closed her eyes.

'Do you need any help, Mat?' Jo said, following him into the kitchen. He seemed to have got everything organised: no washing up piled in the sink, no rubbish escaping from the bin.

'Only if you don't think I can make a cup of tea without it.'

'Sorry, I didn't...'

'I know,' he said. 'Will you get the cups out?'

Jo took three clean mugs out of the cupboard and put them on the counter. Mat lifted the teapot down from above the range.

'I'm not sure she'll be able to drink it,' she said. 'I think she's just gone off to sleep again.'

'Ah. This could be a good time then.' Mat put a finger to his lips and pointed. 'Shut the door will you?'

Jo took a quick look at Blanche. Her eyes were still closed, so she pulled the door to gently.

'What do you think?' Mat asked.

He spoke so quietly that Jo needed to move closer to hear him, and became conscious of the sandalwoody smell of his aftershave.

'She seems a lot better,' she said, 'but sometimes people do rally a bit, before the end, you know. I don't want you to get your hopes up...'

'How long are we talking?'

'It's so hard to say.' Would it really help if she told him that Blanche was going to die on Tuesday next week at two o' clock? How would he feel at half past one? 'It could be a few days,' she said, 'but then things could change suddenly, and we might only be talking a few hours.'

His eyebrows rose. 'Hours? Do you really mean that?'

She nodded. 'I'm sorry.'

'Don't be.' Mat touched her arm. 'I'm just grateful you're here.'

She dare not look him in the eye, in case he could divine her thoughts, but the arm he had just touched was tingling. Was it something to do with the fact he was off-limits that made him so desirable? 'I'm just glad I can be here. Blanche's been my friend ever since I moved in to Station View.'

'Is my tea ready?' Blanche's scratchy voice reached them from beyond the closed door. 'I hope you two aren't talking about me.'

'Of course we are,' Mat called. 'Who else is there to talk about?'

Jo went to get the milk jug from the fridge and felt the cold air sting her face. Phew! She had to get a grip. Not only was Mat off limits as a priest but he was an about-to-be-bereaved relative. Hospice protocol was strict about not getting involved with relatives in a vulnerable state, and for good reason.

CHAPTER 10

April 1204
St Gilles, Languedoc

For the Easter season, Count Raimon's court travelled the one hundred and fifty miles from Toulouse to Saint Gilles, which was near the Mediterranean coast. As soon as Matthieu had settled Catharine and Joana in their rooms at the castle of Mirapetra, and checked that Raimondet was occupied at the archery butts, he rode into Saint Gilles to find his old tutor and mentor, Father Alphonso.

The Abbey was in the centre of Saint Gilles and as he approached, Matthieu looked up at the sculpted frieze that ran around the church at roof height. The life of Jesus was picked out there, in vivid colours, so that anyone who passed that way, especially pilgrims, would know they were on the right track – both temporally and spiritually.

And in these times of ever increasing heresy, Matthieu thought, shading his eyes against the early spring sunshine, that was truly important.

A short, sprightly man wearing the robes of a priest came out of the middle door of the church and ran towards Matthieu, his sandalled feet kicking up spurts of dry dust.

'Matthieu, my son! You're here at last! I thought you'd forsaken me; given me up for dead and gone away for good. What kept you away so long?'

'I'm sorry, Alphonso,' Matthieu said, moving into the priest's embrace.

Sadly, his friend seemed a little older and a little shorter every time he saw him. Matthieu dropped his voice to just above a whisper. 'We had the wedding of Count Raimon and Eleonor of Aragon to attend, in case you hadn't noticed that he has married again – this time being the last time, or so he assures me.'

'Ah, yes, but then it's always the last time with the Count, isn't it?' Alphonso smiled. 'Anyway, wasn't that in January?'

'Yes, and *we've* been here frequently since then, but not you,' Matthieu gave Alphonso a friendly push. 'Do you know why we've come so early, this time?'

Alphonso shook his head.

'The consuls in Toulouse are fighting with the lords around the city again, and Raimon is furious but as usual, unable do anything about it.

He says he prefers it here where he can have a say in how he rules!'

Alphonso grimaced. 'Yes, and Abbot Pons is still struggling to forgive him for building that castle on our land.'

'But he *is* sorry, Alphonso,' Matthieu laughed. 'And he told me you weren't using the land anyway.'

Alphonso spluttered.

'Let's change the subject,' Matthieu said, looking around. They were on dangerous ground if they were overheard, but it was good to have someone to complain to occasionally... 'Anyway, where have you been? Over the Pyrenees again?'

'Ah, yes,' Alphonso said. 'The good Lord saw fit to allow me to return, once again to Compostela.' He made the Sign of the Cross. 'Abbot Pons tires of my prattling, eventually, and he says, 'Alphonso, isn't it time you were going to Compostela again, or Rocamadour, or Rome, or anywhere to give my old ears a rest?"

'Hah! Is that right?' Matthieu said, not believing his friend for one minute. 'I know he misses you when you're gone, Alphonso. Who wouldn't?'

Together they walked into the cool interior of the church and knelt in the choir stalls.

'Can I ask you something, Alphonso?' Matthieu whispered. 'Catharine will be here later to pray for a child. We've been married a little over four years now.'

'And you're wondering if God is deaf to your prayers, is that it?' Alphonso said, nodding. 'Sometimes we have to accept, Matthieu, that what God wishes for us is not what we wish for ourselves. Be glad for what you do have is my advice.' Alphonso took his arm. 'Your health, your wealth, and a very fine teacher in myself – if I may say so.'

Matthieu had to smile. 'For all those things I *am* grateful, believe me – the last especially, but I'm worried about her, Alphonso. Every day she grows thinner and more unhappy. Even the arrival of her sister hasn't cheered her up, but then-' Matthieu looked at the ground. 'Joana brought such bad news when she arrived.'

Alphonso nodded. 'I heard what happened in Tours. Is that why she came?'

'Yes.' Another example of what God wishes for us not being what we might wish for ourselves. 'They're not alike, you know. When you see them together, it's as though one took all the life and the other none.'

'Ah, my son,' Alphonso said, shaking his head sadly. 'Come, let's have some refreshment. You look weighted down with your cares. I'll leave word for Catharine when she arrives, so she knows where to find us.'

They sat in the shady garden of the Abbey courtyard, nibbling honeyed wafers and downing cool draughts of perry.

'Pons authorised these for you himself,' Alphonso said, licking honey off his fingers.

'In Lent?' Matthieu pretended to be shocked. 'And did he authorise you to eat them for me, too?'

'Um, I don't believe he said I couldn't,' Alphonso grinned. 'So tell me. I've watched you grow from a boy into a man, Matthieu, and you're no coward. What is it about the Lady Joana that causes you to turn so pale at the mention of her?'

It was all Matthieu could do not to stutter. Were his feeling really that obvious?

'Mm.' The priest was watching him closely. 'Not good, not good. And what do you propose to do about her? Do you want me to hear your confession?'

'I haven't done anything!' Matthieu said.

'You may think not,' Alphonso said. 'But what about your eyes?'

'My eyes?' Matthieu knew what Alphonso was trying to say: that it was possible to sin in his heart without speaking so much as a word to Joana and therein lay his dilemma. Whenever she came into the room, he made some excuse to leave. Whenever he knew where she would be, he planned to be as far away as possible; yet there were times when he *had* to see her, and then he would seek a window or some hidden place where he could watch but not be seen...

'Ah, my son,' Alphonso said. 'Send her away, for the sake of your soul, and hers. You cannot keep her in your home if that's how you feel. When she's gone, come and let me hear your confession.'

No, no, no! Matthieu couldn't bear the thought of sending Joana away. Not yet.

'Look at me, Matthieu,' Alphonso commanded. 'This will not do.'

'Matthieu! Alphonso! I have wonderful news!'

Catharine was almost running when she came into the garden. Her eyes were so bright, they were close to feverish. 'God has answered our prayers, Matthieu! I saw a vision in the crypt. Saint Gilles was smiling down on me!'

Matthieu mastered his thoughts with difficulty and stood to greet his wife. All of the dark shadows had flown from her face and she looked so radiant that he felt almost afraid of her.

'That's wonderful news, my love,' he said. Surely having a child of their own would put an end to his disloyal feelings?

Alphonso was smiling now. 'Praise be to God,' he said. 'An extra reason to celebrate this Easter: the resurrection of our Blessed Lord, and the promise of a little Matthieu to delight us in the future.'

*

Matthieu and Catharine rode slowly through Saint Gilles. It was a busy day and traders mingled with pilgrims in the market square. Ahead of them walked two men dressed in the long dark robes of the heretics, and as they watched, a young girl came running up and genuflected before the elder of the two

'Bless me lords,' the girl panted, bowing her head. 'Pray to God for my sins so that he makes me a good Christian and brings me to a good end.'

To which both responded: 'God blesses you, child.'

Matthieu bristled. How dare these heretics stroll about the streets so boldly?

'My grandmother is very ill,' the girl said. 'Please, my father says, will you come and see her?'

The older man nodded. 'Take us to her, child.'

'Wait!' Matthieu nosed his mount closer. 'These men are heretics, child. They will lead your grandmother straight into Hell.'

The girl looked at Matthieu, confusion and doubt written on her face.

'Let her be, Matthieu,' Catharine said.

'No. She should go to Alphonso.'

He dismounted and tried to take the girl's hand, but she ran back the way she had come. The younger man started after her, but Matthieu drew his sword.

'Peace, brother!' the elder man said, moving between them.

'There can be no peace,' Matthieu said, angrily. 'Not whilst you pollute minds such as hers!'

'We seek only to help,' the elder said, his face a mask of sadness. 'There is no need to bring a sword against us. We will not fight you.'

Matthieu felt his anger boil over. 'No, you will not even fight for what is right! You only pretend to love peace, and turn hearts away from God.'

'We do not seek to turn anyone from God,' Isarn said, his cheeks suffused with colour.

'So you say,' Matthieu retorted. 'But then why do you preach that there are two gods, one good and one evil? There is only one God, our Father in Heaven.'

The older man shook his head. 'There is evil is in the world, make no mistake, brother. Can you deny it?'

'Man is evil, not God,' Matthieu said, wondering at the man's wits. 'We are given a free choice.'

'But can there truly be such a choice,' the elder replied, 'when man knows not the truth of what he chooses? Look around you.' He pointed to a beggar waiting outside the Abbey. 'If there was only a good god, why would he create a world so flawed?'

Matthieu drew in an outraged breath. That this man could speak so and live was blasphemy...

'Matthieu,' Catharine said, 'can we go, please?'

He was half-blinded by his anger and didn't want to go. He wanted to stay until he had argued this man out of his heretical beliefs; but it was getting late and she did look pale.

'God has given us the Truth,' Matthieu said. 'And if you went to church you would hear it.'

Isarn gave a half strangled laugh. 'Jesus did not found a church. He came to bring the Truth, which your Church has all but obliterated.'

'How dare you insult God's Church?' Matthieu shouted.

'We are not insulting anything, brother,' the elder said, stepping back and pulling Isarn with him. 'Simply stating what we know to be the Truth.'

Matthieu's sword was in his hand again. 'By your lies you are sending souls into Hell!'

'Matthieu!' Catharine called. 'Please!'

'The only Hell we recognise, brother,' the elder said, 'is the one here on Earth – from which death will thankfully free us.'

People had gathered around, several were holding knives and Matthieu could see they had not assembled to help him. Angrily, he re-sheathed his sword.

'Come,' he said, remounting and urging his horse into a canter.

He would speak to Alphonso again as soon as he could. To have so many blatant heretics abroad in Saint Gilles was scandalous.

CHAPTER 11

Sept 19th 1539
Glastonbury Abbey

The sound of galloping hooves made Matthew pause and put down the pail he was carrying. There was much to fear from unannounced visitors these days, for many of the great monasteries had closed after a visit from the King's commissioners, and Glastonbury was the only religious house left open in the whole of the county of Somerset.

As the rider drew near he saw it was Brother John, the Abbey's treasurer, who rode full-tilt up the lane. Spittle flew from the mouth of his horse.

'Matthew! Where is my lord Abbot?' the monk panted, reining in his horse.

'At his grange of Sharpham, Brother.'

'And the Sacristan?'

'In the Abbot's house, I believe.'

Brother John grunted. 'Wait for me in the crypt, Matthew. Tell not a soul.'

The monk rode off and Matthew looked down at his pail. The hens and pigs needed feeding, but Brother John did not seem to have time to wait for him to do that so he tipped the scraps into the pig sty and went to wash his hands at the pump.

Beneath the Abbey, Saint Joseph's crypt was again in darkness. Matthew dipped his fingers into the font of holy water at the entrance and made the Sign of the Cross. As he shuffled forwards to find a pew, he could hear a thudding in his ears and his hands trembled when he thought of the fear on Brother John's face. He offered up a prayer for the repose of his mother's soul – she'd died not long after he returned from Canterbury, an unearthly smile upon her face as she gazed upon what he could not – and then quickly sent thanks and praise to Saint Thomas for the gift of his unfailing intercession.

As the bells of Terce rang, Matthew shifted on his knees. The Novice Master would soon notice he wasn't in church, and the pigs would likely eat each other if he didn't give them more food soon. At last he heard hurrying feet and Brother John came into the crypt, carrying a candle and a bundle. In the flickering light, Matthew could see sweat standing out on the monk's face.

'The King's commissioners are on their way, Layton, Pollard and the rest, so you have to go quickly, Matthew. The Abbot wants you to take this to France.' He thrust the bundle at Matthew.

'But-'

'Don't argue with me,' the monk pleaded. 'I've put spare clothes in there too, but it's the reliquary you brought from Canterbury. They musn't find it.'

'The reliquary?' Matthew's heart missed a beat. All that way from Canterbury he'd been carrying the Saint's remains, unknowingly.

'Are you ill, Brother?'

The monk had a fist against his chest and looked upon the point of expiring.

'I'm sorry. You're not going to like this next bit,' Brother John wheezed. He reached into his sleeve and drew out a parchment. 'Someone will meet you at Weymouth, outside the chapel of Saint Nicholas on the hill. To prevent suspicion, you've to travel as a married couple. The woman knows where to go once you reach France.'

Matthew thought his frustration would suffocate him. Why, oh why was it necessary to hamper him so?

'I have the licence for you here,' Brother John said, handing over the parchment. 'God and Saint Thomas go with you, Matthew, but hurry! There won't time to get away if you dawdle. And remember – nobody here knows anything about where you've gone, or what you carry with you.'

CHAPTER 12

July
Station View, Wesley Village, Yorkshire

Jo blinked back her tears. There was an ache in her chest. Blanche's breathing had become erratic – has-she-gone gaps followed deep, sighing in-breaths. The district nurses were refilling the syringe driver and they stopped to watch as Blanche's breathing slowed again.

'Is her nephew here?' Sarah asked.

'Yes, he's upstairs in bed. I'll call him as soon as you've gone.'

'Good,' Sarah said, still watching for Blanche's next breath. 'Are you sure you're all right, Jo? We'll stay if you want.'

'No, it's OK. I can manage. She's been really comfortable since you increased the morphine yesterday.'

'Yes.' Belinda finished packing the unused needles and syringes back into her bag. 'But if she's not, you know where we are. Don't think you have to do this all by yourself, Jo. You're the same as anyone else at the minute.'

They were being kind, she knew that, but she and Mat had managed to look after Blanche so far and she wasn't going to give in and move her to the hospice now. It had been Blanche's wish to die at home, and die here she would.

The nurses gave a cheery wave as they drove away in Sarah's Mini, but after she closed the door, Jo stood in the hallway, unable to move. Mat came downstairs and she tried to smile at him, but the muscles of her face didn't seem to be working.

'Hey,' he searched in his pocket, 'have this. It's clean.'

He brought out a handkerchief and Jo finally managed a smile. How many men went around with clean hankies in their pockets these days?

'That's better,' he said. 'Can I make you a cuppa? Or how about something stronger? Blanche's got some brandy in the pantry somewhere.'

'No, I'm OK,' she said.

They went into the kitchen and Jo realised that her hands were shaking.

'You go and sit with her,' she said. 'I'll stay here and make the tea. I think she needs you more than me.'

'I'm not sure she does,' he said, looking uncertain all of a sudden. 'I think she needs us both. You sit down and I'll make the tea.'

'Oh, Mat, I'm sorry.'

'Why?' he said, looking baffled. 'For caring for my aunt in a way few other people could?'

'No. Because I'm supposed to be helping *you*, not the other way round.'

He laughed. 'And there was I, thinking I was helping you. Well, I guess the truth of it is, God's helping all three of us. Isn't that good to know?'

She had to turn away. What he said sparked off an anger that she tried not to feel when she was at work, but it was there all the same. Too many of the people who filled the beds at the hospice had worked all their lives only to find that their dreams and plans for retirement were never going to happen. Couples, sometimes young or perhaps having only just met, were painfully dragged apart by an untimely death. Elderly parents could be forced to watch a child of their own body fade and die before their time. Young parents, ill themselves, had to face the nightmare of knowing that they would never be able to help their children grow up. Where was God in all that?

*

The candle spluttered and Jo jerked awake. If she didn't stop falling asleep, she was going to burn the house down. When she sat forwards she saw that Blanche was almost the same colour as the sheet beneath her. Her breathing had speeded up and gurgled noisily in her throat – the dreaded death rattle. Three thirty am the little alarm clock on the bedside table said – a favourite time to go, if you were going.

Mat woke quickly at her knock. 'Yes?'

'I think it's going to be soon. You'd better come down.'

Hearing him get up and move about, Jo tiptoed back downstairs and into the kitchen, as though making a noise would somehow stop Blanche in her progress. Everything was just the same: the harsh rattle of unswallowed saliva, the deep sighs of Blanche's breathing, the sickly smell of impending death.

Mat came in, winding the cord of his dressing gown about himself.

'Do you realise it's a year to the day since Patrick died?'

'Really?' She tried to remember back. Of course it was. How could she have missed that? Typical of Blanche.

'Sit here.' She got up from the wicker chair. 'I'll put the kettle on.'

'But don't you? I mean, don't you want to...'

'I'll only be in the kitchen.' Goodness, he looked almost scared. Surely a priest ought to be used to people dying?

'All right,' he said.

She watched him gingerly pick up and stroke the back of Blanche's hand, then put it down again as if he didn't much like the feel of it, and pull out another handkerchief. The water in the kettle came to the boil and she poured it into the teapot. They would need plenty of this before it was all over.

CHAPTER 13

April 1204
Launaguet, Languedoc

Catharine was in a happy mood all the way back from Saint Gilles. She had taken an enthusiastic part in the Easter rites, her face shining with hope and gratitude, and now she rode beside Matthieu, animatedly pointing out the new growth of spring. For his part, Matthieu couldn't shake off a sense of foreboding. Catharine would be more keen than ever that they share a bed, but the spectre of the birthing chamber haunted him. What if she wasn't strong enough to have a baby? What if she died?

The Count didn't worry about such things, nor did most men that Matthieu knew – so why should he? Why should he try to alter the course ordained by God? Yet there was no denying that women suffered terribly and very often died in childbirth. The Bible taught that God loved His creation, and cared deeply for each of them; but hadn't He also condemned His Son to death at the hands of those who despised him?

Matthieu left the servants and the two sisters to their unpacking and went out into the gardens. He needed time alone and there was a favourite seat of his there, under an arch of clematis, with a splendid view of the Pyrenees.

'Forgive me, if I startle you.'

He looked around. The last person he wanted to talk to was Joana.

'Is anything wrong?' he asked.

'Yes,' she said. 'Actually, I was worried about you. You've looked pale all the way back from Saint Gilles.'

'Really? I'm probably tired, that's all.'

'Of course,' she nodded. 'Well, I won't disturb you.'

She started to walk away, but he called her back. He might as well lay the foundation for her leaving now, whilst he had the opportunity. He patted the bench next to him.

'Come and sit down, Joana. I need to talk to you.'

She swept up the skirts of her gown and sat down, arranging them about herself. It was made of light blue silk, a colour he hadn't seen her wear before, and it made her eyes seem almost turquoise.

A pulse started at his temples.

'Are you sure you're not unwell, Matthieu?' Joana said, frowning at him.

'Yes.'

Before he could stop her, she had laid a cool, white hand against his chest.

'Your heart's racing, Matthieu, I can feel it. See, compare it to mine.'

She took his hand and laid it against the front of her bodice. Dear God! He searched her face. Did she have any idea what she was doing to him? Her lips were very near and it would take but a moment to capture them. Never had he felt so close to paradise, and yet so very near to Hell.

'Joana-' He stood up and faced her.

'Don't say anything,' she begged. 'Please don't, Matthieu.'

'But, Joana-'

He took a deep breath. Her eyes were begging something from him and warmth surged through his body. She stood up too and swayed closer, her face turning up to him, eyes closed, lips half parted. He knew he shouldn't be doing this, shouldn't be here, but his resistance shredded as he felt the heat of her skin near his. Fire raged through him and hungrily he pulled her nearer, claimed her mouth, explored the mounds of her breasts.

'Matthieu?' Joana murmured, as he trailed kisses down the creamy skin of her neck. 'Do you love me, as I love you?'

Her words shattered him, and he jerked away. Joana's hands crossed protectively across her chest.

'Matthieu?'

'Go into the house and help your sister to unpack,' he said, sharply. 'This must never happen again, Joana, do you hear me?'

'But, Matthieu...'

'I know what you thought,' he said, 'but you were mistaken. Now, go back inside.'

'But Matthieu, it's only because you're such a wonderful husband to my sister that I love you,' Joana said, looking so hurt that he felt, absurdly, that he should comfort her. 'You're – I mean – well, I was foolish. Can you forgive me?'

'Just go inside,' he said, dragging a hand through his hair. 'And help Catharine. If you love her and care for her as much as you say, then you must behave better than this, Joana. Do you understand?'

Tears were sliding down Joana's face. She came towards him, her hand held out in supplication; but he brushed it away.

'No!' he said. 'We won't talk of this again. Do as I ask and go back inside the manor, now! And try to compose yourself. The last thing I want is for Catharine to be upset. Not when she's received such good news.'

'Good news?' Joana's tears dried abruptly.

'Yes, did she not tell you?' He hated himself for still desiring her. 'The Saint smiled on her when she was at Saint Gilles. She believes we will soon have a child.'

*

'Will you come to me tonight, my love?' Catharine whispered.

She'd put on one of her best gowns and belted it at her hips with a slender golden chain. Of course he said 'yes', but then he was almost overcome with guilt and couldn't stay in the manor. He asked Bernard to saddle his horse and rode out to the local church, where he knocked for the priest and asked him to hear his confession.

It was dark by the time Matthieu returned home, and Catharine was already in her chamber. Matthieu asked for hot water to be taken up to his room and soaked in a tub of it, taking his time, feeling like a coward. In his heart he wanted Catharine to have the child she so longed for, but he couldn't stop worrying about the effect another pregnancy might have on her. But wasn't that why he'd just spent all that time praying to God? He'd confessed his sins, received absolution, could he not now leave the matter safely in God's hands?

When Ermessinda opened the door of Catharine's chamber, he saw that his wife was already in bed, with her hair falling about her shoulders in shining waves. A strange smile passed between the two women as Ermessinda left, and then they were alone.

Catharine did something she'd never done before; when Matthieu began to undress, she slipped out of bed and asked if he'd like her to help.

'There's no need, my love,' he said, embarrassed. 'I won't treat you like a servant.'

'But I'd like to serve you, my husband,' Catharine said, standing on tip-toe to reach the buttons of his chemise. He was surprised and not a little shocked by this boldness. In all of his life so far, only Bernard and servants had helped him to undress.

Catharine folded his garments carefully and put them aside, until he was clad only in his linen braies. She smiled up at him, clearly enjoying his surprise, and ran her fingers lightly across his chest. The effect was unsettling. He smiled at her, but how guilty he felt at her innocence, and the memory of his loss of control with Joana tortured him. Catharine fetched a light robe and asked if he would like to sup with her. Relieved, Matthieu sat down by the fire and watched the light of the flames flickering through the curtain of Catharine's hair as she bent to pour wine into two pewter goblets.

'I feel so hopeful, my love,' she said, sitting on a cushion at his feet, and leaning herself back against his knees. 'When we were at Saint Gilles and the Saint appeared to me, I was filled with joy. What greater sign can there be that God has chosen to smile on us? I'm going to give you a son, Matthieu, someone to care for us, and this manor, when we're old.'

'Ah, my love,' he said, lifting a tress of her hair and allowing it to fall, silkily, between his fingers, 'there's nothing I could want more than to see you playing happily with half a dozen of our brood. But are you sure...?'

'Of course I'm sure,' Catharine said, taking a gulp of the wine and twisting her fingers through his.

The warmth of the fire and the wine had begun to do their work, and Matthieu stroked the nape of Catharine's neck. She turned to kneel before him and her mouth parted for a kiss. This was a different Catharine he found himself with tonight, one filled with confidence and optimism. As he pulled her towards him, she let her robe fall so that he found himself stroking naked flesh.

Matthieu lifted up his wife and carried her gently to their bed. She weighed no more than a child, but he pushed that thought away. Earlier, he'd felt like a puppet, acting out something he didn't want to do, but now as he pulled off his braies he found himself ready and Catharine urged him to enter her. The release was almost instant and he collapsed against her, shuddering with relief.

'Oh, my love!' Catharine gasped, clasping her arms tight about him. 'Everything is going to be all right this time, Matthieu. I'm certain of it!'

'Did I hurt you?' he asked. There'd been no time for tenderness.

'Of course not,' she said. 'Hold me.'

He lay back and she curled up against him, her head on his shoulder. Shadows from the fire played upon the ceiling and Matthieu pulled the counterpane up to cover them. From now on he would never, *ever* allow himself think of anyone, or anything, other than Catharine – and the fact that their union was blessed by God.

CHAPTER 14

September 20th 1539
Weymouth

Matthew was grateful for the solitude of the road, for he fought a war inside himself. God's will, his will. There could be only one winner, and he knew which one it *should* be, but it wasn't fair! All his life he'd dreamed of joining the monks at Glastonbury Abbey, and now that was impossible. Preposterous though it was, that great Abbey, the oldest in England, was finished. The King's commissioners were on their way and soon the monks would be scattered and sheep roaming the cloisters. And for what? So the King could fill his coffers?

Matthew patted the marriage licence in the pouch under his clothes and urged his horse onwards. There was no point in bemoaning his fate. The only thing to be done now was to make sure Saint Thomas' reliquary was taken to safety, and hope for a new life in a French monastery. After all, how many men could say they had travelled twice in the company of such a great saint?

Matthew had almost got over the shock of learning the scared nature of what he'd carried from Canterbury. It was perhaps as well that he didn't know at the time but – Matthew flexed his shoulders – now he was seventeen, and not only stronger but more versed in God's ways. Just let anyone try to take the Blessed Saint's relics from him now, including King Henry.

The roads were deserted this early in the morning, but sheep moved restlessly around their pasture and he heard the high piping of a shepherd's flute somewhere in the distance. Normally he would have been looking ahead for somewhere to rest, but today he felt too agitated to sleep and thought he would carry on. Dark clouds filled the sky and the temperature fell sharply. Rain pelted his back, and then the sun broke out causing his wet clothes to steam.

'Matthew, I have a most important task for you', *'it's the Becket reliquary you brought from Canterbury'*, *'we've decided you should go as a married couple'*.

The phrases repeated themselves over and over in his head until he thought he would go mad listening to them.

Six months after he brought the reliquary from Canterbury, the Saint's shrine had been cruelly destroyed. It had taken twelve men to carry the chests of valuables away – the gifts of countless pilgrims. Now the King had decreed that Thomas Becket was never a saint, that his martyrdom was a lie promulgated by the Pope, that his bones were to be publicly burned and the ashes put into a cannon and fired into the air. All images of him were ordered to be removed, and his feast day abolished. Every reference to the Saint, whether it be in service, office, antiphon, collect or prayer had been ordered to be scratched out – no matter that it would deface a great many holy books.

Matthew shook his head; he could be carrying the last of the Saint's bones in his saddlebag. Thank God Abbot Whiting had smuggled the reliquary away from Canterbury whilst there was still time. For that, God be praised, but as for why the King hated Saint Thomas so much? The monks had whispered that it was because he had dared to defy his King. Matthew made the Sign of the Cross. May God have mercy upon them all.

The rain began again, blowing directly into Matthew's face and dripped off the end of his nose. At least the cloak Brother John gave him was made of stout wool that kept out the weather. Matthew had insisted on wearing his own clothes and boots for riding, but given in to wearing a smart black felt cap. It turned up neatly at the brim when he first put it on, but now the brim flapped wetly about his ears. To all intents, Matthew looked the picture of a wealthy, if rather wet, traveller; but how he wished he was wearing the simple robes of a monk.

He did a quick check: knife in its scabbard, reliquary in the saddle bag, money in a pouch hidden underneath his clothes. In addition to a goodly amount of gold and silver, the pouch held another marvel – a marriage licence. Although that might mean he was legally married, Matthew knew he could not be so in the eyes of God, for he had given no consent nor taken any vows. He jingled the coins. If he was so minded, with this amount of money, he could have thrown the reliquary into the sea and bought himself a very respectable farm.

At last the coast came into view and the wind freshened, tugging at his clothing. Seagulls piped overhead, and a majestic shingle beach spread out before him, bordering the western side of a peninsula that reached far into the sea. Matthew tried to ease his shoulders, which were stiff from a poor night's sleep. In previous days he might have attempted to take safe lodgings in one of the monasteries on his way, but now they were all in the process of being dismantled.

Avoiding the swampy areas to the north of Weymouth, Matthew detoured out towards the little village of Abbotsbury and finally reached the Weymouth harbour in the late afternoon. The captain of a triple masted caravel named, 'The Promise', readily accepted some of the silver coins in exchange for a passage for two to Sarnac in France the following day. That done, Matthew set off to find the chapel of Saint Nicholas. Fortunately, there was only one hill behind the harbour and one chapel upon it. He tethered his horse at the base of the hill and climbed the steep steps, all the while trying to keep his thoughts under control; but there was no doubt that he was nervous about meeting this, 'wife', whoever she might be.

The bell was missing from the church tower and the dilapidated door locked. As Matthew walked around the outside of the building, he saw the ferry making its way across the river from Weymouth to Melcombe Regis, pulled along by a rope which was slung between the two banks. In the distance, Melcombe Regis' wide white beach curved up the coast towards an outcrop of chalk. Upriver, Matthew could hear the shouts of sailors, from boats clustered about a wharf, unloading cargo. The smell of seaweed was strong, blown off the shingle beaches to the west and, if he squinted, Matthew could see signs of excavations out on the peninsula. Another castle? King Henry was frightened of attack from abroad since he'd alienated himself from the Catholics of France and Spain. Rumour even had it that the Pope wanted to send a crusade against him.

Where on Earth was the woman he was supposed to meet? He'd gone twice around the church now, but then saw someone, sitting on a bench a way off.

'Good day, Mistress, may I interrupt you?' Matthew removed his soggy cap and bowed – observing guardedly that underneath her thick travelling clothes, the woman appeared to be trembling.

'Sir?' As she looked up, Matthew gasped. No mistaking those green eyes and sweeping lashes. 'Lady Johanna? Is it really you?'

'Matthew! The saints preserve us,' Johanna's pale face broke into a smile. 'They said to wait here for my, 'husband', but I was beginning to wonder. Oh, Matthew, I swear it couldn't have been anybody better than you that would arrive.' Johanna let out a sigh. 'I've been so nervous.'

'You must be as downcast as I by this business,' Matthew observed, perching on the bench beside her. 'And I don't pretend to understand half of it. But you're shivering. Come on, let's find some lodgings and then we can talk. My horse is at the bottom of the steps and I've enough money to pay for a good room for us.'

His cheeks burst into flame.

'It's all right,' Johanna said, though there was a blush on her face too. She put her hand on his arm. 'We're doing this for God, Matthew. No shame should attach to us for that. And you needn't worry about a room. The farrier from Amesbury accompanied me here and I have already found one for us in the town. Come on, I think you'll like it.'

*

He unpacked the clothes that Brother John had given him and placed them on a heavy, iron-bound chest in the corner of the room. The monk had done well in such little time: spare breeches and hose, two shirts and another tunic. Matthew pushed the package containing the reliquary further down into his bag and took the marriage licence from his pouch. It was the first time he'd had the opportunity to really look at it.

'Do you think someone had been planning this for a while?' he said, shocked to see both of their names clearly written on it.

Johanna's eyes widened. 'It certainly looks like it, but then why didn't they say? Everything was so much of a rush at Amesbury. I thought Mother Florence would faint, she looked so worried. All she said was that she was sorry, but I had to be willing to do God's work in a different place. Then she told me to go to Fontevraud Abbey with you – only I didn't know it was you then, of course.'

'Fontevraud Abbey?' Matthew said. 'I've never heard of it.'

'It's the mother house of the convent at Amesbury. It's near Chinon.'

'Is that far from Sarnac?'

'About two hundred miles.'

Matthew frowned as he calculated. 'It'll take us the best part of a week to ride there. Holy Mother of God protect us. Have you ever crossed the sea before, Lady Johanna?'

She hesitated. 'I was brought up at Fontevraud Abbey.'

'Ah.' He paused. That was obviously why *she* had been chosen. 'Why didn't you become a novice there, then? Why did you come to England?'

'Because,' Johanna's teeth worried at her lower lip, 'because I was summoned by my uncle to the English court.'

'Court!' The wheels in Matthew's head creaked as he adjusted to this amazing new information. 'You were at *court* before I met you?'

Johanna nodded, but still avoided his eyes.

'But then you left court and went to Canterbury. Why would you go there, when you really wanted to go to Amesbury?'

'I was visiting someone I knew.'

Matthew's eyebrows rose. Johanna seemed to be finding something of enduring interest in the toe of her shoe.

'Father Peter is my mother's cousin.'

'Lady Johanna.' Matthew took a deep breath. 'If you are to be at my side – if we are to trust each other in this venture – then I'm sorry to be so bold, but you must tell me all.'

Still she did not look up, but danced her toe around in a little circle.

'The King wanted me to marry one of his idle-headed courtiers, but I refused.'

'Oh,' Matthew was stunned. 'That was brave.'

'Not really,' Johanna said, finally looking up. 'I told you, my mind was set upon becoming a nun.'

Matthew nodded. So much he could understand. 'But now, with his reforms, the King has made it impossible for either of us to take vows.'

Johanna nodded sadly. 'I've always longed to give my life to God, but my uncle had other plans. I thought I was finally escaping from him when I went to Amesbury, but now my only hope is in France. Once I am there, my soul will be at rest.'

Matthew looked at the marriage licence. An uneasy feeling was snaking its way up his spine.

'Were you *actually* betrothed to this gentleman of the King's, Lady Johanna?' If so, they could add bigamy to their list of crimes.

'No. I managed to escape before it was arranged.'

Matthew's breath came out in a low whistle. 'But you disobeyed the King.'

All the things he'd heard of recently, that had happened to people who were even *suspected* of disobeying the King, crowded gruesomely into his mind.

'Yes,' Johanna said.

'And is he angry with you still?'

She nodded. 'I was desperate when I met you in Canterbury, Matthew,' she said, sitting on the very edge of the bed with hands clasped together. 'If you hadn't helped me to go to Amesbury, I don't know what I would have done.'

Matthew sighed and walked to the window. She'd had a difficult time, that much was obvious. Her uncle had tried to use her as a marriage pawn, and she'd refused. What was truly amazing was that the Prioress at Amesbury had agreed to take her at all. Might there be someone else sponsoring Johanna? Someone more important even than her uncle or Father Peter?

'We're going to have to be extremely careful at the port,' he said, thinking even that was an understatement. 'The King probably has men are everywhere, looking for...' He hesitated. 'Well, looking for people like us who are trying to smuggle Church valuables out of the Country. Might you be recognised do you think?'

'It's possible.'

'By the Mass!' Matthew swung around to face her.

'Matthew, please!' She came up behind him, and lightly touched his arm. A tingle fizzed its way up his arm to his shoulder, and then down into his heart.

'We're a long way from London,' Johanna said, her eyes entreating him. 'I'll make sure I keep as hidden as possible.'

Holy Mother of God! Matthew could barely believe what was happening to him. Despite all his precautions and prayers, warmth was seeping into the whole of his body, as he looked into her pleading eyes.

'Very well,' he said, helplessly.

How was he going to be to spend time in close proximity to this woman? It would require every ounce of self-control that he possessed to ignore the waywardness of his body.

'We'll have to think of a reason why you need to keep away from people,' he said. 'Some illness perhaps?'

'Yes,' she said, 'but not one that makes us unwelcome on board...' She frowned. 'How if I pretend to be with child? Because of that I must rest in our cabin throughout the journey? I could make the reliquary into my bump.'

Matthew froze. 'You know about the reliquary?'

Brother John had insisted that he keep the reliquary's presence *secret*.

'Yes,' she said. 'I knew about it when we left Canterbury.'

'Which was more than I did.' Matthew rubbed at his neck. 'Do you know anything else about it?'

'Only that it contains a relic of Saint Thomas Becket. May I look at it, Matthew, please? So I can plan how best to hide it?'

'My lady-' He looked out of the window. A man was leading a his horse into the stables, which were directly below. Matthew measured the distance. Not too far to jump – if they had to. 'I have to carry the reliquary. It isn't safe for you to be found with it.'

'But if what you say is true and the King's men are everywhere, then they're bound to search us and our bags,' Johanna said. 'I think my suggestion is the only sensible one.' She folded her arms and her chin jutted forwards.

'But, my lady.' He was beginning to feel intimidated by her rank, but still wasn't prepared to give up something he'd been told to guard with his life. 'How can I let you take that risk?'

'Easily,' she said, making an impatient face. 'And for the Saint's sake, Matthew, please stop calling me 'my lady'. Do you want to give us away before we've even left the Country? Listen to me. Everyone is at risk since the King learned how easy it is to rid himself of people he doesn't like; but I'm not afraid of him. I was taking more of a risk than this when I refused to marry the man he'd chosen for me.'

'Were you?' he said. 'The gentleman in question, do we have his enmity to count upon, too?'

'No,' Johanna said, confidently. 'I don't think he was particularly keen to have me either.'

'Are you sure? Didn't you wound his pride?'

She shook her head. 'Now, please, Matthew. Can I see the reliquary?'

'I'm sorry,' he said, 'but I don't believe you.' There was a shadow in her otherwise clear green eyes that told him she wasn't being entirely truthful.

'Why not?' She looked offended.

'I don't know. There's something you're not telling me isn't there?

What is it? Our lives are going to depend upon us being honest with each other.'

For a long moment, they faced each other, but then Johanna went to sit down upon the bed and entwined her fingers.

'Very well. I was a maid of honour to Queen Jane Seymour. It was a position my uncle paid highly for, and he was counting on me helping him advance him at court.'

Matthew nodded. He had heard of such things.

'Whilst I was there, the Queen was delivered of a fine baby boy. The Prince survived, but Jane died twelve days later.'

Tears formed in Johanna's eyes and she reached into her sleeve for a handkerchief before continuing.

'The King-' She wound her fingers ever more tightly, then took a breath and looked Matthew fully in the eye. 'What I wasn't telling you, I'm afraid, is that the King didn't want me to marry one of his courtiers, he wanted me to become his mistress. '

Matthew looked back at the window. People were going about their business in the yard, just as they had done before, but now everything was different. Never mind the reliquary, never mind the crime of trying to smuggle it out of the country, Johanna had just said that she *refused to become the King's mistress*. No wonder she'd been desperate when he first met her. He took an unsteady breath and tried to remain calm, but his heart was hammering for all it was worth. Now she was supposedly married to a woodcutter's son, when her status likely dictated that without the King's blessing she could not marry anyone, especially not someone as lowly as he was. How much danger did they need to be in?

Austin Friars
London

Thomas Cromwell had been writing for hours. His back was stiff and his fingers cramped, but he was determined to finish everything today, for tomorrow, he was entertaining the ambassadors from Cleves.

He pulled the note from Pollard towards him. It had been written whilst the commissioner was in Glastonbury and Cromwell put down his pen as he read the words again.

'*Came to Glastonbury on Friday last at 10 a.m. Went to the Abbot, who was at his grange at Sharpham, about a mile from the Abbey, and examined him on certain articles. As his answer was not to our purpose, advised him to call to mind what he had forgotten and tell the truth. Visited the abbey, searched his study, and found a book against the King's divorce from the lady Dowager, and divers pardons, copies of bulls, and the counterfeit life of Thos. Bequet in print; but could not find any letter that was material. Examined him again on the articles received from Cromwell. His answers, which we send, will show his cankered and traitorous heart. And so, with as fair words as we could, we have conveyed him from hence unto the Tower, being but a very weak man and sickly.'*

Cromwell tapped his fingers as he read. A counterfeit life of Thomas Becket...? What did he have to do to persuade these fools that the man was never a saint? How could they venerate someone who had been not only a violent, selfish man, but had brought about the demise of his King?

Ah, well. The bigger the fool, the bigger the drop.

There was a second, brief letter from Pollard. *'It has come to our notice that one of the young novices from Glastonbury was sent hastily to Weymouth. Will have him apprehended at the port.'*

Cromwell sucked air in between his teeth and shuffled amongst the papers on his desk until he found the short note from one of the commissioners at Amesbury.

'A young novice left the Priory shortly after our arrival. Destination unknown. Possibly the Priory's mother house in France. Have sent word to the nearest ports.'

Two novices leaving for France in a hurry? They were almost certainly carrying something valuable with them. It would be interesting to find out what.

CHAPTER 15

June
Station View, Wesley Village, Yorkshire

Jo kissed Blanche on the forehead and let go of her hand. Mat was in the kitchen and Jo knew he was crying because she could see his shoulders shaking, but he made no sound. She touched him as she passed.

'I'm sorry.'

He turned bleary eyes to her. 'So am I. Sorry for both of us, that is. No one else on Earth could be as wonderful as my aunt. What will we do without her, Jo? Whose ear am I going to bend now?'

Perhaps mine? The thought flitted through Jo's head unbidden.

'I'm just glad we've been able to be here with her, aren't you?' he continued. 'And that the Bishop let me have this time off. She wanted to die in her own home and she's been able to do it – that's something we have to be grateful for.' He wiped his eyes. 'In fact, it's something I want to thank God for right now. Would you like to join me?'

That threw her, it really did. How could she say yes when, since her teens, praying had had no meaning for her? Or would it, in some strange way, have meaning because prayers meant so much to Blanche?

'Give me a couple of minutes,' she said. There were some practicalities that needed sorting out first. 'I should ring the doctor – let him know she's died, so we can get a certificate.'

Jo found Mat sitting at Blanche's bedside with a stole around his neck. It was embroidered with red and gold crosses.

'She did this for me,' Mat said, lifting up one of the tails.

A chair had been pulled up for Jo, and a strange kind of silence descended when she sat down, as though the world was waiting to start praying too. Mat picked up a leather bound book and opened it at a place marked by coloured ribbons. He gave a little cough and then closed his eyes. Jo watched as his hand made movements before his face.

'In the name of the Father, and of the Son and of the Holy Spirit. Amen.'

He stopped and clasped his hands in his lap, then bent his head.

'Eternal rest grant to her, O Lord, and let the perpetual light shine upon her. May she rest in peace. Amen. And may her soul and the souls of all the faithful departed, through the mercy of God, rest in peace. Amen.'

Mat opened his eyes and turned to the book.

'In this moment of sorrow, the Lord is in our midst and consoles us with his word: blessed are the sorrowful for they shall be comforted. Jesus said to his disciples: I say to you, if two of you agree on Earth about anything for which they are to pray, it shall be granted to them by my heavenly Father. For where two or three are gathered together in my name, I am there, in the midst of them.'

He looked at her. 'Do you believe that, Jo? Do you believe that if we're both here, in Jesus' name, then he's here with us?'

What should she say? She forced herself not to look around to see if anyone else was in the room with them. 'I-I don't know.'

'Well, that's the promise, whether we believe it or not,' he said, and bent to the book again. 'With God there is mercy and fullness of redemption; let us pray as Jesus taught us.' He looked up. 'Will you pray this with me Jo, do you know the words to the 'Our Father'?'

Jo nodded. She had prayed it at school when she was little, but never understood why God might lead her into temptation.

'Our Father, who art in Heaven...'

When they finished, Mat put down the book, and kept his eyes firmly closed. Tears spilled from the corners of them, and ran down his cheeks.

'Forgive me,' he said, wiping at his face. 'I'm not myself.'

She thought about trying to comfort him, but the embroidered stole and the book formed a shield that Jo could not penetrate. Finally, he stood up and leaned over Blanche's body.

'Goodbye, Auntie Blanche,' he said. 'Farewell.' He kissed her forehead and sat down again.

Jo had no idea how many deaths she'd been present at, but they'd never had this personal *intensity* before. Perhaps if she'd been there when her own mother died? But that had been a sudden death, a brain haemorrhage, and a memory almost too painful to think about.

She crept out of the room, intending to give Mat some time alone with his aunt before the doctor came. Her turn would come later, when she washed Blanche and put her into a clean nightdress, and made sure she was 'fit to meet her Maker'. Right now she was going to give the birds one last feast before taking the feeders next door into her own garden.

'I won't let them starve, Blanche,' she whispered. 'I promise.'

CHAPTER 16

April 1204
Château Narbonnais
Toulouse

'Sir Matthieu!' Count Raimon greeted Matthieu as he entered the great solar of the Château Narbonnais. 'You're just in time to witness me winning at dice, for once. I'm feeling very pleased with myself, but you,' he clapped Matthieu on the back, 'look as though you've seen the devil himself. What ever is the matter?'

'My lord is too kind,' Matthieu said, silently hoping that this would be one of the days when that was actually true.

'Is it my son again?' The Count frowned. 'Has he been up to mischief?'

'Constantly,' Matthieu grinned, 'but that's not why I'm here.'

'Ah. Well then...' The Count looked around his solar. 'We can go to the window and gain ourselves a little privacy. Is Catharine well?'

Matthieu acknowledged the men sitting at the dice tables. These were not nobles but wealthy Toulousan citizens who cared not a fig about losing money to the Count, because it meant they gained rents and tithes in exchange. Matthieu sometimes worried that the Count would one day gamble away his son's heritage.

'She's much cheered,' he said, sitting down on the deeply-cushioned window seat.

The Count took a goblet of wine from the tray his page held and handed it to Matthieu, who took a long swallow – expecting to need it.

'She had a vision when we were at Saint Gilles, and expects to be with child very soon.'

'Good news then?' The Count plucked a sweetmeat from the same platter. 'Have one of these,' he said, giving the almond-stuffed date to Matthieu. 'They arrived from Marseilles yesterday, and they're wonderful.'

Matthieu savoured the milky nut and sweet, sticky date whilst looking idly at the Count's latest page – a relation of the Bishop of Toulouse, if he wasn't mistaken.

'But I still worry about her health.'

'Matthieu, Matthieu,' the Count put his arm around Matthieu's shoulders, 'has no one told you that women are *meant* to have children. That's why God put them here; and if they don't, well, there's always another one to be had.'

'Wise words indeed,' Matthieu said, forcing a smile. The Count's attitude to women was not one of his most endearing qualities. 'But anyway, it's not Catharine I came to ask you about, my lord, but Joana, her sister. She's seventeen now, and of an age to marry. Unfortunately, the only dowry she can bring is her family's manor in the Touraine, and that land is sorely troubled at the moment, as you know.'

'I don't think it would make any difference in Joana's case,' the Count grinned. 'I can think of a dozen or so rich widowers who'd be delighted to take her to bed. Including me, for that matter. Bring her to court, I'll take care of her.'

The thought of such a godless fate for Joana made Matthieu wince.

'Sire, I want only what is best for my sister. She is of even temperament, an accomplished needle woman, devout in her prayers, and her conversation is lively and well informed-'

'Pah! Who cares how well a woman prattles when she looks as good as Joana?' the Count said. 'You'll make an excellent match for her with or without dowry, of that I'm certain. What does Catharine say?'

Matthieu wasn't prepared to admit that he hadn't even mentioned it to her yet.

'She's happy at the prospect, my lord. As you know, we've been childless all these years and so the prospect of nephews and nieces would please her greatly.'

'Yes, I suppose it would.' The Count was watching him with the same puzzled expression he always wore when they had this kind of conversation. He'd made it plain that Matthieu should divorce Catharine, and if he wasn't willing to do that, take a mistress. 'Did you have anyone in mind for her?'

This was what he had been waiting for. Matthieu took a deep breath. So much depended upon the next few minutes. 'I thought to ask for one of Raimon-Arnald of Astre's sons-'

'No,' the Count said.

Matthieu had dreaded this.'May I ask why, my lord?'

'You know why,' the Count said. 'Raimon-Arnald is a good man but he is not noble, and Joana is the daughter of a lord and knight. I won't have it, and I'm surprised you're even considering it for her.'

'But Raimon-Arnald *is* a good man and a wealthy one too. *And* he's a faithful servant of the church-'

'Yes, yes, I know all that,' the Count said, his face setting into uncompromising lines. 'But *he is not noble.*'

'My lord-'

'No.' The Count stood up. 'Matthieu, you'll have to think of someone more fitting, else leave it to me.'

Matthieu watched the Count's back as he walked towards the dice tables. There *was* no more thinking he could do for he'd already thought long and hard about the matter. What could be more important to him than whom Joana married? In truth, he could hardly bear to think about it, but he was desperate. Ever since that day in the garden, he had tried his best to ignore her and treat her coldly, but he was mortally afraid that one day his resolve would fail. *Ah, God. Why could I not just be left in peace to love my wife*?

'My lord?' he said, following the Count.

'Yes? Have you thought of someone else already?'

'No-o.'

The problem was, practically every one of the noble families were tainted with heresy. Even the Bishop of Toulouse, whose nephew was was here acting as a page to Count Raimon, could barely rouse himself to complain because his 'noble' family was riddled with heretics too. The last thing Matthieu wanted was to save *his* soul by putting Joana's in jeopardy. 'Perhaps we could speak on this another day?'

'Perhaps,' the Count said, and took his arm. 'Try not to be so serious about it, Matthieu. Anyone would think you didn't want her to marry. Look, we'll be going hawking when I've finished here. Come with us and see the new tercel that Pedro of Aragon has just given me. He said he took it from a Moor, and it's a beautiful bird.'

Matthieu nodded and stifled his dismay. How he was going to keep up the pretence of being jolly all afternoon, when he had this heavy burden hanging over him, Heaven only knew.

*

For the feast of Saint John the Apostle, Count Raimon announced a banquet in honour of the Count and Countess of Foix, and requested that Matthieu and Catharine bring Joana to court, in order to introduced her to them.

Matthieu was distraught. He'd been hoping that Joana would be of so little consequence to the Count that he would happily accept whomsoever Matthieu wanted her to marry; but she was beautiful, and obviously hadn't escaped the Count's notice – even though Matthieu had kept her as far out of sight as possible. Now, to make matters worse, Catharine was pleading a headache and begging to be left behind.

He'd got used to his wife's infirmity over the years and if he was honest, it had given him the excuse to stay away from court too; but tonight the Count was adamant that Joana be there, and so Matthieu had no other choice but to take her. By the saints, this matter was not going well! After all he'd done to keep himself away from her; tonight they would be thrown together.

He spent the early part of the day in the school room with Raimondet, teaching him how to form his letters with bold, and hopefully tidy strokes. Now seven years old, the young Count to-be was long of limb and had kept the ruddy, fair colouring of his Plantagenet ancestors, although his hair had begun to darken, and he was taking on the looks of his more southerly kin. In the main, Raimondet's clear blue eyes looked calmly upon his world and they easily creased up in merriment. But, at other times his Angevin temper made its appearance and woe betide the playmate, or plaything, that anger was vented upon!

With tongue stuck out to the side and restless, booted feet making their appearance every now and again from under the table, Raimondet concentrated on his writing tablet. So far, he had showed none of his father's fondness for soft living, and was rapidly developing skills on horseback and at the archery butts. Matthieu felt blessed to be tutor to such an able pupil and the bond between them grew daily – so much so that jealous eyes followed them whenever they were together. Matthieu knew himself to have gained quite a few enemies on account of his closeness with the Count's son and heir.

When he finally returned to his apartment, Bernard insisted on giving him a commentary on the day's events whilst helping him to dress for the evening.

'They've been in Lady Catharine's chamber all day,' the squire said. 'I was sent out to the market at least three times, and the last time they told me to bring the seamstress back with me!'

'Oh?' Matthieu pretended disinterest, but a treacherous part of him was anticipating seeing how lovely Joana would look in her new gown. 'Well, I suppose, it *is* the first time she's been presented at court.' Bernard picked one of the belts that Matthieu had inherited from his father, but he waved it away, seeing its pattern of equal armed crosses. It resembled too much those worn by the heretic priests. 'Find me something else will you?' he said.

What's wrong with this one, sire?' Bernard said. 'I've always thought it was a very fine belt.'

'Yes,' Matthieu said, not wanting to get into a discussion about it, 'but I'll wear another tonight.'

Bernard looked hurt, and was that a spark of rebellion in his eyes? Surely he wasn't in sympathy with those mad heretics as well? Better to have words with him in the morning and find out for sure. No one with leanings that way was going to pollute *their* household.

*

'Take care, dear heart,' Joana called, as she finally appeared from Catharine's bedchamber.

Was it his imagination or did Matthieu see the faintest smile play about Joana's lips, quickly discarded? Self consciously, he stroked his hair. Bernard had needed to use a lot of lavender oil to make it lie straight tonight. Did he look foolish?

'Good evening, Joana, you look... well.'

He could have said more, much more, for the seamstress had excelled herself and Joana's gown fell to the floor in revealing waves of sage-green silk. It was belted at the hip with a gold-linked girdle, and at her slender neck, Joana wore a filigree golden crucifix. Her hair fell loosely down her back, as was permitted of an unmarried woman, but on her head she wore a delightful little jewel-encrusted cap that sparkled nearly as much as her eyes. Matthieu had to look away, for fear of revealing his feelings, and brushed past her to ensure that Catharine was settled before they left.

'Will you be all right, my love?' he asked, taking Catharine's white hand. Her painfully thin body now bulged in the middle, and seeing her like this, Matthieu couldn't help thinking the pregnancy was like a slowly growing gall, eating away her strength; but he tried to shake the notion away. He had enough to worry about tonight.

'Matthieu,' Catharine said, folding her hands protectively across her stomach. 'Joana is so very excited. You will take care of her, won't you?I'm sure both Counts will be smitten.'

'Don't worry,' Matthieu said. 'I'll keep her out of their way as much as possible, and we'll stay only as long as is necessary. The Count knows how important this babe is to me.'

They exchanged kisses, Matthieu straightened his shoulders, and went back outside. Beatrice handed Joana a light wrap, which she pulled about her shoulders.

'Ready?' he said.

'Yes,' Joana said, extending her elbow. 'Are you?'

'Yes,' he said, setting off at an irritated pace and ignoring her arm. The last thing he wanted to do was have her *touch* him.

They strode through the corridors of the Narbonnais, with Joana struggling to keep up and Matthieu refusing to slow his pace. But when they reached the queue to enter the great hall, he noticed she was shivering.

'Is your wrap not warm enough?' he asked.

'No, it's not that,' Joana said, shaking her head. 'It's just there's bound to be so many grand ladies there, and I've never been to court before. What will they think of me?' She looked down at her gown.

Matthieu almost laughed out loud. Any woman could wear fine clothes, but not many would look as wonderful as she did tonight.

'Truly I think you have nothing to worry about,' he said, forgetting himself and patting her shoulder, then swiftly drew back, as if he had burned himself. How was he supposed to treat her as a brother and care for her welfare, when simply being this close was making his pulse race?

'Be careful,' he whispered. 'If any man compliments you, say thank you, but nothing more. Do you understand?'

'No.'

He sighed. 'Please don't be difficult, Joana. What I'm trying to say is there might be lots of men who'll want to make your acquaintance, but we must avoid any scandal attaching to your name.'

'Because I *talk* to someone?' Her eyebrows arched, and her voice rose a notch.

'Yes-' Matthieu was suddenly horribly conscious that Raimon of Ricaud, the Count closest friend and adviser, was walking towards them. He maneuvered Joana into the privacy of an empty stairwell.

'Speak quietly,' he pleaded. 'Didn't your mother teach you anything about being at court?'

'Of course.'

'Well, then...' Sweat trickled down his neck, and the musky, citrus notes of her perfume made his head reel. 'I probably know more about the men of Count Raimon's court than you do, and all I'm saying is, you need to be careful.'

'But I can't pretend to be mute, Matthieu, can I?' Joana said, her eyes glittering defiance.

'Better that than...,' Matthieu let out an exasperated sighed. 'I'm a man and I know how men think.'

'And how *do* they think?' Joana said, the glitter turning to anger.

'For goodness sake!' He tried to think of a suitable excuse for taking her back to their apartment. If they carried on like this, the night was going to be a disaster. 'I'm only trying to protect you.'

'No you're not,' she said. 'You're treating me as if I'm going to act like some kind of a whore, and I won't have it!'

Mother of God!

Joana pushed him away and started off on her own. Matthieu hurried after her, wondering what to do. Until that day in the garden, she'd been quiet and reserved around him; now it was as though a devil had been unleashed.

Fortunately, they arrived in the great hall together and Matthieu forced a smile onto his face as he looked around the room. The Count was sitting at the far end on a raised dais with the Count and Countess of Foix seated beside him. Every tapestry the Count owned had been unpacked and hung about the walls, with not a few extra borrowed ones, by the look of things. The floor under Matthieu's feet was liberally strewn with rushes and sweet smelling herbs, and no less than six chandeliers swung from the roof above his head. Trestles had been laid down the length of the hall, ready for the feasting, and to the side of the dais sat colourfully dressed minstrels, chatting and quietly tuning their lutes and harps.

Matthieu watched as the women noticed Joana and smoothed down their gowns or whispered behind their hands as they were escorted towards the Count; but the men didn't even bother to conceal their interest. Count Raimon's eyes lit up and the lecherous old fox offered Joana his hand as soon as she came up from her curtsey, and led her out to dance. Caught off-guard, the minstrels struck a few discordant notes as they hurried to find a tune. The Count bowed low to Joana and others joined them on the floor, circling left, and then right, crossing and passing. The Count's eyes never left Joana's face as he swung her around, bringing a flush of colour to her cheeks. The minstrels sang and the dancers replied, joining in the chorus whilst they circled. As they finished, the Count swung Joana so hard that she staggered against him, and he slid his arm around her waist.

Matthieu clenched his teeth. It hurt to see Joana being pawed like that, but there was nothing he could do. Before she could return to him, the silver-haired Count of Foix had got to his feet and was bowing low in front of her. Count Raimon withdrew, smiling, and the musicians carried on.

'You'll not have any problem marrying her off, Matthieu,' he said. 'She's exquisite. In fact – to Hell with you. I think I'll make her my mistress anyway!'

Matthieu saw the Countess of Foix watching her husband with wary eyes. As the dance came to a close, the shawms sounded and Eleonor of Aragon, the latest wife of Count Raimon, made an entrance with her ladies. In a gown of azure silk, with exquisite golden embroidery to hem and sleeves, the Countess truly shone, and Matthieu wondered if this could be the woman who would finally capture Count Raimon's heart. Her brother, King Pedro, was not only the King of Aragon and Count Raimon's seigneur, but he was also in good standing with the Pope. Upon her could rest many of the Count's ambitions to keep his lands safe.

The Count welcomed Eleonor with a kiss, and sat her next to him. To Matthieu's delight, his seigneur's face actually softened as he bent to hear what she was saying, and then he personally fetched her a goblet of wine, and held it to her lips.

The dancing began again in earnest, and whilst Joana whirled and twirled, with the Count's cousin – Bernard of Comminges, Matthieu emptied another goblet of wine and leaned against the wall, watching gloomily. He only realised that he was not alone, when a low voice said to him;

'Could she be another, 'Na Loba', do you think?'

'I beg your pardon?' Matthew blanched as he realised that none other than Esclarmonde of L'Isle-Jourdain, the sister of the Count of Foix, was standing at his shoulder.

Her dark hair was shot through with grey, but she was still an exceptional woman and the emerald she wore at her throat sparkled with the same determination as her eyes.

'I said, could she be another Etiennette of Pannautier?' Esclarmonde said. 'So beautiful that all men desire her, but only my brother managed to make her his mistress.'

'My lady,' Matthieu said, trying awkwardly to bow in the restricted space. 'You honour me with your presence, but I should tell you that the lady you speak of here is my sister-in-law.'

'Forgive me,' Esclarmonde said, the corners of her mouth lifting a little. 'I was only talking about the way my brother is looking at her.'

How Matthieu wished he could say that he hadn't noticed.

As soon as the dance was finished, Foix claimed Joana from the Count of Comminges.

'When a woman is admired for her looks,' Esclarmonde said, sadly, 'then she must ever be in fear of a younger beauty. Such is the way of this world. Too many put faith in things that cannot last.'

Matthieu was afraid to hear more. Although one of the greatest ladies of the land, Esclarmonde was known to have leanings towards heresy, just as the court of her brother was well known to be a haven for them.

'We must all put our faith in God,' he said, hastily.

Esclarmonde gave him a mocking look. 'That depends upon the god you are speaking of, of course,' she said.

Matthieu cast about for an excuse to leave, but Esclarmonde indicated that he should join her on the dance floor.

'Come,' she said. 'You look as though you need cheering up.'

She danced well and her eyes watched him seriously as they came together and he bowed to her. What an evening this was turning out to be. Circle to the left and stop, the women curtseyed, to the right – he saw Joana laughing. She was still with Foix, his hand slipping ever lower on her hip as he turned her about. God's breath, why hadn't he refused to bring her here? This was no place for a young woman who barely knew the ways of the world. The dance seemed to last an age, and so lost was he in confusion that he failed to see Esclarmonde studying him.

'Be careful,' she whispered. 'Whatever your feelings are for the lady, they are misplaced here.'

He blushed. 'She is my sister-in-law, my lady. My feelings are solely for her welfare.'

Esclarmonde shook her head. 'In that case, it would have been better to send her to a convent, rather than to bring her to this court.'

When the dance was finished, Matthieu bowed to Esclarmonde, escorted her to the side of the hall, and then went to find Joana. As he approached, Foix slid a possessive arm about her waist – no matter that his wife was standing only a few yards away.

'My lord.' Matthieu bowed stiffly. He was in awe of Foix's reputation, not only as a fierce war-lord but a fine poet. 'I thank you for your kind attention to my sister-in-law.'

'Ha!' Foix laughed. 'If you dared, no doubt you would add, 'keep your hands off her', too?'

'My lord misunderstands me,' Matthieu said, stifling his anger. For the first time ever, he was beginning to regret the generosity that had made Aliénor of Aquitaine send his mother and himself south in the entourage of her daughter. 'I'm afraid I have received worrying news regarding my wife. She is with child and not well. We must return.'

Joana's face fell and Matthieu cursed her silently. Couldn't she at least *pretend* that she hadn't been enjoying herself? Foix gave Matthieu a mocking smile and removed his arm with exaggerated reluctance.

'Not even waiting to eat,' he murmured, sweeping Joana a bow and then kissing her full on the lips – a gesture none could fail to see. 'Farewell, fair heart. I am lonely for you already, and await our next meeting as I await my next breath.'

Matthieu nudged Joana. 'Thank you, my lord,' she said, blushing prettily.

He took her arm and steered her towards the dais. It was unthinkable to leave without Count Raimon's permission.

'My lord,' he said. 'Catharine wasn't in the best of health when we left, which is why she couldn't join us this evening.'

The Count nodded rather absently, but from the twinkle in his eye, it was obvious that he knew only too well why they were leaving. 'One must look after one's wife,' he said, taking Eleanor's hand in his. 'You never know what circumstance will be in waiting. Give Catharine my condolences and tell her that I'll send my physician over to see her tomorrow.'

'Thank you, my lord.' Matthieu stood up.

'Good night, Joana,' the Count said. 'I hope you'll grace our court again, very soon.'

*

Matthieu started drinking with determination after Joana and Catharine retired, but he couldn't erase the memory of the Count of Foix's arm about Joana's waist. So possessive, so sure of himself, a man who was used to getting what he wanted. Esclarmonde was right, even the most celebrated woman in the land had fallen under Foix's spell after rejecting countless love-sick suitors. Now Foix had set his sights on Joana, what could Matthieu do about it? Nothing.

*

When he awoke the following morning, it was to the conviction that he was being beaten over the head with a blacksmith's hammer. Still half asleep, he sluiced his face and allowed himself to be dressed, then grasped the cup of watery wine that Bernard brought, and drank it down in one gulp. But the plate of bread and steamed fish made his stomach heave.

'Tell Raimondet he can have the day off,' he said, thickly, sitting back down on his bed and cradling his head. 'Tell him I'm ill, and remember to look in on me later.'

Bernard bowed to hide his smirk and Matthieu lay down, fully clothed, and went back to sleep.

*

'Sire, sire! Wake up. The Count wishes to speak with you!'

'What?'

'The Count; he's waiting for you in his solar.' Bernard was in some state of agitation and Matthieu sat up groggily.

'What time is it?'

'After-noon. I've brought you something to drink.'

Matthieu took the cup and gasped. 'What is it? Are you trying to poison me?'

'Your mother sent it,' Bernard said, and drew back the bed curtains. 'It's for your headache.'

'Ugh! Did she send anything to take the taste away, too?' Matthieu said, shading his eyes. The sun seemed unnaturally bright.

'I could make you some herb tea?'

'No, I meant wine.'

Bernard poured some into the goblet and topped it up with water.

'You need to hurry, sire. He's been waiting a while. I had difficulty waking you.'

'All right, all right I'm coming,' Matthieu said. 'At least I'm already dressed.'

*

In the Count's solar, there was quite a gathering. The usual gaming tables had been cleared away and all were standing, except for Count Raimon, who sat in the centre of the room with one leg slung over the arm of his chair. Several young pages stood about with trays of sweetmeats, and a wine waiter was kept busy amongst the courtiers.

The Countess Eleonor was the first to greet Matthieu and came forward with her hand outstretched. Unfortunately, as he bowed to her, Matthieu felt his head spin.

'We have good news for you, Matthieu,' the Countess said, her face flushed and excited as she turned to her husband.

'I propose a toast,' the Count said, 'to the betrothal of Matthieu's sister, the beautiful Lady Joana, and Sir Aimeric of Pamiers, knight of the household of my dear friend, the Count of Foix.'

All Matthieu could do was blink.

'God above, man!' the Count said. 'Have you nothing to say?'

Matthieu struggled. Who on Earth was Aimeric of Pamiers? The name was vaguely familiar. Could he have been at the feast last night?

The Count of Foix appeared, trailing his wife behind.

'Well?' he boomed. 'Is it all sorted out yet?'

Matthieu's heart plummeted. Why, oh, why had he brought this upon himself? It was obvious what was being planned here and no doubt Aimeric of Pamiers would be a willing cuckold.

'My gratitude, sire,' he said. Trying to think straight was like trying to push a donkey that didn't want to go. 'May I be permitted to know more of my sister in law's intended?'

'Of course you may,' Count Raimon said. 'Come and sit down. Bring us some wine!' He slapped his hand on the arm of his chair and the young squire, Rebastens, quickly scurried off to do his bidding.

'Aimeric's in my retinue,' Foix said, taking the seat next to the Count and settling himself comfortably into it. 'He's a stout, goodhearted fellow who lost his wife last year in the birthing chamber. He's getting on a bit but he still has some of his own teeth and most of his hair.' He paused to allow someone to titter obligingly. 'But the important thing is, he's inherited his wife's lands and been pestering me to find someone to help him run things. If Joana gives him an heir or two, I don't think he'd object to her lack of dowry. Not at all.'

Matthieu tried not to look appalled. It wasn't possible to demur, not without Count Raimon losing face. Oh, if only he didn't feel so very, very sick.

Jealousy twisted Matthieu's guts. Until this moment he had never realised exactly how much Joana meant to him, and he suddenly couldn't bear to think of life without her. What would he tell Catharine? They'd never even talked about Joana marrying, and now everything was as good as arranged.

'He's a likeable man,' the Countess Phillippa was saying, and her resigned look confirmed Matthieu's worst fears, 'and will no doubt treat her kindly.'

'May I be permitted to share this good fortune with the ladies of my household before I answer?' Matthieu said.

A frown creased the brow of the Countess Eleonor. That she thought him ungrateful was obvious.

'Very well, but make it quick,' Count Raimon said.

'And then we can take her back with us tomorrow,' Foix said, a satisfied smile spreading across his face.

'Tomorrow?' Matthieu stuttered. 'But my lord, why so soon? May we not have time to make arrangements?’

‘Pshaw!’ Foix said. ‘How long does it take to pack a few women’s things? Get on with it, Matthieu. Joana can stay with us until the wedding. What do you say to that?’

CHAPTER 17

20th Sept 1539
Weymouth

Johanna reverently placed the reliquary inside a pillow case and fastened it around her middle with a linen band. When Matthew had agreed, albeit reluctantly, to let her carry it, she'd wasted no time in showing him what she intended to do. He sat with his back turned and she could tell he was scowling. Why did he do that so much? When he smiled, his face looked much younger and his brown eyes softened – in fact it transformed him completely. With thick dark hair and a neat beard, she'd wager more than a few of the lasses of Glastonbury would have been sorry he'd chosen the life of a monk.

There! She rubbed a few ashes from the grate under her eyes and then paraded in front of Matthew, with the 'bump' pulling her green woollen kirtle taut over her stomach.

'What do you think?'

'Hm,' he said. 'You do look a bit unwell.'

He sounded so doubtful that she had to laugh.

'Either I do or I don't. Make up your mind.'

'Well, I just hope it's enough. I'm still not happy that you're the one carrying the reliquary.'

'But it makes sense, doesn't it?' she said, taking a closer look at herself in her little silver mirror. It had been a present from her uncle and Mother Florence had let her keep it when she left Amesbury.

'Go downstairs and see what you can learn. And make sure people know I'm with child, Matthew. Tell them that's why I'm not feeling well.'

'Don't you think they'll find it odd?' he said, still not moving. 'I mean, when you arrived yesterday you weren't – you know...'

'But no one saw me without my travelling clothes. I could have been anything under them. Go on,' she said, again. 'I'm not really with child, you know. You *can* leave me.'

He went, grumbling under his breath, and Johanna lay down on the bed. Oh, but it was wonderful to be on a proper mattress again, wonderful to be away from all the pious exhortations and holy conversations of the Priory, wonderful to be away from the strict enclosure that had grown tedious beyond belief. She let her hands feel their way around the 'bump' and wondered what must it feel like to be carrying a child for real. Although she would never have admitted it to

Matthew, life at Amesbury had been such a disappointment. Yes, she had grown up at Fontevraud Abbey, but being the child of a wealthy family, she'd led a very different life there to the one she'd just been forced to live as a penniless novice.

*

Matthew ordered ale, refused food, and sat alone at the end of one of the trestle tables. Smoke from the fire stung his eyes, adding to the general gloom. Two greyhounds lounged beside the central hearth, seemingly asleep, but their ears pricked up as anyone passed by.

'On your own tonight, are you?' the owner's daughter said, placing a mug of foaming ale before him, and stooping so low that he was treated to an expanse of her creamy bosom.

'My, er, wife isn't feeling very well,' Matthew said, averting his eyes. 'We're sailing to France tomorrow and she's with child, so she's resting whilst she can.'

'Good idea,' the daughter said, 'crossings can be very bumpy if you get bad weather. If she's staying upstairs, would you like some company?'

She smiled and waited expectantly.

'Erm.'

'It can get a bit lonely when your missus is carrying a baby, so I'm told, and I don't mind sitting with you a while. Sarah's my name, by the way.'

Sarah sat down, so close that Matthew could smell beer and cinnamon on her breath, which would not have been unpleasant, had not the whole been overlaid with acrid sweat. On her chin he saw a few, youthful spots and her front tooth was chipped. Could she be even as old as fourteen summers?

'Why's you going to France, then?' Sarah asked, flicking her auburn hair back from her face. Her eyes were a friendly blue, and her mouth stretched easily into a generous smile.

'A visit to family. My wife's.' Matthew shifted as far away as he could, but somehow his arm was still wedged against her bosom.

'Oh, nice. Is she going to have the baby over there?'

'Perhaps.'

'Don't talk much do you?' Sarah said. 'What's the matter? 'Fraid your tongue'll fall out?'

She put out her tongue and waggled it at him.

'Not a bad idea, these days, tho,' she continued, leaning closer. 'You never know who's listening, do you? This place's bristling with spies and the rest'd sell your soul, given half a chance.' She stroked the back of Matthew's hand, where it lay on his thigh. 'Still, we don't have to talk, do we? I can think of better ways of keeping us amused, if you're interested?'

Dear Heaven!

'Sarah,' Matthew said, moving his hand. 'I appreciate your company but I'm not much in the mood for chatting tonight. I've got a lot on my mind at the moment.'

Her face fell. 'Why is it only the old, smelly ones that are ever in the mood – never handsome ones like you? She's a lucky woman, your wife. A man that knows how to be faithful – don't find many like that around here.' She stood up. 'I'll fetch you another ale.'

Matthew found himself sitting in front of another tankard of ale, and he'd only meant to have one. Sarah went on her way, and he'd just about decided to drink up and leave, when the door opened and two travellers came in. By their clothes and accents he could tell they were not from the West Country. As Sarah walked towards them, she smoothed down her apron, and shrewdly calculated their wealth.

'Good evenin' gentlemen,' she said. 'What's it to be?'

'Good evening,' the older man said, taking off his hat. He had the sober robes and demeanour of a lawyer. 'We'll each have a mug of beer, and have you any food?'

'It's a bit late,' Sarah said, 'but I could get you some if...' She looked up at the man cheekily.

'If, what?' he said, shrugging off his rain soaked cloak. 'What have you on offer?'

Sarah giggled and counted on her fingers. 'There be sausage and ham and some slices of mutton. Anything else is strictly extra, sir.'

He turned to his companion. 'We'll have everything I think – don't you, Thomas?'

Thomas, a fleshy, younger version of the other nodded. He had short dark hair and a rubbery mouth which pouted as he scanned the room for somewhere to sit. The only empty table was next to Matthew and that was where he chose. Sarah disappeared into the rear of the inn.

'How long have we been on the road?' Thomas said, settling himself on the bench, and peeling off his cloak. 'My mind can't count the hours but I tell you, Nicholas, my bones remember every minute of it.'

'Aye,' Nicholas agreed, straightening his black doublet. His lawyer's eyes roved the room, assessing, weighing the other customers.

Matthew ducked his head, not wanting to meet his eye.

'There are ports a lot nearer that we could have been sent to. Mind you,' Nicholas said, lowering his voice so that Matthew had to strain to hear him, 'I'll bet that Abbot wished he was coming this way with us, not the other.'

Thomas gave a short laugh. 'No doubt,' he said.

Matthew's heart increased its pace. Which Abbot were they talking about? He craned his neck as far as he dared, but then Sarah arrived carrying two trenchers and sat down with the men. Fearing what might happen if he stayed to overhear more, Matthew got up to leave. He decided to check on the horses and went outside to the stables. The ostler's lad was half asleep, but Matthew woke him and gave him enough silver to make sure their horses would be saddled and ready to leave at first light.

Johanna was already asleep on top of the bed when he let himself into their room. Her face looked clean, and she'd replaced the reliquary in his bag, but she was still wearing her clothes. Matthew took a coverlet from the foot of the bed and drew it up over her body, then went to lie on the truckle bed.

Terrible images crowded into his mind, and he pressed the heels of his hands into his eyes, but he could not stop the pictures forming or the stories coming into his mind: of men who had their limbs dislocated on the rack so they couldn't walk to the scaffold, of prisoners who were kept in such tiny cells that their bodies could find no ease, and of others who had been hung in chains and left outside to die.

He ran a trembling hand over his head. How jealous he'd felt when the older novices had knelt before the Abbot to have the hair on the top of their heads shaved off. But the lack of a tonsure was probably why he'd been chosen to bear the reliquary again. He wedged his hands into his armpits for warmth, but still he shook. Not only were they trying to smuggle something wanted by the King out of the country, but if Johanna's story was true, *he* might be trying to smuggle a wanted person out too.

Matthew soon exhausted all the prayers he could think of, and got up to pace the room. Finally, he took the reliquary from his bag and cradled it in his arms. Saint Thomas had welcomed martyrdom, had known it was coming and had not run away.

And *I* must be the same, Matthew thought: ready to die for God, however fearful I am. He prayed long into the night and eventually fell into an exhausted sleep on the truckle, with the reliquary still in his arms. Strange to think, he'd been so worried about sharing a room with Johanna, but in the end, he hadn't even given it a thought.

CHAPTER 18

August
Saint Bernadette's Catholic Church
Wesley Village, Yorkshire

There were more mourners at the funeral than either of them expected, and Jo had to ask the caterers to bring extra food. Blanche had been well known locally, and many people had been unable to visit in her last days. It looked like every one of them, and their families, had turned up to see her laid to rest.

It was the first time Jo had been inside a Catholic church. Most of the people who looked at home there were elderly but there was a sizeable group of young mothers with babies and toddlers. Jo decided to sit on her own at the back, but smiled at people as they came in, and one or two recognised her and stopped to chat.

The previous evening, Mat had finally put the finishing touches to what he called the 'order of service', and printed it off, with great relief. It seemed unnecessarily long in Jo's opinion, but she liked the picture on the back: Blanche looking absolutely radiant on her seventieth birthday. Only she and Mat knew the photographer had been Patrick McReady.

Everything for the service had been organised by Mat, whilst Jo had contacted the undertakers and caterers, both of whom she knew very well from her work at the hospice. Blanche had asked for low-cost and minimum fuss. She'd said 'no flowers', but that hadn't stopped Mat buying a huge whole-hearted bouquet that overhung the edges of the casket and absolutely danced with colour. They'd put Blanche's olive wood crucifix and her Rosary beads into the coffin too, with the prayer book from Patrick. It seemed a shame to cremate those precious things, but Blanche had been adamant.

'Burn me, burn everything,' she said. 'I'm sure I've been burned often enough before for my beliefs. At least this time I'll be dead before they start.'

Typical Blanche, controversial to the last. Jo hadn't dared ask Mat what he thought of his beloved aunt's belief in reincarnation!

At last people stopped arriving and Jo saw Mat and Father Stephen, the Parish Priest, waiting outside the church door. They were dressed in immaculate snowy vestments; Mat's had a large red cross embroidered on the front and Jo smiled. Blanche had done that. She would be, 'proud as Punch', to know he was wearing it today.

As he passed, Mat gave Jo a little wave and she felt her heart contract. He had never looked more attractive – nor more unavailable.

'*Be still for the presence of the Lord...*'

The organist struck up the first hymn and the two priests walked slowly down the aisle, Mat in front. Both bowed and kissed the altar before taking their places behind it.

Father Stephen raised his right hand and made the Sign of the Cross towards the congregation. 'In the name of the Father, and of the Son, and of the Holy Spirit. Amen.'

Everyone, except the non-Catholics and Jo, obediently made the Sign of the Cross in return.

'The grace of our Lord Jesus Christ and the love of God and the fellowship of the Holy Spirit be with you all.'

'And also with you.'

'A warm welcome to you all,' Father Stephen said, going over to the lectern. 'Please be seated.' He waited until everyone had settled themselves and then carried on. 'We are here today to pray for Blanche Potters, a dear member of our parish, who will be sadly missed. May I take this opportunity to welcome all of you, and to extend an invitation to those among you who are not Catholic, but would like to come to the altar for a blessing during the communion procession. The order of the Mass is in the booklets, and the hymn numbers are here.' He pointed to a board behind him, and then walked back to join Mat. For a moment, he paused, and then raised his arms.

'My brothers and sisters, to prepare ourselves to celebrate the sacred mysteries, let us call to mind our sins.'

What sins would those be, then? Jo wondered. Not being nice to people? Being selfish? Guilty on both counts. Stealing, murder, adultery. Not much of those to speak of – not recently anyway. What kind of way was this to start a 'celebration' of someone's life?

Those who knew what they were doing stood up and sat down in the appropriate places, and the organist and the congregation did their best to fill the church with with song. Father Stephen spoke about the promise Jesus had made to prepare a place amongst his Father's mansions and to come back for them, 'so that where I am, there you may be also'.

Then he held up a disc of bread and asked for it to be blessed by becoming the 'Body of Christ'. Jo knew that Catholics believed that the bread actually became the body of Jesus and watched very closely, but it didn't seem to look any different!

Mat had asked her if she would come up for a blessing, and at the time she'd said, 'yes', but now it seemed rather a long way to go and she couldn't trust herself not to trip over and make a fool of herself. Whilst she dithered, she felt him watching her and suddenly her feet started to make their own way down the aisle. When she reached Blanche's coffin, she touched it briefly.

'Bye, Blanche, dearest,' she whispered, and tears stung her eyes.

Jo stood before Mat, with her arms crossed in front of her chest, hardly daring to look into his eyes. He made the Sign of the Cross in the air in front of her, and she felt a trail of fire upon her skin, as if he'd really touched her. In fact, she was still tingling when Father Stephen gave the blessing at the end and sprinkled Blanche's coffin with holy water. No ordinary man could have had such an effect upon her, Joknew, and the knowledge scared her.

She bowed her head and hoped fervently that Blanche was already sitting in her Heaven, wherever that was. Jo couldn't help thinking back to the last time when Blanche had been well and the two of them were sitting cradling mugs of tea in her kitchen and chatting about Blanche's latest plans for a holiday.

She'd often gone away on her own: 'I enjoy my own company. Why should I take someone along to spoil it?'

Quite suddenly, Jo couldn't wait for the funeral to be over. The dark colours and the formality made her long to be outside in the sunshine. Thankfully, the two priests were coming down the aisle now and the Blanche's final hymn, 'I watch the Sunrise', was being played on the organ. At the chorus, 'for you are always, close to me', Jo dived into her handbag for a tissue. Blanche's faith might not have always been strictly orthodox, but it had never deserted her.

Enjoy your mansion, Blanche, she thought, you deserve it. Goodbye my dear, dear friend.

CHAPTER 19

April 1204
Château Narbonnais
Toulouse

Matthieu and Bernard made their way across the crowded courtyard of the Château just as the servants were throwing out the remnants of the midday meal. Pigs and paupers fought over the scraps and the loud sounds made Matthieu wince. Wagons trundled over the cobbles, bringing wine from the Lauragais, wood from the Ariège, cloth from Cambrai up in the north, spices from the ports at Marseilles, and yet more wine from Bordeaux – which had come on barges up the Garonne.

Matthieu was blind to them, consumed as he was by the twin trials of a headache and the need to break his news to Catharine. Guilt burned brightly in his breast as he remembered how happy the sisters had been since their return from Saint Gilles. Catharine had bloomed in a way he'd begun to doubt she ever could, and Joana had seemed to put behind her all of her jealousy. Now the sisters went about arm in arm, discussing their latest schemes and fancies, and were as close as they'd ever been.

'My lady Joana is to make a good match,' Bernard said, breaking into Matthieu's thoughts. 'One that'll break a few hearts, I'd wager.'

'Oh?' What did that mean? Matthew wondered, dully.

'She's ever looked happy in your household,' Bernard continued. 'It'll be a sad thing to see her go. I think the Lady Catharine will sorely miss her.'

'Um.'

'And *she* might not be the only one...'

Matthieu halted. It would be better to sort this out now. 'Oh?'

'Well, you know we've all been very fond of her...'

'Yes. And so?'

Bernard flushed so brightly that the light finally penetrated Matthieu's wine-addled brain.

'Have you fallen for her lad, is that what you're trying to tell me?' he said, feeling relieved. For a moment he'd feared that his feelings for Joana were open to all.

'Only as a dog yearns to be by his master,' Bernard said, looking away.

Was every man in this world in love with Joana?

'There'll be time for you, Bernard, I promise.' Matthieu said, and reached out to clap the squire's shoulder. 'Your father and I will find you a fine woman, one who knows how to appreciate a good man.'

'Thank you, sire,' Bernard said, still bright red. 'But until then, I'm happy with my dreams.'

The way the men of the south mooned around over women, who were well and truly out of their reach, never failed to amaze Matthieu. The troubadours were always at it – nightly exercising their exaggerated 'Courtly Love' rituals of yearning and song. Yet who was *he to* criticise, when he'd brought all this trouble upon himself by refusing to accept that Joana could never be his?

Matthieu kicked a chicken out of the way as they waited for Beatrice to open the door.

'I'm sorry, sire,' she said, wiping her hands on a cloth. 'I would have opened it quicker if I'd known it was you. I'm not used to you coming in this entrance.'

'We needed the air,' Matthieu said, trying to keep down an acid belch. 'Is my lady well?'

'Yes, sire. She's finishing that new tapestry in the solar. If you can but wait one-'

Matthieu pushed past and took the steps two at a time. The movement jogged his head cruelly, but he was desperate to get the matter sorted out quickly. He found Catharine and Ermessinda seated together on cushions, their heads bent over their needlework. Joana was by the window, looking out.

'Matthieu!' Catharine's hand flew to her throat and her eyes widened in alarm. 'I didn't know you were back. Whatever is it?' She turned to Ermessinda. 'Leave us, please.'

The servant packed up her needles.

'You, too, Joana,' Matthieu said. 'I have news for you both, but I must speak with Catharine first.'

Joana looked as if she might refuse, but Catharine shook her head. Matthieu watched sadly as she walked from the room, bewildered as to how he was going to say all that he had to say to the sisters.

'Beloved, I have wonderful news,' was how he started, dropping to one knee before Catharine. It was surprising how easily the lie came. 'But first let me ask, how you are?'

'Well, my love, thank you,' Catharine said, shifting in her seat. 'But tell me, why are you so serious, Matthieu? Is something amiss?'

He took the cushion beside her and sat down. He could do it if he didn't think too much.

'Quite the opposite, my love,' he said. 'It seems Count Raimon and Foix have found a husband for Joana. His name is Aimeric of Pamiers.'

Catharine covered her face with her hands and gave a cry

'What is it, my sweet?' he said. 'Isn't this good news? We could have hardly hoped for a better match for her.'

'But, Matthieu, it's so sudden! Who is he?' She pushed his hand away as Matthieu sought to soothe her, and stared angrily at him. 'We've never even spoken of Joana's marriage before.'

'Americ's a knight in the service of the Count of Foix,' Matthieu said, willing himself to stay calm, 'a wealthy man by all accounts. At least enough not to worry that she doesn't have much dowry. And she'll only be going as far as Pamiers. You'll still be able to see each other.'

Catharine continued to stare at him. 'Pamiers? Matthieu, that place is filled with heretics. Surely you can't want her to living amongst them? For all we know, this man may be one of them too.'

'Joana has been brought up as a good Catholic,' Matthieu said. 'I don't think we need to fear for her soul. So long as she continues to go to Mass and keeps well away from them, no harm can come to her.'

'But what if *he* is one of them?' Catharine persisted.

'My love,' Matthieu said, (trying to reassure her about the very point he feared so much himself), 'the heretics despise marriage, so it cannot be possible if this Aimeric agrees to marry Joana.'

Catharine nodded slowly. 'But he could allow them to visit his house. You know how often even Catholics whom we have seen regularly at Mass, ask for the heretic priests when they are dying.'

'True. If it turns out he has leanings towards the heretics, then I think we can justifiably complain to Count Raimon, and ask him to bring her back to us.'

'Do you think so?' Catharine's face was filled with anxiety. 'But what if she listens to them, Matthieu? They're so persuasive. Only last week, one of my friends had to dismiss her serving woman because she'd called for the heretic priest when her mother was dying.'

He sighed. 'Do you really think Joana could be persuaded that there are two gods, that Jesus wasn't real, or that our souls wander through the heavens when we die and come back again, time and time over? It makes my tongue uncomfortable even to voice such untruths.'

'And my ears uncomfortable to hear them,' Catharine said.

'Listen to me.' Matthieu was hardly able to believe that Catharine was agreeing with him. 'Joana is seventeen now. You can't have expected her to remain unmarried much longer? I know this has come as a shock to us both, but it has the promise of being a good match for her. I'll think of a way to break the news to her gently, don't worry, but I'm afraid I must do it quickly.'

'But why? What's the hurry?' Catharine frowned. 'I've barely absorbed it myself yet.'

'Perhaps she'll be pleased,' he said. 'Had you thought of that? She must have been worried about not having a dowry. Both Countesses have had a hand in this matter, and they say Aimeric is an excellent match for Joana. He can give her everything she'd want. Don't weep my love. We've been happy together. Why wouldn't you want the same for Joana?'

'Matthieu,' Catharine said, gulping back her sobs, 'of course I want the same for Joana, it's just...'

'Listen to me, he said, taking her hand. She did not resist this time. Why not stop worrying? Everything has been taken care of. The Count and Countess of Foix want Joana to go with them when they return to Foix in the morning, so she can get to know her new husband whilst she's living with them.'

'Matthieu!' Catharine was on her feet now. 'She can't leave tomorrow. There are a million things we have to do first. Whatever are you thinking of?'

'Hush my love,' Matthieu said, thinking of the servants who would no doubt be listening outside the door. 'I cannot say otherwise when the Count himself has requested this, and nor can you. If they say she has to go tomorrow, then tomorrow it has to be. Why would we want Joana to miss this chance of happiness and a family of her own? I need you to be strong for this, Catharine, as I am trying to be. Pamiers is not far away. She'll be able to visit, our children will see each other and grow up as cousins...'

'But,' Catharine shuddered, 'what if he's *old*? We've never even seen him. How can we do this to her?'

'Because we have no choice?'

So many emotions raged inside him, but most of all he was angry with God that his desire to do the right thing and remove Joana from his life had led to *this*! He was torn between the need to comfort Catharine and his need to hurry. If only he could show his feelings as honestly as she had, but he *must* appear to approve of this match.

'What about her clothes?' Catharine said. 'We haven't got anything ready. She'll need a new dress and veil at least. I'll have to send for the dressmakers.'

'She could wear your wedding dress, couldn't she?' he said, thinking that if they had to wait for dressmakers, they'd never have Joana ready for the morning. 'You looked wonderful in it on our day, and as for the rest, we can always send things on.'

'Wear mine? Oh, Matthieu, I can't believe it's you who's saying these things.' Disbelief was etched into every part of her tear stained face. 'What if she refuses to go?'

Matthieu said nothing. Catharine knew as well as he did that Joana's refusal wouldn't change anything.

'Send for my ladies,' she said, and there was a note in her voice that he'd never heard before. 'And don't worry. I'll break the news to her myself. You can allow me that?'

He nodded, his relief enormous.

'The Count of Foix has had many mistresses,' Catharine said. 'Joana told me how he behaved towards her at the banquet. Can we believe that this marriage is not simply a ruse, so that she can become a whore to him?'

'Catharine!' Matthieu was as shocked at her words as her cleverness. 'To the best of my knowledge, the Count of Foix does not make a habit of forcing noble women into a relationship they're not willing to have. You must talk to her. Tell her that her behaviour at the banquet left a lot to be desired, make sure she guards herself against any brazenness on her part that might encourage him.'

'Brazenness on her part?' Catharine's eyes flashed fire now. 'What are you saying, Matthieu? My sister has a beautiful heart. She would never deliberately draw attention to herself, and she deserves a loving husband, just as I *did*!

'Just warn her that's all,' Matthieu said, deliberately ignoring the barb. His head throbbed unbearably and he really didn't want to continue the conversation any longer. 'And make sure she's ready to leave by tomorrow morning.'

*

From his chamber, Matthieu watched sparrows darting about the gardens, now in, now out of the shade. How wonderful it must be to be free, to move where and when you wanted, and to be bound by no man's whim. He was struggling to understand was why had everything gone so awry when he was only trying to do what Alphonso had suggested when they were at Saint Gilles, what he thought God wanted of him. So why was he now facing the prospect of forcing someone he loved into a marriage not of his choosing, and in a region seething with heretics? Why had God allowed this to happen?

Matthieu clenched his fists. Esclarmonde had been right, it *would* have been better to send Joana to a convent than to take her into that den of wolves.

'Sire?' It was Bernard. 'The Lady Joana wishes to speak with you.'

Matthieu thought about it, but he could hardly refuse. She stood uncertainly in the middle of the room, her hair covered by a gauzy veil and her hands clasped so tightly before her that the knuckles were white.

'Do you really hate me so much, Matthieu?' she said.

'What?' He stumbled at the question. How could she believe that?

'Isn't that why you're sending me away?'

Every particle of colour had drained from her face and she swayed towards him, entreating him to touch her; but Matthieu stood where he was, horribly aware that he had no control over the feelings that surged inside him. How much longer he could keep up the pretence of being happy with what was happening, he did not know.

'The Count has found a husband for you, Joana. Aimeric of Pamiers is a better match than I could ever have hoped for you,' he said, but he was unable to stop his voice breaking. 'You'll be wealthy, in a prominent position at court, and you'll have a family of your own. What more could you want?'

Joana crossed the distance between them faster than he could have imagined. 'What more could I want? Matthieu, you know what I want!'

He drew a ragged breath. 'But it can never be, can it?'

She sought his gaze, held it, beseeched – nay demanded – some truth of his feelings for her; but he could only turn away, the future suddenly looming harsher than the bleakest winter.

'Do I have to give you my answer yet?' she asked.

'I'm afraid there's only one answer you can give,' he said and quailed before the scorn in her eyes. 'Joana, listen to me. This is a good match for you. The wedding won't take place until some time off. We can send things on to you but the important thing is you go tomorrow. I know that isn't much time-'

'It isn't *any* time, Matthieu!' she howled. 'I can't leave so soon!'

'You must,' he said, thickly. 'Can't you see that? Listen to me: if you'd been wealthy when your father died, where do you think you would be now? King Philippe would have soon found you a husband of *his* choosing. At least you've had the freedom of living with your own family until-'

'Tell me this has nothing to do with what happened that day in the garden?' The colour had returned to her face in an angry flood.

'Of course it doesn't-'

'But you saw how Foix treated me at that banquet, and you know what will happen to me if I go there. So, I ask you again, Matthieu. Have I angered you so much that I must be sent away because you fear for your *precious* soul if I stay?'

'Joana!' How right she was. 'I care for *both* of our souls, and I tried to warn you not to flirt. Why didn't you listen to me?'

'Why didn't I listen to you?' Her eyes blazed and his jealousy, released like the pent up demon that it was, hung nakedly in the air between them.

'And-it-is-for-that-you-would-punish-me!' she hissed. 'Because I paid another man more attention than you?'

'No!' For all he knew, Bernard and the other servants could be just beyond the door. 'For pity's sake, Joana. For what it's worth, this match is not of my choosing either. I'd hoped you could live a comfortable life near us in Toulouse, but last night changed everything. If only you'd taken heed of what I said before we went in, matters would not have been as they are today. Now, I cannot refuse this. What you did has taken everything out of my hands, can't you see that?'

Joana glared at him and he glared back until he could bear it no longer.

'Please,' he begged. 'Foix may have a reputation for bedding women, but to the best of my knowledge he has never taken a noble woman against her will. So don't encourage him, cleave to your husband, remember your prayers and if you've a whit of sense, have nothing to do with the heretics that swarm in his lands. That's my advice, if you'll take it – for once. Now, I suggest you get ready to leave.'

'Matthieu,' Joana's voice dropped so low that he was forced to move nearer to hear her, 'I ask you once again. Do you truly care so little for me?'

It was all he could do not to cover her face and neck with kisses, tell her not to worry, that everything would be all right, that he'd take care of her.

'Of course I care about you,' Matthieu said, summoning up one last lie, 'that's why I'm so pleased with this match.'

CHAPTER 20

Sept 1539
Weymouth

Matthew was up before first light, pacing the room, not wanting to wake Johanna but anxious all the same and wanting to wake her up so he could tell her what he had overheard. He picked up the reliquary, unable to believe that he had fallen asleep with it in his arms. How could this wonderful saint have enraged King Henry so much that his name was erased from every place, his feast days forbidden, and his sainthood mocked?

He glanced across at the dark shape that was Johanna. Her breath whistled softly through her lips and she lay perfectly still. How could she be so relaxed? It was as though they were travelling for pleasure, rather than trying to escape a terrible fate. He offered up humble prayers for their safety, sorely missing the regular rhythm of prayer that had become his life at Glastonbury; and prayed Saint Thomas as well, for hadn't he given Matthew's mother the most gentle end to her suffering? Wouldn't he now protect them as they sought to preserve this last relic of his blessed body?

Dawn began to creep through the partly opened shutters and he went to wake Johanna. There was no doubt she was a very beautiful young woman, especially unguarded in sleep. He stood for a moment, wondering what his life might have been like if he'd made the choice to become a family man; but he knew there was no point in imagining what would never be, and definitely no point in wondering it about a woman as far above his station as she was. No. His heart and mind were made up. He belonged to God alone.

'Johanna? It's time we were going.'

She rolled over and stretched. Embarrassed, Matthew looked away and hastily pulled the curtains around the bed. There was a knock at the door and he hesitated, unsure what to do. The knock came again, lightly and timidly. Cautiously, Matthew unbolted the door and opened it a crack. Sarah stood waiting.

'Can I come in?' she whispered.

Matthew glanced behind quickly. His truckle bed was still out upon the floor and it would be obvious they hadn't slept together.

'Er.'

'Please, it's important. They mustn't see me or I'll be in trouble.'

'Just a minute.'

He closed the door and pushed the truckle as quietly as he could under the bed.

'Johanna?'

'Mm?'

'Will you stay there for a minute?'

'Why?'

'There's someone at the door who wants to come in. It's the owner's daughter.'

'Made that good an impression, did you?'

'No. Look, just wait there. She says it's important.'

'All right. But take care there's no one with her.'

He opened the door and beckoned to Sarah. Her eyes were tired and her face pale. She stood, clasping her hands nervously, as though wondering what to say.

'What is it?' he asked. There was a purple bruise on her neck that hadn't been there last night and he wondered who could have put it there – Nicholas or Thomas?

'I'm sorry,' she said, 'but you mustn't go by ship to France this morning.'

'Why not?' Matthew said, instantly on guard. 'Is it the weather?'

'No, it's not the weather.' Sarah hesitated and looked down at the ground. 'It was something I overheard last night. Something those men said, the ones who've come from the King.'

'From the King? Which men?' Matthew forced his breath to remain steady.

'The two that came late on. I think they might be looking for you.'

'Looking for me?' His heart beat painfully. 'What makes you say that?'

He hoped his shock didn't show. If Nicholas and Thomas were really looking for him, then why hadn't they apprehended him last night?

'Because, because-' Sarah looked pointedly beneath the bed. 'Because they said they're looking for a monk.'

'A monk?' Matthew's mind whirled. 'But I'm a married man!'

'So you say,' Sarah said, 'but in my opinion, you ain't. Not properly. Married men don't usually spend their evenings downstairs – begging your pardon.' She gave him a direct look. 'Normally they has their meals sent upstairs, and not only that-' Sarah blushed, but carried on, 'you turned me down, even though I could see you was interested, and it got me to thinking. Was there something wrong with you, or her – we've barely seen your missus. And then when I heard them talking-'

'What did they say?' Matthew tried to still his agitation, even as he wondered quite how, exactly, she'd come to the conclusion he was interested in her.

Sarah started to recite from her head, the way she'd done with the food last night.

'They said they'd been at the Abbey at Glastonbury, looking for something that was supposed to have been there since ancient times, or something, but they couldn't find it. They was laughing about how they'd dragged the Abbot off to London, and how he'd be regretting not telling them where it was. Nothing like a 'stretch' in the Tower, they said, to help a man remember where he's put his nicknacks – isn't that horrible? But then they said it was all right because now they'd found out where it was from one of the other monks and all they had to do was stop it getting to France.' Sarah waited, a greedy expression forming on her face.

'God's breath,' Matthew said, hoping his legs wouldn't give way. 'Did they say anything else? I know the Abbot at Glastonbury. He's a good man. May God protect him.'

'Not really,' Sarah said, darting sly glances at the purse on Matthew's belt. 'Am I right, sir? Is it you they're looking for? Only, you was decent to me and I don't want you to getting dragged to London. I didn't tell them anything but...'

Here was the girl who had gone around the hall last night, shrewdly calculating the worth of her customers. Rather than being helpful, Matthew suddenly realised she was hoping to earn herself some money.

'And if you've any decency you still won't,' Johanna's voice said, from behind the bed hangings.

Sarah squeaked and looked towards the bed as Johanna pushed the hangings back. She was wearing her linen chemise with a robe over it, and her waist looked prominently thickened.

'But since my husband is *not* a monk and there's nothing wrong with either of us, then that's not going to happen, is it?'

'I won't tell anyone I told you,' Sarah stammered. 'I swear it. God save me, if they knew they'd send me to London too. Oh, good dame, I'm sorry. I knew I was taking a risk, but he'd been so nice to me, you see!'

'There's no need to worry,' Matthew said, placing a protective hand on his money purse. 'We won't tell anyone, Sarah. It was brave of you to come, and we'll see you rewarded for that. But, as you can see, I *am* a married man – although if I was this monk of which you speak, you would have just saved my life.'

'Thank you, sir,' Sarah said, and her eyes gleamed as she watched Matthew dip into the pouch; but her disappointment was great when he brought out a wooden crucifix.

'If you will swear on the sacred body of Our Lord,' Matthew said, 'that you'll not tell anyone, I will do the same. Does that reassure you?'

When Sarah hesitated, he rummaged again, pulling out one of the golden crowns. That did it, her eyes sparkled with triumph.

'And there's another one in here,' he said. 'It's yours when we come back if you keep your silence. Do you understand me?'

Sarah placed her hand on the crucifix, rather too confidently Matthew thought, and swore to keep her silence. Then she curtseyed and backed towards the door, her hand tightly wrapped around the coin.

'What do you make of that?' Johanna whispered, as soon as Matthew had closed and bolted the door again.

He could not answer her and stood uncertainly, his body paralysed with foreboding.

'Come on.' Johanna jumped up and started pushing clothes into her bag. 'Didn't you hear what she said? We need to get going.'

'I'm sorry. The news about the Abbot has sent me sick.'

'I'm sure it has, but we need to get out of here, *fast*, Matthew. Come on!'

'But-'

'Pack!'

He started collecting his things, but when Johanna tried to take the reliquary, he held it fast. 'I promised that I would take it to France.'

Johanna's green eyes glinted. 'Listen to me! If they know someone from Glastonbury is trying to smuggle something valuable out of the country, they'll be searching every man!'

'Aren't you forgetting something?' Matthew said. 'Sarah said they're looking for a monk and I've got a certificate and a wife to prove I'm married; *and* I don't have a tonsure. How could anyone mistake me for a monk?'

Johanna gave him a pitying look. 'You're a monk, Matthew. It stands out a mile when you're with women – you heard her. Come on. It's not worth the risk.'

'And what if they search *you*?'

Johanna hesitated. 'They wouldn't dare search a pregnant woman.'

Still, he held on to the reliquary. 'Do you think she's right, that we shouldn't take that ship? If we don't turn up, we've as good as said we're guilty.'

'There might be another way,' Johanna said.

'What?'

'I have a kinsman who lives further down the coast, with people who are loyal to the old ways. We could go to him.'

'How far?' Matthew was moving now, the energy flowing back into his limbs.

She bit her lip. 'We could make it in little more than a day if we really tried. What do you say?'

He swung his bed roll onto his back and picked up his bag. 'Let's go. The sooner the better.'

‘Aren’t you forgetting something?’ Johanna held out her hand.

‘What?’ He looked all around the room.

‘The reliquary!’ she hissed. ‘Give it to me!’

They heard the clatter of hurrying feet on the stairs and the sound of men’s voices. Matthew threw the reliquary to Johanna and ran to open the window. The stable roof wasn’t far below them.

‘Hurry!’

Johanna was still trying to stuff the reliquary into the pillow she wore beneath her gown. Matthew dragged the iron-bound chest across the door.

‘Are you sure we can climb down there?’ she said, looking over the sill, her eyes wide.

‘We don’t have any choice. Hold on to me.’

Matthew swung one leg over the sill and then the other. There was a pounding at the door and Johanna pushed him forwards then climbed behind him. They half-fell, half-skated down the lower roof onto the ground, landing in a heap.

‘Come on!’

Matthew dragged Johanna to her feet and ran with her into the stables. Please God the ostler’s lad had not overslept.

But both horses were saddled and ready, and Matthew flipped the surprised lad a silver coin. They mounted as if the devil himself were on their trail and Matthew lowered his head over his horse’s neck. He gave it free rein as they left the Inn, glad that Johanna could ride as well as he.

‘Stop! In the King’s name!’

But that was the last thing they were going to do. It would take a while for their pursuers to ready more horses, and the first place they were likely to look for them would be the port – but in the meantime they would be on their way to the West, where with God’s grace there would be people to help them.

*

As night closed in and they were still free, Johanna started to feel exhilarated; that is until Matthew insisted they carry on because the moon was full, and there was still enough light to see.

She rubbed at her back, glad she wasn’t really pregnant.

‘What about smugglers?’ she said. ‘Surely they could be about and it wouldn’t be good to stumble upon them.’

Matthew’s hand went to the knife at his belt. ‘How much further do you think?’ he said.

‘Four or five more hours at least. There’s no one following us now, Matthew. Can’t we stop soon, please?’

He shook his head and Johanna sighed. She found herself dozing off several times, only jerking awake when she slipped in the saddle. A brisk wind had started up from the south-west and eventually the moon was all but obscured by dark clouds.

'We'll have to stop now,' she said. 'The horses are going to stumble if we're not careful.'

If she didn't get some sleep soon, she would likely fall off.

'As long as we're up before daylight,' he said. 'I want to be on the road before anyone else is.'

'Will you help me down?' She feared that she was so stiff she might fall.

Matthew came to her side and she swung out of the saddle, feeling his strong arms tighten about her as he lowered her gently to the ground. A feeling of warmth pulsed through her and stayed there, and Johanna had to fight the desire to lean against him. She was tired, that was all, and his nearness was comforting.

They hobbled the horses and lay down in a thicket, a little way off from each other.

'In the name of the Father-'

'Matthew?'

'Yes?'

'Can we pray together?'

Silence. 'You want us to say the same prayers?'

'Yes.'

More silence and then a sigh. 'Very well.'

She shuffled her blankets a little closer. It was very dark now there was no moon. 'Shall we say the Rosary together?'

'Yes. Will you lead?'

'Of course.'

They whispered the Mysteries of the Rosary into the night and as they finished, Johanna lay back to sleep.

'Might it be a good idea for us to sleep nearer, do you think?' he said, surprising her.

'Why?'

'Because, I've been thinking about what Sarah said. If we're found, we *are* supposed to be married; but more than that, I want to know you're safe.'

Pleasure suffused her body as she heard him shuffle towards her and felt his breath near her cheek. The desire to reach out for him and to be held safely in his arms was almost overwhelming. What on Earth was happening to her?

'I bid you a good night,' she said, but there was no answer. Matthew was already asleep.

Johanna lay awake long into the night. Her back and thighs ached with fatigue and her head throbbed dully, but she could not sleep. Whilst they were riding, sleep had been her only thought, but now she stared up at the blackness of the sky and wondered what would become of them both. Since the day she'd been summoned to Queen Jane's court, her life had closed around her until all she could see of her future was a prison sentence subject to the whims of her sickeningly ambitious uncle; but now she had managed to escape, and once she became a professed nun at Fontevraud, even his long arms wouldn't be able to reach that far.

She'd been staying with her friend, Anne Basset, in Calais when the message came. Anne's mother, Lady Lisle, had been horrified when Johanna said she didn't want to go to court.

'Whatever are you thinking of?' she said. 'You must be out of your mind not to want to go. Your mother, God rest her soul, would have been ecstatic! Why, it's such an *honour*!'

It was no secret that Lady Lisle had been trying everything she could think of to obtain positions as Maids of Honour for her own girls, but despite sending vast quantities of fat quails to tempt pregnant Queen Jane Seymour, none had been forthcoming.

After much fuss about gowns, head dresses, veils and the like, which had been paid for by her uncle, Johanna arrived in London and was welcomed by Queen Jane at court. But, Johanna soon realised that it wasn't the kind of place she would find it easy to relax or to be herself. For one thing, she knew hardly anyone and for another, the ladies of the court were pleasant to each other when the Queen was present but in private their kind words could turn to bitter sarcasm.

Fortunately it had proved easy to love the kind, gentle Queen, who took a personal interest in all of her Maids. But after the triumph of giving birth to King Henry's long awaited son, and being forced to sit for hours receiving boring people – when anyone with eyes in their head could see she wasn't well – Jane succumbed to the fever that eventually killed her.

Johanna scrubbed at the tears that dripped down the sides of her face and shuffled to find some ease for the ache in her back.

She'd barely had time to mourn for the Queen before Henry had started fawning over her, as if she was a child's comforter, bleating of his grief and pain. And all because Jane had apparently told him that she trusted Johanna. The King sought to share his loss with someone he thought sympathetic – which was understandable – except that he soon began to transfer other feelings on to Johanna, ones she was ill-prepared to deal with.

Johanna shuddered. Thank God Lady Lisle succeeded with the quails shortly before Jane's death and Anne Basset finally became a Maid of Honour. Anne had the knack of telling funny stories and was exceptionally pretty, a combination which eventually diverted the King's attention away from Johanna.

'You little fool!'

Johanna winced at the memory of her uncle's face. His eyes had been full of fury and he had shaken her so violently that her teeth crunched against each other.

'Why do you think I went to all the trouble of getting you to court? Don't you realise Henry has married two of his wives' Maids of Honour already? And you could have been the third! I could kill you for this, Johanna. Truly I could. Get out of my sight!'

The next day there'd been dark bruises on her arms, which she'd hidden from the other women out of shame; but none of them had much time to notice because they were all packing up to leave. There would be no Queen's court until a new Queen was chosen, and judging by the King's bereaved state, that wasn't going to be any time soon. Johanna had no idea what she was going to do. No instructions had been sent by her uncle. She was effectively homeless.

Whilst she tried to keep up a brave face, her situation frightened Johanna so much that she felt permanently sick. She could have gone to the King, as Anne did, asking leave to remain on account of her family difficulties, but he was unlikely to agree in Johanna's case because he was still displeased with her.

If only she had not *minded* so much, the thought of becoming Henry's mistress; if only her father had not died of the sweating sickness; if only her mother had loved her father a little less and not died of grief; if only her uncle could have been more like his brother...

Those dark days had left a scar she would never forget, and she vowed that she would never, *never,* turn her back on another's plight as long as she lived.

In the end it was her faith that saved her. God would not abandon her, even if everyone else had, and so she went to the only person who might be able to help – her mother's cousin in Canterbury. Father Peter had been dismayed to see her initially, and he'd gone away muttering that he needed to talk it over with someone. When he returned, he looked even more uneasy.

'You're to become a novice at Amesbury priory,' he said.

Which was how she had met Matthew. Johanna smiled into the darkness at her memories of his reluctance when they first met and how he'd fretted about how she would manage on the road. Little did he know then that she was desperate enough to have slept in a cess pit if it was the only way for her to get to Amesbury.

Matthew snorted in his sleep and turned over and Johanna snuggled up closer to his warmth.

When the King's commissioners had arrived at Amesbury, Mother

Florence had flown about, rounding the novices up and giving them exact instructions on to how to behave. When she came to Johanna, she had thrown up her arms in horror and made her hide in a confessional. The commissioners had gone away grumbling because Mother Florence refused to allow them to close the Priory, and told them that it was not within her power to do so until she had orders from the mother house in France.

Undeterred, they returned for a second time and were more brutal in their demands. All the nuns were to be turned out – the sisters must either return to their families or, if their families were too poor, live together in small groups dependent upon whatever pension the King could afford to give them.

At a stroke, Johanna had been made homeless again; but that night Mother Florence had come to her and told her she was to go to Fontevraud with a very important package. And when she met Matthew at Weymouth, Johanna began to suspect that some unseen hand was at work behind it all, one that had first directed her to Amesbury and was now sending her to France. But as to who that might be? She had no idea – but thought it most likely whoever Father Peter had spoken to in Canterbury. Obviously, the safety of the reliquary had been uppermost in their minds when she arrived, and they had used both her and Matthew to smuggle it first of all away from Canterbury and now, out of the country.

Johanna wriggled under her blankets and turned around so that the heat from Matthew's body warmed her back. A bright light shot across the sky and then another and another. It was as though the universe was celebrating and she took a deep, steadying breath. God was on their side. They would reach France and take Saint Thomas' relic to safety. Nothing was more certain than that.

CHAPTER 21

August
Osmonton, Yorkshire

The firm of solicitors, 'Jackman, Stirk and Feather', had their offices on a busy main street in Osmonton. Surrounded by charity shops and hairdressers, they never-the-less managed to maintain an old-worldly gentility. The receptionist even wore a crisp white blouse and had her hair pinned into a bun.

'Good morning,' Mr Stirk said, rising from his leather arm chair and holding out his hand as Jo and Mat were ushered in.

They sat opposite him, Mat instantly at ease but for some reason, Jo felt unsettled, agitated. What was wrong with her? Her eyes wandered over the shelves of books, the neat, polished surface of the desk, the signet ring on the solicitor's little finger, the expensive fountain pen in his hand, the rheumy eyes above his glasses.

Sometime in the past, Blanche must also have sat in here and given instructions for this will. Was she now hovering around in the ether to see it read out to them? Jo had never expected to be involved, but Mat had told her that she was both an executor and a beneficiary; and all that she could think was perhaps Blanche wanted to formally bequeath her the bird feeders.

'This is the last Will of me, Blanche Eleanor Potters, of 3, Station View, Wesley, Yorkshire. I hereby revoke all my previous Wills and testamentary dispositions and declare this to be my last Will.' Mr Stirk looked over his glasses. 'With me so far?'

They nodded. He said that they had been appointed as executors, which they already knew; that Blanche wished to be cremated, which they also already knew; and that she owned an apartment in France as well as her house on Station View, and would like to divide her estate equally between them – which was a complete surprise. Oh, and would they also take her ashes to be interred in the garden of the said apartment in France?

'You probably need permission for that,' Mr. Stirk said, pushing the papers together neatly and tapping them on his desk.

Mat was the first to recover. 'Don't worry,' he said. 'We'll get it.'

CHAPTER 22

January 1205
Château Narbonnais, Toulouse

Matthieu watched snow swirling outside of the window of the school room. It had been a terrible winter. The rivers were swollen, ready to overspill their banks at any moment, threatening to add flooding to the region's woes. He looked at Raimondet, hesitantly flicking beads across his abacus. The boy would need to grasp arithmetic. Power came to those who understood how to grow money – just look at the mill owners of Toulouse who were earning fortunes by using the water from the Garonne to grind grain into flour. They were able to use this cash to buy up land and property from the Count, who was always short of ready money. No, Raimondet must become a modern prince, have the skills to prosper in changing times – not just excellence on the battlefield. Yet it seemed that as the lad grew older there was less and less time for his studies.

Of course, Matthieu had always had to contend with competition from the tilt yard and the archery butts, where the lad was more than at home. Just this month, however, he had been betrothed to another of the King of Aragon's sisters, Sancha, with all the feasting that had entailed. In effect, both father and son were marrying King Pedro's sisters. Strange to think they would become brothers-in-law when the marriage finally took place!

Matthieu looked out across the courtyard, watching in case one of his servants should come hurrying in this direction. Catharine had been feeling unwell that morning when he left. She had managed to carry this pregnancy for well-nigh eight months, but the spectre of the birthing chamber so oppressed him that he felt his dread growing daily. Why did he find it so hard to put his faith in God? After all, hadn't Catharine become pregnant after seeing a vision at the tomb of Saint Gilles?

Raimondet looked up.

'What is it?' Matthieu asked.

'How is it my friends don't have to join me in the schoolroom, as often as I'm here anymore?' the boy said.

'Because we want you to be more intelligent than they are. You'll be be the next Count, they won't.'

'Hm.' Raimondet flicked a few beads randomly. 'I'm already more intelligent than they are. People are always telling me so.'

'But are those people merely seeking to flatter you? That is what you must always ask yourself, my lord.'

The boy regarded Matthieu innocently enough, but there was a glint of anger in his blue eyes.

'And yes, I will always tell you the truth,' Matthieu laughed. 'Unfortunately for you.'

'Can we do something else, please?' Raimondet said. 'I haven't been on my horse for days.'

'Yesterday morning.'

'Please?'

'Finish those sums first and then we'll see.'

Raimondet bent his head back to his work and Matthew looked out of the window again.

What kind of world would they be living in when the lad grew to manhood? Everything they had taken for granted for years had been swept away so quickly, and all that had gone before took on the semblance of a dream. The mighty Plantagenet empire, which had held sway for over fifty years was now being dismantled, piece by piece by the French King, Philippe, and who was to say where he would stop? Meanwhile John of English, seemed to be sleepwalking through it all because rumour had it that he was obsessed with his very beautiful, very young, wife.

At least it wasn't Joana, and for that Matthieu was thankful. John's eye had lighted upon Isabella of Angoulême, a girl of twelve summers who was promised to Hugh Lusignan – the Count of Marche. He had whisked her away from her betrothed, just as he had whisked away his nephew, Arthur of Brittany after capturing him at Mirebeau when Arthur was besieging Queen Aliénor. John had left all the knights in Arthur's retinue to starve to death in the dungeons of Corfe castle in England; and although no one had any doubt that John had also played some part in the disappearance of Arthur, no one had been brave enough to call him to account for it.

Matthieu sighed and chafed his hands. The heat was dying in the fire and no one had been in to throw more logs on. He would have words with the steward.

Count Raimon considered John a close ally, but then the Count held his lands from no less than four liege lords – the kings of England, France, and Aragon and even the Pope himself. Not a comfortable position to be in at all.

'There, I've finished!'

Raimondet stood up to stretch and Matthieu went to check his answers. They were all correct, the lad was learning fast.

'Very well, you may chose what you want to do now.'

Raimondet's eyes lit up. 'Can we go hawking?'

'No,' Matthieu said, chiding himself for offering too openly. He needed to look in on Catharine before he did anything else, for his unease was growing steadily. 'It'll be too dark before we can get everyone ready. Why don't you go down to the archery butts?'

'But you said, I could chose what I wanted to do!'

'So I did,' Matthieu said, 'but I was distracted. My wife has not been very well today.'

Raimondet's petulant look changed to one of sympathy and Matthieu's heart gladdened. The lad might strong and valiant but he also had a good heart.

'Then you must go and see to her,' Raimondet said. 'And I'll go to the butts with my friends, as you suggested.'

'Sire?' It was Bernard who walked briskly into the room, without knocking. 'Can you come quickly? The Lady Catharine is asking for you.'

There was no need to say more, Bernard's expression said it all.

'Look after Raimondet,' Matthieu said, picking up his cloak. 'He wants to go to the archery butts.'

*

Beatrice met him at the door.

'I've tried to get her into bed, sire,' she said, 'but I can't move her. She's in the solar. We've already sent for the doctor.'

Matthieu dashed along the hallway to Catharine slumped in a chair, with great gouts of blood soaking the hem of her gown and making a crimson lake upon the floor.

'Catharine!' he cried, falling to his knees. He wrapped his arms around his wife, but it felt as if every bone in her body had dissolved to nothing. 'Speak to me, my love,' he said. 'Everything's going to be all right.' Desperately, he looked around at the maid. 'Fetch the doctor!'

'I've already sent for him, sire,' Beatrice said, twisting her hands together. 'Will she be all right, do you think?'

'Get Bernard to bring a mattress in here,' he ordered. 'And cloths and blankets, and hot water! Didn't you think to stop the bleeding?'

'I – we couldn't, it was all so sudden-' Beatrice fled and Matthieu heard her shouting for Ermessinda.

'Matthieu?' Catharine's voice was a mere whisper, and he had to put his ear next to her lips to hear her.

'Matthieu, I'm sorry. There never was a vision. I lied to you, and now I'm dying. Forgive me.'

'Catharine!' Matthieu shook her. 'Don't say that. I won't let you go.'

'I'm so cold, Matthieu.' Catharine's lips had turned the colour of plums and her breath came out in a sigh. ' Say goodbye to Joana, tell her I'm sorry...'

'No!'

Catharine's eyes stayed open, but they had lost their focus forever and her head rolled back. Matthieu gathered her to him.

'I've sent for blankets to warm you up, Catharine. They'll feel my wrath for not looking after you better than this.'

She was already wearing an amulet about her wrist, one that contained a thread from the Virgin's girdle, but Matthieu pulled his own from about his neck and strung it around hers. Why was God punishing them like this? Were their sins too great to be forgiven?

'Catharine,' he begged, trying to straighten up her head and patting her pale, pale cheek, 'please don't die.'

A sudden, great gasp sent hope coursing through Matthieu; but there were no more.

'Catharine!'

People arrived then: Pons, the Count's physician, Beatrice, Bernard, and, unbelievably, Arnald of Fanjeaux.

'Get that filthy heretic out of here!' Matthieu bellowed.

'Peace,' Pons said, trying to extract Catharine from Matthieu's arms. 'Arnald only wants to help. Let me take her, Matthieu. I might still be able to do something.'

'No. She stays with me until *he's* gone!' Matthieu said, pointing an unsteady finger at Arnald. He grasped Catharine even more firmly to himself and turned on Beatrice. 'Get me a proper priest, now!'

Arnald put up his hands and started backing away. 'Apologies, brother,' he said. 'It was the Count who thought I could be of service to your lady. Think nothing of it.'

Matthieu wanted to boot him in the backside but he wasn't going to let go of Catharine. How dare *he* come in here, lusting after her soul?

'Matthieu,' Pons said, gently. 'Please let her go. I might be able to save – the child.'

'What?' It was as though fog enveloped his brain. Only slowly did the doctor's words filter through.

'Catharine's dead,' Pons said. 'Put her down.'

Still he clung to her.

Pons turned to Bernard. 'Give me a hand.'

They dragged Catharine away from him and Matthieu felt as if they were taking his body too. Everything took on the semblance of a bad dream and he saw a look pass between Pons and Bernard but could not understand it. What were they doing?

They laid Catharine upon the floor as though she were already upon her funeral bier, and the long hair that he loved so well suddenly escaped from its net and cascaded about her shoulders. Why, Matthieu wondered, suddenly noticing a few strands of grey, had that happened to one so young?

Pons tapped him on the arm. 'Do you want me to do this?' he said, holding a gleaming knife and gesturing towards the bulge in Catharine's stomach.

Matthieu's mind refused to think.

'Well?'

'Do what you have to,' he said, bile already rising into his throat. 'And send for me if the child lives.'

CHAPTER 23

September 1539
Devon

The following morning, Johanna shook Matthew awake and he grumbled about having only just got to sleep. She smiled to herself. For the last hour or so he'd been snoring softly into her ear.

'Just tell me again how you know there'll be people who'll want to help,' he said, as they readied themselves for their journey.

'I had a letter from my cousin, Gerald,' she told him, 'whilst I was still at Amesbury. He was a monk at Saint Nicholas' priory in Exeter, until they were turned out. Father Peter must have told him where I was. He wrote to me, asking for money.' She blushed. 'I had to tell him I didn't have any.'

'And where is he now?'

'At a fishing village along the coast from here, so he said. They worship in secret.' She stopped and bit her lip. 'You have some money, Matthew, haven't you? We could help him, couldn't we?'

'Yes,' he said, checking over his shoulder. 'Someone needs to keep the old traditions alive, even if it has to be in secret. I pray God protects them.'

It was a little after noon when they reached the village and, after finding stabling for their horses at the inn, they walked down to the harbour to see if there were any likely vessels for the crossing to France. Johanna felt rather bold and gave Matthew a peck on the cheek to remind him to keep up the pretence that she was carrying their first child. He coloured furiously, but eventually put his arm about her and then seemed to relax. She, for her part, felt that same flow of warmth from him, but told herself that it would have been the same, whoever he was – they were merely actors.

'How will we find out where your cousin is?' he asked. 'If people are risking their lives to say the Mass here, they will not be easily given away.'

'I've thought of that,' she said, smiling up at him. 'Gerald gave me the name of a man called Reginald Mossby, if I was able to send money – someone he trusts. We can ask for him at the Inn.'

Matthew looked impressed and wearily stretched the muscles in his back and neck. 'I wish I could be as confident as you,' he said.

Two fishing vessels lay at anchor in the tiny harbour. Either one looked capable of the crossing to France, but neither were big enough to take the horses. Johanna and Matthew walked back to the Inn with heavy hearts. Being without horses when they arrived was a big disadvantage, but at least they had enough money to buy fresh mounts. When they enquired the whereabouts of Reginald Mossby, they were told he was a blacksmith and directed to a cottage on the outskirts of the village. A woman was sitting outside, spinning wool.

'Good day, Mistress Mossby,' Matthew said, removing his cap. 'Is your husband at home?'

The woman watched warily from beneath her mop cap, and her hand grasped at the collar of a large mastiff dog, which strained towards them.

'Can I ask who wants him?'

'We're family of Gerald Grenfell, late of Saint Nicholas' in Exeter,' Johanna said, stepping forwards.

The woman's expression changed from suspicion to fear and she scurried off around the side of the cottage to where they could hear the ring of metal upon metal. Reginald Mossby was not long in coming to greet them, wiping the sweat off his big, ruddy forehead.

'Forgive me,' he said. 'But I wasn't expecting you.'

Johanna pulled Gerald's letter from her bag, but the farrier only put his work-roughened hand to it and then pushed it back, his face reddening further.

'Um, that's all right,' he said. 'Father Gerald told me he was writing to you. Lady Johanna, is it?'

She nodded and Reginald's wife gave a squeak, then disappeared into the cottage.

'Don't mind her,' Reginald said, shaking his head. 'She isn't used to fine ladies. You'll be wanting to see him?'

'Yes, please,' Johanna said. 'We have something for him. Can you show me where he is?'

'Not rightly,' Reginald said. 'But you can wait here and I'll fetch him. I won't be long. Mags!'

Mags Mossby poked her long nose out of the door.

'Bring our visitors something to eat, woman.'

He strode over to where a bay gelding was cropping a patch of grass and jumped onto its back, urging it forwards into a trot. Mags Mossby took a long time to bring out a tray with cider and bread, and two small slices of cold mutton. A young lad with a shock of black hair followed her, and grinned when Matthew flipped him a coin. Mags, however, scowled as if she was worried he'd corrupt the lad.

As they neared the end of the bread, which was surprisingly good, and the mutton, which wasn't, Reginald returned leading his horse. Sitting astride was a man wearing a much faded and well worn tunic over rough woollen hose. He vaulted lightly down and came over to kneel in front of

Johanna.

'Oh, get up, Gerald, do,' she said, laughing. 'I hardly recognise you without your tonsure. Come and meet Matthew."

'Greetings, Matthew,' Gerald said, his eyes straying almost unwillingly to Johanna's swollen belly. 'I hope you bring good news, but I fear there is little of that these days.'

For an embarrassing moment, Matthew looked to be on the verge of tears.

'Come now,' Gerald said, taking his arm and casting another brief peek at Johanna's belly. 'There is no problem too large to lay before the Lord, and we must all hope for better times in the future.'

Matthew's face had turned bright red. Gerald obviously thought he was responsible for Johanna's condition; but before either of them could say anything, Mags brought out more cider, and Gerald settled himself comfortably against the trunk of a birch tree. By the way he kept looking about, it was clear he was as wary as his hostess.

Johanna waited until Mags had gone away and then came straight to the point.

'Gerald, we need your help,' she said. 'We have to get to France as soon as possible. I can't tell you why, but it's nothing you would be ashamed of, and things are not what they seem.' She pointed to her belly. 'Only please make sure that His Majesty never gets to hear of this.'

Gerald blanched, and a look of puzzlement stole across his face. 'Is it his, Johanna? I heard he was bereft when you left court.'

Johanna's jaw dropped open. 'Gracious, Gerald! I told you, all is not what it seems. Anyway,' she lowered her voice, 'I hear Henry is struggling to find someone prepared to marry him – no one has a long enough neck.'

'Johanna!' Gerald said. 'Be careful what you say, please.' He looked over towards the cottage. 'People have been arrested for less – believe me.'

'I know,' she said. 'Forgive me.'

He nodded. 'Where are you bound?'

'Fontevraud Abbey,' she said, and his eyebrows rose. 'I'm to complete my novitiate there.' Johanna looked around. 'And I'm carrying a reliquary in here.'

His eyebrows rose further. 'A reliquary of which saint?'

'Thomas Becket,' she whispered. 'Matthew and I brought it from Canterbury last year, before the shrine was destroyed. Matthew was a novice at Glastonbury. So as you can see, we're on a mission of great importance.'

Gerald paled, but quickly made the Sign of the Cross over them both.

'Then God speed you, for surely there was never a darker time in our

Church's history than this. Whatever you do, may the Lord bless you.' He turned to Matthew. 'Do you intend to complete your novitiate at Fontevraud too? I must say, the idea of serving under a lady abbess is a novel one.'

Matthew looked nonplussed and Johanna wondered if his plans had ever gone beyond delivering the reliquary; for at times on this journey, even that had seemed a doubtful possibility.

'God has His will for me,' he said, simply. 'And I am his servant.'

'Indeed. Well,' Gerald looked around again, 'I'm sure we can find someone to put you on a ship, that's not a problem, but,' he looked embarrassed, 'do you have the money to pay for it?'

'Enough,' Johanna said. 'How soon can we sail?'

'As soon as the next tide, I suppose. Reginald will see to it.'

He called out for Reginald, who came at once, and after a brief conversation set off towards the village.

*

Mags was still inside the house so Matthew decided to look around, leaving Johanna and her cousin to talk. He had already given her some of the Abbot's gold coins and instructed her to give them to Gerald. There would be plenty left to pay the ship's captain, and once they reached Fontevraud...? He sighed. Once they reached Fontevraud he would give all of what he had left to the Abbess in the hope that she would accept him; but in truth, now Glastonbury was finished, there was nowhere else he wanted to be.

As he turned around the back of the house, he saw the glowing fire and tools of the farrier, but he also saw the young, black haired lad running away in the direction of the village. Perhaps Reginald had forgotten something or he was on an errand? Matthew hoped they weren't putting Reginald's wife to too much trouble, for she was clearly unhappy at them being there. The bay gelding was pulling at a rack of hay and looked well and content. Matthew stroked the mastiff dog, which was quiet now, and hunkered down beside it. He could not deny the tension building inside of him. Didn't he believe they would succeed? In his head and his heart he did, but it was as though his body knew otherwise. Finding a sheltered spot, he knelt to pray, offering up his doubt and weakness to God and receiving solace and comfort in return.

Johanna and Gerald were laughing together as he returned, and Matthew paused before rejoining them, feeling suddenly out of place. Whilst he was with her on the road, and her clothes were as travel-stained as his, it was easy to forget that she was a lady – someone who had been at court and a favourite of the King. With her cousin, she held herself differently, spoke differently. Matthew picked up a fallen branch and threw it for the dog.

'Matthew,' Gerald said, coming over. 'I want to thank you for your very generous donation. I believe God warned you of the danger in Weymouth and sent you here today. He has brought you to me so that we can benefit from His support. I will put the money to good use, have no fear of that.'

Fighting the lump in his throat, Matthew bowed his head. 'May God's Kingdom come.'

As soon as Reginald appeared, everything was bustle and saying farewell. They left both horses with the farrier in thanks for his help and then were on their way to the cove, where the larger of the two fishing vessels was getting ready to leave. Reginald introduced them to Brent, the skipper, and told Matthew how much to pay.

Brent was a huge-shouldered man in his late thirties, with a face badly marked by smallpox scars. He had bright eyes, like the sea on a summer's day, and looked them both over thoroughly before showing them to the small cabin at the stern of his ship. There was no proper bed but someone had laid down woollen blankets and with their bed rolls on top, it was passably comfortable. There was nowhere safe to hide the reliquary though.

'You'll just have to keep it on you,' Matthew said.

'For three days?'

'Or stay in here all the time. That would probably be a the best idea anyway,' he said, knowing how easily she talked to people. 'The less we come in contact with others, the better. You know that.'

'Oh, Matthew!' Johanna said. 'We're among friends now, can't you feel it?'

'No,' he said, shaking his head. 'I can't trust people I've only just met, Johanna, and remember, you're the one who insisted on carrying it.'

'Very well,' she said. 'If I must carry on pretending I'm with child I'd better put my feet up and rest. Would you see if they've got any refreshments on board?'

Matthew fought back his bewilderment. Why did she insist on behaving as though this was a game? As he went back on deck, he noticed that some of the sailors were watching the quayside and at first looked interested, but then worried. Now they were now looking directly at him. Matthew hurried back into the cabin.

'Johanna,' he said. 'Give the reliquary to me. Now!'

'No,' she said.

'Someone's coming. I heard voices and it sounds like trouble. If they come aboard. I'll jump over the side with it.'

'What?' She came towards him. 'Who's coming?'

'I don't know, but from the way the sailors were looking at me, it must be something to do with us. I'm sure we've been betrayed.' He thought about the farrier's lad hurrying away from the cottage and his fear mounted. 'Johanna, please. Give me the reliquary!'

'No,' she said, again. 'I won't let them arrest you, Matthew. If they do, I'll never see you again.' Her voice broke. 'If they take me – well, I have some connections.'

'Johanna, don't be such a fool!' Matthew desperately wanted to shake her. 'Give me the reliquary. At least then there'll be a chance of saving it from the King's men.'

'Saving it?' She stared at him. 'If you jump off the ship, how far do you think you'll get?'

He looked around hopelessly. There wasn't enough time. He would have to drag it away from her.

Four men burst into the cabin. Two of them seized his arms and locked them painfully behind his back.

*

'Leave him alone!' Johanna said. 'What has he done? I'll have you know you have no right to do this!'

The men ignored her and started dragging Matthew out of the cabin.

'No!' she shouted, running up to them. 'Help me someone! Stop them! My husband hasn't done anything!' She tried to grab the arm of one of the men but another thrust her away, roughly.

'If he's done nothing then you've no need to worry,' he said.

'Johanna,' Matthew pleaded. 'Let it be, my love. Carry on to France. Your mother needs you. I'll be there soon. I promise.'

'No! I won't let them take you!' She tried again to stop them, but the other man gripped a handful of her hair and pulled her away. The last Johanna saw of Matthew was through the door of the cabin as he was forced down the gangway.

'Brent!' she called. 'Is there anything you can do?'

But the captain, who had watched everything from the deck, now turned his back and strode away. Whilst one of the remaining men held Johanna fast, the other made a thorough search of the cabin, up-ending everything into a jumbled heap on the floor. She couldn't conceal her distress and tears cascaded down her face. This was all her fault. She'd been the one to suggest they'd be safe if Gerald helped them and Matthew had been right – she *was* too quick to trust.

The man's eyes lighted upon her stomach and he looked up at his mate. Johanna froze. He moved forwards, as if he were going to touch her, but then the man holding Johanna shook his head.

'Let her be,' he said. 'It's a bad enough business as it is.'

They left abruptly and Johanna rubbed at her bruised arm, trying to gather her wits; then she rushed after them. The sombre-faced sailors carried on at their tasks as she passed and didn't look up. Johanna thought she would be able to get off the ship, but then an iron arm stayed her progress and drove the wind from her lungs.

'Oh, no you don't,' Brent grunted. 'You'll be no help to him where he's going.'

'But he hasn't done anything. Please let me go. I need to stop them.'

Brent leaned closer to her ear. 'Shut up you little fool! There's nothing you can do for him now. Do you want to put the rest of us in jeopardy as well? I'm going to raise anchor as soon as I can and get away to France. Isn't that what you wanted?'

He searched her face and she stared back, half frightened out of her wits.

'I know someone in Sarnac who can help you,' he continued. 'I'll tell you how to find her later. Forget your friend, he's gone – understand?' He started to propel her towards the cabin.

'But,' she said, 'I can't just leave him!'

'Yes you can!' Brent gave a sharp laugh. 'The country's not what it was. Wake up! People listen out and make profit by reporting on their neighbours. I'll find out who was responsible for this, you can rely on that, but we have to get away whilst we can, and just hope they don't ask any more awkward questions.' He put his face close to hers. 'Are you going back into that cabin, or do I have to throw you in there?

Johanna risked a look out over the gunwale, but Matthew was nowhere to be seen.

'Very well, I warned you.'

Brent pushed her so hard in the direction of the cabin that Johanna skidded along the deck. Tears stung her eyes and she curled her fists. How dare he treat her like this? But when she would have turned around and argued further, she felt him at her back and he gave an almighty shove that sent her straight through the door of the cabin. She heard it shut behind her and the sound of a bolt being drawn across. Brent was taking no chances. She was now effectively a prisoner.

Johanna straightened her bed and lay down upon it in a curled ball, her thoughts in turmoil. What would happen to Matthew now? Images forced themselves into her mind, horrible ones, and she squirmed where she lay. Oh, Matthew, Matthew, I'm so sorry. She couldn't bear the thought that she would never see him again. Dear, dear Matthew. Not many men were as good and true as he was.

After a while, she felt the motion of the ship and soon her stomach started heaving. She banged hard on the door, and as soon as someone opened it, rushed out onto the deck.

'Excuse me,' she gasped, pushing her way past one of the sailors.

There was still some land visible in the distance, but night was closing in fast. When she turned away from the gunwale, Brent was watching her.

'Bit late for the early sickness, isn't it?' he said.

'What would you know,' she said, irritably, wiping her mouth. 'Have you ever carried a baby?'

He laughed. 'No, thank God. I take it you won't be wanting anything to eat, then?'

'No, thank you,' she said.

'I'll send a lad with some ale for you to drink and some water to wash,' he said. 'Get your head down if you can, and sleep away the sickness. That's the best idea.'

Johanna returned to the cabin and threw herself down on the makeshift bed. At least the reliquary was safe. She cradled her pillow-stuffed belly and tried to pray. For whatever reason, God had seen fit to send the reliquary but not Matthew to France. That decision was His and His alone. Who was she to question the will of God?

But, however hard she tried to tell herself that, she missed Matthew with every fibre of her being. He was... she struggled to put into words how she felt.... was she in love with him? She didn't know. What was being in love like? Surely it ought to be more than this heart-sick feeling? Certainly, he was a dear friend; but even though Johanna told herself that God was looking after Matthew, losing him felt much, much worse than just losing a friend. Her shoulders shook and every wave churned her stomach. Worse still, every wave took her farther and farther away from Matthew. Tears slid down her face as she remembered his final words to her. 'I'll be there soon. I promise.'

But that wasn't going to happen. Merciful God, she prayed, please don't let them hurt him.

*

After a fitful night, Johanna awoke to find the deck still pitching underneath her. Her stomach lurched and evil tasting liquid forced its way into her mouth. Johanna sat up groggily and then staggered to the door, needing to relieve herself. To her relief, someone had pushed in a bucket; and grateful not to have to join the men at the bilges, she used it then banged to be let out to empty it. Spray flew into her face as the door was grudgingly opened by one of the sailors, and the wind whipped at her travelling cloak as she stepped out on deck. In the sky, dark clouds were massing. Where was Brent? Apart from her cabin, the only other accommodation aboard was likely to be below the deck and she dare not go down there.

'You're about early,' the sailors said. 'Most passengers are too sick by this stage to come looking for breakfast.'

Johanna put a hand to her mouth. The mere thought of food was appalling. 'Thank you,' she said, 'but you're right. I'm really not hungry. I wanted to speak to Brent.'

'Ah, Brent.' The sailor smiled, showing her his blackened teeth. 'Women never can resist him.' The stench of liquor on his breath made Johanna's stomach heave even more.

'Excuse me,' she said, making for the side.

Eventually she spotted Brent near to the prow, talking to one of his men. Johanna staggered crab-wise across the deck towards them.

'Good morning!' Brent said, swaying easily with the motion of the ship.'You're up early.'

'I couldn't sleep because I was worrying about my husband,' Johanna said.

He gave an irritated sigh. 'You and I need to talk.'

The ship crested a particularly large wave and Johanna retched. Brent pushed her towards the side where she hung miserably, thinking it would be better to be dead.

'Best stay in your cabin,' he said. 'Looking at those clouds, I would say the sea will get a lot rougher before we reach France.'

'But I want to go back to England. Please, turn the ship around. How can you expect me to carry on to France when I don't know what's happened to my husband?'

Brent took a step nearer and whispered into her ear. 'All right, *Lady* Johanna,' he said. 'You can stop the acting now. I know why you're here. You have a reliquary don't you, of the Blessed Saint Thomas Becket?'

Johanna stared at him in shock and couldn't think what to say. Who had told him? Did Gerald trust the sea captain? Yesterday she might have done the same herself, but not today.

'What would I want with that papist nonsense?' she said.

Brent looked unimpressed. 'That's what I was told. Why else do you think I was willing to take you when the King's men are offering bribes in every port, and looking for a monk who's escaped with something the King wants?'

Johanna felt the colour drain from her face.

'Word came just before I got the message to take you,' Brent continued. 'It's only my love of the old ways that got you on board at all. Your cousin told me you was a novice nun. Isn't the safety of that reliquary more important than the monk?'

Johanna's cheeks began to burn. How dare he speak so highhandedly?

'Oh, I see,' Brent said. 'Like that is it? You two thought you would elope together and the reliquary be damned. Is that it?'

'No! It's just...'

She shook her head. She couldn't even explain it to herself.

'It's just I can't bear to think what they might do to him.'

Brent shrugged. 'You knew you were taking a risk. Thank God you got away with it at all.' He eyed her belly. 'I take it that's not really a babe in there?'

'Of course not,' Johanna said. 'I was in my novitiate at Amesbury Priory.'

'By the saints!' Brent said. 'I've never had a nun on my ship before.' His expression softened. 'I've been a devotee of Saint Thomas all my life, my lady, and I'm sorry for hurting you. It's just that when I saw you two travelling together...'

'Our superiors permitted the deception in order to safeguard the reliquary,' Johanna said, tartly, relieved that she seemed to be gaining some advantage over the man.

He nodded. 'I'll do everything in my power to make sure Saint Thomas arrives safely in Sarnac. You can be sure of that.'

Johanna thanked him and went back to the cabin, her mind working furiously. Matthew had been carrying most of their money and she barely had enough to buy another horse and claim a night's lodgings in France. Once again, the yawning fear of homelessness stalked her and she thought feverishly back over the last two days. What error of hers had brought this calamity upon them? Most likely she'd angered God by being glad to be away from the priory, or could it have been because she enjoyed the warmth of Matthew's sleeping body? Feeling suddenly unworthy, Johanna took the reliquary from its hiding place in the pillow and placed it into her bag.

The pitching of the ship increased and soon she heard the wind gathering strength outside. Everything in the cabin started sliding around and Johanna struggled to keep even herself in one place. Her stomach continued to heave wretchedly but, thankfully, nothing came up; which was lucky because the empty slop bucket was also rolling around on the floor. Never in all of her life had she felt so wretched, and so cast down. The ship's timbers creaked and groaned, and the sailors shouted to each other above loud bangs and crashes, the cause of which she could only guess. Her bag came flying towards her head and she ducked. To her horror, when everything righted itself again, the reliquary lay broken open upon the floor. Johanna edged towards it, her back contracted against the punishment she knew must come from above. How could she have allowed such sacrilege to happen?

Desperately, she scrabbled the contents together, convinced she was destined for Hell even if this voyage did not end in disaster. In went a faded purple velvet pouch, a fold of yellowing linen, and four rather large gem stones. Johanna took a sharp breath. Gem stones – were they diamonds? Her mind whirled. Why would diamonds be inside the saint's casket?

For an age, the ship bumped and tossed as if it had gone mad; and now the men outside were barely audible over the rage of the storm. Consumed with the need to keep the reliquary safe, Johanna wedged the slop bucket against the door and managed to secure herself to the side of the cabin.

Finally, blessedly, the ship's motion calmed. The sounds outside diminished and eventually she could hear gulls calling. On legs that shuddered, Johanna got up to use the bucket. Not long afterwards, Brent opened the door and looked in briefly, presumably to see if she was still alive, and satisfied that she was, left again without a word.

Johanna knelt and asked for God's forgiveness, and offered up thanks for the safe deliverance of the ship. Then she asked for guidance and support in what she was about to do – and opened the reliquary again.

The casket was lined with the same faded velvet as the pouch. She picked up the four diamonds and let them nestle in her palm. The largest was the size of a dove egg and even in the dim light of the cabin, emitted an entrancing fire. She sat back on her heels, stunned. Could these be the real reason she and Matthew had been hunted across the country? Everyone knew the King loved jewels, especially diamonds. Hadn't his younger sister, Mary, bought off his anger when she secretly married the Duke of Suffolk, by giving Henry the famed, 'Mirror of Naples'? By rights, the diamond belonged to the French crown, for Mary Tudor had only been Queen in France for eighty two days before her elderly husband died. But she had smuggled the Mirror away with her on her return to England, knowing that it could buy something for her that she very much desired. How right she had been, and the word was that the King was in no hurry to give it back!

Johanna shuddered. The Abbot of Glastonbury may have put these diamonds into the reliquary as a way of saving some of the Abbey's wealth; but she knew of no particular links between Fontevraud and Glastonbury, so why would they wish to send their wealth there? No. There must be another reason. She swallowed hard. What if the, 'unseen hand', who had been guiding her progress was at work here? What if she was being used and these diamonds were destined not for Fontevraud, but for the King of France?

She sat back on her heels. Many of the clergy bitterly opposed Henry's break from Rome and longed to reinstate a Catholic monarch. Could these diamonds could be part of a plot to replace Henry with the French King Francis? In which case, if she and Matthew had made the crossing at Weymouth, there would likely have been someone waiting for them at

Barfleur.

Johanna's hands trembled as she reached into the reliquary again, feeling strangely reluctant to separate herself from the largest diamond, which fitted into her palm as if it belonged there and gave a most welcome feeling of calm. She picked up the velvet pouch and felt a ring in there, perhaps two. More treasures, 'hidden' from the King? She tipped the contents onto her lap and caught her breath as two rings and a fragment of bone, the size of a cockle shell, landed there. Seeing the bone made her shiver and the back of her neck began to prickle. By its shape it looked to be part of a skull. Ah, Saint Thomas, forgive me, she prayed, terrified that the saint, who had not been known to suffer fools gladly, might materialise in front of her and chastise her for her irreverence.

When nothing of that kind happened, Johanna kissed the fragment, placed it back into the pouch and then back into the reliquary, amazed to think that she had actually touched a relic of the great Saint's body. She picked up the rings, one a man's – with an emerald the size of a thumb nail, and the other a woman's – with a large, milky opal. These and the diamonds she didn't return to the reliquary but slipped them into the money pouch which hung about her neck, underneath her clothes.

The yellowing linen caught her eye as she started to close the casket and she wondered if it was a part of the Saint's vestment; but there was hair peeking out of the fold and when she started to tuck the hair back inside, she realised that it was part of a lock of long dark hair tied with a decaying silk ribbon. Johanna blinked. What now? No man had ever worn his hair this long, especially not a priest.

Questions tumbled about in her head. Who did the rings and the hair belong to? Could Mother Florence and the Abbot of Glastonbury have been sweethearts? Was this how they had chosen to hide their guilt? She thought it unlikely. Mother Florence patently disliked men, even priests.

There was a knock at the door and she scrabbled to hide the reliquary under her bedding.

'Come in.'

Brent opened the door. 'I'm sorry to disturb you, my lady,' he said, 'but we can see land and I thought you might like to come out on deck.'

Johanna followed him outside, pulling her cloak about her and taking great lungfuls of the cold, salty air. The sun glinted off a low land mass in the distance and her breath came out with a sigh. How she had longed for this! What irony then, that her first task was going to be to find a way back to England.

'Still feeling sick?' Brent asked her.

'No,' Johanna said, giving him her sweetest smile. She would cause as few problems as possible from now on, meekly accept whatever he told her to do and keep quite – because she couldn't risk him finding those diamonds. Like Mary Tudor, she had a very important use for them, which was not what those who had sought to hide them would have intended. She was going to buy Matthew's freedom.

CHAPTER 24

August
Station View, Wesley Village, Yorkshire

Jo percolated coffee and tried to find the words she needed. Mat was through in her lounge, sitting on the sofa with his legs stretched out, eyes closed. He looked utterly weary, which was why she'd suggested a coffee; and she had wanted to drink it in her own house because Blanche was so conspicuously absent next door. Her own house. It really hadn't sunk in yet that she now owned half of Blanche's house, and half of an unknown apartment in France, as well as all of the bird feeders and a sewing machine...

'Mat?'

There was no answer. She popped two Kit-Kats onto the tray and took it through, pausing as she did, to look out of the window. There'd been so little time to plant anything this year, with work and looking after Blanche; but last year's calendula was flowering again, albeit on straggly stalks, and there was a brave showing of self-sown nasturtiums, nigella and California poppies. In fact, the garden was surprisingly full of colour.

Mat gave a grunt and settled himself further down on the sofa. He looked so comfortable that Johanna's heart gave a little leap but she squashed it immediately. Why torture herself with what could never be? She sat in the armchair, sipping at her coffee, and looking over the rim of it at his sleeping form. She felt quite guilty, stealing these precious moments, and being able to observe him without him knowing. He *was* wasted as a priest, she decided. Blanche was right. No man so attractive ought to be locked away forever.

She ought to offer him her half of Blanche's properties. He was, after all, Blanche's blood relation – although she had to confess to a burning curiosity to see the apartment. What a dark horse Blanche had been. The solicitor had given them a big brown envelope containing keys and directions, along with the information that a man called Jean-Yves lived downstairs and was looking after it for them.

Mat sighed and gave a yawn. 'Oh, my goodness,' he said, looking at his watch. 'Jo, I'm so sorry. How rude of me. And you've made the coffee. Have I let it go cold?'

'No, it's still OK,' she said, handing him his mug. 'You looked like you needed a nap. Don't worry.'

He took a sip and grinned. 'Thanks, I need this as well. There's too much to do to sleep the day away; although I can't really remember when

I last had a full night. Can you?'

She shook her head. 'But there'll be plenty of time to catch up now. I've asked if I can take the balance of my annual leave before I go back to work.'

'Oh, that's marvellous,' Mat said, picking up one of the Kit-Kats. 'Why don't we use the time to take a look at Blanche's apartment and bury her ashes whilst we're there?

Jo didn't know what to say. Even the thought of going to France with him had set her pulse fluttering. 'Mat, can I talk to you about something?'

'Go ahead,' he said, with a grin. 'I don't normally go to sleep in people's houses, to be honest, if that's what's worrying you. I won't do it again, promise.'

'It's not that,' she said, returning his smile. He knew how to disarm people didn't he? 'I'm glad you feel comfortable. It's just that, well, the house next door and the apartment in France – they're nothing to do with me. They're yours. You're Blanche's nephew. I was only a friend.'

'Not just a friend,' he said. 'You were the nearest thing Blanche had to a daughter. I know what you're trying to say, and I appreciate the offer, but I'm not penniless, you know.'

'I-' Now she felt terrible. 'Mat, I'm sorry. I didn't, that's not what I meant-'

'Aren't you looking forwards to us becoming neighbours when I'm in my dotage and need somewhere to retire to?'

'But we, you can't. I mean...' Jo shrugged. What did she mean?

He came and knelt before her.

'Jo,' he said, taking her hand in his.

Delicious tingles streaked all the way up her arm. His eyes were calm and friendly, but there was a hint of mischief in them. If only he knew the effect he was having on her!

'Blanche knew what she was doing,' Mat said. 'So, how can you deny her wishes? The house next door belongs to both of us, and what we do with it is up to both of us. And as for the apartment in France; we haven't even seen it yet. For all we know it could be a ruin, and I'll be glad to have you help me get rid of it.'

Jo couldn't help pulling her hand away. The sensation of him holding it was just too confusing. He stood up abruptly, looking concerned.

'What I'm saying is, don't make any hasty decisions, will you?'

'But you'll have to go back to Scotland very soon won't you?' she said, hoping it didn't show that the thought of living here without him or Blanche to be about as miserable as a long, cold winter.

'Yes. Which is why I suggested we should go to France now. But I'm sorry. I should have realised you needed to get some rest first.'

What should she say? Here he was, without a trace of guile, offering her the chance to spend time with him in France. Were Catholic priests supposed to do things like that with single women?

'I-er-' She stopped. Why not just say yes? What else could she possibly want to do other than get herself deeper into trouble with this man?

*

They took the train to Poole, on the south coast, intending to hire a car once they reached France. That night they stayed in single rooms in an anonymous hotel whilst they waited for the early morning ferry. Mat was in high spirits as they strolled along the harbour.

'Tell you what,' he said, turning up the collar of his mac against the breeze and pointing to one of the racy Sunseeker yachts that were moored there. 'These boats are fantastic. Look how aerodynamic they are. Why don't we sell everything and buy one of those? Then we could sail around the world – and worry about the rest when we got back.'

'As in finding new jobs and homes, you mean?' she said, squinting against the sun. Now what was he up to?

'Ah, where's your sense of adventure?' he said, raising an eyebrow. 'Wouldn't you like a break – to sail away from it all? Looking after dying people must be draining.'

'Wouldn't there be a few questions asked of you?' she said, disturbed to be having this conversation with someone who was a priest.

'Nah,' he said, with a shrug and a grin. 'Catholic priests take off on round the world sailing trips with attractive young women all the time. No one, especially not the newspapers, would be in the slightest bit interested.'

She felt sweat forming on her palms. If she didn't know better, she'd say he was flirting with her. 'I'm surprised you haven't done it already,' she said. 'There must be millions of attractive students at the chaplaincy, who'd jump at the chance of a trip around the world with you.'

There, let's see how he dealt with that...

But Mat only sat on a bench in front of the moored yachts and patted the seat next to him.

'Perhaps,' he said, as seagulls landed nearby and watched them eagerly. 'But then I've never really felt like asking any of them.'

The breath caught half way out of Jo's chest. 'Mat,' she said, 'are you trying to tell me something?'

'Only that it's nice to dream, sometimes.' He didn't look at her but gazed into the distance. 'Being ordained doesn't take the feelings away, you know. It just helps you deal with them. If I'm honest, there are plenty of days when I wish I was an ordinary man and could walk along this sea-front, hand in hand with my wife, and know what it's like to be a 'father' to my blood children.'

Jo stared ahead, frightened to say the wrong thing. He was opening his heart to her and she really didn't know how to respond.

'I guess what I'm trying to say,' he said, straightening up, 'is that you're a wonderful person, Jo; kind, funny, intelligent...'

She studied her feet. Didn't he realise that even saying the words was giving her false hope?

'Your God is a hard task-master,' she said, eventually. 'Harder than the Church of England's.'

He let out a long sigh. 'And that's just it. We share the same God. So who's right?'

'Couldn't you, I mean, if you wanted all of those things, isn't it possible for you become an Anglican priest?' She hesitated, sure that she'd said the wrong thing; but he nodded for her to continue. 'Wouldn't that be an answer?' She held her breath. She'd heard of priests having mistresses, children even with them, all whilst still pretending to be celibate. Was it so important to them to stay Catholic that they preferred to live a lie?

'But I can't be what I'm not,' he said, shaking his head. 'Many of my brother priests have fallen in love. Some left priesthood, some became ministers in other faiths, some took mistresses; but none were ever *themselves* again. Can you understand that?'

She could tell by the sadness in his eyes that it was important for him to talk to her about this, but she had to stop him. All he was doing was burdening her with his feelings, without any thought for *hers*.

'Well, that's only to be expected, isn't it?' she said, a little more sharply than she intended. 'I mean, that's what you sign up to before you become a priest, and I suppose you have to think about these things before you say 'yes', don't you?' She shifted away to give herself some breathing space. If she wasn't careful, she could assume a whole lot of things that weren't true, just because he was telling her all this.

'Ah, Jo, I'm sorry,' Mat said, picking up her hand. 'I'm sure you think I'm just talking. I've wanted to be a priest ever since I was a young lad. You might not believe this, but one day Jesus set his hand on my shoulder and said, 'come on now Matthew' – Matthew's my Sunday name of course – 'I want you to follow me'. I felt Him, Jo, just like I'm feeling your hand now. It was as real to me as that. How can I ever turn away from Him? Can you understand what I'm trying to say?'

Embarrassment flooded her. 'I'm sorry, Mat,' Jo said, standing up to go. 'I think I need to be on my own for a while. Shall we meet back at the hotel?' She didn't wait for an answer but walked away briskly, tears and the breeze stinging in her eyes.

CHAPTER 25

January 14th 1208
Saint Gilles, Languedoc

Matthieu got up from where he had knelt for the past two hours, and made the Sign of the Cross. Outside it was barely light, dark grey clouds scudding across a dark grey sky. Icy rain stung his cheeks, promising snow to come. Everything seemed to be in waiting, even the animals in the byres hardly stirred, for the office of Prime had just finished and the morning had not truly arrived.

He hastened through the cloister, hugging his robe about him, a sense of foreboding weighing down his steps.

'Alphonso, do you have a minute?'

He called to his tutor who strode up ahead, and the priest turned, his body bent against the bitter wind that funnelled through the open sides of the cloister.

'A minute? Before breakfast – or afterwards?'

'Before, if you don't mind,' Matthieu said. 'I need to speak with you. Privately.'

'Words before we break our fast? You don't exactly tempt a man, Matthieu. Especially not on a morning like this. Where do you want to go?'

'My room, it's nearer than yours.'

His room was a simple cell near to the rear of the Abbey of Saint Gilles. Since Catharine's death, Matthieu no longer slept at the castle of Mirapetra when Count Raimon's court visited Saint Gilles. He had given up his suite at the Narbonnais, and made a gift of his manor and all that went with it to Bernard. Only his lands in Poitou had he retained of his old life, because the revenue from them kept his mother in relative comfort as she lived out her last days at the Abbey of Lespinasse.

In the three years since Catharine's death, Matthieu had found refuge as often as possible with Alphonso. He found that the time he spent in the company of the monks gave him some release from the guilt that tortured his nights.

'My heart is heavy, Alphonso,' he said. 'Yesterday was a terrible day. No good can come of it, I fear.'

Alphonso nodded. 'The Pope will come to a decision soon, how could he not? He may even call for a crusade, had you thought of that?'

'Of course,' Matthieu replied, 'but how would crusaders tell who amongst us is Christian and who is heretic? All look the same.'

'I am praying, Matthieu,' Alphonso said, 'as must we all, and then we can leave the rest to God.'

'Of course.' He could say no other, and yet he still doubted. The Bible reassured him that every hair on his head was counted and important to God, yet still people were still raped, maimed and murdered on a daily basis – and that was when the country *wasn't* at war. 'Alphonso, can't *we* do something?'

His tutor sighed. 'Greater minds than ours have spoken here with the most eloquent of tongues. Even the great Bernard of Clairvaux himself came here, half a century ago; and yet the people pounded upon the doors of the church so loud that his preaching couldn't be heard. No, my son, I'm afraid the time for words is over. The people of these lands must realise the error of their ways, or perish.'

Matthieu shook his head. 'We can't just turn away. Speak to the Count again, Alphonso, please. Surely he can't want there to be a crusade here? I know he lost patience with Castelnau yesterday, but in truth, the Legate was half to blame himself, wasn't he?'

Alphonso scratched his bald pate. 'Haven't you been listening, Matthieu? The truth, since you mention it, is that Raimon is powerless in this matter, however many legates the Pope sends. So many heretics here are drawn from noble families, and I don't have to remind you how little control he has over them at the best of times. He simply couldn't, 'give up', his heretics, even if he had a mind to.'

Matthieu nodded. 'So why does the Pope keep asking him to do just that?'

'Politics,' Alphonso said, his voice fading to a whisper, 'and you can't have failed to notice that Raimon keeps a heretic nearby himself at all times?'

As long as he lived, Matthieu would never forget Arnald of Fanjeaux arriving whilst Catharine was dying in his arms. 'But the Count still attends Mass, and I've never seen him bow down to the heretics like others do, nor let them spout their filthy lies at him.'

'Of course not,' Alphonso said, 'because he needs to find himself on the winning side, whichever that happens to be. He keeps a heretic nearby so that if he's dying he can receive their sacrament, as well as one from our priests.' Alphonso shook his head. 'The Pope knows Raimon can't solve this problem by himself, which is why he's asking the King of France for help. But Philippe claims he's too busy fighting his Plantagenet enemies. If Raimon would even just agree to co-operate in driving out the heretics, that would keep the Pope happy; but so far the legates haven't even been able to get him to do that.'

Matthieu watched a beetle freeze halfway in its slow progress across the floor of his room. Did it believe that if it didn't move it couldn't be seen? That was certainly how the Count was behaving, but surely he could see that by doing nothing he was condemning the innocent to suffer?

'Come now,' Alphonso was saying, 'don't look so dispirited. The Almighty always gives us hope, and I am famished. Let us break our fast. Everything looks better from the other side of a full stomach.'

In the refectory they sat with Brother Sylvester, the chorister, who was planning the music for the Feast of the Presentation of Jesus at the Temple. Alphonso's talk of a crusade had troubled Matthieu deeply, not that his thoughts hadn't got that far already; but after the Count's argument with the Papal Legate, Castelnau, that prospect came ever nearer.

They heard the sound of hooves coming to an abrupt halt outside the Refectory, and then Brother Stephen hurried in, his face ashen.

'He's asking to see the Abbot!'

'Who is?' Alphonso said, getting to his feet.

'The messenger. He's in a terrible state. Says Castelnau's been stabbed!'

'No!' Matthieu followed Alphonso to the door of the Refectory. His heart had started hammering, and all his foreboding crowded back.

'Talk to him yourself,' Brother Stephen said. 'He's just here.'

Several monks had already gathered around the bedraggled messenger. His horse's flanks heaved and his travelling robe was spattered with mud.

'Where's the Abbot?' the man panted. 'Castelnau's dying and they want to bring him here.'

'The saints preserve us,' Alphonso said, making the Sign of the Cross. 'Matthieu, warn Abbot Pons. Brothers, bring some warm clothes and drink for this man, and care for his mount. You,' he said to the messenger, 'must come with me.'

Matthieu ran to find the Abbot. Here was horror indeed. Who could be responsible for this outrage? *Please don't let it be anything to do with Count Raimon*, he prayed, *please*! All he could see was the anger on the Count's face as he argued with Castelnau before driving him out of Mirapetra. Could he really have been foolish enough to command the murder of a Papal Legate, so close to Saint Gilles? And yet it was said that the second Henry of England had carelessly brought about the death of Thomas Becket by his angry words. Perhaps someone had heard the Count raging, and thought killing Castelnau would win himself favour? Holy Mother of God! If the Legate died... it didn't bear thinking about. Pope Innocent would have the justification he needed for bringing a crusade upon the South, sooner rather than later. *Dear God and his saints preserve us!*

CHAPTER 26

23rd September 1539
Sarnac, France

Johanna lifted her skirts high and jumped out of the rowing boat. Splash! She missed the beach by inches and sea water soaked eagerly into her boots. Ralph, one of Brent's men, hefted her bag onto his shoulder and Johanna squelched after him down a sandy track that ran beside the dunes. Grey haze covered the sun and the temperature dropped sharply as they walked.

As they neared Sarnac, Johanna saw children playing in the dirt by the side of the road and heard the sounds of men drifting from the harbour. At a crossroads on the outskirts, she saw a few men standing together, disconsolately, as if they had hoped for a day's hire and had been disappointed. Ralph led her through some narrow lanes to a two storey timber house, where an elderly greyhound sat before its sun bleached door. The dog pricked up its ears at their approach.

'Hello, boy,' Ralph said, reaching down to stroke the long, thin flanks.

The dog sniffed and licked at his hand. Ralph knocked in a little rhythm upon the peeling door and looked over his shoulder once or twice as he waited for an answer. There was the sound of shuffling feet and a woman's head came around the door. Her eyes were heavy with sleep and an annoyed expression creased her already heavily lined face.

'What is it? Haven't I told you not to come pestering me this early?'

Johanna wondered if this was perhaps the mother of Brent's friend. She didn't look at all pleased to see them.

'Madame Mathilde!' Ralph said, taking off his cap. 'I've brought someone with me. Brent wants you to look after her. He says he'll see you right.'

Johanna shivered as the wind picked up; but strange to say, her body felt quite warm.

'Is that so?' Madame Mathilde squinted at Johanna. 'Why are you here so early? Your ship's not due for a week.'

'I can explain if you'd just let us in,' Ralph said, patiently.

To Johanna's surprise, the young lad spoke passable French. He took a purse out of his shirt and handed over a gold coin.

'Why didn't you say so before?' Mathilde bit into the coin professionally, and her expression changed. 'Come in,' she said, turning to lead them into the house. 'Why stand freezing your arses off out there? What can I do for you?' She looked at Johanna with narrowed eyes.

'You're shivering like a bird and stink of seaweed. I suppose they made you swim to shore did they?'

'No, Madame.' Johanna shook her head, aware that her teeth had started chattering.

'Would you like a bath to warm you up?'

'A bath would be lovely,' she said, feeling a surge of pleasure at the prospect. The last time she'd soaked in a hot bath was when she was in Queen Jane's retinue at Hampton Court.

Mathilde bustled about, filling the big old cauldron over the fire with water, and feeding the embers beneath it with tied up bundles of wood. As she worked, she hummed a tune unknown to Johanna and pushed her straggly grey hair back up into her cap.

'Madame, I have to go soon,' Ralph said. 'Brent's waiting for me. Can I talk to you in private?'

Mathilde tutted, but took the boy out of the kitchen, leaving Johanna alone. She looked around, wondering what kind of place Brent had sent her to. A rope of Rosary beads hung from a crucifix attached to the rear wall, above a crudely carved statue of the Virgin with partially burned candles before it. A tub sat in the corner, heaped full of mugs and platters, that were obviously waiting to be washed. Did a lot of people live here? Johanna frowned to herself. Somehow she had expected Brent's friend to be some *amour*, not this ageing scold who was happy to heat water for a bath but not to wash dishes.

Mathilde's voice grew louder, until Johanna could hear snatches of what was being said.

'It is unreasonable! What about my business?'

'... only for a couple of days...' Ralph's voice was lower, pleading

Johanna felt uncomfortable but what other option did she have than to hope Mathilde would let her stay for at least one night? The fire soon heated up and she moved towards it, holding out her hands. Sweat started to trickle down her back, even though she still felt cold, and when Mathilde and Ralph eventually returned, Johanna's whole body was shivering.

'What are you waiting for, now?' Mathilde said, glaring at Ralph, who looked wistfully at the ale tankards on the shelf by the window. 'I thought you were in a hurry?'

Ralph replaced his cap and gave a disappointed shrug. 'Good luck,' he said, nodding to Johanna, and left quickly through the kitchen entrance, pulling the door closed behind him.

Johanna felt an immediate tug of loneliness. Now she was definitely on her own. Mathilde muttered to herself whilst she searched in a chest and pulled out clean linen. Then she sat down at a trestle by the table and indicated that Johanna should do the same.

'I hear you are taking a reliquary to Fontevraud Abbey.' Mathilde's pencilled eyebrows rose as she spoke.

Johanna stifled her anger. How dare Brent let Ralph and now this woman know about the reliquary?

'Yes,' she said, stiffly.

'And he says I am to find you a horse and food.' Mathilde tutted. 'And I'm to look after you like a lady...' She looked suspiciously at Johanna. '*Are* you a lady?'

Johanna raised her chin. 'I am, but I was also a novice at Amesbury Priory.'

Mathilde made an unimpressed noise. 'Ralph says Brent seems to think you're the next best thing to the Holy Mother herself, and I have nothing better to do than look after you on account of Saint Thomas. What about my chores? That's what I want to know. When am I supposed to do those? And my business? What will become of that?' She stopped for a breath. 'Oh, don't tell me. I know he's the captain of a ship. What does he know about chores?'

'I'm sorry,' Johanna said. 'It's only for one night and I could help you, if you like. After that I won't trouble you again.' She swayed on the bench and felt that if she closed her eyes it might be days before she woke up. 'I was travelling with someone else, a novice monk, but he was arrested...'

Oh, no, the tears were impossible to hold back.

Mathilde's mouth turned down. 'Don't distress yourself. I know about him too. Brent says you were travelling as a married couple?'

Johanna nodded, not trusting herself to speak.

The other woman gave her a long look. 'I think you'll feel a lot better after a hot bath,' she said. 'I've never dared to go to sea myself. I'm so afraid of being sea-sick. Come and help me fetch the bath from the cellar.'

Together they lifted the wooden bath tub and carried it up to the kitchen. Johanna's whole body was shaking now.

'Are you sure you're all right?' Mathilde said. 'You look flushed to me.'

'I'm fine,' Johanna said, hoping that she indeed was. *Please God, don't let me be ill now. Not when every minute counts if I'm going to be able to help Matthew.* If she could get a boat to take her to Calais, and then to London, there might be a way she could save him.

Mathilde pulled her washing off the creel hanging from the ceiling and folded it carefully. 'Were you in love with him, this monk?'

'No,' Johanna said. 'But I was fond of him.'

'Only fond? Are you sure?' Mathilde smiled.

Johanna turned away, unable to meet the older woman's eyes. Why couldn't she answer that question?

'Do you know what's been happening in England, to the Church?' she said, hoping to change the subject. 'Our monasteries and convents have all been closed down. That's why they sent me to complete my novitiate at Fontevraud.'

'Yes. We have our own problems here with Reformists putting up notices and the like, but so far our King still bows to the Pope, Heaven be praised.' Mathilde dipped a finger into the hot water. 'It's nearly ready. I'll fetch some soap – you smell like you'll need it.'

Mathilde also left out a clean petticoat and kirtle for Johanna. They were coarser than her own but ironed neatly, and smelled of rosemary. 'You don't dress much like a lady,' Mathilde sniffed, eyeing the salt grimed boots, 'do you?'

'I gave up my best clothes when I joined the priory. As a nun, I wasn't expected to need fine clothes.'

'Hm.' Madame was barely listening. She searched on her shelves and pulled down a few bottles, tipping a little from each into the bath. Delicious smells rose in the hot steam: rose, bay and cloves. 'There. You should smell better after that. Come on, then. What are you waiting for?'

Johanna undressed and sat in the deep tub. She scooped up some of the sweet smelling Marseilles soap and rubbed it into her grimy skin – what a luxury! No doubt about it, this was just what she needed. She slipped down until the hot water came up around her ears and tried to shut out her thoughts, at least for a while. There would be plenty of time for them later.

After drying herself with linen towels, Johanna pulled on the fresh clothes and tried to squeeze the last of the water from her hair. Her body still felt quite hot and she was light headed from the bath. Perhaps Madame would allow her to sleep now. That was what she needed more than anything, and then, she would find that ship to take her to Calais.

Austin Friars
London

Pollard had come to give his report personally; and in between escorting the Cleves ambassadors about town and running errands for the King, Cromwell eventually found time to see him. The news was as expected; money and plate hidden in the walls and vaults of Glastonbury Abbey and more conveyed to other places in the country. They had jailed both treasurers and some of the monks, for robbery, and were awaiting his instructions.

If he had his way, he'd hang them all. Avaricious scum.

Pollard also said that they'd apprehended the young monk, and he was on his way to the Tower. (It was getting to be quite a party in there), but as yet, there was no sign of the novice nun.

Cromwell picked up a herb-stuffed bag and held it to his nose. Would it be enough to shut out the stench of the Thames today?

CHAPTER 27

August
Poole, Dorset

Jo spent a sleepless night in her room at the hotel. In the corridor outside, groups of revellers arrived back at all times through the night; but even if everything had been perfectly silent, and the bed the most comfortable in the world, she wouldn't have been able to sleep. Never had she felt so confused about a man, and that was saying a lot. Over the years she'd had relationships that started well, but ended in tears. This one hadn't even started, but the tears were here.

Jo leaned over and pulled another tissue from the box by her bed. Twenty-nine wasn't exactly over-the-hill, but there were occasions when she felt like she'd missed a high speed train. Most of her school friends were married, and there'd been a time when she was engaged herself; but her fiancé had left her for a woman he met at the gym.

She dried her eyes and shook her head. What she ought to do now was tell Mat that she didn't want to go to France. The more time she spent with him, the harder it would be to accept that there was no hope. She'd known from the moment he'd suggested this trip that it was a bad idea, but had gone along with it because some bit of her wondered if he *might* fall in love with her and change his mind about wanting to be a priest. But after what he'd said yesterday, though, that was clearly impossible. How could she expect him to give up an essential part of himself, just so that she could have what she wanted?

The alarm clock said six am. They were due at the ferry port at seven thirty. If she was going to cancel, she really ought to get ready now.

At least the shower was worth paying for. It bombarded her back with hot water and she soaped her hair, sighing at the knots. Why couldn't she find someone to have an uncomplicated relationship with? Other people managed it. She turned off the shower and wrapped herself in the fluffy hotel towel. If she really did care about Mat, and herself, then going home was the right thing to do. He could carry on without her and send her some pictures of the apartment. That would have to do.

Jo picked up the hair dryer and as the warm air dried her hair and she noticed that, today of all days, it was looking particularly shiny. In fact it was styling in a way that it almost never did and before she knew it, she was looking at herself and feeling good. So good in fact that she felt a surge of optimism. Why *did* it have to be a problem going with Mat to France? Was she so desperate for a man that she had to make a fool of herself over one that wasn't available? Not a bit of it. If he could manage to behave himself, then so could she.

Her mind made up, Jo packed away her things and cast a last look around the room.

'Are you sure you know what you're doing?' said the sensible voice in her head. Of course, she thought airily, pushing aside the other little voice that whispered, truthfully, that she'd rather have her toenails pulled out than give up the chance to spend a week with Mat in France. Whatever it cost her.

*

The taxi dropped them off outside the buildings of Poole ferry port and Jo took her documents from her hand bag. Inside, the reception clerk looked up and smiled.

'May I see your passports?' she said.

Mat had his ready and handed it over. Jo fumbled in the plastic pouch that contained all her important bits of paper. They'd barely spoken to each other so far, and he looked like he'd spent a sleepless night too. Around his chin she counted no less than three razor nicks and the collar of his shirt was spotted with blood.

'I'm sorry, madam,' the clerk said, looking at her apologetically, 'but I'm afraid your passport is out of date.'

'What?' Jo looked at her picture. Surely that couldn't have been taken ten years ago? How could she have been so stupid? Her world went into free-fall as she tried to deal with the next few minutes. The car hired in France, their air flight back. Everything would have to be cancelled. Would the insurance cover them when it was her mistake? Stupidly she blinked at her passport. What on Earth were they going to do?

'I can make a telephone call,' the girl said, trying to be helpful. 'It may still be possible for you to sail.'

'Oh, no, don't do that,' she said, her mind beginning to work again. 'We're flying back and we can't do that without my passport. You'll have to go on your own, Mat.' She turned to him, convinced that this had happened for a reason, that she wasn't meant to go with him. 'It's only me who can't travel. There's nothing to stop you from carrying on.'

'No,' he said, taking her arm. 'Excuse us.'

He guided her away from the reception desk to a more private part of the check-in area. She could still feel the sympathetic looks from the reception girls, whispering to each other behind the counter.

'Sit down,' he said, and she noticed she was trembling. 'I'm beginning to regret not driving down here, aren't you?' he said, but she barely heard him.

'Carry on without me, please. I've no idea why I didn't check my passport and I'm really sorry for messing this up. At least if you still go, it won't be a total disaster.'

Could God have intervened? To save his priest from her?

'Jo,' Mat said, sitting down and sliding his arm along the back of the bench behind her. 'I've no intention of abandoning you here, however bad you might feel. We all make mistakes – it's called being human. I even make a few myself, would you believe?'

'But all that money wasted. It doesn't bear thinking about.'

'Well, we don't know that for sure. We might get some of it back. But that's not the important thing, is it?' he sighed. 'Listen. We can go another time. I just need to make a few phone calls, ring the car hire and the airline. Please don't worry. It could so easily have been me that messed things up. I've just remembered that I haven't brought the insurance documents.'

She couldn't believe he was being so calm about all this.

'They're on the dressing table back at Blanche's.' He gave a wry smile.

'At least we'd have managed without the insurance documents,' she said. 'But because of me...'

'Hey,' he said, angling her face towards him. 'Stop it.'

'But-'

'No. I won't have you blaming yourself. There could be a very good reason we're not going. God works in mysterious ways, you know.'

So he thought the same as her. Jo shivered and Mat brought his arm down off the back of the seat to give her a cuddle.

'Don't,' she said, sitting forwards. 'What if someone knows you and reports you to the Bishop or something?'

'What if they do?' he said, looking hurt. 'It isn't a sin to comfort someone who's had a shock. Not as far as I know.'

Jo stood up and wrapped her arms around herself.

'All right,' he said, standing up too. 'I've decided what we should do. I think we should hire a car. We can drive it back to Yorkshire. It'll be cheaper than buying rail tickets today.'

He was even making sensible plans, whereas she was still overcome with guilt. Damn it! She thought she'd said goodbye to all that religious nonsense years ago.

'In fact,' Mat said, suddenly looking pleased with himself. 'Why don't we take a couple of days to explore the south coast whilst we're here? To be perfectly honest, it would be miserable to turn around and go straight back, wouldn't it? We could make the best of it. What do you think?'

CHAPTER 28

June 18th 1209
Saint Gilles

No fewer than three archbishops and nineteen ordinary bishops assembled on the steps outside the Abbey church of Saint Gilles. Matthieu was inside, with Raimondet. The boy hadn't wanted to be there, but the new Legate had insisted. Matthieu put his arm, briefly, around Raimondet's steadily broadening shoulders. It was impossible to believe that today the lad's father was going to be whipped before his people – much as had happened to the second Henry of England when he sought to make reparation following the death of Thomas Becket.

Matthieu shook his head. The parallels were there to be seen.

The two of them peered around the open door of the church. A large crowd had assembled and there was a considerable amount of jostling to find a good view point. Some had brought empty barrels to stand on, while others stood on carts, sat in trees, or hung from windows around the square.

He heard the sound of 'Veni Creator Spiritus' and pulled Raimondet aside to let the Abbot process out through the door of the church. Abbot Pons was dressed in his finest vestments and flanked by monks swinging thuribles of smoking incense. He carried a consecrated host, clearly visible inside a rock crystal compartment at the heart of his golden crucifix. Behind him came Alphonso, bearing a gilded casket containing the relics of Saint Gilles and many other priests followed, carrying cases and boxes of holy relics. All of these were placed reverently onto a stone table, which had been placed outside for the purpose, and then the churchmen stood in an arc around it. A murmuring grew up, became louder, and then the crowd started to part.

Raimondet pulled back and Matthieu looked down at him. He was twelve years old now, and well able to control himself in public, but...

'Don't worry,' he said. 'It'll soon be over and then your father will be able to go to church again with you.'

Raimondet didn't answer, but cautiously craned his neck around the door, then gasped. His father had appeared amongst the crowds, stripped to the waist, and the new papal Legate, Milo, was leading him by a rope around his neck. Matthieu watched the boy put his knuckles to his mouth.

'It's all right, they won't hurt him,' he said.

Milo led the Count to the relics and then read out a list of the church's grievances against the Count. As he did so, the relics were placed one after another into Count Raimon's hands and he swore reverently to uphold the Church and to keep his promises. Then Milo picked up the crucifix with the consecrated host and held it before the Count for his kiss.

When the Archbishop of Arles handed Milo a birch whip, Raimondet started forward, but Matthieu pulled him back out of sight. The crowd surged forwards eagerly.

'I thought you said they weren't going to hurt him?' Raimondet said.

'It's only a token,' Matthieu said. 'A sign that your father's been punished and then forgiven.'

There was a whistle and slap as the birch twigs hit bare flesh and the Count grunted. Matthieu counted twelve strokes with the Count's breath coming in heavy bursts and Raimondet jumping at every lash. Sweat formed inside his clenched fists – and then there was silence. Milo put a cloak around the Count's shoulders and led him into the church. Matthieu placed a warning hand on Raimondet's shoulder, to stop him rushing towards his father, and when the Count reached them he managed a grin. There was a sudden rush of onlookers towards the church doors; several of the monks hastened the rest of the clergy inside and then shut them fast. Angry shouts and jeers came from outside.

Raimon was ushered to a special kneeler, which had been placed before the altar. Milo and the other priests stood on the altar with their backs to him, their robed arms raised like rays of the rising sun. Matthieu and Raimondet crept into the choir stalls and sat amongst the monks, Raimondet with his head down, sniffing every now and then and rubbing his nose on his sleeve. How must he have felt to see his father humbled like that? When Raimondet eventually looked up, Matthieu blanched. He could see only anger in his face.

After the service, Count Raimon was led down into the crypt below the Abbey, to where Castelnau, the murdered Legate was interred. All the churchmen bowed their heads and the Count was forced to do so as well. Milo prayed to the Blessed Virgin for the repose of the Legate's soul, and looked significantly at the Count as he did so.

*

Later, Matthieu found Raimondet walking in the gardens of Mirapetra.

'I just don't understand it,' he said, his youthful voice breaking. 'If my father had truly wanted to kill Castelnau, he would have made sure someone did it far away from Saint Gilles, wouldn't he? So why does the Pope treat him as though he's guilty?'

'I'm not sure he does,' Matthieu said, carefully, 'but this matter is more than whether your father is guilty of murder or not. The Pope wants your father to do something about the heretics in his lands, and so far, he's refused.'

'But he told them he would help today, didn't he? He swore it on blessed relics – I saw him.' Raimondet kicked a pebble at a dove that was pecking in the vegetable garden. 'So why are people saying there's going to be a crusade? *We're* not infidels. Doesn't the Pope know my great-great grandfather led the first ever crusade into Jerusalem?'

'Of course he does,' Matthieu said, hearing the father's bewilderment in the son's words.

All in all, Count Raimon was in an unenviable position; but his inability to keep his previous oaths had now brought the wrath of the most vigorous Pope for decades down upon his shoulders – literally.

The Count came out to join them then, dressed in a fresh chemise and breeches. He sat down gingerly, and did not lean back against the seat.

'Do you think they'll be happy now?' he said, giving his son an affectionate hug. 'I've made a spectacle of myself in public, prayed for the soul of Castelnau – who must have been the most obnoxious man to ever walk the Earth – and I've said I'll join their crusade, whenever and if ever it arrives. At least that way my lands cannot be forfeit whilst I'm doing God's work.'

The Count grinned wickedly, showing his yellow teeth, then winced.

'Papa!' Raimondet said. 'Did they hurt you?'

'No.' His father's face grew serious. 'The only way they could possibly hurt me is by hurting you, chicken. As long as they leave you alone, I don't care what they do to me.'

'But it went on a long time,' Raimondet said, his lip trembling until he bit down upon it. 'I wanted to grab that whip and turn it on the Legate. Let him see how it felt.'

'Well, I'm glad you didn't,' the Count said. 'That wouldn't have pleased them very much. I'd probably be excommunicate forever, if they thought I was training my son to whip Legates! No, it's over and done with now. Let them get on with their agreements and their crusade – if they must. After today, the only person likely to suffer is my nephew, the young fool. I asked him to stand with me, before they came, but would he listen? Does he ever listen? It's hard to believe my sister's blood runs in Trencavel's veins.'

Matthieu kept his silence. By his actions today, the Count had, at the eleventh hour, managed to divert the crusade away from himself and towards the lands of his nephew – the young Viscount Trencavel.

'Does that mean you'll be a crusader?' Raimondet said, his eyes shining, 'and wear a red cross and everything? Can I be your squire?'

'No,' the Count said. 'And if you think I'm going to be fighting against my own flesh and blood – however stupid he is – you can think again. You, Raimondet, are not going anywhere near a battlefield until you're knighted.'

'But Papa,' Raimondet said, 'I could sharpen your sword, and polish your armour like the squires do. I'd make sure it was the best ever!'

'Which would be a waste of time because I won't be using it.'

'But, Papa!'

Matthieu held his breath. How could the Count confess to such cowardice before his son?

'Listen,' the Count said. 'No good is going to come of me wasting my life on this fools errand. People won't give up their beliefs just because someone brings a sword against them. All that will happen is they will strengthen them.'

Raimondet looked crestfallen, but Matthieu found himself nodding in agreement.

'Perhaps Bishop Foulques might be able to help?' Matthieu suggested. 'Now he's fully installed in Toulouse?'

The Count scowled. Pope Innocent had sent Foulques to replace Bishop Raimon of Rebastens, an appalling churchman but a friend and confidant of the Count's.

He wagged a finger at Matthieu. 'Thank you for reminding me of that fact,' he said. 'And don't think I let you move into his palace because I think he's a wonderful bishop. You're there to keep an eye on him.' The Count spat on the ground. 'As far as I'm concerned, the man is an arrogant, jumped-up nobody, like all the other churchmen who haven't a noble bone in their body but think they rule the world. Tell me again, what did he do before he became a bishop?'

Matthieu had to smile. It was well known that Bishop Foulques had been a troubadour before entering the Cistercian order.

'I believe it was you, sire, who told me that he used to 'sing a few songs' and run after women-'

'That's right,' the Count laughed. 'I do believe I have mentioned it before. Anyway,' he continued, getting to his feet, 'it's far too pretty a day to spend it talking about churchmen, especially when we'll be spending all our time in a tent with them soon. Best make the most of our comforts whilst we can, eh, Matthieu?'

'My lord?' Matthieu's heart gave a great thump.

'You're going to come with me if there's a crusade,' the Count said, 'because you get on so well with bishops and the like, and speak their language. In fact, you're practically one of them; whereas I can't seem to say anything without getting myself into a mess.'

'But Papa!' Raimondet said. 'If you're taking Matthieu, you've got to take me too. He's almost got to the end of the Song of Roland and I want to know what happens. Please don't take him away, or let me come too!

Even in the midst of his consternation, Matthieu was touched by the boy's words, but the Count merely laughed. 'I've told you already. I'm leaving you in Toulouse, where it's safe. Ricaud will look after you. No, Matthieu is coming with me because I need him more than you do at the moment. I want him to stop me letting my tongue run away with itself again. Otherwise, I'm sure to earn myself another flogging. From now on, I think I'll let him do all the talking.'

CHAPTER 29

23rd September 1539
Sarnac, France

Madame Mathilde insisted on carrying Johanna's bag upstairs and she agreed reluctantly, not wanting to arouse suspicion. It was a hard climb up the narrow stairs, and when they arrived at the little room that was to be hers, Johanna was on the point of collapse. She saw Madame eyeing her shrewdly, and knew she would have to find a very safe hiding place for the reliquary and the diamonds, when the other woman had gone.

Johanna waited until Mathilde's footsteps faded down the stairs and then began to search for a hiding place; but it wasn't easy with such a thick head. Oh, God, please help me, she prayed, as even her vision began to blur. Eventually she noticed that the hem on one of the drapes was frayed and when she knelt down, found there was a small opening in the turning which would conceal the diamonds and the rings, and what few silver coins she had left. But where would she put the reliquary? Eventually Johanna settled for wrapping it in one of her stockings and hiding it between the mattress and the wall, below the place where her head would be. At least then, Mathilde would have to wake her up if she attempted to take it. Finally, Johanna placed her money pouch and the few coins that were now left in it under her clothes at the bottom of her bag. It held only a few groats, and if Mathilde looked for it, as Johanna was sure she would, then it was not too much to lose.

After that she lay down, thankful for the softness of the deep feather mattress. She tried and tried, but every time she started to slide into the welcome darkness of sleep, a cough would well up in the depths of her chest, and then she was awake again. Groaning, Johanna turned over and tried to find some ease, but her body was trembling and her teeth chattered.

Wicked faces visited her, their mouths grinning evil. They chased her, mocked her – so you wanted to be a nun, did you? How long did your faith last? Only long enough to find yourself a comely lad. Ha, ha, ha. Their laughter echoed inside her head and Johanna saw Matthew stretched out upon a wooden frame, his face twisted in agony. He was being watched by herself, and she was wearing the diamonds in a crown. People were bowing before her, looking to her for something, but she didn't know what. Johanna plunged to dark depths, wanting to cry out but no noise came for she was suffocating, choking, drowning. Madame Mathilde's hand was over her mouth.

‘Hush, child,’ the woman hissed. ‘Are you trying to wake the dead?’

‘Don’t let them torture him, Madame,’ she said. ‘It isn’t his fault. He had no idea what he was carrying.’

Cold water wetted her lips and Johanna drank greedily, surprised at how good it tasted.

‘Why wouldn’t a monk know what he was carrying?’

At that her lips clamped shut. Even though she dearly wanted another gulp of the water, Johanna didn’t trust herself to speak or open her mouth again. Was the reliquary safe? How long had she been ill?

Some time later, the sun burned its way through the chinks around the window drapes and Johanna awoke, her thirst a ravening sensation in her throat. She felt strong enough to sit up and the first thing she did was check that the reliquary was safe behind the mattress. It was, a reassuring bulge marking the place where she’d hidden it.

*

Another time when Johanna awoke, Madame Mathilde was wiping a damp cloth around her face.

‘Thank you,’ she said. ‘You’re very kind.’

*

Sometimes she was so hot that she fought to pull off the bed clothes. Other times she shivered with a cold so profound that she wondered if she’d been taken up in the mountains. Sometimes she felt Matthew’s arms around her, and then it was her mother – her sweet mother, bouncing her on her knee. Maman! As always, it was too late. Her mother slipped away, looking back regretfully.

At one point Johanna got up to find the privy, but was so dizzy that she fell to her knees.

‘Johanna.’ Madame Mathilde’s hand slid beneath her neck and raised her up to take a drink.

‘It’s all right,’ she tried to say. ‘I won’t be staying much longer.’ But the liquid bubbled into her throat before she got the words out.

‘Don’t worry,’ Mathilde said. ‘I won’t be keeping you here much longer. You’re bad for my business.’

*

‘Johanna, Johanna!’

The voice was urgent, forcing its way into her dream. Her mother had come back for her, she hadn’t died after all.

‘Wake up! Someone is coming. From England!’

‘What?’ Gone was the beautiful dream. Johanna opened her eyes to find Madame Mathilde bending over her, anxiety in every line of her face.

‘Thank God,’ Mathilde said. ‘Do you feel well enough to get up?

Johanna stretched. She was warm, but not too warm, and her head was clear.

'Yes, I think so,' she said.

'The saints be praised. Get up. I don't know who's coming but I won't have your King Henry's men marching in here looking for you.'

'Looking for me? Here?' She gaped at Mathilde. 'I thought I would be safe in France.'

Mathilde snorted. 'Apparently not. The message came this morning. Come on. I've packed some food for you and found a horse. It's not a bad one either – considering how little I had to pay with. Come on. You need to be on your way. Get up, now!'

'Madame.' Johanna put a hand to her forehead. Everything was happening so suddenly. 'Thank you for taking care of me and I'm sorry to have been such a burden. How long have I been ill?'

Mathilde put up her fingers and counted. Five days!

To her dismay Johanna saw that her bag was empty. 'Where are my clothes?' She scanned the room. 'I need to get dressed.'

'No use looking for your things,' Mathilde said. 'I had to sell them. Brent only sent money for the one night and he hasn't been back since. You can have some of the girls' things. They'll do for now.'

Mathilde dropped some patched clothes onto the bed and left. As soon as she was alone, Johanna reached for the reliquary. With hands grown useless and fingers fumbling, she opened the lid and sighed with relief. The velvet pouch was still there, and – she shuffled over and bent dizzily to the curtain hem, so were the rings and the diamonds. But the money pouch in her bag was gone as she had suspected.

Johanna slowly laced up the unfamiliar kirtle and then looked for her silver mirror – but it was gone too, of course. She had been too ill to remember it. There was a broken comb on the table and Johanna dragged it through her hair until she could make a plait and coil it up under her coif. Then she put the reliquary into the bottom of her empty bag, and covered it with a pillow case.

Downstairs, Mathilde handed her a cup of watered wine and an oat cake. She took them gratefully, realising she was very hungry.

'This should keep you going for a while,' Mathilde said, handing her a leather food sack, 'but you'll have to stop for more on your way. You don't have much money, do you?'

Johanna shook her head.

'You're not thinking of going back for him, are you?'

She shook her head again, surprised at the woman's frankness.

'No, that would be foolish. I know what I must do, Madame. The reliquary is more important than my feelings. Once again, many thanks for your help.' She got to her feet and the room began to spin. Johanna grabbed for the side of the table, and held on tight, waiting for it to stop.

'Ah, child,' Mathilde said, coming towards her. She stroked the side of

Johanna's face. 'I had a daughter, once, as beautiful as you. She died of the small pox. She was with child. I lost them both.'

Mathilde's eyes clouded.

'I'm sorry, Madame. That must have been hard to bear.'

'Hard? Yes, it was hard. Sometimes I thought I'd never survive, sometimes I didn't even want to.'

'There was a knocking at the front door and Mathilde stiffened.

'Quickly!' she said. 'Hide in the cellar.'

CHAPTER 30

August
Poole, Dorset

Mat threw their bags into the back of the hire car and Jo climbed into the passenger seat. Never had a vehicle seemed more like a refuge, especially since the rain had started and it was blowing directly off the sea. Jo's cropped pants and open toed sandals suddenly seemed more optimistic even than believing she could blithely go off to France with a man committed to being a Catholic priest.

She marvelled at Mat's composure as he sat beside her. No anger, no blame, only understanding.

'Where are we going?' she asked, as the Dorset scenery flashed by – wet, but still full of summer colour.

'No idea,' he said. 'We need to buy a map.'

He turned left and drove, seemingly at random, away from Poole until they came to the sea. She could see the sweep of Chesil bank, with its strange lagoons sheltering behind a long spit of shingle. The mound of Portland was in the distance and to the east, the white cliffs of the Jurassic Coast.

'It's beautiful, isn't it?' Mat said, drawing the car into a lay-by.

He got out and walked towards the grass verge, shading his eyes against the sun, which had just disentangled itself from the clouds. Johanna wondered what he was thinking. There was an innocence and lack of sophistication about him that was endearing; but celibacy was such a ridiculous prohibition these days. What was wrong with sex anyway? She sighed. It was truly beautiful on this coast, especially now the rain was clearing. If she could only manage to accept that he was a priest, and that was that. Then she could stop dreaming.

'Right,' Mat said, getting back into the car. 'I'm sure once we find the M5, it'll only take us six hours or so to get back to Station View.'

Johanna panicked. She was suddenly not at all sure that she wanted everything to be over so quickly. Once he dropped her off and went back to Scotland, there was no telling when she'd ever see him again.

'Mat,' she said, 'it would be lovely to spend a couple of days here. That is if you're sure it's OK with you?'

*

They reached the fishing village of Revellyan, and found there was a youth hostel there, set in its own grounds. Single sex rooms and no ambiguity – just what they needed. Jo slung her bag onto her bunk and read the 'what to do in a fire' notices. It was years since she'd been in a youth hostel, but there was still a faintly institutional smell about it.

She rummaged around in her case and lifted out a pair of linen trousers and a gauzy, embroidered top. It was pretty and if she had been any other man, she wouldn't have worried if her bra showed a little; but this was Mat. If she was going to behave herself, she had better find a vest top to go underneath.

Half an hour later, after a brisk shower, Johanna applied a final flick of mascara and a slick of gloss to her lips. It was raining again, and grumbling to herself, she picked up her waterproof jacket.

Mat was in the foyer, chatting to the receptionist and Johanna hung back, noticing how much of a public person he was. He talked to people everywhere; easily, naturally, and they opened up to him, asked his opinion, treated him with respect – and all that whilst he wasn't even wearing a 'dog collar'.

'Mat?'

He turned and she saw his face soften. 'You look lovely,' he said. 'Aren't I the lucky man tonight?'

They walked down the main street of the village. Cheerful notices advertised community events, film shows, dancing. They checked the menus in several restaurants and settled on a pub at the end of the village, overlooking the sea.

'What will you have?' Mat asked, looking at her over the top of his menu.

Johanna's appetite was minimal, and she was as aware of him as it was possible to be of another human being. Everything about him fascinated her; his smart-to-the-point-of-old-fashioned clothes, his composure under stress, the way he seemed to become all things to all people. She could imagine old ladies sighing over, 'what a lovely young man', he was.

'I'll have the sea bass,' she said.

'No starter?'

'Er, no. I always get too full up.'

'If you're worried about how much it's going to cost, forget it. This is the least i can do to thank you for looking after Blanche. You were there every minute when you weren't at work. I'm just sorry we're not in France but, hey – that doesn't mean we can't enjoy ourselves and – who knows, there could be a perfectly good reason why we weren't meant to go today.'

'Do you really think that?' The doubts were back. Should she have gone home? Would there be some punishment for this, 'tempting of fate?' 'How can you be so fatalistic about a disaster?'

'It's not a disaster,' Mat said, his eyes faintly mischevious. 'Not from where I'm sitting, anyway.'

Johanna ducked down behind the menu, not sure what to make of that. Not fair, not fair, she wanted to say, but what she actually said was, 'Do you fancy sharing one?'

'OK. You choose.'

*

Afterwards they walked along the cliff edge. Jo zipped up her rainproof and pushed her hair out of her eyes. The smell of salt and seaweed was everywhere, and the fishing boats were drawn up high in the harbour. She looked out to sea, thinking of warm French evenings, large glasses of ridiculously cheap wine, and *tarte tatin*.

'Where have you gone?' Mat said, ducking into a sheltered cove.

'Nowhere,' she said.

There was a bench there, facing east, and she sat down. 'Just saying goodbye to the dream of being in France, that's all.'

'We still have Blanche's ashes to take,' Mat said, sitting down beside her. 'We'll have to try again sometime.'

Jo edged away, and turned to face him. 'Mat, she said, 'answer me truthfully. Do you think it was ever a good idea for us to go to France together? In fact, do you even think its a good idea for us to be together at all?'

'Well now.' He was silent for a while and looked out to sea, and she thought she saw a tremendous sadness overcome him. When he turned back, he lifted a strand of stray hair from her face and let it run through his fingers.

'Stop it,' she said. 'That doesn't help. Mat, you're here but not here – if you know what I mean. Sometimes you're a priest and sometimes an ordinary man. It's hard to deal with.'

'I'm sorry,' he said, dropping his hand. 'I'd like to think I'm always a man?'

She started to get up.

'OK, OK.' He took a deep breath. 'Don't go, Jo. The truth is, I've thought of little else but you you for weeks now, despite Blanche being ill; and I can't tell you how guilty that makes me feel. So help me God, I think I'm in love with you.'

The shock was intense. Johanna sat back down and stared at him. How could he say it – just like that? 'You're in love with me?'

He nodded.

'Oh, Mat.' If she moved, even so much as a millimetre, it would happen. She could feel it. They would kiss and goodness only knew where that would lead, even on this windswept cliff; but if she stayed still? The moment would pass and they would leave, as friends.

CHAPTER 31

22nd July 1209
Outside the walls of Béziers, Languedoc

Brightly striped pavilions spread out along the sandy plains before the cité of Béziers, and silky pennants flapped in the warm breeze. People milled about; erecting tents, unloading chests of armour, setting up kitchens, tending to the horses, polishing armour – a million and one tasks to be completed before nightfall.

Many of those who wore the gold or red cross on their garments, and now stood assessing the walls of the cité, were churchmen. Matthieu had seen the Bishops of Cahors and Agen at the Count's wedding to Eleanor of Aragon. With them stood the Bishops of Limoges, Autun, Clermont and Nevers, and the stately Archbishops of Sens and Bordeaux, all of them wearing garments stiff with embroidery and brocade.

As he wandered about the crowded meadows, safely out of arrow range, his ears picked out the familiar accents of Burgundy, the Limousin, Poitou, Gascony, the Agenais, Provence, Auvergne. Many were less familiar – Norman, French, Germans and Lombards, groups of Basque and Aragonese mercenaries thrown into the mix. He shook his head. Mercenaries were not known for meekly going home when they were no longer required, which was why the Pope had reprimanded Count Raimon for his use of them. So why were they here, taking part in this crusade? He looked in wonder at the amount of armour and weapons being unloaded, and at the battle-hardened men – many of whom had already been to the Holy Land – sitting calmly, sharpening their swords and axes.

Suddenly Matthieu's attention was caught by a procession heading towards Count Raimon's pavilion. It was the papal Legate, Arnald-Amalric – the Supreme Commander of the crusade – and his entourage. Matthieu picked up his pace, hoping to get there before they did. But there was to be no such luck. The Count didn't even stand to welcome the Legate, but slouched in his chair with a goblet of wine beside him.

Arnald-Amalric's huge head was scattered with wisps of white hair, and his white tunic was picked out with gold embroidered crosses. On his finger he wore a garnet and pearl ring, the finest Matthieu had ever seen. A scribe informed Count Raimon that this was a courtesy visit to to enquire whether the Count, as the uncle of the Viscount Trencavel, might be able to bring some pressure to bear upon his nephew. The Viscount, who had hurriedly decamped to his fortress of Carcassonne, was convinced that his townsfolk were safe behind the walls of Béziers; and the Bishop of Béziers had brought the crusaders the answer that the townsfolk would rather be drowned in sea salt than surrender to the crusaders.

The Count sniggered when he heard this, and Matthieu's stomach turned over. He watched the snake-like blood vessels dilating at Arnald-Amalric's temples.

'Then the people of Béziers are foolish indeed,' Matthieu interjected. 'Perhaps they think themselves safe behind their walls, so that they have no need to listen?'

All eyes turned to him.

'And, who is this?' Arnald-Amalric asked.

'My son's tutor,' Raimon replied. 'Matthieu's been well trained, by the monks at Saint Gilles, and he's a good scribe – should you need one, of course.'

Arnald-Amalric nodded in a rather bemused fashion. 'I shall keep that in mind, thank you.'

Count Raimon sighed. 'And as for my nephew's people, I confess myself at a loss. Trencavel is young, as you know, and treats everyone as a friend – except me. Mind you, for that I blame the man who brought him up after the death of his father. Bertrand of Saissac is a heretic through and through; certainly no respecter of the Church, as I'm sure you're well aware.'

Matthieu looked at the Count. Was he deliberately making things worse for his nephew? If Arnald-Amalric hadn't yet heard that Bernard of Saissac had dug up the dead Abbot of Alet, and made the corpse 'preside' over the election of his successor so that they could get a candidate favourable to the Trencavels, then he soon would.

'Quite,' the Legate said, grimacing. 'I've been fully appraised on that man by Milo and Bishop Foulques. An unsavoury character, indeed. Well, my dear Raimon, if you've nothing else to suggest on the matter, the lords of the crusade will be meeting after lunch in my pavilion.'

'Good,' Raimon said. 'I hope you come up with something.'

Arnald-Amalric blinked. 'I was rather hoping you'd join us too.'

'Matthieu will,' Raimon said. 'He can tell me what you decide.'

Matthieu saw Arnald-Amalric stiffen.

'Here in body, but not in soul, eh? Is that it?' the Legate said.

'Trencavel is my nephew,' Raimon said, spreading his hands, 'and he has not declared war on me.'

The Legate's breath escaped impatiently. 'So you would have your scribe attend our councils of war, rather than you yourself?'

'Matthieu is a knight of my household; he's not just a scribe.'

Matthieu's blood ran cold. Why was the Count doing this? Had he learned nothing from his scourging? Arnald-Amalric turned on his heel and walked out of the tent. The Count threw an empty wine skin after him and then told Matthieu to get out and not come back until he'd been to the meeting.

*

The sun climbed high into the sky as midday approached and cooking fires were lit adding the smell of roasting meat to that of horses and sweat. Everyone was in good humour, cheered by their numbers and the thought that in forty days' time they would have earned an Indulgence from the Pope, and be on their way home again – with their sins forgiven.

Every bit of shade had been commandeered by the great lords. The Duke of Burgundy had the largest camp, which sprawled beneath his azure and gold banners; but the Counts of Nevers, Saint Pol, Auxerre, Genevois, and Clermont were not totally outdone, and made a spirited showing with their multicoloured pavilions and gaily caparisoned destriers. Matthieu shaded his eyes, it was as though every grand thing in the world was on display and the noblemen merely gathering for a summer tournament, rather than a crusade to do the work of God.

Matthieu's attention was diverted to some young lads and hangers-on who had decided to cool off down by the river and were splashing about in the water. Matthieu longed to do the same, but he would not go so near to the wall, even though sweat soaked freely into his thick gambeson. Already arrows and stones had been launched from the cité – falling short of their targets – but he was taking no chances.

He made his way back to his own tent and threw off the stifling jacket. He sat to eat his lunch under the shade of flap that he'd rigged to the side of his tent, enjoying what little breeze there was. Eventually he saw the Duke of Burgundy make his way to Arnald-Amalric's pavilion and, sighing, picked up his gambeson. It stank, but he dare not be without it in case of surprise attack, and shrugged into it as if he were shrugging into his shroud. As he neared the Legate's tent, he saw that the rabble in the river had started to exchange insults with those who stood on the ramparts inside the cité, and bits of rotten food and stones were raining down on them. Then something happened that he could scarce believe. The gates of the cité started to swing open. What on Earth was happening?

Yielding pick axes, shovels, broomsticks – anything they could lay their hands on – the young bloods of Béziers raced out of the gate towards their tormentors in the river. Their cries and whoops alerted the armies of the crusaders who, seeing their chance, snatched up their weapons and raced towards the cité. For every lad that ran out, many, many more fighting men cut them down, and the screams of those who still stood on the ramparts, chilled Matthieu to the marrow. Hearing the commotion, the Duke of Burgundy hastened out of Arnald-Amalric's pavilion, closely followed by the other lords, and seeing the gates still open, shouted for their horses.

Arnald-Amalric watched the spectacle in silence. Count Raimon arrived at a run and pushed his way towards Arnald-Amalric and Matthieu.

'What did you tell them to do about the Catholics inside?' he panted.

The Legate didn't answer, but continued to watch as the crusaders threw brushwood into the ditches and men fell screaming off the walls. Ropes snaked into the sky and were caught by those crusaders who had, incredibly, already fought their way onto the walls. In a short space of time, scaling ladders were erected and men swarmed up them like angry ants.

'I didn't tell them anything,' Arnald-Amalric said. 'There wasn't time.' With shaky hands, he made the Sign of the Cross and looked up to the sky. 'May God know his own.'

In their haste to get into the cité, several knights plunged into the half-filled ditches and had to re-mount before they even got inside. Screams rose into the air like devilish prayers; flames and black smoke billowed above the towers and Count Raimon got down on his knees. Matthieu joined him. It was the feast day of St Mary Magdalene and he prayed that the good folk of Béziers would find refuge in her church. Oh, why had they spurned the offer of their bishop?

Crusader men-at-arms and mercenaries started streaming back out of the cité, all the while harried and harassed by the knights who were still trying to get in. Matthieu looked on in confusion as they were run through or speared by the knights and then plundered. Why was that happening? Where were the townsfolk? Why were they not running from the flames too?

*

It was to be many hours later before Matthieu and the Count learned the reason, and heard first-hand what had taken place inside the cité. Count Adhémar of Poitiers, count of the Valentinois, brought them the news. The normally immaculately dressed count stank of smoke and sweat, and his face was smeared with soot, but he seemed too tired to care.

When he'd seen all the other knights rushing into Béziers, he said, with not so much as a bucket of boiling water being thrown at them from the battlements, it had spurred him on to follow. But once inside, the mercenaries started looting and the townspeople had gathered, as Matthieu had hoped, in the church of Saint Mary Magdalene. Adhémar shook his head. There must have been a thousand souls crammed into Saint Mary Magdalene, he said, but it had been no refuge for them, even such a holy place. Count Raimon's mouth thinned.

'They killed everyone,' Adhémar said. 'Men, women, children, babes, priests. The horses fared better – at least the scoundrels had the sense to keep them alive.'

'Bring me more wine,' the Count said, handing the wine-skin to his squire, Rebastens. 'I can't hear this sober.'

Peire of Rebastens, nephew of the deposed Bishop of Toulouse, sped off to do the Count's bidding. When he returned, Adhémar immediately held out his goblet.

'Those thieving mercenaries gathered up just about every bit of gold in the place, so then the knights set about killing them too, to get it off them. Can you believe it?'

'What about that big Basque captain?' the Count asked. 'I wouldn't have thought anyone could take gold off him.'

'No, you're right,' Adhémar said. 'And there were a lot more like him. So then they decided to torch the cité, to drive them out of where they were hiding with the loot. A lot of innocent people burned to death today, Raimon.'

The Count exhaled heavily. 'And the other churches?'

'I told you,' Adhémar said. 'They killed everyone.' He stood up unsteadily. 'I can't think about it any more, I'm sorry. I'll see you in the morning.' He took a skin of wine and made his way out of the tent.

'Well, Matthieu,' the Count said, sourly. 'A great victory for God, today, wouldn't you say?'

Matthieu didn't answer. He'd known this sort of thing might happen, and his heart was weighed down by grief for the innocent souls who had been betrayed by those who should have spoken up for them. Why had they not accepted their Bishop's offer and driven the heretics out? How many lives would that have saved? Why on Earth were the people hereabouts so intent on protecting the heretics and their insane beliefs?

When the arguing and score-settling had finally settled down, and the knights were celebrating beneath the soot-charred walls, Arnald-Amalric sent for Matthieu. It was the first time he'd been inside the Legate's pavilion and did not know what to expect. A great lord such as the Legate was, could not be expected to humble himself, even on crusade, but Arnald-Amalric seemed to have gone to the other extreme. Embroidered cushions, brocaded drapes, real silk carpets – now blackened by the tramp of sooty boots – everywhere was gilt and splendour. And in the midst of it sat Arnald-Amalric.

'Matthieu, my son, come and sit with me,' the Legate said, indicating a stool next to him. 'Brother Alphonso at Saint Gilles speaks highly of you. A very gifted pupil so he tells me, with leanings to become a monk, am I right?'

'Thank you, my lord,' Matthieu said, hoping Count Raimon would never get to hear what the Legate had just said. 'I love the Church, but am happy to be a tutor to the Count's son. Raimondet is a very fine boy. It's a pity you've never met him.'

'Perhaps one day?' Arnald-Amalric said, his bushy eyebrows rising. 'Tell me, I'm writing to tell the Pope of our great victory today. You've lived in these parts a while, Matthieu. How many souls would you say lived in Béziers? How many shall I tell him perished?'

For a moment, Matthieu was unable to speak. 'Ten, twenty thousand?' he said, struggling to keep his face impassive. 'I know a great many left with the Viscount when he went to Carcassonne.'

'Call it twenty,' Arnald-Amalric said, turning to the scribe who sat cross-legged at a bench near the side of the tent. 'Read me out what you've got now.'

The scribe unwound himself and held up the parchment.

'While discussions were still going on with the barons, about the release of those in the cité – who were deemed to be Catholics – the servants and other persons of low degree and unarmed, attacked the city without waiting for orders from their leaders. To our amazement, crying 'to arms, to arms!' Within the space of two or three hours they had crossed the ditches and the walls, and Béziers was taken. Our men spared no one, irrespective of rank, sex or age, and put to the sword almost 20,000 people.'

'That will do for now,' the Legate said. 'We'll finish it later. I need to say Mass, Matthieu, before everyone gets too drunk. Come along, you may serve me at the altar.'

CHAPTER 32

Early August 1209
Carcassonne

After leaving Béziers, the smell of burning and charred flesh followed them on the prevailing winds towards Carcassonne. Matthieu rode behind Count Raimon, his conscience troubled. It was as though Raimon was deliberately trying to make as much trouble for his nephew as possible, and had been deep in conversation with Arnald-Amalric along the way, pointing out this and that place where heretics may be found – all of them on the Viscount Trencavel's lands.

From the crusaders' point of view, the victory at Béziers had been nothing short of a miracle. No one could have dreamed that it would take any less than months of dedicated siege to wear down the defenders; but they had been able to capture the cité in a few hours! The countryside they travelled through trembled with the fear of what would happen next; and as they rode towards Carcassonne, one noble after another, even a deputation from Narbonne, approached them, all anxious to make their peace and promising a full and complete submission to the Church. Arnald-Amalric grew in stature with every surrender, an emissary from God that none could withstand.

Up ahead, the advance party of crusaders had already captured the northern approach to Carcassonne, and commandeered the water supply. What must it be like inside the walls now, Matthieu thought, with everyone packed in for safety, including those who had fled from Béziers? He brushed away a cloud of flies and realised they were almost there.

As the ramparts and towers of the cité came into view, he whispered a *Pater Noster,* praying that the Viscount would see sense and offer up the heretics before Carcassonne met the same fate as Béziers. In Matthieu's mind there was no doubt that the Almighty could vanquish this fortress, however invincible it looked, should the townsfolk prove as stubborn as their neighbours.

He searched for some shade to wait whilst his tent was being readied, and took a wafer from his satchel. In the main camp, an ox was being spitted and hung over the fire, but Matthieu could summon no appetite. What he needed now, as much as anything, was sleep. If his dreams before the crusade had been disturbed, with guilt about his dead wife, then the dark fears that now stalked him were even worse, and robbed his body of ease. He settled his head on his bed roll but immediately heard a shout, and sat up to see people pointing. Matthieu squinted into the far distance and could just make out a mass of fluttering red and gold pennants. The King of Aragon was on his way!

'My lord, my lord,' he called, racing to Count Raimon's tent; but the Count was already on his way out.

'Something to thank God for I suppose,' Raimon said, still fastening his breeches and pulling on his robe. 'I hope my nephew listens to Aragon more than he did to me, because if they do here what they did at Béziers, they're going to come for us in Toulouse next. Do you realise that, Matthieu?'

Matthieu searched his seigneur's face, struggling to understand his meaning. Of course he realised the crusade would not end until all the heretics were driven out of the south, but whilst Raimon was with the crusaders, his lands were under the Pope's protection. Was the Count already preparing himself *not* to give up the heretics in Toulouse?

The King of Aragon cantered into the camp on a magnificent grey destrier and after greeting the dukes and counts, and bowing before the churchmen, he made his way to his brother-in-law's pavilion and they embraced. Raimon's servants set out tables in the shade, meat was brought up from the main camp, and wine from their own stores. For a while, Matthieu thought, it was as though they were having a pleasant family picnic.

Count Raimon was a good twenty years older than his brother-in-law but they looked very much alike, having the same arrogance of bearing and thick dark hair – now greying in the case of Raimon. They were alike in other ways too, Matthieu noted. King Pedro's eyes roved the camp, pausing at every pretty camp-follower that he saw.

'What do you think?' Pedro asked, after the food had been cleared away.

'I think someone needs to talk to young Trencavel,' the Count said. 'I tried before they arrived, but he wouldn't listen. Too hot-headed for words, that's my nephew. Mind you, the Trencavels were ever the same.'

'Who's in there with him?' Pedro asked, looking towards the massive ramparts and towers of Carcassonne.

'Cabaret, I think,' Raimon said, frowning, 'and Saissac, of course. I'm sure they're the only reason the young fool hasn't come out to fight already.'

Pedro laughed. 'Have you forgotten what it's like to be young, Raimon?'

'I was never young,' the Count replied. 'My father and your father saw to that.'

'Ah,' Pedro said, grimacing. 'This is not the time to nurse old wounds, my friend. Every defeat we've ever suffered will be as nothing if we don't find a way to end this crusade. Let me talk to the Legate. He's a Catalan man, so I've been told, and wants glory for God more than he wants bodies on the street.'

'Hm.' The Count looked sceptical. 'You'll have to make your own mind up about that. Take Matthieu with you. He seems to like him, which is a lot more than can be said of his feelings for me.'

Matthieu tagged behind King Pedro and his entourage as they made their way to the Legate's pavilion. Never had he expected to be thrust into such a situation. He was a tutor, not a diplomat. What if he said the wrong thing? The Pope had crowned Pedro as the King of Aragon himself, and Pedro was considered to be a good servant of the Church; but Trencavel was his vassal. What good seigneur could stand by and see him trampled upon without objecting in some way?

They found the Duke of Burgundy and the Counts of Nevers and Saint Pol lounging on cushions inside the Legate's pavilion. Arnald-Amalric's scribe sat cross-legged again, quill at the ready. Matthieu watched the King's eyes survey the interior of the tent, inspecting the brocade hangings and silk tassels.

'Listen,' he said, after the greeting formalities were finished. 'Trencavel cannot be held responsible for the actions of his subjects. It's the heretics you need to attack, not genuine lords like him. Accusing him of being a heretic is like accusing me of adultery, just because some half-wit in my entourage can't keep his breeches fastened.'

Matthieu looked away to hide a smile. King Pedro had a formidable reputation with women. Any accusation of adultery was likely to be true, whatever his men had been doing.

'My dear Pedro,' Arnald-Amalric said. 'I understand what you're saying and nothing would please me more than to grant the Viscount a safe conduct out of Carcassonne with... perhaps twelve of his knights?'

The King stared at Arnald-Amalric. 'Are you mad? Carcassonne is his by *right*. Why should he leave it? Ask him to send out the heretics and do with them what you wish, but you cannot take away his birthright!'

'We've already asked him to give us the heretics,' Arnald-Amalric said, reasonably, 'and I think you can guess his answer. He believes himself safe behind the walls of Carcassonne.'

'Then talk to him again,' the King said, beginning to pace the floor.

'We have many dead, shot by his archers from the walls.' Arnald-Amalric said, and his eyes flicked to the noblemen.

'Well, let me talk to him,' the King said. 'There must be some answer to all this.'

'As you wish.' Arnald-Amalric gave a shrug. 'You have my blessing, but our terms stand as I said.'

The King glared and the muscles at the side of his jaw bunched, then he turned and walked out of the pavilion.

‘My horse,’ he shouted to the men waiting outside. ‘I’m going into the cité.’

They brought him a fine bay palfrey, with a mane that shone like silk in the mid-afternoon sun. Pedro took two of his men, and Matthieu – to act as interpreter if necessary. They rode into the cité without shield or weapons, and although the sun was past its zenith, the heat had built up so much within the walls that Matthieu finally had to take off his gambeson. They were among friends here, at least for now.

People came out to greet the King, and he nodded to them graciously, a figure of hope amongst their fear and grief. Matthieu could barely look into their faces; the nightmare of Béziers was too fresh in his memory. At least there were plenty of animals still about, so food and water couldn’t be a problem – not yet.

When they reached the Viscount’s palace, Peire-Roger of Cabaret came out to greet them. He looked strained and tired, and he was barely able to disguise his relief at the sight of King Pedro. They were led to the Viscount’s personal chambers, the first time Matthieu had ever been at the Trencavel court, and he was surprised at the familiarity with which the Viscount’s courtiers addressed their.

King Pedro made it obvious that *he* wasn’t about to tolerate such liberties and sat in the largest chair, waiting for the knights to pay him homage. Then and only then, did he allowed the Viscount to pour out his heart, telling how the crusaders had butchered everyone in Béziers and devastated his lands.

The King let out an impatient sigh and got to his feet, clasping the Viscount’s shoulder.

‘In Jesus’ name, you need to deal with these heretics. The fools have brought terrible danger and distress to your people. Tell them to go, and we’ll work out something with the Legate, because if you’re hoping to hold out, look around you. Carcassonne is crammed with hungry mouths. If it were otherwise then, yes, I could see you’d have some hope. But, my friend, think about this, please. There’s nothing I wouldn’t do to help you, but in the end, you need to save yourself.’

Tears glinted in Trencavel's eyes as he listened to his seigneur, but it was obvious to everyone standing around that there was no last minute reprieve being offered and that their young leader was going to have to make a hard decision. He stood up and embraced the King.

‘All I have belongs to you, and before that it belonged to the King, your father, who loved us dearly. If you can reach an agreement on our behalf, then we would be deeply grateful.’

King Pedro nodded, but he couldn’t meet the Viscount’s eyes. ‘I’ll do what I can.’

*

No one spoke on the ride back to the camp. Matthieu couldn't imagine what King Pedro was going to do now, because Arnald-Amalric had already laid out his terms. They called first at the pavilion of the Duke of Burgundy and the two men greeted each other cordially enough, but the Duke said there was nothing he could do without Arnald-Amalric, and Matthieu was sent to fetch him.

The Legate was sitting outside his tent, enjoying the sunset and a goblet of wine. At the sight of Matthieu, Arnald-Amalric's face lit up.

'Ah, you're back, my son. Have you good news for me? Has the Viscount seen sense?'

Matthieu steeled himself. 'Viscount Trencavel has asked the King to negotiate on his behalf. King Pedro is with the Duke of Burgundy and they respectfully request your presence, my lord.'

Arnald-Amalric frowned. 'But I've told the King our terms already. They haven't changed just because he's been to see the young whelp. Didn't he tell him what I said?'

'My lord, I would rather you question the King directly,' Matthieu said, keeping his face neutral.

The Legate sighed. 'Oh, very well. The Lord give me patience with these stupid men, Matthieu. Gone are the days when a man became a prince because he was the one most fit to rule. Now we're saddled with whoever is born first, half-wit or no.'

Matthieu said nothing, but inside he was shocked. Did the Legate not believe that all rulers were anointed by God?

Arnald-Amalric commanded his servant to bring his cream robe and he fastened it with a huge ruby brooch. When they entered the Duke's pavilion, King Pedro did not rise to greet him, but Arnald-Amalric affected not to notice.

'My vassal wishes me to negotiate for him on his behalf,' Pedro began. 'As Count of Barcelona, I am overlord of Carcassonne, and as a faithful son of the Church, I have the right to be consulted before you wage war on my lands.'

Arnald-Amalric's eyes locked onto the King. 'No one wants to wage war on your lands,' he said. 'All we want is to stamp out heresy and save innocent souls from eternal damnation. If you can help us do that, then we're prepared to listen.'

The King was obviously baffled. 'I don't think you're listening,' he said. 'Why should the legitimate, *Catholic,* seigneur of Carcassonne leave his vassals and turn them over to you when he has done nothing wrong. Why?'

Arnald-Amalric shrugged and sat down with an air of finality. 'If he's done nothing wrong, then you have our terms. He can leave, with twelve of his knights.'

Matthieu thought King Pedro might strike the Legate, so angry did he seem. He leaned forwards, practically spitting his words. 'If that's all you're prepared to offer, then I tell you, it'll happen when donkeys fly!'

The King left the tent and called again for his horse. Not knowing what else to do, Matthieu followed him back into the cité. This time, there was only anxiety on the faces of the people who watched them make their way to the Viscount's palace. Trencavel was on his feet, walking agitatedly about his chamber. When he heard the Legate's terms, all colour vanished from his face. Cabaret thrust a goblet of wine into his seigneur's hand and went to look out of the window, crushing his fist into his palm.

'But, that's impossible!' Trencavel said. 'I would rather be flayed alive than accept these kind of, 'terms'. They can't expect me to abandon my vassals. Good seigneur, I thought you were going to help me?'

Pedro's eyes narrowed. 'I've already told you what to do. You must drive the heretics from your lands. I'm sorry, I truly am, but this is what you and these crazy people have brought upon yourselves. Can't you see that?'

'Crazy people?' The Viscount turned to the knights who crowded around him. 'Look at them. They're not crazy, they're my friends, my family. Even our bishop has a family the crusaders would call, 'heretic'. And, here,' Trencavel put his hand on the shoulder of a grizzle haired man, 'is the man who raised me and whom they call heretic because he once confronted a nest of corrupt churchmen with their own perfidy. Should I turn my back on him, too?'

'A man who digs up dead abbots?' the King said, shaking his head, sadly. 'Is that whom you would call sane? I should tell you now, I've always thought it a pity your father didn't chose a better guardian for you. But if it grieves you, then make him one of those you bring with you and have done with it.'

There was utter silence. The Viscount and the King stared at each other.

'Enough,' King Pedro said. 'I can see I'm no longer welcome here, and if you're simply not going to listen, I'll take my leave. May God show you mercy, my son.'

CHAPTER 33

28th September 1539
Sarnac, France

Johanna grabbed her bag and ran down into the cellar, looking for somewhere to conceal herself. She started to lift the bath off the wall but realised that was too obvious. Where then? Mathilde had barrels of wine stacked high against the walls of her cellar and Johanna saw that it might just be possible to slide in behind them. Taking a breath she squeezed herself into the narrow gap, so that her ribs were pressed tight back and front, but at least she was hidden.

A long time went past, and she grew light headed from taking shallow breaths, but eventually she heard Mathilde's voice.

'Johanna?'

For a while she hesitated. Were they waiting to arrest her upstairs? Could she trust Mathilde not to betray her?

'Johanna? Are you all right?' Mathilde said. 'The person who was coming from England is here. He says he's your cousin, Gerald.'

*

Johanna could hardly believe that Gerald was there, smiling, giving her a hug. Then he asked about the reliquary – was it safe?

'Yes, but...' She looked uncertainly at Mathilde. They were speaking in English but perhaps the woman could understand them. 'Matthew was arrested.'

'I know,' Gerald said. 'I came as soon as I heard.'

'Thank you,' she said. 'Do you know what happened to him?'

Gerald shook his head. 'No one is saying, but thank God you and the reliquary are safe.'

'Yes, thank God for that,' Johanna said, carefully, 'but what about Matthew? What do you think they'll do to him?'

'For the love of God,' Mathilde interjected, confirming Johanna's suspicions about her understanding of English. 'What does it matter? Now your cousin is here, there's nothing to stop you taking the reliquary to Fontevraud now.'

'But I'm not going,' Johanna said.

'Mon Dieu!' Mathilde said.

'I have to go back for him because they'll take him to the Tower and probably torture him.'

Gerald put his hand on her shoulder. 'Johanna, I know you were fond of him, but Matthew *does* know what he was doing and he was willing to give his life to keep the reliquary safe. Do you think he'd want you to put yourself in danger on his account? Isn't the safety of the reliquary more important?'

How could she explain, in front of Mathilde, that she'd found the diamonds inside the reliquary and they had changed everything?

Mathilde gave an exasperated sigh. 'You're an imbecile, Johanna. What is the use if you are in prison too?'

'I won't end up in prison-'

'How can you say?' Mathilde's eyes glinted. ' Have I slaved for this, keeping my girls away, so you can run after a *man*?' Mathilde made a face. 'I tell you, he is not the only man who can stoke your fire, Johanna. Forget him! That's what I say.'

Johanna felt her face burn, not at Mathilde's anger, but because she finally understood what the woman's business must be, and that Mathilde had no idea who Gerald really was. She glanced at him. What would Mathilde say if she knew she now had not only a novice nun but a priest in her bordello?

'Anyway,' Mathilde said. 'Both of you must go, *now*.'

'Madame,' Johanna pleaded, 'may I have just a little time with Gerald? Alone?'

Mathilde sniffed. 'Very well,' she said, 'but be quick,'

As soon as Mathilde left, Johanna pulled Gerald into a corner of the kitchen

'Brent's ship was caught in a storm,' she whispered. 'The reliquary was thrown against the wall of the cabin and burst open.'

'Go on,' Gerald said, watching her closely.

'There were diamonds in it.'

'Diamonds?' His eyes widened. 'What were they doing there? How many?'

'Four,' she said. 'Huge ones. Someone put our lives at risk, Gerald, not just for the sake of the relic, but to smuggle those diamonds out of the country. Now do you see why the King's men were looking for Matthew?'

'Sweet Jesu.' Gerald made the Sign of the Cross.

'The thing is, Matthew doesn't know anything about them. However much they torture him, he can't tell them anything.'

Gerald stroked his beard. 'What difference will it make if you go back to England? What can you do?'

'I can give the diamonds to the King and ask him to release Matthew.'

Gerald's breath whistled between his teeth. 'And you think he will?'

'I have to try,' she said. 'I can't turn my back on Matthew; but listen, if I go back to England, will you take the reliquary on to Fontevraud for me?'

*

Mathilde grudgingly agreed to give Gerald the horse and the food in exchange for a few silver coins. Johanna watched until he was out of sight, her heart heavy as she contemplated what now lay before her. There were more obstacles than solutions, that was for sure, and perhaps she *had* taken leave of her senses as Mathilde and Gerald seemed to think.

'I'll go now, Madame,' she said. 'I'm sure I'll find someone at the harbour to help me.'

'And I'm sure you will too,' Mathilde said, her hands on her hips. 'But I'm equally certain you'll never reach Calais if you try it on your own.'

'Why not?'

Mathilde sighed. 'Sit down,' she said.

Johanna did as she was bid.

'I can get you onto a ship, but convince me it's worth it-'

'Oh, it is, Madame!' Johanna said. 'Matthew is a good man.'

Mathilde gave her a sceptical look. 'Do you really think you can help him?'

Johanna hesitated. 'I was a maid of honour at King Henry's court,' she began.

Mathilde sat up straighter.

'I hated it, but I loved the Queen. After she died...'

The tears were there again, always when she thought of poor, tragic Jane.

'Go on,' Mathilde said. 'Remember there's not much time.'

'The King started to make advances towards me.'

'Ah...'

'But I couldn't, I mean, she'd only just died...'

'Holy Mother of God,' Mathilde said. 'You turned down a king? Johanna, you're even more of a fool than I thought. You turn down a *king*, but lose your heart to a penniless monk?' She shook her head. 'If you stayed here a while, I'd teach you how to handle men.'

'But I don't want to know how to handle men!' Johanna said. She was starting to become angry now. 'I saw what he did to her! She was nothing but a brood mare for him.'

'Of course,' Mathilde shrugged. 'What did you expect?'

'That he would care about her. After all, she'd just given him a son, what he'd always wanted...'

'A son was what he wanted. Your King Henry seems not to esteem wives so much. And then what happened?'

'I started my novitiate at Amesbury. Matthew helped me to get there. Why are you laughing?'

'Nothing. It's just I haven't had many nuns sleeping here,' Mathilde said.

'Yes, well.' Oh, why did she have to colour so easily?

'So you think your King will still be so keen to bed you that he'll do anything for you?' Mathilde asked.

'No!' Johanna said. 'No, I mean…' What did she mean? She hoped that Henry would be much more interested in the diamonds than her. 'I just want to talk to him.'

Mathilde shook her head again. 'Then you're even more of a fool than I first thought, but then I think you know that, don't you?' She gave Johanna a long look. 'But, don't ask me why, there's something about you makes me want to help. Come on.'

When they arrived at the quay side, Mathilde hailed one of the sailors and the brawny young man flushed to his hairline.

'Imbecile boy,' Mathilde muttered. 'Does he think no one else knows what he does with his spare time?'

'Madame?' The lad took off his cap and stood unwillingly before them.

'Now, Gui,' Mathilde said. 'You remember how much you owe me, I hope?'

He nodded and his embarrassment deepened.

'Well, here is a young lady who needs to go to Calais. You *were* going there today, weren't you?'

He looked appalled. 'But, Madame, we're only going a short way out today. The fish are so close, we can practically see them.'

'Tush,' Mathilde said, taking him aside. She whispered something in his ear and the man looked at Johanna with a mixture of pity and fear. 'That's what you *were* doing,' Mathilde continued, 'but now, of course, you're going to Calais – aren't you?'

Gui looked down sullenly. 'As you wish,' he said. 'But then I've paid you everything, right?'

'Right,' Mathilde said, her eyes bright with triumph. 'After this, Gui, with me your slate is clean.'

CHAPTER 34

August
Devon

Jo couldn't help it. She swayed forwards, her mouth turning up to his, lips parting. Mat groaned, pulled her towards him, his arms sliding tightly around her. It was a long time before they finished exploring, savouring, and then he ran a trail of kisses down her neck. Jo's body came alive in a way she had never experienced before and she felt like a teenager again – kissing in the park because there was nowhere else to go, lost in the headiness of new experience. She stroked the nape of his neck and nuzzled up under his ear, inhaling the scent of him. Surprisingly, he seemed quite normal this close to, not intimidating or strange – just sexy and inviting...

'Let's go,' he said, thickly, pulling away from her. 'I was crazy to think I could handle this.'

'What?' Her eyes struggled to focus and disappointment crushed her. 'Mat...' She was so dizzy, she could barely think.

'I can't,' he said. 'I'm sorry, but I can't. What a mess. Come on, we have to go.'

'But – wait a minute.' Jo's thoughts were scattered, her lips and skin still on fire. 'I'm not sorry,' she said.

'I know,' he said, 'but I am.'

'And is that all that matters? You and that ridiculous church of yours?' She had begun to feel angry. 'Who do they think they are, telling people how to live their lives? What about *my* feelings? Don't I get any say in this?'

'Of course you do,' he said. 'You have a perfect right to be angry and I should never have let it get this far.' Jo flinched at the guilt in his eyes. 'The fault is mine, not the Church's. I know the rules and I knew how I felt abut you even though I've been denying it to myself. I shouldn't have brought you here.'

'But Mat!' she wailed. 'I've never felt like this about any other man. What just happened was wonderful, beautiful. Please don't say it wasn't.'

'I'm not saying it wasn't beautiful, but I should have known better.' He shook his head. 'That's why the older priests warn us about this time and time again – be scrupulously honest and don't get involved. I'm sorry. I didn't mean this to happen. I didn't mean to hurt you.'

'Hurt me?' She could see the pain etched on his face. 'Oh, Mat!'

They walked back to the Youth Hostel without speaking. When Jo glanced across at him, Mat's head was held high but there were tears rolling down his cheeks.

'Mat-'

He pulled a handkerchief from his pocket and wiped it across his face. 'I'm sorry,' he said, again. 'Terribly sorry.'

What could she say? She felt utterly wretched. 'I had no idea it would be this bad for you.' She tentatively put a hand on his arm. 'I want to be with you and I don't really understand why I can't but if this is the way it has to be, then it does.' Her heart was fluttering in her chest like a trapped bird.

'I'm sorry.' He shook his head as if to be rid of his thoughts. 'But there we have it. I can't be like other men. I knew that at my ordination. I'm a priest, and that's all there is to it.'

He looked so miserable that she longed to wrap her arms around him and comfort him; but how could she do that without making things worse?

'OK,' she said, quietly, taking a deep breath. 'That's clear enough for me. Let's get some sleep, shall we? It's been a heck of a day.'

CHAPTER 35

Mid August 1209
Carcassonne

The weather only got hotter. Matthieu anxiously scanned the walls of Carcassonne as flies buzzed everywhere, maddening the horses and finding their way into men's mouths. What must it be like within the walls, with the numbers of sick and injured increasing day by day?

The suburb of Castellar, which lay before the cité, was now ruins. It had been garrisoned by the crusaders; but the young Viscount Trencavel, in a fit of bravado, had come charging out one night and hacked them to death. Far from a victory, Matthieu knew Trencavel had just sealed his fate.

He wandered away from Count Raimon's pavilion, feeling his mouth to be dry and sticky, and sweat was trickling down his back. The Count now spent most of his days sitting glumly in there, often with his head in his hands, with the knights he'd been obliged to bring lounging around, their faces grim. Matthieu couldn't bear just sitting and waiting with them, so he walked around the camp, overhearing conversations and trying to learn as much as he could. As a member of the Count's household though, he was virtually an outcast amongst the crusaders, especially as he was yet to bloody his sword. It was only his position of favour with the Legate that enabled him to be part of the interminable meetings in Arnald-Amalric's pavilion. Count Raimon refused to attend any of them and his relationship with the Legate deteriorated daily. Matthieu lived with the expectation of disaster, for that was all he could see facing his seigneur now.

A new star was rising amongst the crusaders. Taller, stronger, braver, and even better looking than most of them, Simon of Montfort had leaped to the defence of a wounded soldier during the attack on Le Castellar, defying a rain of stones and arrows, and emerged unscathed to carry the man to safety. No wonder he drew so many glances from the women who followed the camp; no wonder the soldiers looked at him with admiring eyes – a knight who cared about ordinary people. What would they not do for a leader like that?

Matthieu shook himself, not at all sure of where his thoughts had led, and saw a squire running towards him from the direction of Arnald-Amalric's pavilion.

'Sir Matthieu of Poitiers?' the lad panted.

When he nodded, the squire told him he was wanted by the Legate.

'His scribe has the flux and his Lordship would like you to take over.'

*

Inside Arnald-Amalric's pavilion, Matthieu was surprised to see Simon of Montfort standing to one side, stooping a little to manage the slope of the roof.

'Excuse me,' Matthieu said, his eyes struggling to focus after the glare of the sun. It was unbelievably hot in the tent, and the stench of sweating men overpowered the incense that the Legate had burning.

'Matthieu!' Arnald-Amalric was dabbing at his face with a linen cloth. 'You're just in time. Come and sit down.'

Matthieu blanched. All the bishops and the lords of the crusade were packed in there, excepting Count Raimon, and to a man their expressions were grim. Quickly, he took his place at the scribe's bench and readied his quill.

'Are we all agreed, then?' Arnald-Amalric said. There was a good deal of strained nodding. 'Who shall we ask to offer this parley?'

'Trencavel has a kinsman in my company,' said one of the French lords. 'If we send him up to the gates, they might let him in.'

'Good,' Arnald-Amalric said. 'Are you getting this, Matthieu?'

'So we're going to give him another chance to surrender, is that it?' The Duke of Burgundy said, and then wiped the sweat from his long nose onto his sleeve.

'Of course. You don't seriously think we'll be able to reduce that citadel by force, do you?' Arnald-Amalric said.

'It would certainly suit our purposes,' Simon of Montfort mused, 'if we could keep the walls intact. Much easier for us to defend it that way later.'

'Have I got this right?' Hervé of Nevers said, his rumbling voice deepening with anger. 'Are we still hoping Trencavel will surrender and let us walk in there?'

'Not really,' Arnald-Amalric said, cheerfully. 'That's the last thing he's likely to do; unless we persuade him it's in his best interests, of course.'

'And just how are we going to do that?' Burgundy asked.

Arnald-Amalric looked around at the lords as if he were a school master waiting for his pupils. 'Well?'

The silence stretched into a dozy hum of flies, but no one spoke. Finally Simon of Montfort took a deep breath and everyone turned to him. 'Shall we tell him that if he surrenders, we'll let everyone go?'

'Have you lost your wits?' Gaucher of Saint Pol asked. 'That cité is seething with heretics. We can't just let them go. Have you forgotten why we're on this crusade?'

'Not for a minute,' Simon said. 'I'm as committed to the crusade as you are; but speaking plainly, if I had a garrison of men in there, not thousands of hangers-on, I could defend that citadel until you were all in your dotage. Do you see what I mean? We can always root the heretics out later, wherever they've gone, but we'd find it a lot harder to come up with a better base for this crusade than Carcassonne.'

'But it'll take months to find them all again-' Nevers stopped, realising he had given himself away. Knights were only compelled to offer forty days service to the crusade. After that, it was obvious he intended to go home, whether the crusade had been successful or not.

The Duke of Burgundy shook his head. 'I don't see he's got any other choice because we control the water supply. In this heat, people die fast without it. I don't think Trencavel has got what it takes to throw out the useless mouths, and he's obviously not going to give up the heretics. No, I think Montfort's right. Let's offer him a full surrender. He's probably foolish enough to accept it.'

"You're giving him everything he wants, apart from his castle!' the Count of Nevers said.

'No we're not,' Simon said. 'Let everyone go, but they can't take anything with them. After Béziers, we can't afford everything going up in smoke again. We have to have money to keep an army this size going.'

'I take it that's agreed, then,' Arnald-Amalric said, smoothly. 'We offer Trencavel a full surrender, but make sure we know where all the heretics go. I think that's a wonderful idea.' He looked around, smiling. 'Let's find this kinsman, whoever he is, and send him out to parley.'

As soon as he could, Matthieu went to Count Raimon's pavilion. On hearing the news, the Count flew into a rage.

'If Trencavel gives himself up then that's the last we'll ever see of him,' Raimon said, clenching his fists. 'But you know, Matthieu, it's his son I feel most sorry for. That young lad has a father with wax for wits!' The Count put his fists to the side of his head. 'For goodness sake! If he could just hold out, that's all he needs to do. Those French peacocks will be gone when their forty days are up. If he surrenders now, they'll think it's God's will again, and there'll be no stopping them after that – this madness will swallow us all up.' He threw himself down onto his chair. 'I suppose we should thank God that Cabaret and Saissac are in there with him. Let's hope he listens more to *them* than he did to King Pedro.'

Matthieu shuffled his feet, not wanting to cast more fuel on the Count's fire, but knowing he must report everything he'd heard. Hesitatingly, he told his seigneur what Simon of Montfort had said about using Carcassonne as a base for the rest of the crusade.

'Simon of Monfort?' The Count had gone quite pale, despite the heat. 'Wasn't his grandfather an English earl?' He thought for a while, scowling. 'John of England has forfeited the lands of those nobles who still support the French king, which means Montfort may have much to gain by staying here – my lands for one. This is not good news, Matthieu.

I had counted on them tiring quickly, and going home.'

Matthieu nodded.

'Send for my son,' the Count said. 'There are kinsmen of mine on this crusade. My mother was a princess of France. Surely, once they meet Raimondet, and see just what a good son of the Church he is – none more nobly born. Once they see whom they seek to disinherit, they will think differently about invading my lands?'

'But sire,' Matthieu said, 'are your lands not protected by the Pope whilst we're on crusade here?'

The Count looked broodingly at Matthieu. 'If only it were that simple,' he said. 'This crusade isn't just about rooting out heretics, even someone as keen to be on his knees as you are must see that?'

Matthieu looked down at the floor and tried to deal with the pain in his heart. What the Count said was true. The events at Béziers had gone far beyond dealing with heretics.

'Arnald-Amalric thinks he's bringing God to the godless,' the Count said. 'But I know what he really wants. Think you he'll be content to go back to his monastery with a pat on the back from the Pope? That man wants this crusade to make him a cardinal, at least. And Montfort is probably wondering right now how he can carve himself a dynasty of *my* lands, since John has taken away his own; and what's worse, the Pope has given him the perfect excuse for it.' He sighed heavily. 'Matthieu, Matthieu, do you know what I think? I think I must go to Rome myself and talk to this Pope. They say he's an intelligent, listening man. Let's see if I can't give him something worth listening to for once.'

*

On the 15th August, Raimon-Roger Trencavel, Viscount of Béziers and Carcassonne, gave himself up, and the people of Carcassonne fled the city with only what they were wearing. Arnald-Amalric climbed onto a marble plinth inside the cité to address the soldiers, and there was grumbling when they realised that the booty they'd helped to capture was destined only for the powerful lords who, the Legate said, 'With God's grace, will hold and keep this country so that the wicked heretics can never retake it.'

The neighbouring towns of Montreal and Fanjeaux were quickly garrisoned. When the soldiers arrived they found not one person still living there. Matthieu grieved, not least when he learned that in a twist of fate, the young Viscount was now manacled to the wall of his own dungeon.

'Can't you do something to help him?' he asked Count Raimon, only to be met with snapping, red eyes.

'What do *you* think?' the Count said. 'Just thank God I'm not as stupid as he is, or I'd be sitting on my arse in my own dungeons too.'

'Forgive me, sire,' Matthieu said, suddenly deeply moved. 'I spoke out of turn.'

'Yes, you did, and you keep doing that, Matthieu,' the Count said. 'I don't understand you any more. Can't you see what I see? I've never come across such a character as this Legate – 'may God know his own', isn't that what he said – instead of trying to stop them slaughtering the innocent people inside Béziers? Well, I can tell him that God *does* know 'his own' when it comes to it, and that butcher of a priest is going to be in for quite a surprise when he meets his maker, I can tell you that.'

Matthieu said nothing, but stood with his hands folded, eyes downcast.

'And you know something else, Matthieu? It doesn't matter how much time you spend on your knees with them, you'll never belong. You're tainted by me, belong to me – that is unless you think otherwise?'

The knights in the retinue had slowly made their way into the pavilion and were listening, their eyes hostile – especially the young squire, Peire of Rebastens.

'My lord?' Matthieu stammered. 'I'm indebted to you for everything I have,' he said, kneeling before the Count, uncomfortably aware that his enemies in the court were celebrating behind him.

'Yes. Don't forget, when you're scribing for them in his tent, that you're *my* subject, Matthieu,' Raimon said, his finger wagging.

'Yes my lord, of course,' Matthieu said, searching his mind for something to distract the Count who could harangue his courtiers at great length, once he got going.

'In fact I don't really know why I trust you to look after my son,' the Count continued. Matthieu looked up sharply, unable to disguise his distress.

'Hah! You might well look at me like that. I'm warning you, Matthieu. I understand more about this crusade than you do.' Raimon took a breath and looked around at the waiting faces. 'What are you all doing in here? Haven't you got anything better to do? Get out! Go and find some heretics to torture.'

The knights shuffled out and then Raimon beckoned to Matthieu, his eyes narrowed. 'I want you to go to Toulouse and bring Raimondet back here.'

'Are you sure it'll be safe, sire?' Matthieu said. He knew it was suicidal to argue with the Count right now, but he couldn't bear to think of Raimondet getting caught up in this tangled web of a crusade.

Raimon shook his head. 'He's only a boy. I have to do what I can for him. I want to show him to Montfort, let him see the calibre of my son, and then...' Raimon trailed off and looked around as if he couldn't believe how he came to be there, '...and then, I'm going to ask him to marry his daughter to my son. If we can't beat them, then we must join them – eh Matthieu?'

CHAPTER 36

29th September 1539
Calais

It took a night and most of the next day to reach Calais but Johanna was less sick on the voyage – something she put down to her exhausted state. There was nowhere comfortable in the small fishing vessel, but Gui had done his best for her, draping a tarpaulin across part of the stern. She shivered there, despite her travelling cloak and an old woollen blanket. A sea journey in weather such as this, when she was barely recovered, was lunacy; but at least she no longer had to pretend she was with child.

Johanna dozed fitfully, until she became aware that the wind had dropped and the pitching of the vessel had lessened. She crawled out from under the tarpaulin, and saw the walls of Calais and the Lantern Gate coming into view. Johanna looked down at the grubby sleeves and stained hem of her cheap kirtle. No one would believe her if she said who she was – however high she raised her chin.

Gui walked towards her, still looking uncomfortable. 'Are you ready, Mademoiselle?' he asked. 'We do not want to stay long.'

'I'm ready,' she said. 'Thank you for bringing me here. Will you go straight back to Sarnac?'

Gui looked around and shrugged. 'This is Calais,' he said. 'For now it belongs to you English. Why should we want to stay here?'

*

Johanna entered the great walled city through the Lantern Gate and headed for the market. The impact of the crowded streets and noise was almost overwhelming. Everything was for sale hereand she pushed through the throng towards a stall selling buttons and Venice braid. Gerald had been able to give her a few more coins and she spent some of these on a length of ribbon.

As she turned around, she caught sight of a woman she recognised and shrank back, hiding her face. It was Lady Margery Shelly, a lady in waiting to Lady Lisle, and Johanna remembered her from when she had been living with the Lisles in Calais. Had God sent her here to help? But would the noblewoman even recognise Johanna in her impoverished state?

Lady Margery walked briskly towards the stall and commanded the seller to cast out a length of silk brocade. After smoothing the fabric and holding part of it up to the light, she satisfied herself and turned to ask her page for the purse he carried. As she did so, her eyes met Johanna's and widened in surprise. Swiftly, Lady Margery completed her purchase and bid the page take it away for her, then she came towards Johanna wearing a puzzled frown.

'Goodness, Johanna!' Lady Margery said. 'I thought I was seeing a ghost. Why are you here?' She leaned closer and whispered. 'I heard you spurned the King. Whatever were you thinking of?'

It came as no surprise to Johanna that her business was known, even here. After all, Lady Lisle's daughter, Anne Basset, had been at court with her and kept her parents well-informed of events happening in London. Also, the Lisles kept a man, Husee, in London who made sure they were up to date.

'Forgive me, Lady Margery,' Johanna said, curtseying briefly, 'it is wonderful to see you here. How does my lady Lisle?'

'Well enough,' Lady Margery said. 'His Lordship is in London at the moment and her Ladyship always frets about him whilst he is away. I'm afraid he isn't getting any younger.'

Johanna nodded. The Lisles were both in their second marriages, but a devoted couple. Lord Lisle had received his prestigious placement in Calais because he was the only one of the King Plantagenet relatives that he trusted, and that only on account of him being a base-born son. 'Do you think her Ladyship would receive me?'

Lady Margery's eyes narrowed and she looked Johanna up and down slowly. What she thought of the shapeless woollen kirtle, Johanna could only imagine.

'What would your business with her be, Johanna? We dare not arouse the displeasure of the King, and there's your uncle to think of...'

Johanna winced. 'Lady Margery, I promise no harm will come to Lady Lisle, and I won't take up much of her Ladyship's time. All I need is some help to get to London.' She risked put her hand on Lady Margery's arm. 'Please. I beseech you.'

Lady Margery dithered. 'You know I've always had a soft spot for you, Johanna, but I could be forgiven for wondering if you have lost your senses. It's common knowledge that the King is angry with you, and your family have disowned you. Why on earth would you want to go to London?'

'I need to speak to the King.'

Lady Margery gawped, and Johanna drew the purse from under her kirtle, then selected the emerald ring.

'Give this to her Ladyship, will you, Lady Margery? And remind her of my love for her and recommend me to her good grace?'

Lady Margery examined the ring. 'Why, this is a fine gift Johanna, one his Lordship might be right glad to wear.' She looked at the ring a while longer. 'I'll do my best for you, but I cannot predict how her Ladyship will react. Where are you lodged?'

'I...' Johanna looked around, flustered. 'Nowhere yet, I've just arrived.'

'Nowhere?' Lady Margery hesitated, and then made up her mind. 'I still have lodgings on Whethill Street. Do you remember where they are?'

Johanna nodded.

'Well, go and wait for me there. I'll do what I can.'

Austin Friars
London

Cromwell surveyed the very long list of the things he would have to organise before the Princess of Cleves arrived, one of which was making repairs in Calais so that the port was fit to receive their next queen on her long journey to London. Arthur Lisle's requests for money to mend the fortifications had become quite poignant of late – but that was the King for you. Make do until it was almost too late. Henry hated spending money unless it was on one of his pet projects.

Cromwell's eyes strayed to a note sent from Amesbury priory. Why did that set off an alarm? One of the nuns had confessed to overhearing a conversation about diamonds. Heaven help the old crows if they were hiding diamonds from the King. He *loved* them and could smell a diamond out quicker than a bloodhound. Cromwell remembered being subjected to an hour or so of stories about them, how they all had names and came from this God forsaken country or that – often stolen. He couldn't remember the King mentioning any significant diamonds that were housed at Amesbury, but then there was no telling what papists were capable of hiding under their altar cloths.

Amesbury. Amesbury. Cromwell stirred the parchments on his desk. Where was it? Ah yes! '*A message from Amesbury*'.

'*A young novice left the Priory urgently before our arrival. Destination unknown. Possibly the mother house in France. Have sent agents to apprehend her.*'

Cromwell sat back and stretched. Could the novice have been carrying diamonds? Smuggle these out of the country because God commands it, no matter what might befall you if you're caught. How cynical.

Cromwell began to write.

*

Matthew was finally brought to the Tower by wherry, shooting under London Bridge, whilst the great stone starlings that supported the arches churned the water into rapids. He knew where he was going, had known ever since he was arrested, and his only question was: would Abbot Whiting be there too? Matthew took comfort from the thought that if they were incarcerated together, then he could at least join the elderly abbot in his pain.

In the moments when he was not praying for the Abbot, Matthew thought of Johanna. Dear Johanna. The last he had seen of her, was her face as he was taken away. How far had she managed to get? Had she been arrested, too, or had she reached France? His most fervent prayer, was that she and the reliquary had found safety; but it would have been difficult for her travelling alone, with so little money.

Severed heads on pikes decorated the south tower of the bridge and Matthew looked away. His might be there in the not too distant future. The wherry steered towards a gate with a raised iron portcullis, just as rain started to fall from a lead-grey sky. Nicholas, the older lawyer, had left them further up the river, and now his companion, fleshy, young Thomas, un-cramped his knuckles and pulled at the manacles that held Matthew's arms pinioned behind his back.

They were escorted inside by a Tower warden, and led to one of the many buildings that surrounded the central courtyard. Matthew was pushed into a room where a man wearing a black doublet sat at a table stacked with parchments. He looked up, eyebrows raised.

'Greetings, Master Knevitt.' Thomas made a show of taking off his hat. 'This is the lad we were asked to find.'

The man behind the desk nodded and held out his hand, palm upwards. Thomas handed over a scrolled parchment and the man read it, tapping at his teeth with his index finger. Matthew looked around. No one was holding him now but if he ran, where was he to go?

There was a fire in the grate and he longed to stand by it, to dry his sodden clothes.

'Right, you can leave him with us,' Master Knevitt said, placing the parchment to one side. Matthew's knees began to wobble.

Thomas replaced his cap, screwing it onto his head with finality, his job done.

'You,' Knevitt said, pointing at Matthew. 'What have you got to say for yourself?'

Matthew gave a start. 'Nothing,' he said.

Master Knevitt flashed a look of annoyance. 'Don't you even want to know what you're accused of?'

Matthew willed his heart not to beat so fast, it was making him feel faint. 'I'm innocent, sir,' was all he said.

'Of course you are,' the man said. 'So is everyone until they're found guilty.' He read from his parchment. 'Theft of the King's property and treason. Not much , eh? Mark!'

A door at the side of the room opened and a youngish man in dark-blue livery came marching in. He nodded briefly to Master Knevitt and then took a key proffered by Thomas, to open Matthew's manacles.

‘Strip!’ he said. ‘Now!’

Matthew massaged his sore wrists and started to take off his clothes, his hands trembling. He looked around for somewhere to put them.

‘Down there will do,’ Mark said, pointing to the floor.

As he dropped his clothes, Mark picked them up and searched through them. Naked and exposed, Matthew could have told him there was no point in looking. Thomas and Nicholas had taken all he had.

‘Open your mouth,’ Mark ordered, and Matthew complied. ‘Right, that’s everything. Nothing on him.’

‘Very well, you can take him away now,’ Knevitt said. ‘Put your clothes back on.’

Matthew dressed hastily, grateful to be able to cover his body again.

‘Right, come with me,’ Mark said, snapping the manacles back into place again, but this time with Matthew’s arms before him.

He was pushed out of the room and along a corridor, then down two flights of spiral steps and along another corridor. All the while Matthew’s surroundings changed from well-kept to dusty and disused, with broken bits of furniture in the corners, and the floor became dirtier and wetter as they descended yet another level. As he walked, keys jingled on Mark’s belt and he whistled, bits of a tune Matthew did not know.

‘Will I be here long?’ he asked, knowing it was useless to ask, but still wanting to hear in this man’s voice, some recognition of his humanity.

‘Depends,’ Mark said, ‘on how long it takes you to tell us what we want to know. Could be as little as a couple of days.’ He shrugged. ‘It’s really up to you.’

They stopped before a low, iron-bound door and Mark selected a large key from the bunch at his belt. He opened the door, and propelled Matthew forwards to forcibly that he stumbled and fell. Without another word, Mark closed and locked the door, the sound of the key turning in the lock sounding as final as the Crack of Doom. Matthew wanted to rush to the door and plead to be let out, but he forced himself to stay calm and looked around. The room was virtually dark and smelled of damp, piss, sweat and – something even more unpleasant. There was a little grille, high up on the wall and from that came all the light there was. It took a while for his eyes to adjust and then he could see that the room was almost empty, except for a dirty mattress in one corner and a chipped and stained wooden bucket in the other. Matthew’s stomach churned at he saw the thick metal hoops on the wall and the chains that hung from them. Thankfully they hadn’t attached him to those, yet.

From outside the room came the sudden sound of screaming, high and wild, and Matthew covered his ears, his heart nearly bursting out of his chest; but then he heard laughter and Mark’s voice.

‘Bet that made you piss yourself, didn’t it?’

Matthew wrapped his arms about his body. How someone could find that funny was beyond him. As he walked around the room, he trailed his hand on the wall, reluctant to do that which he knew he would have to do: sit or lie upon that filthy mattress. His fingers felt indentations in the stone, here and there – not deep, just about the depth a man could scratch. He paused and went back, ran his finger tips around the shallow trenches, reading without seeing the words scratched there. Names, dates, prayers – some in Latin.

Well educated men must have been housed here too, he thought. '3 years, 2 months – 1156 days. God, when will it end?' His blood ran cold in his veins. Who was the wretch who had written that? Had he died here?

It had been afternoon when Matthew arrived at the Tower but he had no idea of the time now. Would someone feed him? He sighed. There was one way to make the waiting easier, one way to blot out some of his fear and give himself comfort. He knelt on the damp earth floor and made the Sign of the Cross, then started to pray.

CHAPTER 37

August
Devon

Jo undressed in the dorm of the Youth Hostel, keeping to her corner, whilst three new arrivals walked around the room, chatting to each other across the bunks. When she pulled out her pyjamas, they produced short dresses and sparkly flip flops. Suddenly she felt very old. She was going to bed, their night was just beginning.

As their voices faded down the corridor, Jo got into bed and turned onto her side, trying to make sense of what had just happened. Mat had said he loved her! But he had also made it plain that he was a priest, so what she was trying to understand was how they'd got into this situation. Why had he let her get so close? It had been as if he couldn't help it, and she blushed as she remembered how aroused he'd been.

Her body was still tingling from where he'd touched her and she wanted to be with him now, not alone in this narrow bunk. Her lips were swollen with his kisses and she couldn't bear to believe she was never going to experience them again. Despite being as attracted to a man as she'd ever been in her life, and despite him obviously feeling the same way about her – it wasn't going to happen.

She slammed her pillow and shifted uncomfortably on the bunk. For a few, sweet moments she allowed herself to fantasise about what could never be; having Mat's child and sitting in the garden at Station View watching father and son play together. Stop it, she told herself. It's not going to happen, don't torture yourself.

She must have dozed off, because the next thing she knew there was a loud knocking and she staggered towards the door in the dark. The three girls were outside, full of apologies for losing their keys. Numbly, Jo muttered 'don't worry' and went back to bed. They'd obviously had a fantastic time and could hardly suppress their giggles. Had she ever had so much fun? If she had, she couldn't remember.

At seven thirty the following morning Jo got up and went for a shower. The girls were still asleep and she tiptoed around until she realised it was going to take a nuclear explosion to wake them. After that she didn't bother and dried her hair, then pulled it into a pony tail. She rubbed at the mascara smudges under her eyes until she realised they were dark shadows and swore. It was going to be hard to get through this day.

Mat was already in the dining room, sitting at a table by himself and reading a newspaper. Jo's anger flared when she saw him looking so calm. Was that it then? She'd been put to the back of his mind already?

The sight of bacon and sausages did nothing for her appetite. Perhaps she'd start with coffee. She even flirted with the idea of sitting at another table but when Mat looked over and smiled at her, all of her anger vanished and tears sprang into her eyes. For goodness sake, she was an emotional wreck. The sooner this was over, the better. She slid into the chair opposite him.

'Good morning,' Mat said, searching her face anxiously. He was probably worried she'd make a scene. 'Did you sleep all right? Those bunks are surprisingly comfortable, aren't they?'

'No,' she said. 'I damned well didn't?' She looked around. It was perhaps a bit strong, for a public dining room. 'I was sharing a room with three young girls who all went out as I went to bed, and then knocked me up at goodness knows what time because they'd forgotten their keys. Can you believe it?'

He laughed in a half-hearted, relieved, kind of way. 'I guess that's why they call it a youth hostel.'

'Are you trying to say I'm not young?' she said.

His face reddened. 'Not at all,' he said. 'What I'm trying to say is maybe you've got used to more luxury. Anyway, ' he looked around, 'it's a lovely hostel, isn't it?'

'Yes.' She had to agree. The gardens outside the dining room window were delightful. 'I'm sorry,' she said. 'I'm not at my best this morning. Just ignore me.'

He put one of his lovely brown hands over hers. 'You know I can't do that.'

The anger started again. 'Mat,' she hissed, 'you've got to stop touching me. You're driving me mad. I know we can't be together. All it does is make things worse. When we end up like last night, neither one thing nor the other, I feel like Jezebel. I want it to stop. Now.'

He fell silent, regarding her with troubled eyes. 'You're right,' he said, eventually. 'It won't do.'

'But all you have to do is go to confession when you get back. Right?' She couldn't feel pity for him. Not when her heart was close to breaking. 'And then carry on as though I never happened?'

'In theory,' was all he said, looking down at his hands and then out of the window.

She watched him withdraw from her as completely as if he had just got up and left the room.

'Oh, you're impossible!' She got up to leave. He *was* already making plans to forget her, had as good as admitted it.'

'Jo!'

She didn't look back but pushed open the main door and walked outside into the gardens. To her annoyance, he followed her. 'Jo! Stop a minute and let me try to explain.'

There was a bench, a way off, and she couldn't decide whether to head for it and give him a chance to talk, or to keep on walking and never look back; but she couldn't do that. He was clearly distraught and she tried to remember how innocent he was in relationships. Beginning to calm down, she went and sat on the bench.

'This is terrible, Jo,' he said. 'Can you ever forgive me?'

'Of course,' she said, wanting so much to be in his arms that it took all of her willpower not to cry out for it. 'But I don't want to have to give you up. Can't you see that? I want to know I mean something to you.'

Mat dragged a hand through his hair and sat down on the bench. Their arms went around each other and the kiss became urgent. They clung to each other, tears and kisses mingling, and when the need abated long enough for them to draw breath, Mat held her tightly cradled against him.

'Oh, Jo,' he said, his voice muffled by her hair. 'What on Earth are we going to do?'

CHAPTER 38

Late August
Pamiers, Languedoc

It was a relief to be away from Carcassonne and the devastation of the land thereabouts. Nearer to Toulouse, everything looked as it always had; yellow, soft earth contrasting with the greenness of the vineyards and tall cypress trees, all over-arched by a clear turquoise sky. In the distance, the hulking Pyrenees filled the horizon end to end, freshening the air and enabling Matthieu to take what felt like his first deep breath in weeks.

The Count had instructed him to journey to Toulouse via Pamiers, in order to keep the purpose of his mission secret. If anyone asked, he was going to see his sister-in-law. Matthieu's heart was heavy as he contemplated the thought of seeing Joana again. She had come alone for Catharine's funeral and from the moment she arrived, Matthieu hadn't been able to drag his eyes away from her. Afterwards, he'd felt obliged to ask her to stay with him at his apartment in the Château. Once there, she broke down and he asked Beatrice to put her in Catharine's chamber, then called in later, to see how she was feeling.

He found her sitting before the fire, cradling a goblet of spiced wine, and wearing one of Catharine's night robes. It put Matthieu in mind of the night Catharine had been in that same chair, drinking wine, bold with the promises of the Saint. A bitter taste filled his mouth when he remembered how he'd allowed himself to believe everything would be all right. But who was he to know God's reasons?

'Will you take a cup, before bed, Matthieu?' Joana asked.

Her eyes were still swollen from crying, and the wine had reddened her lips. Pity stirred Matthieu's heart and he brought up a coffer to sit by Joana. Her hair lay unbound about her shoulders, the first time he had seen it so since she was a young girl, and he breathed in the tantalisingly familiar scent of her. Despite the rigours of Catharine's death and the misery of her funeral, he couldn't help himself responding.

'Joana-'

'Shh,' she said. 'Whatever you're going to say, don't say it. Just sit with me for a while and be friends. I've missed you so much.'

She put out her hand to clasp his and he twined his fingers in hers, bringing her hand slowly to his lips. Their eyes met and her tears started to fall again. Groaning, Matthieu pulled her into his arms, holding her as if she were the most precious thing on Earth, and their lips met. Fire blazed through him, kindling all the long submerged passion that he held for her. Before he knew what he was doing, he had lifted her into his arms and carried her to the bed. The robe slid off her shoulders and he kissed the erratic pulse at the base of her neck.

Behind the heavy curtains, their quickly naked bodies entangled – the only other human who knew how he felt, the only other human who cared. Passion engulfed Matthieu in a drowning wave. Never had he allowed himself to imagine what it would be like to do this, to run his hands over her nakedness, to experience the exquisiteness of entering her. All thoughts, fears, regrets ceased to matter as he emptied himself into her, and she responded: her hands clasping around his back and her body arching against him. Never had he experienced such ecstasy, such release, such... love.

Afterwards, he slipped from the bed whilst she was still sleeping – sliding his arm from under her head, and feeling the silk of her hair brushing against his inner arm. He left the warmth and the scent of her behind, and tiptoed carefully past Beatrice's sleeping figure.

When she awoke, he knew that she would be hurt; that she would have to go back to her husband without saying goodbye and that Beatrice would look at her and know what had happened. But how could he face her when they had just committed the greatest sin of their lives?

As soon as he could, Matthieu went to Saint Gilles to see Alphonso and begged him to hear his confession. As he knelt in the darkness his mouth ran dry. Alphonso asked if he was ready, but Matthieu couldn't answer. Perhaps he should have chosen a different priest?

'My son,' Alphonso said, 'think how long I've been a priest, and how many years I've listened to the frailties of the innermost human heart. Do you really think there is anything you can tell me that will shock me now? And remember, the Lord *already* knows what you have come to tell me. I am merely here to offer you His grace.'

Matthieu clasped his hands tightly and tried to clear his mind. 'Bless me, Father, for I have sinned,' he said, but still the word *adultery* stuck fast in his throat. Tears ran down his cheeks. Alphonso waited.

'Would it help to say a few prayers together, my son?' the priest asked.

Matthieu took a deep breath. 'No, it's all right, Father. I'm ready now. If I wasn't ashamed to sin, I should not be ashamed to confess.'

*

Matthieu's horse kicked up dust from the dry earth as he rode south. The broad valley in which lay the town of Pamiers opened before him and Matthieu paused for a moment to look down upon the modest manor that was now Joana's home. How well everything looked. After the mayhem of the crusade, and living in cramped conditions for so many weeks, the sight of the farm was balm to his eyes.

As he cantered up to the main entrance, chickens scattered before him and a pair of hunting dogs rose from their place in the shade, slinking towards him, hackles raised.

His horse pulled restlessly on its reins, nervous of the dogs, but in response to the noise Joana came around the corner of the house with a maid and a young child. Her hand flew to her heart when she saw who was there.

'Matthieu!' The colour drained quickly from her face. 'Is there bad news?'

'Can I get down?' he said. 'The dogs look like they think I'm their next meal.'

'Of course.' She called the dogs away, and shut them in a hut. 'Aimeric insists on them being out, now there's so many soldiers about. Agnes, take Guillem and prepare some food for our guest.'

Matthieu dismounted. 'How are you?' he asked.

For a moment they stood close together and Matthieu's breath caught in his throat. So familiar, the same scent, the same longing. Her green eyes drew him and he steeled himself. They were outside her husband's house and he had spent too much time praying to let his thoughts stray down that road again. Unbelievably, there was no trace of anger in her face and his heart lightened. Had she forgiven him?

'We're all well,' Joana said, giving him a welcoming kiss on both cheeks. 'I expect your horse will want some water.'

He watched her, mesmerised, as she took a pail and tipped water into a trough. She was still as beautiful as ever, and her movements lithe and quick. The horse drank deeply from the trough, whinnying his gratitude. Joana wiped her hands and pushed wisps of hair back into her linen bonnet.

'You'd better come in,' she said, looking more wary. 'Aimeric's asleep but I'll wake him.'

The boy came running out into the yard again. He was a serious faced youngster with wavy brown hair curling to his shoulders and startling green eyes. Joana took his hand and steered him before her into the house.

'Come on, Guillem,' she said. 'Let's wake papa and show him our new visitor.'

Papa? Matthieu felt shock race through his body. This was Joana's child? How could he have been such a poor brother to her that he didn't even know she had a child? Curiously, he studied Guillem, trying to work out his age; and as he did, the breath suddenly left his body. Could it be? He almost banged his head on the lintel as he followed Joana into the flagged coolness of her home. They'd only made love that once, although it had certainly been more than once on that occasion – but surely the child was more likely to be Aimeric's or even, Matthieu took a deep breath, a Foix bastard.

He handed over his dusty cloak to the maid and Joana led him into their hall.

Aimeric lay asleep before the unlit fire Sunlight made stripes across his body as it filtered through the shutters. To Matthieu's eyes, his brother in law had aged rapidly in the five years since he and Joana were wed. His grey hair was sparse, and in his relaxed state, folds of skin drooped from his neck over the collar of his chemise; but neither Aimeric nor even Joana could hold Matthieu's attention at the moment. All of his thoughts were of Guillem.

The young boy regarded him steadily, half hiding behind his mother's skirts. The serving woman brought in hot water and a towel for Matthieu to wash, then a tray with wine and food. That done, she held out her hand for Guillem and he took it; but his eyes never left Matthieu's face. Were visitors such a rarity here, or could the boy possibly sense what was running through his mind?

'Come on, Guillem,' Agnes said. 'It's time to feed the piglets.'

'A handsome boy,' he said, turning to Joana as they left. 'I had no idea.'

Her smile broadened. 'Of course you didn't. But I'm glad you've seen him now.'

She lifted two earthenware goblets off a shelf by the window, and poured wine into them.

'This is our wine. Tell me what you think.'

He towelled his hands and face and then took the goblet from her. Their finger tips brushed and she looked directly into his eyes. Was there a hint of challenge there, or amusement? He swallowed.

'It's excellent,' he said, and truly it was.'I'll let the Count know. If he ever gets away from this crusade, I'm sure he'd like some at the Château.'

Every breath felt an effort. Why had she not told him? But, of course, he knew that answer only too well.

Joana's smile faded. 'Have you come to tell us what's happening with the crusade, Matthieu, because every word I hear terrifies me. Is it true they killed everyone at Béziers, even babes and children?'

Matthieu nodded slowly. 'The fools there refused to surrender. Carcassonne was different, thankfully.' He bit into a fresh fig and licked his lips. 'This is a welcome change from camp food. I thank you.'

Their eyes met again and he felt his body stirring. Would he ever be immune to this woman? Even now, with the memory of his sin burning like a hot brand on his conscience, he still desired her. 'They let everyone go, except the Viscount,' he said. 'And now he's imprisoned in his own dungeon. Count Raimon is furious.'

'What made Trencavel give himself up?' she asked. 'I heard

Carcassonne was well defended. Was it treachery?'

'No,' Matthieu sighed. 'He gave himself up to save the heretics.'

'Ah.'

There was a snort from Aimeric and disappointment flickered across Joana's face. 'You'd better talk to my husband now,' she said, drawing away. 'I'm sure you'll have plenty he's keen to hear.'

If Aimeric was surprised to see a visitor waiting for him, he didn't show it. Whilst Matthieu told him of the events at Béziers and Carcassonne, Aimeric sucked annoyingly on the gap between his front teeth.

'Carcassonne could have held out for months,' he said. 'What happened?'

Matthieu hesitated; how much should he tell him? Joana may be still listening, and he didn't want to frighten her. 'All they wanted the Viscount to do was hand over the heretics. That's all they asked, at Béziers and Carcassonne. But he refused.'

Aimeric shook his head. 'So what made him change his mind?'

Matthieu hated remembering the hope on the faces of the people of Carcassonne. 'They were running out of water. So many people packed in there it was impossible. The Legate said that the Viscount could go free with some of his knights. But...'

'They put him in his own dungeon instead.' Aimeric's round face sank into a deep scowl. 'Foix's not going to like this one bit. Ah, Matthieu. All this on account of beliefs. It's not as if the Goodmen and women mean any harm.'

'Not on the face of it,' Matthieu said, feeling his anger rise. As far as he was concerned, heretics were very far from being 'Good men.'

'They say they have the truth,' Aimeric said, with a shrug. 'What do you think of that? The truth as taught by Jesus. They're convinced of it.'

Matthieu took a deep breath. 'Can you believe, as they do, that God's creation is evil?'

Aimeric looked around his hall. 'What would I know? This crusade is not pretty either, and when I hear of the wickedness of priests, or see people suffering horrible diseases, or hear that supposed men of God have put babies to death... sometimes I think they may have a point.'

Matthieu sighed. 'And those things grieve me too.' More than he would care to admit. 'But it was man who first brought suffering into God's creation when he committed the first sin. *We* are the agents of the evil you describe, not God.'

Aimeric squinted at him. 'In that case, why doesn't God just punish us and have done with it?'

'Aimeric,' Matthieu said, 'I'm no theologian, but I believe that God doesn't punish us for sin, but forgives us.'

‘Really?’ Aimeric frowned into his empty goblet. ‘Is there any more wine? You wouldn’t think we made the damned stuff. Agnes!’ he turned back to Matthieu. ‘If God doesn’t want to punish people, why did the priests put Trencavel in prison after he gave himself up?’

Matthieu regarded Aimeric steadily. How could he stand here, pretending to understand the workings of God, when he was the biggest sinner alive? ‘I’m afraid that’s a matter only the leader of the crusade can answer.’

Agnes came in with a jug, and Aimeric held out his goblet. ‘I’m sure you’re right,’ he said, tasting the wine and spitting it back into his cup. ‘Bring something better, Agnes, out of those barrels at the back of the cellar. Mind you,’ he said, ‘I think there’s more to this crusade than heresy, however the Church sees it. What about that cunning spider who is sitting on the French throne? He’s biding his time, isn’t he? Look how much territory he’s taken from John of England. Why wouldn’t he look here next?’

‘King Philippe has refused to join the crusade,’ Matthieu said. ‘In fact he was reluctant to let any of his knights come at all, according to the Duke of Burgundy. Said he was too busy fighting the English and the Germans.’

‘Humph.’ Aimeric scratched at his belly. ‘You mark my words. He waits and watches – exactly like a spider. Anyway,’ Aimeric stood up and banged his goblet on the table, shouting for Agnes again, ‘enough of this dismal talk. Let’s eat and then find you a bed. You must be exhausted. Where is it you’re going anyway?’

*

That night, Matthieu lay on a comfortable mattress for the first time in weeks. His pillow smelled of lavender and his body and hair had been rinsed with lemon and rosemary scented water. As he stretched out his feet under the sheets, he couldn’t help picturing what life would have been like if he and Joana had been able to marry. She wouldn’t have had to work so hard if she was married to him. Aimeric was a lazy man, he thought, bitterly. No wonder he’d been so keen to marry again. The farm owed its smooth running to its mistress, not to its master, that was for sure.

‘Matthieu?’

Her voice came from the corridor.

‘What is it?’ he whispered, getting up quickly and opening the door. ‘For the love of God, why are you here?’

Joana pushed her way into the room and he saw that she was only wearing a thin linen shift. Her hair hung luxuriantly down her back and her eyes gleamed at him, cat-like, in the dim light of the candle.

‘I have to talk to you,’ she said. ‘Don’t worry – no one knows I’m here.

Agnes has gone to home to her mother and the others sleep away from the house.'

Matthieu let out his breath as quietly as he could. 'And Aimeric?'

'He sleeps,' she spat, 'like a dead pig.'

The temptation to hold her was almost unbearable. He could see her body outlined in shadow form beneath the shift: her breasts still full and high, her waist slender. Matthieu swallowed. It had been a long time.

'He won't hear us,' Joana said, coming towards him and sliding her hands up around his neck. She touched his cheek and he turned his mouth into her hand, pressing his lips against her palm.

'Forgive me,' he said.

She clasped him tightly, and he felt her breasts pushing against his chest.

'Matthieu,' she said, hoarsely. 'I've missed you so much.'

She drew his head down until their lips met and it was as though the years had rolled away and they were together for the first time. His hands slid down her back, cupped her buttocks, and lifted her up into his embrace. She clung to him and their kiss deepened. Two strides to the bed and they were together; their bodies entwined, and he stroked the wonderful softness of her curves, felt the hardening of her nipples beneath the soft fabric. Slowly, she raised her shift until she was naked before him, and now the skin of her body was smooth and warm beneath his hands. The puckered tips of her breasts invited his mouth, and he teased them until she groaned and pulled impatiently at the cords of his braies, freeing him into her hand.

'Ah...'

As the last vestiges of Matthieu's will crumbled, Joana opened her body to him and he knelt above her, anticipating the ecstasy, feeling the urgency in his loins to be almost out of control...

'Maman?'

They froze in horror. Matthieu was the first to react and tore himself away from Joana. She leaped to her feet and snatched up her shift.

'It's Guillem,' she whispered. 'Perhaps he's unwell. Give me your night robe.' She shrugged into it and went to the door, opening it a fraction. 'Guillem?'

There was no answer, so she threw the robe behind her and disappeared into the corridor. Matthieu sat down with his head in his hands. What had he been about to do, *again*? If it had not been for the cry of a babe... had he no shame? Disgusted, he picked up his belt and whipped the buckle end of it over his bare shoulder. It bit hard against his skin and the pain jolted his body. He gasped and whipped again, and again, biting his lip to stop from crying out. Eventually, the buckle ran with blood and he fell to his knees, his heart and soul in agony.

CHAPTER 39

30th September 1539
Calais

'This just came for you, my lady,' the maid said, handing over a note. 'Shall I wait in case you've instructions?'

'Yes, please,' Johanna said, and gave a long stretch. Her body felt stiff and sore, but the rest had helped her spirits revive and she felt hopeful again. She read quickly, her heart giving a little leap – Lady Lisle would see her.

'This is wonderful news,' she said, swinging her legs off the bed and getting up quickly. 'Will you help me dress, Isobel? Lady Lisle wishes to see me as soon as possible.'

Isabel combed out Johanna's hair and then plaited it and wound it at the back of her head. 'Do you have a veil, my lady?'

Johanna shook her head. 'Alas, when I was crossing from England, the weather was exceedingly stormy and most of my luggage was lost. I have a ribbon that I bought in the market yesterday...'

Isabel nodded, curtseyed, and then slipped away. She came back with a gauzy veil.

'Lady Margery will never miss this,' she said. 'It's her fourth best and not likely to be worn again.' She fixed it to Johanna's head with the ribbon and then stood back to admire. 'Looks lovely, I think,' she said.

Johanna went to the mirror on the wall, hardly daring to look; but there was no doubt the girl was right. Johanna eyed the kirtle that Mathilde had given her and which lay over a stool by her bed. However well-dressed her head was, it wouldn't make up for wearing something so coarse.

Isabel picked up the kirtle. 'I took the liberty of giving your clothes a bit of a clean, whilst you was sleeping, my lady,' she said. 'But there's a stain on the hem of this I couldn't get out. Lady Margery told me about your difficult sea-crossing. I think salty water has done it. Perhaps I can find you another?'

Jo nodded, grateful for the maid's tact. Two minutes later the girl was back with a fine woollen kirtle, a gown to go over it in Johanna's favourite shade of pale sage green, and a pair of worn but still elegant silk slippers. Isabel helped her to dress, and although it felt strange to have a maid again, it was very pleasant to have someone to chat to. Johanna learned that the maid was to be married soon.

'His name is James,' Isabel said, 'and he works for my lord Lisle, in the stables.'

Johanna nodded, remembering the grandeur of the Calais stables. What made them truly notable was their size. At very little notice the garrison in Calais could be asked to supply horses for large parties of visiting dignitaries travelling either way over the Channel, which might even include the King himself.

'Congratulations,' she said, feeling wistful. 'I hope you'll both be truly happy.'

Isabel beamed at her. 'Lady Margery says he can live here when we're wed. At least then we'll be together.'

Looking at the happiness on Isabel's face, Johanna felt more than a twinge of envy. How wonderful it must be to marry for love.

*

'My dear,' Lady Lisle said, embracing Johanna pleasantly, but formally. 'How lovely to see you.'

Johanna blushed and curtsied deeply. 'It's good of you to see me, my lady.'

Honor Lisle had the most pleasing apple-round cheeks and merry blue eyes. She was in her early forties and had brought to her marriage with the King's uncle an amazing seven Basset children – of whom Anne Basset was Johanna's favourite.

'Not at all, not at all,' Lady Lisle said. 'I've been anxious about you, Johanna. Anne writes to me, of course.'

Johanna didn't miss the flicker of a look towards Lady Margery. Lady Lisle was doubtless of the same mind – that she was a fool for refusing the King.

'Come and sit next to me. Ladies...'

All, except Margery, picked up their sewing and melted from the room. A little squirrel in a cage by the window came to stare at Johanna through the bars, as if glad of the distraction.

'There now.'

Lady lisle indicated a cushion near to her feet and Johanna lifted her skirts to sit upon it. Lady Margery poured wine for them all into pewter goblets.

'I hear you've had quite a journey,' Lady Lisle said.

Johanna nodded and tried not to gulp at the wine. Lord Lisle kept a good cellar, far better than most in England, and the ruby liquid warmed her blood. She must remember her manners and not to come out with her request boldly – however much haste she felt on Matthew's account.

'How is his Lordship and yourself? Well I hope?'

'Well enough,' Lady Lisle said, nodding, 'although I could wish we were getting younger.' She smiled a little crookedly and Johanna's heart went out to her. She had tried hard to give Viscount Lisle, who had only daughters from his first marriage, a Plantagenet heir, but with little success.

'And your children?'

'Philippa is here and is well,' Lady Lisle said. 'And John and Frances are happily married. She had her baby in May and they've called her after me. Isn't that nice? Anne, as you know, is still in London. She's lodged with her cousin, Mistress Mewtas, until the new queen arrives. She writes that she's been ill of late, I'm afraid – headaches and chestiness. I sent over some of my codiniac and she offered it to the King. Seems he liked it very well and has asked for more! Johanna remains with Lady Rutland, although the Earl of Hertford has asked for her; and Mary is here.' Lady Lisle broke off with a sigh and looked up at the ceiling. 'As pretty as ever but suffers terribly with fevers. She's had them ever since you were here. George remains with Sir Francis Bryan and James remains in the service of the Bishop of Winchester, and always writes to me in French – which I still cannot read. But anyway, my dear, enough of us. What brings you to Calais?'

Lady Lisle looked expectantly at Johanna, who took a deep breath. It was now, or never.

'I wondered if you could help me to get to London, my lady?'

Lady Lisle choked a little on her wine. 'Really? Margery told me you wanted to go to England, which I thought difficult enough, but London! Johanna, have you thought about this?'

'Yes, my lady,' she said. She had been expecting this and steeled herself. 'I have some business with the King – of the most urgent nature.'

'You're not carrying his child are you?' Lady Lisle said, frowning at Johanna's stomach.

'No,' she said, ignoring the slur. 'I have something of great value that I know the King wants.'

Lady Lisle paused and appraised Johanna carefully. 'Something Henry wants badly? May I ask what it is?'

'I'd rather not say.' The fewer people who knew about the diamonds, the better.

Lady Lisle's mouth tightened. 'I see. Johanna, I hope you're not expecting to be restored to the King's favour, because I think that would be unlikely in view of what Anne has told me. He's terribly angry with you.'

Johanna trembled. 'I regret with all my heart that I have angered the King,' she said. 'But I simply couldn't agree to become his mistress, no matter how much upset that has caused. In my heart, you see, I have always longed to give myself to God...'

Lady Honor clicked her tongue. 'You girls have such fantasies. Who would want to be a nun when you could have a home and children of your own? In any case, there are precious few convents left now. Just where did you hope to become a nun?'

'At Fontevraud Abbey, where I came from, my lady. I was on my way there just now, but my companion was arrested. I'm hoping I can persuade the King to release him.'

'Release *him*?' Lady Lisle looked first astonished, and then suspicious. 'Perhaps not so ready to be a nun after all, is it?' she murmured.

Johanna was unable to stop herself from blushing. 'Matthew was accompanying me to Fontevraud, my lady, because *his* greatest wish was to become a monk at Glastonbury Abbey. That place, as you most likely know, is in the process of dissolution.'

'Yes, I know that all too well,' Lady Lisle said, 'along with many others around my lands in that area. Do you have news of Gerald, by the way?'

Johanna nodded. 'He's well, my lady, but I may not tell you of his whereabouts.' She looked quickly at Lady Margery.

'You have no need to fear speaking in front of Margery,' Lady Lisle said, putting a hand on her woman's arm. 'We are both fond of the old ways, although we scarce mention them now. So, you are going to petition the King to release this young friend of yours. Why was he arrested?'

'We had been ordered to carry a reliquary with us, to safety at Fontevraud,' she said, carefully.

'A reliquary?' Lady Lisle's eyebrows rose. 'You're not going to offer that to the King, are you? Something like that's not going to buy your friend's freedom. Cromwell would only have him destroy it.'

'I realise that, my lady,' Johanna said, trying to keep her voice steady. She was so nervous she felt like she might faint. 'The reliquary is safely on its way to Fontevraud, as we speak. No, it's something else I have in mind for the King, and I am confident he will be well pleased with it. In fact I think he may actually be angry if I didn't bring it.'

Lady Lisle paled. Everyone feared the King's temper. 'But you're not going to tell me what it is?' she said.

'It would be better if I didn't, my lady.'

The older woman tapped her fingers on the arm of her chair. 'Dear, oh dear,' she said. 'Every day seems to bring a new trial, and it's not as though we don't have enough all ready. Mary Boleyn is here, did you know that? We've been forced to shelter her for long enough; and Cromwell speaks in platitudes to my husband about the state of the fortifications here in Calais, but stops short of sending us any real help.' She lifted her goblet and Lady Margery obligingly refilled it. 'And of course there's this marriage-' Lady Lisle stopped short and Johanna's curiosity was aroused. What had she been going to say? Surely the marriage didn't involve one of her children or she would have mentioned it earlier.

Lady Lisle shook her head. 'Never mind,' she said, 'I may not speak of that, yet.'

*

For supper Johanna was invited to join Lady Lisle in her private dining chamber. Many sly glances thrown Johanna's way and a few behind-hand conversations took place, but Lady Lisle frowned so sternly that these eventually they ceased.

The evening passed slowly. Johanna was only too aware that she needed to hurry if she was going to be able to help Matthew, and impatiently made conversation whilst she longed for the night to be over.

After the meal, some of the ladies took up the lute and virginals, until finally, it was time to retire. Johanna joined Lady Margery in her litter and they sat comfortably together, with Lady Margery's hand laid upon Johanna's arm.

'Johanna, my dear,' she said. 'Will you be terribly upset if you cannot save your young man? One hears such tragic stories, these days, hard to believe...'

'I know,' Johanna said, trying to sound more confident than she felt. 'But there's been a grave misunderstanding, Lady Margery, one I can easily put right.'

'But how can you be so sure?' Lady Margery said. 'What has her Ladyship advised you to do?'

'She's given me a letter,' Johanna said. 'Her man, Husee, will see that his Lordship receives it.'

'Oh, dear,' Lady Margery said. 'You do realise this could go ill for the Lisles?'

'It won't, I'll make sure I tell the King that this was all my own idea.'

'Well, make sure you do,' Lady Margery said. 'I don't want the Lisles to lose their place in Calais. I like my life here.'

*

Johanna ate a hasty breakfast of fish in almond milk, with manchet and a little light ale, then said a tearful goodbye to Lady Margery and Isabel. The wind was brisk as she approached the port, and brief showers pattered against the side of the litter. Johanna prayed fervently to Saint Christopher – hoping that the weather turning would not turn against her.

The litter took her up to the ship and its Captain greeted her cordially enough then showed her to her cabin. What a relief! Thanks to Lady Lisle's generosity, she would be comfortably housed for the duration of this journey. Her spirits rose. Now she had some decent clothes again, she could do this. The King would listen to her, he was bound to. Everyone knew how greedy he was – and God willing – she would be able to buy Matthew's freedom.

God's help was already waiting for Johanna when she reached Dover, in the shape of John Husee. He had arrived with a delivery of items for Lady Lisle, which were to go back with the vessel on the next tide. Johanna gave him her letter and he dispatched it straight away to Lord Lisle who, Husee said, was with the King at Hampton Court. Now all Johanna had to do was wait.

Austin Friars
London

Another exhausting day with the Cleves ambassadors but at least some things were becoming clear. The Duke of Cleves was in desperate financial straits and couldn't afford a dowry for his sister – which was not a problem for a King growing alarmed at the dearth of foreign princesses willing to accept his overtures of marriage. Also, the bride-to-be would have to travel overland for most of the journey, because it was winter and the seas likely to be rough. That meant someone would have to negotiate her safe passage with the Emperor...

He sighed and rubbed the heels of his hands up over his forehead. So much to do, and daily Henry grew increasingly ill-tempered.

Cromwell perused the end-of-month accounts and his eyes lighted upon those of the Wardrobe. Significant sums had been spent on enlarging the King's clothes. What, with his game leg, expanding waistline, and sudden unpopularity with the princesses of Europe, it was no wonder the King was in a bad mood most of the time.

CHAPTER 40

August
Devon

They drove away from the fishing village and made their way to the M5. Why, why, why? Jo struggled with her frustration. There were millions of men in the world. Why did she have to fall for one she couldn't have?

'Why don't you tell me about it?' she said. 'Tell me why this can't happen. What's wrong with a priest getting married?'

'OK,' he said, settling back after negotiating the slip road, 'what do you want, the long or the short version?'

Jo watched the cars in the outside lane speeding by, just as life seemed to be passing her by – or at least the prospect of what most people would call a life.

'The long version,' she said. 'We've plenty of time before we get back to Yorkshire, and I want to understand this.'

'Right. Hang on a minute.' Mat overtook a lorry and then pulled back in. 'First of all,' he said, 'celibacy is not dogma, you know. It's Canon Law. Does that mean anything to you?'

'No.'

'All right. Canon Law is the law of the Church. It's something that was adopted by the Apostles in the first century and expanded afterwards. Dogma, on the other hand, is divinely revealed teaching. There's no arguing with that.'

'OK,' she said. 'So God didn't say priests had to be celibate?'

'No. Jesus only said if you could live like a eunuch for the sake of the kingdom of Heaven, then you should. It's in Matthew's Gospel – 'For there are eunuchs who were born that way from their mother's womb; and there are eunuchs who were made eunuchs by men; and there are eunuchs who make themselves eunuchs for the sake of the Kingdom of Heaven. He who is able to accept this, let him accept it.' But he didn't actually say you had to.'

'That's a lot of eunuchs!' Jo muttered. 'So he didn't come down on one side or the other?'

'No-o. But he himself never married.'

'So the Church says. What about Mary Magdalene?'

Mat pulled out to allow the traffic coming in from a busy junction.

'Mm, remind me how we got there when we were supposed to be talking about celibate priests?'

'Because Jesus wasn't really celibate?'

'Ah!' He gave her an apologetic grin. 'I'm afraid I've got to stick to what's in the Bible, Jo. It's OK for people like Dan Brown to make things up. That's his job – writing fiction.'

'But don't you think there's something in it? What about all the stories about them taking bits out of the Bible and making other bits up?'

'By 'them', I assume you mean the Church fathers?'

'I don't know,' Jo confessed. 'I haven't really looked in to it.'

'Well, if that's the kind of thing you want to go into then I'm afraid it really will take a long time; but whatever the outcome of that particular argument is, all I have to go on is what actually *is* there.'

'OK,' Jo sighed. 'Carry on where you were. I shouldn't have diverted us onto Mary Magdalene.'

'Well, it is sort of relevant – whether Jesus was actually married or had a partner. But, what I'm really trying to tell you is that priests *choose* to be celibate.'

'Which is all right if that's what they want.'

'Yes, of course. When I was thinking about becoming a Catholic priest, I didn't think, 'Oh, I want to become a Catholic priest but, rats! I have to be celibate', you know.'

'Didn't you?' she said, unable to imagine why a young man would freely choose to cut himself off from half of what it meant to be human.

'No. But I did give it a lot of thought.'

'So what made you decide?'

That was what she really wanted to know, what she desperately *needed* to know. What was it about becoming a priest that trumped over ever wanting a relationship with a woman?

Mat let out a sigh. 'Well, don't get me wrong. I believe that God's calling of a couple to marriage is a high calling. It asks for everything that being a priest asks for – dedication, self sacrifice, honour, duty. When I became a priest, I married the Church and through her married God. When a couple marry, they're seeking union with each other, aren't they? It's a yearning inside to be together.'

Jo couldn't take her eyes away from his face.

'Well, I felt that yearning, Jo – to be one with God. When a couple marry, then they become celibate in the sense that they commit to keeping themselves pure for each other. I became celibate because I wanted God to always have the best of me.'

'So what you're saying is that having a relationship with me would be like committing adultery?'

This was terrible. Even if the Pope changed the rules tomorrow, there was no future for them, if that was how he felt.

Mat held the steering wheel with whitened knuckles and stared straight ahead without answering.

‘Isn’t it bad for you?’ she said.

‘Bad?’

‘Repression and all that. Isn’t that why priests become paedophiles?’

‘Aw, come on, Jo,’ he said. ‘You’re a nurse. You know better than that. Are married men never paedophiles? And, it’s not confined to Catholic priests either. The Anglican church is having its problems too, with the same issue.’

‘OK,’ Jo said, perhaps that had been a bad example. ‘Talking of Anglican priests, how do they manage their calling and still get married?’

‘I don’t know,’ Mat said, suddenly braking as the traffic slowed to a stop. ‘I find it taxing enough being a priest and not married. Goodness knows how they cope. I only have God to please, but they often have a wife and children too!’

*

Mat helped Jo carry her bag inside, but then stood in the doorway of her house, looking uncertain.

‘Are you going?’ she said, fighting the urge to plead with him to stay.

He nodded.

‘Setting off for Scotland straight away?’

He looked at his watch. ‘I’ll get a shower next door and then pack up. I can be back before it’s dark.’

‘That’s a lot of driving.’

The reason they’d decided to take a train to the south coast in the first place was to save on driving, and now he was proposing to drive the whole length of the country in one day.

‘If I’m tired, I’ll stop at a Travelodge. Don’t worry.’

She put her handbag down and hugged her cold hands to herself. This was it then. He couldn’t wait to be away from her.

‘Goodbye,’ she said, but even though she was really trying, her voice wobbled.

‘Jo-’

‘No! It’s OK. Don’t touch me,’ she said, backing away. ‘It’s best if you just go.’

‘Will you be all right?’

Would she? It was too painful to think about. ‘Of course. Send me a text to let me know you’re safe, will you?’

‘Of course. And,’ he hesitated, ‘I’ll contact you about the ashes.’

She nodded. If he didn’t go soon she would crumble.

‘Bye, Mat,’ she whispered and turned away. Let him stand there as long as he wanted but it wouldn’t make any difference. He wasn’t going to change his mind. How could he? He was married to God, and how could she ever compete with that?

CHAPTER 41

August 1209
Toulouse

The sun sent sloping shadows before Matthieu as he passed Saint Catharine's hospital for lepers, and he begrudged a smile to himself. Joana was no saint, but she ran the farm at Pamiers well – something he couldn't thank Aimeric for because he was obviously fond of sleeping away the afternoons. And she was a good mother to their son.

Their son! Although he would never be able to publicly acknowledge Guillem, Joana had confirmed that the boy was his, and what he'd seen of the lad so far made Matthieu feel proud. When the crusade was over, he would visit them more often and see Guillem growing up. Even if it meant seeing more of Joana? He sighed. No woman would ever hold his heart as she did, especially now she was the mother of his son. With Catharine, his love had come slowly, but with Joana it was an altogether different kind of love – wild and uncontrollable – which was why he would always have to guard himself when he was with her. But at least now he knew Guillem was at the farm, he would have some distraction from his feelings. Matthieu resolved to pray harder for the strength to resist Joana, because if he couldn't, then he would never see his son grow up. Joana had told him how the boy made her life with Aimeric more bearable, and gave her the reason she needed to work hard on the farm. She deserved better, far better, Matthieu knew; but in truth what woman ever married the man she deserved?

She had come to say goodbye, standing outside the house with Aimeric and Guillem. He could still see her waving. Fear rose in his chest at the thought of what could happen to them if Foix refused to hand over his heretics. According to Aimeric, since the crusade started the Goodmen and women had been pouring into Pamiers, for they saw the Count of Foix as their protector. For had he not allowed his sister, Esclarmonde, to join them and now his wife, the Countess Phillippa?

Matthieu shook his head. When heresy was as tolerated as it was in these lands, what choice did the Pope have, other than to send a crusade?

The cool breeze from the Garonne was welcome as he rode into Toulouse, past the Château Narbonnais and headed towards the Cathedral of Saint Étienne in the east of the city. The Cathedral had been allowed to decay scandalously under its last two bishops, but Foulques had taken a firm hand and at last things were beginning to improve. In fact, building work looked to be already in progress.

As Matthieu dismounted, he saw Bishop Foulques come around the side of the Cathedral, followed by Sir Aimeric of Castelnau and Sir Peter of Saint-Rome. He was showing them the new building work.

'Matthieu!' The Bishop's ruddy face broke into a grin.

'My lords,' Matthieu said, dropping to one knee and kissing the Bishop's ring.

'How are you, my son?' Foulques asked, urging Matthieu to rise. 'I'm pleased to see you. We've just been admiring the plans for the refurbishment of the Cathedral. Work started this month on the nave, praise God.'

It had been April when Matthieu last saw the new Bishop of Toulouse, and in the interim Foulques had filled out somewhat and now looked sleek and content. There was obviously something about his new post that was suiting him – not least the continued absence of Count Raimon.

'You look well, my lord,' he said.

'Yes, I feel it,' Foulques said. He threw an arm casually about Matthieu's shoulders. 'Have you brought us news of the crusade?'

Matthieu knew what Foulques was expecting, but how could he describe the slaughter and destitution of so many as 'good news'? Why had the heretics never paused to think about that, when they so wilfully brought this crusade down upon them all?

'I'll be pleased to give you a full report, my lord,' he said.

'Excellent,' Foulques said. 'But first we have something rather important to attend. You're welcome to join us and perhaps afterwards we can all hear your news?'

Matthieu nodded and led his horse into the run-down stables behind the Bishop's palace. Foulques had offered him an apartment at his palace in the nightmare days after Catharine's death, and Matthieu had seen it both as a way of avoiding his bitter memories and Arnald of Fanjeaux, the ever-present heretic who seemed permanently attached to Count Raimon's court.

His apartment had only a tiny solar, overlooking the gardens, and a bedroom with a kneeler on which he could pray. Everywhere inside the palace was now freshly decorated and had intricately scrolled friezes of vines and grapes atop the white painted plaster.

Downstairs, the walls were adorned with bright frescoes of Biblical scenes, and Matthieu had to pass under the stern gaze of Moses holding out the Ten Commandments, to take his seat at a long wooden table where sat an astonishing assemblage of Toulousan citizens and churchmen. Amongst them were many men of goodly calibre that Matthieu called friends. If he had known then why these good people had assembled, and what import it would have for him in the days to come, he would have walked out there and then before he became a party to it;

but by the time he learned what they were about, it was too late.

There was a smell of fresh bees wax polish and Matthieu noticed sanding marks on the table where someone had sought to smooth out its previous hard living. He accepted the jug of wine that was passed to him and poured some into his goblet. It was not made of silver, like the one he'd drunk from in Arnald-Amalric's pavilion, but earthenware, and as he raised it to his lips, Matthieu felt a stab of shame. Although he didn't believe that churchmen should live in luxury, he cursed Raimon for not taking more interest in the Cathedral before it got into such an impoverished state.

'My dear men,' Foulques began raising his own goblet. 'May I propose a toast to our new brotherhood.'

Matthieu swallowed hard. Brotherhood? The men sitting around the table had all raised their goblets. Was this a brotherhood of committed Christians, or something more sinister?

Foulques looked around. 'Shall we get down to business, gentlemen? As you know, I agreed to petition our Holy Father, the Pope, and,' he said, 'he has agreed with me.'

Smiles broke out on all the faces.

'He acknowledges that you are as much a part of this crusade as those who stand outside the gates of Carcassonne, and he wants to reward you for your steadfastness. He know that daily you live your lives in the face of terrible heresy and wants to reward you for refusing to take part in the evil practices that the heretics encourage.' Foulques paused.

'I'm talking here of money-lending, as I'm sure you realise. Our Holy Father has pleaded, nay begged, for an end to the despicable practice of usury and yet what do we find these heretic vipers doing?'

There was no answer but everyone nodded as if they knew the answer anyway.

'When our beloved Pope tried to finance action against the infidel in Jerusalem, what did he find?' Foulques looked around, his eyes gleaming, and Matthieu reflected that the years as a troubadour had given Foulques skills that few could match. Every eye in the room was locked on him. 'The money he needs is held fast in the hands of greedy, evil Jews and heretics who think nothing of asking for outrageous amounts of interest. And I know I do not need to remind you that all they own was placed on Earth by God himself.'

There were nods and murmurs of agreement.

'Well, today brothers,' Foulques continued, 'we are going to take a step towards destroying these evil practices. We are going to cleanse Toulouse of its sinners and make it a place where *godly* men can thrive. Do I need to remind you who holds all the wealth in Toulouse? Do I need to remind you who sits down to eat with them? You won't find any of them here, because they're too busy kneeling at the feet of those so-called 'Goodmen', and adoring them. As if any other than God can be described as good or worthy of adoration!' Foulques banged his fist on the table. 'Those damnable heretics encourage the money lenders and their wickedness because they *all* make money out of it, and then make use of it to further their depraved ends.'

He held out his hands in an attitude of supplication. 'Tell me, brothers, when those poor souls upon whom they prey are ready to give up their earthly lives and pray for God's forgiveness, what do they do?' He looked around. 'We've all seen them all, haven't we, hurrying and scurrying to the bedsides of usurers and fornicators? But they can only secure for them a trip to eternal damnation by refusing the Church's offer of salvation and insisting on their own so-called sacrament-' Foulques had to pause for breath and his eyes burned with righteousness. 'I tell you, brothers, the Pope *has* listened to me and there *will* be indulgences for your efforts. Until Toulouse is cleansed of heresy, we will stand up to them in the streets, and in their homes, at the Consulate and, yes, even at the court of the Count himself. If Count Raimon cannot extinguish the life of these serpents in our midst, then we must do it *ourselves*!'

The men around the table were on their feet now, but Matthieu wanted to hide his head in his hands. The sooner he could be away from here, the better. Foulques was half a step away from encouraging a full-scale rebellion against the Count: and if Raimon ever found out that Matthieu had been part of this gathering, his head would be on a pike before he knew it.

CHAPTER 42

1st October 1539
The Tower of London

At intervals through the night, Matthew was woken by a loud hammering upon the door. He would jolt awake, sometimes having barely drifted into sleep, but then – nothing. No one unlocked the door or said anything, and he would lie back upon the thin mattress and try to still his galloping heart. Time after time it happened, until he understood. They meant to weaken him.

Morning appeared as a slight change in the grey light entering his cell, and after relieving himself Matthew was surprised to hear the turn of the key in the lock. Mark walked in, pointed to the bucket and then to Matthew. By that Matthew understood that he was to follow and picked up the bucket. If he'd not been manacled, he would have been tempted to upend it upon the man's head; but then, what might be the punishment for that?

Mark led the way to the jakes and Matthew managed to pour the contents of the pail into the running water beneath, without spilling too much on himself.

'All right, back to your cell,' Mark said.

A bowl of thin pottage and a husk of bread so dry no mould could ever have grown upon it, had been left outside the door. Mark pushed Matthew in, slid the pottage and the bread after him, then locked the door.

Matthew looked at the pottage despondently. How could he eat when his bowels churned constantly and his stomach seemed strangled? The lumps floating on top of the greasy liquid made him heave. When Mark returned and saw the uneaten food, he wagged his finger.

'You haven't eaten anything,' he said. 'Well, that's all right. I won't bother bringing you any more.'

After he left, Matthew looked at the door with new feeling. Did that mean the next time somebody opened it, they would be coming to interrogate him? He stretched his manacled hands above his head, as far as he could – higher, up on his toes, reaching, reaching... What would it feel like to be stretched more than that, an inch at a time? Would he cry, faint, plead, scream? Probably all of those. If he fainted, they would likely wake him with a bucket of water, not even allowing him the peace of insensibility. He knew that his joints and sinews would rip and pop as they were stretched beyond their limits. Dear God, don't think like that, he urged himself, shaking. You're doing their work for them.

He sat down upon the mattress and sniffed. It didn't smell too bad now. Perhaps he was getting used to it. Automatically, he began to pray, chanting the wods inside his head until he felt a little more calm. *Et ecce ego vobiscum sum omnibus diebus, usque ad consummationem sæculi* – I am with you always, even unto the end of the world.

Matthew thought back to the day he had finally entered the gates of Glastonbury Abbey as a novice, glad with the knowledge that he didn't have to leave again. His mother had died peacefully, all thanks be to Saint Thomas, and was now taking her well-earned rest in Heaven. He remembered even further back, to the very first time he'd seen Abbot Whiting – a wonderful, godly man, with the wisest, kindest face. Now the blessed Abbot might be incarcerated here too – but please God in a better cell than this one.

The rattle of the keys sent his guts into spasm. Mark walked in.

'Get up,' he said.

On shuddering legs, Matthew staggered before Mark to the spiral staircase and up one flight to an iron-bound door, where Mark knocked.

'Yes?' said a deep voice.

'I've brought the prisoner for you, Sir William,' Mark said.

'Come in then, the door's open.'

They walked into a room so brightly lit that Matthew had to close his eyes, but he struggled to open them quickly so that he could scan for the contraption, cruelly nick-named 'The Duke of Exeter's daughter' - after the Constable who introduced it into the Tower. But there was nothing resembling its description. One wall sported an array of hooks, which he didn't like the look of, and a fire burned hotly in the grate with an assortment of pokers near to it – surely not all necessary to prod the coals?

But in truth the room was cosy, rather than threatening, and his heart calmed a little.

'Sit down,' Sir William said. He was smartly and expensively dressed in a black velvet doublet and his cloak was turned back with a sleek lining of black genet. 'I am Sir William Kingston, Constable of the Tower.'

Matthew's fear abated a little. He had expected some brutish torturer, not the Constable himself, but his confusion grew. Surely he wasn't important enough to warrant the attention of the Constable?

'Good day, Sir William,' he said, as politely as he could, taking the stool indicated to him.

'And good day to you, too,' Sir William said, unscrolling a parchment and pursing his lips. 'Now then,' he said, looking up briefly, 'let's see if we can't get this sorted out quickly and then we can all get on with what we were doing. There are matters of state coming up that will keep me very busy soon. I don't want this to drag on any longer than it has to.'

'I'll help you as much as I'm able,' Matthew said, 'but I have no idea why I'm here.'

'No idea, eh?' Sir William looked up benignly and nodded to Mark. A heavy blow near knocked Matthew's head from his body and he struggled to right himself, his ears ringing.

'Right, then,' Sir William said. 'Shall we start again?'

*

After they had finished with him, Matthew spent another night on the foul mattress. This time the banging on the door echoed the banging in his head. Whenever he tried to open his swollen eyes, bile leaped into his throat, and he drifted back into a nauseated stupor almost straight away.

Sometimes he dreamed that he was on the rack and his body had been stretched beyond recognition. Sometimes he dreamed that he was back in the crypt at Glastonbury where the man with the strange moustache now regarded him sadly. I did my best, he wanted to say; but the silent stranger merely shook his head and looked away.

When his bladder could no longer be ignored, Matthew heaved himself up and stifled a groan whilst he peed into the bucket. Mark had given him a good kicking, that was for sure – no mercy in his strangely unfocussed eyes, no hint of what he was thinking as he put all that effort into his swinging boot.

They hadn't seemed much interested in the reliquary at all, and only wanted to know *where* had it come from – *which abbey*? He told them that he wasn't a monk, that he was a married man and had given the King's agents a marriage licence to prove it. Thank goodness Johanna had left with the ship – or he wouldn't have dared to mention her name before them.

He lay down, wincing as his bruised back made contact with the mattress. If this was the treatment they gave him, what of the Abbot? Would they be so brutal with a man of his age? Matthew fought back his tears. If only he knew the Abbot was well. It would make everything more bearable – that and knowing Johanna and the reliquary were safe in France.

CHAPTER 43

July
Station View, Wesley village, Yorkshire

The large brown envelope was addressed in Blanche's handwriting, contained directions to the apartment in France and two sets of keys. Next to it were Jo's travel documents, including an up-to-date passport. Blanche's apartment was in the village of Saint Gilles de Loire, not far from Chinon, and the downstairs neighbour, Jean-Yves, would arrange to meet her if she let him know when she was arriving.

Jean-Yves had sent a message to say that a Monsieur Moreau was interested in buying the apartment and could one of them come out to advise? Jo didn't trust herself to actually speak to Mat and was unwilling to risk any misinterpretation through e-mail; so she wrote to him. It had taken a long time to get the words right – friendly but neutral, and it seemed an age before she got a reply from him – carefully phrased, giving nothing away. How was she, how was the house next door (it had been rented out to a middle aged couple who said they loved living there) what did she think about selling the apartment in France?

Waves of longing swept over her. She could imagine his hands as he wrote – how she loved those hands. Dammit. Why was her life still so entangled with him? Even now, her body ached at the thought of him. You did me no favours, Blanche, she thought, watching the birds squabble over the feeders outside her window. The sooner they sold the apartment the better. It would be one less reason to have to communicate with him.

*

She decided to drive all the way this time and once off the ferry, the road flew by. She wondered how often Blanche had visited this apartment. It was strange that she'd never mentioned it before and it definitely wasn't like her to be so reticent. Blanche was normally only too keen to share stories about her holidays.

The Loire came into view at Saumur and Jo followed its sleepy flow eastwards towards Saint Gilles. The village was on the south side of the river, a collection of half-timbered houses that seemed incredibly well-preserved and little changed from medieval times. She pulled into a car park and found a boulangerie that was still open, its low door nestling beneath the overhanging corbel.

'*Bonjour, Mademoiselle*!'

The proprietor's smile was warm and welcoming and Jo looked into a glass counter crammed with mouth-watering confections. She chose a tart tatin and two croissants, then sat in the car munching them whilst watching the Loire and the occasional traffic flow past. Blanche had sketched a map of how to get to the apartment and Jo squinted at it. Rue Saint Gilles, yes, she was on that now. Drive towards the centre and then take a left turn. Why, the apartment was practically on the river! Jo decided to walk and chose a path leading down to the river's edge. Warm air blew around her bare legs and the geraniums that clustered on every terrace, ledge and step bloomed like an entirely different species from the ones she'd left at home.

Blanche's apartment was number twenty-two. Most of the houses Jo had passed were set back behind high wrought-iron gates; but there was a sign on the wall of an old warehouse for numbers twenty-one and twenty-two that pointed down a narrow road. Jo checked Blanche's map again. Yes, that would be them. Number twenty-one was the ground floor and twenty-two the upper. The whole building looked very old – perhaps even another warehouse – for there was a gantry high up on the wall that bordered the waterfront. To Jo's delight, she saw that Blanche's apartment had a window overlooking the river, and there was a walled space behind the building that must be a garden. Twenty-two's entrance was a cream painted door with a single pane of bulls-eye glass. It was covered by a trellised canopy that supported a rambling white rose, and in front of it was a faded coir mat saying 'Welcome'. To the side stood a cast iron boot-scraper in the shape of a hedgehog – Blanche had one just like it back at home. Very Yorkshire, Blanche, Jo thought, a tear starting in her eye.

She looked around for the entrance to twenty-one. Despite the sign pointing down the lane, the neighbour's door was back on the riverside. Three cats lay dozing on the doorstep and Jo bent down to stroke their sun-warmed fur as she waited for Jean-Yves to answer. They arched lazily against her hand and she smiled to herself. Oh, to have as few cares as a cat. Jean-Yves opened the door and held his hand out towards her.

'You are here, at last!' he said, in accented English, and gave her a kiss on both cheeks so that she caught the lingering smell of cigarettes. He had dark hair and a deeply tanned face with a very white, welcoming smile. 'I've wanted to meet Blanche's niece for many years. We were sorry to hear about her death, and so soon after her husband – it's terrible, *non*?'

Jo froze. Husband? Had she heard him correctly? Fortunately, Jean-Yves had gone ahead to unlock the door of twenty-two so she was glad he couldn't see her confusion. Mistaking her for Blanche's niece was understandable, but *husband*? They climbed the flight of stairs inside the entrance and Jean-Yves led her into the lounge, where a large casement window overlooked the Loire.

'What a wonderful view!'

'It is beautiful, *non*?' Jean-Yves said. He walked into the kitchen and pulled open the door of the fridge. 'My wife has put some coffee and some milk in here and there is an Intermarche in Saint Gilles, opposite the main parking.'

'Thank you,' Jo said, looking around with delight. The kitchen had a distinctly retro look with an old fashioned stove and duck-egg blue cabinets. 'I'll go there later. I've already had some croissants from the boulangerie. Thank your wife, for me, will you?'

'Of course,' he said, giving her a little bow of his head. 'Enjoy your stay, Mademoiselle. Er, Monsieur Moreau-'

'Yes?'

'He asked if he could come tomorrow, to speak to you.'

'Do you know him?' Jo asked. She was already beginning to wish it was possible to keep the apartment. It was in such a lovely setting. If only things had been different between her and Mat.

'Not well. He is a friend of my friend, but since you didn't visit, I wondered if you wanted to sell the apartment?'

'It's certainly a possibility,' she said. 'Tell him I'll speak to him tomorrow. In the afternoon? I'd like to do some exploring in the morning.'

'Exploring? Ah, yes,' he said, 'we have some of your royal family near here, did you know?'

'No.' She hadn't had the time to do any research about the surrounding areas.

'Yes, Richard, '*Cœur de Lion*', Henri Plantagenet and the beautiful Aliénor of Aquitaine. Their, effigies, I believe you call, them-'

She nodded.

'Are found in Fontevraud Abbey, not far from here. Poor Henri died just along the water at Chinon, betrayed by his sons. As a father, I can imagine how he felt.'

Jean-Yves closed his eyes, theatrically, and she smiled, liking him.

'How many children do you have?'

'Six,' he said, opening his eyes again. 'Three boys and three girls. All married now. Two *en Angleterre*, two *en Australie*, and two *au Canada*. We are proud, of course, but we wish we could see them more often.' He shrugged. 'But what can we do, it is the way of the world.' He walked to the door. '*Au revoir*, *Mademoiselle*. If you need anything, please...' He mimed knocking at the door.

'Thank you, Jean-Yves,' she said. '*Vous êtes très gentil.*'

'*Pas de quoi*. I will ring you when I hear from Monsieur Moreau.'

After he had gone, Jo collected her car and then continued her exploration of the apartment. When she put her head in at the bedroom door and saw the double bed and two dressing gowns hanging behind the door, she could not put off her suspicions any longer. Why, the wily old bird! All those holidays 'on her own', and not telling any one about this apartment. Could the 'husband' have been called Patrick, by any chance?

The iron bedstead had a netted canopy over it, and someone had laid out clean bedding. On the bare painted floorboards lay two colourful rag rugs, one at either side of the bed, and on the walls Jo spotted some beautiful floral still-life paintings. When she went over for a closer look, she recognised Blanche's signature. Another secret!

Jo sat down before the white painted dressing table. It had a speckled mirror and she tried to imagine Blanche sitting here with Patrick looking affectionately over her shoulder. Should she have been able to guess? But they had kept their secret very closely. Jo thought back over the years she had known them; the birthdays, the anniversaries of Patrick's ordination, Christmas even. Blanche had often been there, in the background perhaps – but there none-the-less.

Suddenly impatient, Jo went into the bathroom and turned the taps on the roll-topped bath. Jean-Yves had showed her how the heating worked and she found some lavender oil in the Lloyd Loom cabinet. Lying in the deep tub, watching the clouds skim by outside the window, Jo willed herself to relax. Blanche's apartment was a charming place and she could be here for a full ten days if she wanted.

But inevitably her thoughts strayed to Mat. He was unable to help with the selling of the apartment, he'd said, because he'd been transferred to a new post in Rome. Did she mind going by herself to sort out the sale? She'd been disappointed at the time. No matter how often she told herself it was better not to see him, she still yearned for him; but now he was in Rome he was more closely bound to his Church than ever. It was like having a rival with limitless charms, an underlying threat to her happiness which she knew would never lessen until she managed to find another outlet for her feelings...

Simon, one of the administrators at work, had asked her out a few weeks ago and she'd thought hard about whether to take him up on the offer. She was fearful of having to work together if things went wrong, but they had a perfectly pleasant evening, saw a perfectly pleasant film at the cinema, went for a drink afterwards and shared a perfectly pleasant goodnight kiss. The next weekend they'd gone for a perfectly pleasant walk on the moors. The weather was pleasant – not too hot, not too cold – the conversation flowed and they shared a perfectly pleasant picnic in the shade of an overhanging rock. Simon had pulled her towards him and they had another, perfectly pleasant kiss.

Aargh! Jo slammed her fists into the water and it fountained over the sides of the bath and onto the floor. She didn't want perfectly bloody pleasant! She wanted heart stopping kisses, a feeling of being where she was meant to be… she wanted Mat!

CHAPTER 44

August 1209
Toulouse

As early as possible, Matthieu left the Bishop's palace and rode to the Château Narbonnais. It was still grey dawn and the smells and bustle he normally associated with Toulouse were absent. Heavy rain during the night had washed the gutters clean and Matthieu took a breath of air, fresh from the river, then squared his shoulders. If Raimondet was ready to leave, they could be at Carcassonne by tomorrow evening.

As he rode he worried about the events at the Bishop's Palace. Was Foulques aware of just how many spies Count Raimon had in Toulouse, or did he simply not care, now the crusade had been so successful? He caught sight of Bernard waiting with a hunting party in the courtyard of the Château. His one-time squire was now a lord in his own right and was mounted upon a chestnut gelding and carried a sparrowhawk upon his fist. Excited dogs milled around the legs of the horses, panting and whining to be off.

'Matthieu!' Bernard's eyes were alight with pleasure. 'How are you?'

'Well enough,' Matthieu said.

'How goes the crusade?' Bernard said, his pleasure fading quickly.

'It all depends upon where you stand,' Matthieu said.

The hooded bird had hunched down into its shoulders as though expecting a great weight to fall upon its head.

'I heard what happened at Béziers,' Bernard said, quietly, 'and Carcassonne. What do they they intend to do next?'

'I don't know, but if I were you I should look to your family and see they're safe,' Matthieu said. He was still unsure of Bernard's leanings, ever since the incident with the belt. 'It's hazardous to have any truck with heretics now, however closely related they are to you. Do you understand what I'm saying?'

Bernard frowned.

'What I mean is,' Matthieu said, 'look to your affiliations, Bernard, make sure they're safe.'

'My affiliations?' Bernard pulled his horse's head around. 'Are you saying they're in question, Matthieu?'

Matthieu shook his head. 'Not as far as I know, but soon everyone will be under scrutiny. Believe me, they're going to start burning anyone they suspect of heresy.'

'So you think they're coming here next – to Toulouse – do you?'

Bernard's face had paled. 'I thought the fact that the Count is with them meant his lands were safe, whilst he's on crusade?'

'Yes,' Matthieu said, spreading his hands. The last thing he wanted to do was start a panic. 'But that doesn't mean the heretics are safe, does it?'

Bernard's mouth slipped into a sullen line. 'The Goodmen mean no harm to anyone. They set up schools and hospitals for the poor, which is more than the Roman church has ever done here.'

Matthieu sighed. 'Don't you see that they only do these things because they want to lead people away from the true Church? They laugh at the cross and the sacraments, and are enemies of the true faith. Nothing they do or say can be truly 'good', can it? Only God is good. Those schools and hospitals merely seek to ensnare the unwary. Listen to me, Bernard, the crusaders are going to burn heretics because they want to show people what will be waiting for them when they die. And it isn't Heaven! '

Bernard's friends started calling to him, urging him to hurry, and Matthieu was suddenly seized with a terrible vision of the flower of Toulouse's youth, lying dead outside the broken walls of their city. Above their blood soaked bodies flew the triumphant banners of the crusade. He shuddered, shaking the vision away.

'Listen to me, I beseech you,' he said, putting a hand on Bernard's arm, 'if you care for your family. Have nothing to do with those mad people.'

'Good day to you, Matthieu,' Bernard said, turning away. 'I will think on what you've said, but I still say the Roman church has a lot to learn from those they call heretics. Good day.'

Matthieu watched the hunting party leave, and waited for his heart to slow down. The vision had been so vivid. Was he simply tired and his mind playing tricks? For weeks now his dreams had been full of awful portents, but this was the first time he'd been troubled with them in daylight.

After arranging for the stabling of his horse, Matthieu went to find Raimon of Ricaud. He was the Warden of Toulouse, the Count's closest friend and adviser, and his rooms were adjacent to the Count's. Two armed guards stood at his door. Matthieu knew both men well by sight but they still insisted on taking his sword and dagger, and kept him waiting whilst they checked with the Warden before allowing Matthieu to enter.

The Warden's dark eyes had sunken into his sallow face and he looked as though he rarely saw life outside the Château these days. About him towered stacks of parchments, piled so high that he was almost hidden behind them. Being next in command to a man like the Count of Toulouse was an onerous task.

'Ah, there you are,' Ricaud said. 'I've been expecting you.' The Warden stood up and Matthieu couldn't helpadmire the quality of the velvet gown he wore casually belted at his hips. 'I hear we're to travel to Carcassonne together, with Raimondet?'

Matthieu nodded, musing that the Count had obviously not trusted him to deliver the message himself.

'Indeed,' he said. 'When will you be ready to leave?'

The Warden looked out of the window and permitted himself a smile

'Very soon, but I'm waiting for Raimondet to wake up.'

With some alarm, Matthieu realised that the smile had stopped short of the corners of Ricaud's mouth. Had the Warden already heard about the meeting at the Bishop's Palace?

'Tell me about the crusade while we're waiting,' Ricaud said. 'Of course I've had word from the Count, but I'm sure you can add the details.' He sat down and gestured for Matthieu to sit at the other side of his desk.

Matthieu told him what he knew, ending with the imprisonment of the Viscount Trencavel.

'So they put him in chains, in his own dungeon...' The Warden shook his head in wonder. 'Even though they'd guaranteed his safety. What did the Count say?'

'It's not repeatable,' Matthieu said.

The Warden gave a bitter laugh. 'Too close for comfort, eh? Luckily for us, Raimon is more cunning than a fox on heat.' Ricaud paused and looked up at the ceiling. 'Why does he want Raimondet over there? I would have thought the boy was safer here.'

Before Matthieu could answer, Raimondet bounced into the room, yawning loudly. He'd grown at least two inches since Matthieu last saw him and there was a smudge of dark hair beginning on his upper lip.

'Matthieu! You're here!' The young count-to-be hurried over and embraced his tutor.

Matthieu saw Ricaud's face slip and sighed inwardly. Jealously of his close relationship with Raimondet had made him some unwelcome enemies.

'But I'm going to Carcassonne today,' Raimondet said, frowning. 'I thought to find you there. Now I shall miss you.'

'Except, I'm coming too,' Matthieu said. 'Your father sent me to escort you, along with the Warden here.'

'Really?' Raimondet's sulk evaporated. 'Then you'll be able to tell me the rest of the story of Roland whilst we ride, won't you? Are we leaving soon?'

'As soon as you're both on a horse,' Ricaud said. 'I'll meet you in the courtyard.'

*

Matthieu swung into his saddle, and counted the armed men assembled with them. No wonder Count Raimon was always short of money. These men were all mercenaries. He pursed his lips, remembering how he had witnessed the Count swearing on sacred relics that he wouldn't use mercenary fighters again, and yet here were at least a dozen of them.

The first night of their journey was spent with one of the lords of the Lauragais, bedded down in a strangely hushed household. To Matthieu, it seemed that the whole of the countryside was holding its breath, wondering what the crusaders would do next. They reached Carcassonne the following day, flying the Cross of Toulouse and with Raimondet in a cheerful mood. Matthieu felt boosted by his young lord's good humour.

'Why did Roland refuse to send for help when he could?' Raimondet asked, as Matthieu finished his recounting of the Song of Roland.

'You tell me,' he said, ever the tutor.

Raimondet frowned, trying to work it out. 'Did he think they were too far away and wouldn't hear him?'

'I don't believe so,' Matthieu said, and held his breath.

'So he must have thought he could beat the Saracens on his own?'

'Yes.'

'But he was wrong?'

'Yes.'

'So he was stupid?'

'Is it always stupid to get things wrong?'

Raimondet flashed a smile. 'He was very brave.'

'He was responsible for a lot of his men losing their lives.'

'Yes. He should have thought about his men, not just about being brave.'

Matthieu could have embraced the lad there and then. 'If he'd blown his horn he could have saved his men, but then he'd have had to admit that he couldn't win by himself.'

They continued a while in silence and Matthieu smiled to himself. The lad was only twelve years old, but he was developing a wisdom far beyond his years, and he loved him as though he was his own.

From the outside, the citadel of Carcassonne was the stuff of legends; and when it came into sight, Raimondet stirred restlessly in his saddle, looking at Matthieu with shining eyes. Built high above the river, the walls of the cité were punctuated by towers almost beyond number, and looked invincible. Yet, Carcassonne had held out less than a month.

That's what I was trying to explain to Bernard, Matthieu thought. No thing and no one can hold out against God.

The crusaders, bored since the taking of the cité, had set up lists and quintains, and were riding around on horseback, trying to unseat each other. Matthieu watched a young rider charge towards the quintain, his lance held steady and level, and winced as the lad hit the shield full-on. He could almost hear the crunch of teeth.

'Look out!' he shouted, just as the lad was buffeted off his horse by the counter weight. Raimondet laughed delightedly.

'Come now,' Matthieu said, but he was amused too. 'Let's see how much fun you think it is when you're the one getting knocked off.'

'But I shan't get knocked off,' Raimondet said, his chin lifting arrogantly. 'I'm soon to go to the court of my Uncle of England, where I shall be taught by Sir William Marshal himself.'

'Are you indeed?' Matthieu said, wondering what political manoeuvring of his father lay behind that particular promise. William Marshal was said to have defeated five hundred knights during his time on the tourney circuit. 'A worthy tutor,' he said, 'and one with many stories to tell, I don't doubt. Do you know he was the only man to ever manage to unseat your Uncle Richard?'

'No!' Raimondet's eyes grew round with wonder.

'Yes. And it wasn't in a tournament, it was for real.'

'Tell me!'

So he told Raimondet the story of how his grandfather, the second Henry of England, had fallen out with his sons, and how Raimondet's Uncle Richard, 'the Lionhearted', and Philippe of France had attacked Henry at Le Mans.

'Your grandfather was getting old by then,' Matthieu said, 'and the barons knew it. They were looking towards the coming of the new king, who was most likely to be Richard. So they held back – but not the Marshal. He guarded your grandfather's back as he fled for his life.'

'I could never imagine fighting *my* father,' Raimondet said.

'And I pray God you never will,' Matthieu replied, fervently.

'So how did William Marshal unseat my Uncle Richard?' Raimondet prompted.

'Richard was in the party pursuing your grandfather and the Marshal engaged him on the road. He charged straight for your uncle who shouted out that he was unarmed – as if any man would go about unarmed in a war.'

'And then?'

'William Marshal killed your uncle's horse with his lance, and knocked Richard to the ground.'

'Poor Uncle Richard!'

'Hardly,' Matthieu said, trying to conceal his mirth. 'The Marshal could have done a lot worse.'

'What do you mean?'

'Well, he could have killed Richard if he'd wanted to, or even if he'd misjudged his aim.'

'Surely he wouldn't have dared?' Raimondet looked astounded.

'I wouldn't be too sure. Anyway, when your grandfather was buried at Fontevraud Abbey, Richard and the Marshal met at his funeral. Everyone expected a confrontation.'

'What did my Uncle Richard say?' Raimondet asked. 'Did he challenge the Marshal to a duel?'

'No,' Matthieu laughed. 'He gave him a position.'

'What?' Raimondet's eyebrows drew together in puzzlement. 'Wasn't he angry? Especially as the Marshal *could* have killed him if he'd missed.'

'Yes, that's what your uncle said; but the Marshal said that if he'd really wanted to kill Richard, he would have done so – which is true because he's such a capable knight. You see?'

Raimondet lapsed into silence for a few moments. 'But I'm still not sure why he offered him a position.'

Matthieu looked at his pupil kindly. 'In addition to his jousting feats, the Marshal is also famous for his loyalty. That's why Richard wanted him; and in your time, I hope you'll look for such men too, and rightly reward their loyalty. Men like that are more valuable to you than riches.'

Matthieu caught Raimon of Ricaud looking at him, and the unease he'd felt in Toulouse grew. Ricaud's loyalty to the Count was beyond question, but Matthieu couldn't help wondering about himself. If he was in the Marshal's position, could he honestly say he would favour the father over the son?

*

Raimondet received an affectionate welcome from his father and Matthieu left them alone whilst he wandered along the river, looking up at the battlements of the cité, which were now manned by the crusaders army. He was only half surprised the Count hadn't chosen to take up more comfortable lodgings inside the walls, as had the other lords. After all, who would want to live on top of his imprisoned nephew? Matthieu didn't want to go inside either; the memories of the day he'd ridden in with King Pedro were still too vivid in his mind. At least here people had escaped with their lives, if not their possessions. Had Jesus not said it was easier for a camel to go through the eye of a needle than for a rich man to enter the Kingdom of Heaven? Perhaps in many ways they should count themselves lucky.

Matthieu stripped off and bathed in the river then tried to doze in the shade of a huge willow, but the next thing he knew, Raimondet had landed on his chest and started a play-fight. The boy was clearly excited and after Matthieu managed to fight him off, he listened to how the all the great lords had wanted to meet Raimondet and how the Count of Saint Pol had even offered to let him ride his destrier – except his father would not let him.

Perhaps the Count's plan was working after all, Matthieu marvelled. Whatever quarrel the Church had with the father, anyone could see that Raimondet was different, would *be* different in his time as Count – if only that time were allowed to come.

*

In the days that followed, Arnald-Amalric offered the Viscountcy of Béziers and Carcassonne to the Duke of Burgundy and then to the Counts of Nevers and Saint Pol, but they all declined, saying they had enough lands of their own and would not want to take another's birthright. Matthieu was much cheered by this and wondered if the Viscount Trencavel might even be freed, but then he heard that someone *had* agreed, and that someone was Simon of Montfort.

Count Raimon was inconsolable. He refused to let anyone near him, for two whole days, except his son and Ricaud, and when he emerged from his solitude he looked years older. His hair hung limply to his shoulders and his expression was that of a cornered animal.

'I have to speak to Montfort,' he said, not quite meeting Matthieu's eyes. 'I want you and Raimondet to come with me.'

The Count mounted his horse like a man going to his own funeral. They rode in single file into the citadel, with a party of armed knights at their back.

Simon of Montfort had made himself quite at home in the Viscount's chambers, and was directing everything with an air of brisk functionality. His eyes narrowed as he saw Count Raimon and Matthieu sighed inwardly.

'My congratulations,' Raimon said, without warmth, 'on becoming the new Viscount of Carcassonne and Béziers.'

Montfort smiled thinly. 'Thank you,' he said, indicating a seat for the Count but not taking one himself. 'I hope I can rely on you in the next stage of the campaign? Arnald-Amalric is pushing me to do more to catch the heretics, but the northern knights have completed their forty days service and want to be on their way home.'

The Count tried hard to look regretful, but failed. 'In my capacity as the Count of Toulouse and Marquis of Provence,' he said, 'I can assure you that every assistance will be made available to you. And as for the heretics in my own lands, you've no need to waste time and men for I gave my assurances to the legate, Milo. All I need is enough time to go home and make the arrangements myself.'

Montfort took his time replying, watching the Count's face and weighing every nuance of his words. 'Of course. May I say that I too would like to offer every assistance to you, as far as my resources will allow. I hope that we can become better – friends.'

The Count held up his hand. 'I hope for more than that, Viscount. May

I propose an alliance between our two families. What do you say? A betrothal between my son and your daughter?'

Raimondet's body stiffened and Matthieu could barely hide his shock. Raimondet was already betrothed to the sister of the King of Aragon!

The new leader of the crusade took in a slow breath and rocked gently on his feet as if calculating a sword thrust. 'I'm sure my little Amicie would be a perfect match for your son,' he said, looking at Raimondet. 'Anyone can see what a splendid young man he is.'

'Thank you,' the Count said. Raimondet's face stayed blank but Matthieu could see a resentful muscle working at the corner of his jaw. 'And then our lands will be united into one; something I was never able to achieve whilst my nephew held sway.'

Matthieu barely managed to stop his jaw from falling open. Not content with vanquishing his nephew, Raimon was now plotting to take over his lands!

'I'll have my scribes draw up an agreement,' Montfort said. 'I take it you'll be able to sort things out with the King of Aragon?'

Matthieu found his breath stuck somewhere between in and out as he tried to imagine King Pedro's response.

'Of course,' the Count said. 'Leave everything to me.'

CHAPTER 45

3rd October 1539
England

The messenger returned as they neared London. Lord Lisle would soon be on his way back to Calais, he said, but was presently at Hampton Court with the King. Johanna listened to this news with a mixture of anticipation and dismay. The last time she'd been at Hampton Court was when Queen Jane died. How ironic that, of all the King's palaces, she would have to elicit his aid in the very place she had refused him.

It was now eleven days since Matthew had been arrested – and all because of four diamonds which he knew nothing about. Poor Matthew! Johanna was finding it hard to forgive Mother Florence and Abbot Whiting. How could they have knowingly put their lives in jeopardy like this? It was one thing to suffer torture in order to safeguard the precious relic of a saint; yet another to be tortured for the sake of baubles.

Husee and Johanna took a barge upstream and eventually reached the red brick walls of Hampton Court. As always, it was a busy place and the sounds of voices and horses hooves echoed around its walls. A group of mounted men were setting off to hunt and Johanna scanned them quickly, but the King was not amongst them. Did that mean he was unwell? It wasn't like Henry to miss a chance to go hunting.

Husee took his leave and went to locate Lord Lisle. Johanna waited nervously, rehearsing what she would say to his Lordship, her frozen fingers curled into numb fists. Time passed so slowly that she began to feel incredibly tired. A delicious aroma of roasting meat wafted its way towards her from the nearby kitchens and she longed for a good meal and some warmth to curl up in. She patted the diamonds in the pouch under her clothes, checking for the umpteenth time that they were still there, feeling again a sense of calm emanating from the largest stone. Why did it do that, she wondered? What about that stone, as opposed to the others gave it that power?

She looked around impatiently. What was keeping Husee? Johanna pulled her cloak tightly around her and tried to still her chattering teeth.

Eventually she saw him coming towards her.

'His Lordship is with the King in the Privy Chamber and cannot receive you, but says you may wait on him in his rooms.'

The suite of rooms designated for Lord Lisle was not far from those of the King, an honoured position. In the solar, Johanna sat on a velvet covered chair and presently a page came to offer her refreshment. Husee disappeared, and she sat alone, warming herself before the fire and sipping a cup of Lord Lisle's excellent Burgundy wine. What happened from now on was in God's hands, of that she was sure. If she could manage to be received into the King's presence, she would throw herself on his mercy. Henry might have many faults, but she knew he could be kind – if it suited him.

She chewed her lip, fighting despondency; and then she heard the door of Lord Lisle's solar start to open and quickly pulled back her feet from the fire. But it was Anne Basset who entered.

'Johanna!' Anne came to embrace her. 'I can't believe you're here.'

'Anne!' Johanna stood to accept Anne's embrace, noting that her friend's smile did not quite stir her deep brown eyes. 'How are you?' she said, admiring Anne's crimson taffeta gown and the long rope of matching pearls at her neck.

'Improving,' Anne said, sitting down, 'but the King is sending me to stay with my cousin, Denny. There are plenty of good walks where she lives and the air is clean – I hope to feel fully well, soon. And how are you, Johanna?'

'Well,' Johanna said, 'though nervous. Has his Lordship told you why I'm here?'

'Yes,' Anne said, frowning. 'May I be frank with you, Johanna? I don't really know why you've come. The King was incredibly angry when you disappeared without telling him, and I'm not sure he's forgiven you.'

Johanna's heart trembled. 'I know, Anne, but once he knows what I have brought him, I know he'll thank his Lordship.'

'How can you be so sure?' Anne said, glancing at Johanna's middle.

'Oh no. It's nothing like that,' Johanna gasped, crossing her arms over her belly. 'How could you think such a thing?'

'He *was* very fond of you before, is all,' Anne shrugged. She signalled to the page to pour her some wine. 'Whether he'll see you rather depends upon how he's feeling, but Johanna, I won't forgive you if you put our family at risk-'

'I'm not putting anyone at risk,' Johanna said. 'I'm trying to save someone, if you must know.'

Anne made a little face. 'Some monk or other, so I heard. Are you sure he's worth all the effort, Johanna?'

She stared at Anne, unable to believe how callous her friend had become.

'He hasn't done anything, Anne. It's my fault he was arrested so the least I can do is try to help him. They'll torture him in the Tower, but he doesn't know anything about why he's there.'

'And you do?' Anne's eyes gleamed. 'My mother says he must be an exceptionally handsome chap to merit all this devotion on your part. If I were you, I'd have stayed in France, where I was safe.'

Johanna bit back her anger. Matthew *was* handsome; enough to turn women's heads, but she was appalled at what Anne was suggesting.

'Oh, never mind,' Anne sighed. 'I can see you're hell-bent on this mission of yours.' She waved her hand, dismissing the page. 'His Majesty has been in poor spirits of late on account of his leg, and he walks with a limp – that is unless there's someone near-by to impress.' She lowered her voice. 'Sometimes his whole leg swells up and the smell is terrible. Sometimes he can barely take the pain and that's when we all try to stay out of his way. Pity poor Heneage and the others in the Privy Chamber. There's no escaping for them.'

The King had always been proud of his physique and he must be devastated to be so handicapped.

'I suppose it's been hard for him since Jane's death,' Johanna said, taking another sip of wine. She longed to down the whole cup, but knew she would need all of her wits about her if she had any hope of petitioning the King.

'Yes, it has, ' Anne said, 'and you can be sure the Howards have been parading their daughters in front of him as often as possible, hoping to 'cheer him up'!'

'I hear His Majesty has been very kind to you,' Johanna said, watching Anne carefully. The last thing she wanted to do was provoke her friend's jealousy.

'He has,'Anne said, carefully arranging the skirts of her gown, 'but I dare not ask him for favours, not even for my mother or sisters.'

Johanna paused, registering the point. 'Do you hope to marry him, Anne?'

'Gracious, no!' Anne shook her head. 'I am of the opinion that the King should marry a foreign princess – someone with royal blood who knows how to behave at court.' Anne sighed. 'Won't you tell me what you have for him?'

'I'm sorry,' Johanna said, sadly. 'That's something I can only tell the King.'

Anne's eyes narrowed. 'You are a mystery, Johanna. Do you really think Henry will be so interested in whatever it is that he'll free this monk of yours? Or are you hoping to tempt him, as you did before?'

'No!' Johanna said. 'I refused to become his mistress then, Anne, and I'll refuse him now – if he asks me, which I doubt!'

'Oh, Johanna, you're such a *fool*!' Anne said. 'Why don't you save yourself, and us, a lot of trouble by going back to France?'

Before Johanna could think of a suitable answer, Husee walked in.

'Ah, Lady Anne,' he said, sweeping a bow. 'Your lady mother has sent several jars of the codiniac and damson conserve the King said he likes, and she wishes you to be sure to tell him that she made them for him herself.' He stopped and stared up at the ceiling with a finger to his mouth, as though trying to remember something.

'And?'Anne leaned forwards eagerly.

'Oh yes.' Husee smiled. 'She's also sent you the lace you asked for and three gold crowns.'

'Husee!' Anne clapped her hands. 'At last! Let me see the lace, do. I can hardly wait to sew it onto my gown. No one here can make lace like my lady mother. Let's hope the King notices and asks for some for his new queen.'

'That would be wondrous,' Husee said, somewhat drily.

'What would?' said a deep voice.

The man who stepped into the room had a shock of grey hair, but his back was still ramrod straight.

'My lord.' Johanna and Anne got to their feet and curtseyed. Lord Lisle scowled at them both.

'May I introduce the lady, Johanna Grenfell,' Husee began.

'I know full well who she is,' Lord Lisle said. 'What I don't know is why she's here.'

'Her Ladyship has written to you, has she not?' Johanna asked, dismay tightening her chest.

'Lady Honor writes to everyone,' Lord Lisle said. 'It comes of being abroad most of the time.'

Johanna was taken aback. Anne's step-father had been so kind to her when she was in Calais.

'Forgive me,' she said, eyes downcast.

'For goodness sake, Johanna!' Lord Lisle said. 'I've read the letter, but it didn't make any sense to me. Something about you having something the King really wants, and I should ask for an audience for you.' Lord Lisle put his hands on his hips. 'And what's all this nonsense about a monk? I won't be party to any of this, Johanna. In fact, I want you gone from here now.' He poured himself some wine and went to stand by the window.

Johanna felt the burn in her cheeks and turned to look at Anne, but her friend seemed suddenly fascinated by a stray thread on her sleeve. She looked at Husee, but he was already moving towards the door.

'Escort her back to London,' Lord Lisle said, over his shoulder, 'and Johanna, I don't want you to associate with my household ever again – do I make myself clear?'

'But, my lord...' Johanna cast one last look at her friend and was shocked to see Anne hiding a smirk. Could she have turned her step-father's mind against her, despite Lady Lisle's recommendation? Was she so frightened of losing her place in the King's favour?

She followed Husee out of the door and for a wild moment considered rushing into the King's Presence Chamber and demanding to see him; but she knew such behaviour was more likely to get her thrown into jail than obtain an audience. Tears pricked at her eyes but she clenched her teeth and fists, and held her head high. This was not a place to show weakness, she remembered that well enough. As she descended the great staircase, some men were on their way up and she recognised the thick set man with dark greying hair as Baron Cromwell, the Lord Privy Seal. She turned her face away quickly, overcome by the notion that Cromwell might well have interrogated Matthew by now, and be looking for her.

Outside the palace, the sun was shining but she couldn't enjoy its warmth. She'd failed and now Matthew would die a traitor's death. Husee marched her straight to the riverside, but whilst he was readying their luggage she pulled the pouch from under her kirtle and took out the smallest of the diamonds. It was the size of her thumb nail and glistered in the afternoon light.

'Husee,' she said, 'will you please go back and give this to his Lordship? She slipped the diamond into his palm and he lifted it up to get a better look.

'Is this what I think it is, my lady?'

She nodded.

'Where did you come by it?'

'I may not say,' she said, 'not until I'm with the King.'

Husee looked at her. 'Are there more?'

Johanna took a deep breath. 'I may not say until I am with the King.'

He shook his head. 'You've always been an enigma to me, Lady Johanna. Wait on!' he shouted to the steersman. 'I'll be back presently.'

Johanna laced her fingers together and tightened them painfully. Since finding the diamonds it had been hard to pray because she had felt so betrayed by those who should have cared for their welfare, but now the prayers came naturally, with a feeling of relief.

She was still praying when Husee returned. 'His Lordship says you'd better come back inside and explain yourself.'

Relieved, Johanna followed Husee back into the palace. It was God's will now. She had surrendered to Him completely.

*

Lord Lisle was on his own when Husee ushered her back into the solar. He looked tired and scratched at the back of his head.

'Johanna,' he said, 'will you please tell me what you mean by this?' He held up the diamond. 'How can you expect me to help you if I haven't the faintest idea of what's going on?'

She dropped him a low curtsey. 'Your Lordship is gracious to receive me again. I only ask that you show the diamond to His Majesty, and ask if he'll see me.'

'Sit down,' Lord Lisle said, irritably. 'Husee, bring us some more wine.'

As the heat began to thaw her limbs again, Johanna realised she'd made a miscalculation by expecting Lord Lisle to help her with so little information – and there was the matter of whatever poison Anne had managed to pour into his ears.

'My lady.' Husee brought the wine and Johanna took a gulp, feeling the ruby liquid burn her gullet.

'Leave us please,' Lord Lisle said.

After his man had gone, Lord Lisle drew up a stool and Johanna studied him fondly.

'Forgive me,' she said, 'if I've picked a poor time.'

Lord Lisle sighed. 'Yes, you have I'm afraid. I can't tell you much at the moment but, please God, if all goes well we shall have our old Henry back...' He trailed off, looking wistful.

Johanna pressed her hand nervously against the pouch under her clothes. 'My lord,' she began, but he stopped her by putting up his hand.

'There's only one thing I want you to tell me now, Johanna, and that's who gave you this?' He twirled the diamond in front of his face. 'Beautiful, isn't it?' He held it up to the light. 'Lady Lisle would think Heaven itself had smiled upon her if I was to give her a diamond of this size, and Husee tells me you have *more*, but are not saying?'

She nodded. 'It is a matter for the King's ears only. Will you take that to him and ask if he will see me? I promise this is not some poor attempt to win his favour.'

Lord Lisle gave her a sharp look. 'Please tell me where you got this, Johanna. Henry was so angry when you disappeared without permission. He doesn't take slights lightly, as you know.'

'I know, I know,' she said, plaintively, 'and if I could undo that which happened, then I would be only too happy; but in truth I do not believe that *anyone* has the power to command me to give that, which in my heart, I have already given to God.'

Lord Lisle rubbed the back of his neck. 'You know I was fond of you when you were in Calais – you always seemed such a sensible sort to me.' He took a few paces around the room, making the boarding creak. 'So what would you have me say to the King?'

Johanna could barely believe her ears. 'That I send the diamond as a token of my deepest respect and love for him, and that there is a matter of great interest which I seek to discuss with him.'

'A matter of great interest? ' Lord Lisle shook his head in exasperation. 'God's blood, Johanna, you make it sound more of a riddle!'

He strode towards her and she shrank back, thinking he might strike her. 'If you want me to risk the King's displeasure, then you'll have to give me a better story than that because, believe me, I'll not put my head in the lion's mouth until I get one.'

Johanna scrambled to her feet. She'd never seen him this angry before. 'If it pleases you, my lord,' she said, 'you may tell him that I found it in a reliquary. Will that do?'

CHAPTER 46

September
Saint Gilles de Loire, France

Wood pigeons woke Jo the following morning and when she looked at the clock, it was already eight thirty. In the little kitchen, she heated coffee and drank it at the table in the sitting room, watching the river. Birds looped and dived around the banks and a grey heron took flight, dangling a shiny fish from its beak. On the table, the road map lay open and she studied the route to Fontevraud Abbey. It looked relatively simple, and she would pick up some breakfast from the boulangerie on the way out of Saint Gilles.

Munching mouthfuls of crumbly, fresh croissant Jo soon reached the small village of Fontevraud. No one was around as she walked to the entrance gate of the Abbey, enjoying the warmth of the sun on her back and grateful for her straw hat. At the other side of the air-conditioned *Accueil,* the sun reflected off the Abbey's bright, white walls and made her screw up her eyes. Once inside, her attention was drawn to the four figures lying in the nave, and she looked at her guidebook. They were effigies of Eleanor of Aquitaine, her husband the Plantagenet King Henry II of England, their son, Richard "the Lion Heart', and Isabella of Angoulême – the wife of King John of England. Fascinated, Jo moved closer and scanned the still faces. Henry and Richard's were coldly handsome, Eleanor was holding an open book in her hands and appeared calm and relaxed, but Isabella of Angoulême was less distinct and darker than the rest – her effigy made from wood rather than stone. Jo lingered, went round them again, took photographs and asked herself what would it have been like to be them; but no matter how long she looked, or from what angle, the effigies offered only a tantalising glimpse of who they might really have been.

She wandered to a pillar that stood between the nave and the choir. The lower legs and feet of a knight were painted on the plaster, but the rest of his body had been torn away. The plaque told her that the feet were thought to belong to Count Raymond VII of Toulouse, the only son of Joan of England – a daughter of Henry Plantagenet and Eleanor of Aquitaine – and Count Raymond VI of Toulouse. It also said that Joan had been married twice, the first time being to the King of Sicily, and that she had died in 1199 wearing the 'cloth of the Order of Fontevraud'.

Jo was intrigued. Why had Raymond chosen to be buried in Fontevraud with his mother and not in Toulouse if he had been Count there? She turned to her guide book. It said that Joan, sometimes called Joanna, had died following the birth of another male child, and been buried at Fontevraud along with the infant, whom she'd named Richard, after her beloved brother. But it didn't say anything about the son who became Count of Toulouse after his father, and why most of him had been ripped away from the wall. She looked around for a plaque commemorating the Countess Joan, but could find nothing.

Outside, Jo wandered around the cloisters and visited the many-sided kitchen, designed so that a fire could be lit in any orientation to take advantage of the prevailing wind. She enjoyed a snack in the Aliénor café and walked around the herb garden revelling in its scents. When her phone rang, she scrabbled to answer it, her heart thumping – but it was only Jean-Yves. Could Monsieur Moreau visit around 3.30 that afternoon?

*

Jo visited the Intermarche on her return to Saint Gilles and it was almost three by the time she let herself into the apartment. She unpacked the shopping – delicious fruits and salad, unusual cheeses, a ready-made Coquille Saint Jacques and a luscious strawberry tart. She put on some coffee and pulled the cork on a ridiculously cheap, but excellent-looking bottle of red wine.

At exactly three-thirty she heard a knock on the door downstairs and went to answer it. Jean-Yves had arrived with Monsieur Moreau – a man of medium height, in his mid-thirties with short, black hair, brushed back over his ears. He wore a light-weight beige suit and shiny leather shoes and came forwards immediately to shake her hand. Then he surged past her and up the stairs as if he owned the apartment already.

'Er, excuse me-' She stared after him. Was this how people did viewings of houses in France?

He didn't wait to be asked but went straight to the kitchen and opened the door that led down to the garden.

'A nice garden', he said to her, in English with a strong French accent.

'Er, I haven't been out in it at as yet,' Jo said, looking past him to the large garden which was mainly set to lawn, but had three pear trees in the middle. She smiled when she saw both trees festooned with bird feeders. 'Would you like to look at the bathroom?' she said, determined to take back the initiative.

He nodded, and Jean-Yves said something very quickly in French. Monsieur Moreau shrugged. The bathroom seemed to interest him for only a few seconds, so much for her efforts to clean it up that morning, before he zoomed into the bedroom, looked at the fireplace, and then into the sitting room where he looked long and hard at the wall surrounding the stone fireplace.

'Would you like some coffee?' Jo asked, faltering. 'Or wine?'

'Non, merci.' Monsieur Moreau sat down on the window seat and started rolling his thumbs. 'At what price you would like to sell the apartment?'

'We haven't decided yet,' she said. 'Did you have a figure in mind?'

Monsieur Moreau frowned and Jean-Yves broke in.

'Mademoiselle,' he said. 'There is *un agent immobilier* in Saint Gilles. They are similar to your estate agents. You should ask them to give you a valuation.'

Monsieur Moreau glared at Jean- Yves.

'Thank you,' she said. 'And I suppose I would have to find a solicitor, too-'

'*Un notaire*,' Monsieur Moreau said. 'I can find someone for you.'

'Your aunt used a local man,' Jean-Yves said. 'I can give you his name.'

Monsieur Moreau's teeth clicked impatiently and he said something to Jean-Yves, then stood up to go.

'Thank you, Mademoiselle,' he said, making his way towards the stairs. 'We are leaving, now.'

Even after she'd watched them both out of the door and gone to flop on the sofa in the sitting room – Jo's heart was still beating fast. Monsieur Moreau's presence had left an unpleasant feeling and she got up to open the window. Sounds floated up to her and she realised she could hear the two men arguing but couldn't understand what they were saying.

When Jean-Yves had asked if she would meet a prospective buyer, Jo'd assumed it was someone he knew well, a friend even; but from the sound of their argument, that could hardly be the case. Had Monsieur Moreau had hoped to get a knock-down price for the apartment? If so, Jean-Yves was having none of it. Well, thank goodness for that. At least someone was looking out for her, even if Mat couldn't be bothered to come.

Restlessly, Jo roved around the apartment. She'd brought Blanche's ashes with her, intending to bury them, but felt increasingly reluctant to do so if they were going to sell the apartment, especially to Monsieur Moreau. Already she disliked him thoroughly. In fact, if he was the last person alive, she thought, I wouldn't sell Blanche's lovely apartment to him. What she really wanted to do was keep it. The only problem was, that meant she would have to talk to Mat.

CHAPTER 47

September 1209
Carcassonne

After a few more days, the Counts of Nevers and Saint Pol took their leave. Matthieu and Raimondet watched them set out along the road towards Montpellier. Count Raimon was due to leave for Toulouse soon, but already the storm clouds were gathering. The Legate and he could agree on nothing and, caught in the middle, Matthieu began to despair. Arnald-Amalric demanded that Raimon make good his promises to hand over the heretics in his lands and rid himself of mercenary troops. The Count responded by stating that he needed more time, and pointed to the fact that even the crusaders had brought mercenaries with them. The Legate then reminded the Count that he had made his promises in June, that it was now September, and he had done nothing; at which point the Count exploded.

'Are you blind?' he ranted. 'I've been here. *Here*! In front of you for all of these months!'

To make matters worse, Bishop Foulques arrived to congratulate the crusaders, and with him came the deputation that Arnald-Amalric had sent to negotiate the surrender of the heretics in Toulouse. Soon afterwards, the Legate sent messages to the Count requesting him to attend his to his pavilion.

Matthieu was playing chess with Raimondet.

'I'm not going,' the Count said, bluntly. 'Tell them, if they want to talk, they can come to me.'

Matthieu tried to conceal his surprise and quickly ushered the messenger out of the pavilion, whilst the Count muttered about low-born, trumped-up churchmen who had no right to demand his presence anywhere. Matthieu found it hard to suppress his anger. No good would come of this, of that he was sure.

By and by, the messenger returned, announcing that the Legate and the Bishop were waiting outside, requesting admission. Sulkily, the Count said they'd have to wait, but then he sat brooding, his expression dark.

'My lord,' Matthieu ventured, 'do you wish myself and Raimondet to be present for this meeting or shall we go out?'

'What?' the Count looked up as though he'd forgotten they were there.

'Shall I take Raimondet away, until your meeting is over?'

'No.' Raimon's eyebrows drew together so that they looked like one. 'I want *you* to stay here. Peire!'

Peire of Rebastens was instantly at the Count's side. 'Sire?'

'Take my son to the Warden's tent.'

Matthieu helped Raimondet to pack up his chess men. They could all hear the clinking of bridles and the low murmur of impatient voices outside, but still the Count sat, unmoved.

'I suppose you could tell them to come in,' he sighed.

Arnald-Amalric and Bishop Foulques were both wearing brocaded silk garments, all-over emblazoned with gold crosses. Whilst the Count picked dirt from under his fingernails, Matthieu rose to greet them and both extended their rings for his kiss. He knelt before them, but was horrified to see his seigneur's face turn from sullen disregard to fury

'The consuls have brought no assurances for us regarding the heretics in Toulouse,' Arnald-Amalric began. 'And they have replied to us that they wish to appeal to our Holy Father in Rome. What do you say to that, Count Raimon?'

The Count barely looked at the Legate. 'I think it's a good idea,' he said. 'In fact, I'd like to do the same myself.'

Arnald-Amalric took an irritated breath. 'May I remind you, Raimon, that I was sent by the Pope himself?'

'That may be, but I'd rather talk to someone...' The Count gave Arnald-Amalric a look of disdain, '... like my *cousin* for instance, the *King* of France, or my wife's *nephew*, the *Emperor*, before I give my answer to you.'

'For why, may I ask?' Arnald-Amalric had developed spots of high colour in his cheeks. 'Why not trust me? I am authorised to speak for the Pope.'

'So you say,' the Count said, bitterly, 'and I agree. If I *could* trust you, then there would be no need to go to such lengths.'

The two men glared at each other and all Matthieu could do was tremble. If a lightning bolt had descended from Heaven and reduced the Count to ashes upon the floor, he would not have been surprised.

Arnald-Amalric made a startled noise and turned on his heel. Foulques flung Matthieu a sympathetic smile as they strode out.

'And you can get out, too,' the Count said.

'My l-lord?' Matthieu stuttered.

'Get out before I throttle you! You're a grovelling swine, Matthieu, and I want you out of here!' The Count stalked towards Matthieu, dagger in hand. 'I've been lenient with you. Oh yes I have, but today you've finally overstepped the mark.'

Matthieu tried to move back, but Peire of Rebastens was suddenly behind him, blocking his way.

'My lord, I-I-'

'Shut up!' the Count yelled. 'If I hadn't seen what I've just seen with my own eyes then I might not have believed what they told me you were doing when I sent you to *my city*!'

Ice ran down Matthieu's back.

'You just couldn't stop yourself, could you?' The Count nudged his dagger towards Matthieu's throat. 'Couldn't stop abasing yourself before those – *carrion crows*. You treat them as if they were God himself. Tell me, Matthieu,' the Count said, inching the dagger forwards so that the tip bit into Matthieu's skin, '*why* did you go to the Cathedral in Toulouse, when I sent you to fetch my son?'

'My lord,' Matthieu stammered craning his neck backwards, 'you knew I'd taken lodgings with the Bishop when Catharine died. You even gave me permission-'

'Shut up!' the Count snarled, and Matthieu winced as the dagger dug deeper.'You know what I'm talking about. You're a knight of *my* household but you spend all your time with my enemies. You owe allegiance to *me*, but every time I turn round you're with *them*. Think carefully on this before you answer, Matthieu. Where are your loyalties, with them, or with me?'

Blood trickled down Matthieu's neck and he shivered.'I'm surprised you even ask, my lord,' he stuttered. 'Everything I have I owe to you.'

'Yes, you do!' the Count said. 'And yet you were planning to raise a militia against me, weren't you, when you were in Toulouse!'

Whatever way he answered, Matthieu knew that his life in the south, his role as tutor to Raimondet, and even the chance to see his son grow up, had vanished. Even if the Count was to spare his life, which looked increasingly unlikely.

'My l-lord,' he said, searching the Count's eyes for some vestige of their old friendship, but he saw only cold fury. 'Let me bring Bishop Foulques here to speak for himself about what took place-'

'Bring him here?' The dagger jabbed forward. 'Get out before before I cut your lying throat out,' before I have you flayed alive. Get out! Get out!'

Matthieu fled, with Peire of Rebastens' triumphant grin following him. Outside the pavilion, the other lords were standing about; Matthieu knew better than to speak to them. He went straight away to his tent where he gathered up his few belongings, his first thought being to go to Arnald-Amalric's pavilion, but thankfully, enough of his wits returned before he committed that particular act of suicide. He threw his saddle packs on to his horse and rode to the only place he knew he could be welcomed, even if it was only for a short while. As he galloped away from Carcassonne, tears rolled down Matthieu's cheeks and the shock and loss jolted him as it permeated into his mind and his heart. He remembered what Foulques had told him after the meeting broke up at his palace that night – something which at the time had seemed impossible – that if Count Raimon refused to uphold the promises he made to the Church, then devastation on an un-dreamed of scale would be brought down upon the south. He swallowed and gripped his horse's reins so tightly that the veins stood out in knots upon the back of his hands. What would that mean for Joana and Guillem now he was no longer in a position to protect them?

CHAPTER 48

3rd October 1539
Hampton Court, England

Although Johanna rejoiced that Lord Lisle was going to help her, there was no telling how long she would have to wait for an opportunity to speak to the King, and Matthew's plight weighed heavily upon her. She settled herself down as best as she could, the fire had burned low in the grate, but it was still giving out a lot of heat and the page had been in to close the shutters. She changed her boots for the slippers Lady Margery had given her, knelt on the carpet and, illuminated by the glow of candles and the embers of the fire, sent up her most heartfelt prayers for his safety.

The next thing she knew, Husee was shaking her by the shoulder. 'Wake up, my lady. Wake up. His Lordship is asking for you.'

Groggily Johanna tried to focus on what he was saying. 'All right. I'm coming,' she said. 'Where is he?'

'With Baron Cromwell,' Husee said.

Her heart plummeted. Lord Lisle had not gone to the King after all, but to the most hated and feared man in all the land.

'Come on,' Husee urged. 'This is your chance.'

Johanna stood up in a panic, trying to straighten her clothes and hair. It was the third day she'd worn the green gown and she hurried about the room, scooping up sprigs of lavender from bowls laid out there, and rubbing them over her clothes to freshen them.

Husee led her through the outer rooms of the King's apartments, her slippered feet tapping across the floors. Cromwell would never let her see the King, of that she was certain, but Johanna reminded herself that she had put everything in God's hands, and resolved to keep as calm as she could. Now they were in the Presence Chamber, its priceless tapestries barely visible in the dim light, and now the outer door of the Privy Chamber. Johanna's breath stuttered in her chest. Even if she wasn't able to see the King, she was at least getting very close. Peter Mewtas opened the door to them and came out to greet her, a tall, athletic man and one of the King's gentlemen of the Privy Chamber. He was also married to Jane Astley, who had been another of Queen Jane's Maids of Honour.

'Good evening, Lady Johanna,' Peter said, bowing politely.

'Good evening, Peter,' Johanna said. 'How wonderful to see you. How is Jane, may I ask?'

'Very well,' Peter said, his grey eyes regarding her neutrally. 'We have a son. Did you know? We named him Henry.'

'A fine choice.' She smiled. Of course they would call him Henry. 'I'm afraid I've been at the convent at Amesbury. Little news reached me there. I know I may be rather late, but you both have my congratulations.'

'Thank you.' Peter raised an eyebrow. 'How did you enjoy the convent? Was it better than being at court?'

'I liked it very well,' she said, conscious of the lie.

'Interesting.' Peter seemed without much curiosity. He led her through the sumptuously furnished room towards a door at the far end. 'The Baron will see you now, but please don't keep him. We still have work to complete.'

Johanna nodded, her heart hammering against her ribs. The dazzling furnishings and gilded walls were beginning to have an effect upon her, sapping her morale and making her feel like an insignificant fool. Who was she to come begging favours from her King? A knot of fear twisted in her belly, but she fought to keep her head up and back straight, even though her legs were shuddering.

'How is His Majesty?'

'In good spirits, you'll no doubt be pleased to hear,' Peter said.

Johanna willed herself to relax. Peter was opening the door now, the one that led into the King's Bedchamber, but the King didn't sleep in there, of course. Sir Thomas Heneage was waiting inside and Cromwell nowhere to be seen.

'The Lady Johanna, Sir Thomas. Do you remember her?'

Heneage nodded. As the Groom of the Stool, he was the King's closest confidant and the second most important man at court.

'I do indeed,' he said.

He indicated a velvet chair, placed a short distance away from a magnificent, gold-covered Chair of State that, as far as Johanna knew, served only for the King to sit upon whilst getting dressed. She sat down and arranged her skirts as neatly as possible, hiding any stains in the folds, thankful that she could not be seen so clearly now that it was evening. Her mouth was dry and the shaking hands that she clasped in her lap were as cold as those of a corpse. Whilst she concentrated on breathing slowly, she prayed a decade of the Rosary for Matthew, wondering as she did, if he thought of her as often as she thought of him.

A side door opened and Baron Cromwell came into the room, mopping his brow with a linen kerchief. Even in the candlelight Johanna could see he was flushed. When he caught sight of her, he stopped and shook his head.

'Not here, not now,' he said. 'Find her somewhere to sleep, Sir Thomas and I'll see her in the morning.'

'Baron Cromwell,' Johanna said, finding courage from somewhere.

She wasn't going to give up when she was so near. 'May I be allowed to see the King, just for a moment? I have something I'm certain he'll be interested in.'

'No,' Cromwell said.

'But-'

'Sir Thomas,' Cromwell grunted and indicated the outer door.

Heneage nodded and came to take Johanna's arm.

'Until the morning, Lady Johanna,' Cromwell said.

'But-'

Another door into the room slowly opened and a fat gaudily dressed man limped in, holding one hand to his head.

'Crum, Henny,' he said, 'I have the most awful megrim. I don't think I can look at any more parchments tonight.'

Cromwell and Thomas Heneage looked at each other and then at Johanna, who shocked to recognise the King, scrambled to her feet and dropped into a deep curtsey before him. He was *here*, in the same room with her, but where was the sprightly man she had known when she was at court?

'God's breath, Johanna,' King Henry said. 'What on Earth are you doing here? I never thought to see you again.'

'Good evening, Your Majesty,' Johanna said, unable to stop trembling.

The King sat down heavily on his Chair of State and winced as he stretched out his left leg.

'They tell me you have something of importance for me,' he said, tiredly. 'Well, let's have it; and don't think I've forgiven you for leaving court without my permission.'

'Please accept my apologies, Your Majesty,' Johanna stuttered. 'I was a young and foolish-'

'Did you really run away to a convent?' the King asked. The deep rumble of his voice made her tremble even harder. 'Am I so repulsive?'

Fear nearly made her faint upon the ground. *Please tell me what to say*, she prayed.

'No Sire! Not at all! Your Majesty is fair beyond comparison,' she gabbled frantically. 'I regret giving you the impression that I was running away from you for that reason-'

'Ah!' The King sat back with a satisfied smile. 'So you *do* admit you were running away from me! What do you think of that eh, Crum, Henny? Whatever you've brought, Johanna, it will have to be something exceptional for me to even consider forgiving you for such an insult.'

Johanna's legs were screaming with pain, for she was still in a curtsey, but the King hadn't told her to rise. 'Your Majesty is most kind,' she began, 'and even more gracious to be willing to overlook my unforgivable behaviour...' She stopped. He hadn't actually said he would forgive her yet. Dear God – help me! She risked a look through her lashes and saw that there was no hint of warmth in his expression. His great fat fingers drummed upon the arm of the chair, and he watched her, much as a cat watches a mouse it has caught.

'May I be permitted to show you what I have brought, Your Majesty?' Johanna said.

'Please do, and get up for goodness sake. Unless you want to stay like that 'til your knees give way?'

Johanna tried to rise gracefully, but her knees *were* stiff.

'You don't *seem* to have brought anything with you,' the King mused, looking her over. 'Or perhaps-' he leaned forwards and his voice dropped a fraction, 'perhaps you've hidden it somewhere I can't see?'

Heat flared in her cheeks. Matthew's life depended upon her right now.

'Your Majesty is too clever for me,' she said, giving the King a shy smile. 'I'd hoped to keep my secret a little while longer, but now I'm afraid you've guessed.'

'Ha!' The piggy eyes crinkled and Johanna noticed that the King had grey hairs in his beard now. 'But I haven't guessed exactly...' He put a finger to his lips, pretending to consider. 'Wait now, where would you..?'

'Ahem.' This from Cromwell. 'I could send for someone to search the Lady Johanna, maybe?'

The King waved his hand. 'That won't be necessary Crum. Off you go, both of you. The lady Johanna and I have some – business to attend to.'

Cromwell and Sir Thomas exited backwards, their faces blank, but their disapproval palpable. As soon as they were alone, the King patted the knee of his good leg.

'Come and sit down, Johanna, and tell your King where you've hidden his surprise.'

Caught off guard, Johanna hesitated. Being alone with the King this quickly was the last thing she had anticipated, and he seemed to have some erotic game of hide and seek in mind.

'Come on,' the King said. 'You've kept me waiting long enough, you naughty girl, but I'm not going to bite you.' He patted the knee again, and with a feeling of dread, Johanna went to sit upon it.

This close, she could smell the King's pomade and the herbs he used to freshen his body and clothes, but they could not disguise the putrid odour of his rotting leg. She felt an arm slide around her waist and give her a 'friendly' squeeze, and then the King leaned in towards her ear and whispered: 'I'm so pleased to see you, Johanna. Why did you run away from me? I wouldn't have hurt you. Heaven forbid that I should have so little understanding of a maiden's modesty.'

The squeeze got tighter and the King's breath hotter.

'I'm sorry, Majesty,' Johanna said, almost squeaking. 'I was a foolish young girl, with foolish imaginings. Can you forgive me?'

In answer Henry trailed his fingers from her throat to the top of her chemise and a sick feeling welled up in Johanna's stomach.

'We'll see,' he said. 'Never let it be said that your King has no mercy.'

'Then if you will allow me,' she pulled as far away as she dared. 'I will show Your Majesty that which I have brought.'

'Very well.' Henry released her and Johanna slid off his knee, then turned away to pull the pouch from the front of her kirtle.

When she turned back, she almost gasped because there was the innocence of a young boy in his face, waiting eagerly for his surprise gift. Johanna's heart softened as she remembered that the King had lost his beloved mother when he was only eleven years old.

'Hold out your hand, please, Majesty,' she said, feeling a little more bold.

The King held out his hand, palm up, and closed his eyes. Johanna emptied the contents of the pouch onto it

'Can I open them now?'

'Yes.'

For a moment, there was utter silence as the King gazed at what was in his palm, and then he brought the diamonds nearer to his face.

'Johanna, sweeting,' he said. 'Do tell me where you found these.'

CHAPTER 49

September
Saint Gilles de Loire, France

Jo awoke to a knocking at the door. Hurriedly she checked her watch. It was a quarter past nine and she'd slept in, again, but then there was hardly anything to get up for – if you didn't count the beautiful day being held at bay behind the curtains.

'Who is it?' she called, standing at the top of the stairs.

'Monsieur Moreau. Pardon, Mademoiselle, but I have a question for you.'

Now what? She wanted to tell him to go away, but didn't exactly know how.

'I'm, sorry,' she said. 'It's not convenient right now.'

'Pardon?'

'I said, it's not convenient.'

'Pardon? I cannot hear you. Can you open the door?'

She pulled yesterday's clothes on over her pyjamas and dragged a hairbrush through her hair, then went downstairs and opened the door a crack. 'Bonjour, Monsieur.'

'Mademoiselle.' Monsieur Moreau's eyes took in her hair and the crumpled state of her clothes. 'Did I wake you? I'm sorry, but there is something I need to speak to you about.'

'Monsieur, I'm sorry but it's not convenient right now. Could you come back later?'

'When?' He tapped his fingers against the door-jamb.

The later the better, she thought. 'This afternoon? About four o' clock?'

'Mademoiselle,' he said, stiffly, 'I would like to buy your apartment and you are making things very difficult for me. Are you sure I couldn't come back in...,' he looked her over again, 'an hour? I will visit Jean-Yves, until then.'

What could she say? 'Oh, all right,' she sighed. 'Monsieur Moreau, will you bring Jean-Yves with you when you come?'

'You don't trust me?' he said, smiling. 'Je comprends. I will bring Jean-Yves. In an hour?'

'Yes, in an hour. Goodbye.'

She shut the door and stomped back upstairs, cross with herself because she hadn't said 'No.'

*

Barely three-quarters of an hour later, whilst Jo was still munching her way through a pre-packaged croissant from the Intermarche – so much for fresh croissants and lazy breakfasts overlooking the Loire – there came a knock again at the door. At least Jean-Yves was there, looking apologetic. Both men came upstairs and, to her annoyance, Monsieur Moreau made his way into her bedroom and started tapping on the walls.

'Er, look here,' Jo said following him, then stopped in disbelief. He'd pulled open the door to the built-in wardrobe and was tapping on the back wall.

'Can I help you?' she said, uncomfortably aware that she was on her own in the apartment with two more-or-less unknown men.

'That is not necessary,' Monsieur Moreau said. 'Finish your breakfast, please.'

'But, you're in my wardrobe-'

'A precaution,' he said. 'This is an old house.'

'Monsieur Moreau-' Jo was about to tell him to get out and never come back, but he interrupted her.

'Not now,' he said, holding up a hand to her and moving to tap the wall around the fireplace. 'I am listening.'

The cheek of the man! 'I've, er, well I've been thinking that perhaps now is not the right time to sell the apartment. It seems so soon after Blanche's death, and it's the first time I've been here and I think it's lovely-'

Suddenly Monsieur Moreau started stamping his heels on the floorboards, as if about to start an Irish dance and Jean-Yves let loose a torrent of French. For a few minutes they argued back and forth and then Monsieur Moreau shrugged and left, his feet echoing down the stairs.

'Mademoiselle,' Jean-Yves said, shaking his head regretfully. 'I should not have brought that man here. He has deceived me.'

'He has? How?'

Jean-Yves gestured towards the sitting room. 'Come, sit down and I will tell you.'

They sat at the table and Jean-Yves fumbled in the breast pocket of his shirt for his cigarettes. Jo went into the kitchen to put on the kettle, hoping that he wouldn't ask if he could smoke – because she would definitely say 'no', however kind he'd been. The encounter with Monsieur Moreau had unsettled her, and her hand shook as she lit the gas. What was all that tapping about? Was the apartment about to fall down around her ears?

'Jean-Yves,' she said, coming back with a pot of coffee and two cups. 'Is there something wrong with this apartment?'

'Non,' he said, emphatically. 'Your aunt and uncle fixed it. There *was* a problem, after they bought the apartment.' He spread his hands. 'But my cousin is a builder. He made everything strong again and there has not been a problem since.'

'So why was Monsieur Moreau tapping?'

'Je ne sais pas,' he said, taking a sip of the coffee. 'Originally he told me he wanted to make you a very good offer for the apartment, but that was not true, and he was 'impoli'. So I told him to leave. I hope we don't see him again.'

'Yes, I don't really like him very much-'

Jean-Yves nodded. 'Don't worry.' He squared his shoulders, and then tapped his cigarette on the packet.

'Pardon,' he said, obviously realising what he was doing and putting the packet away again, 'I wasn't thinking. I shall make sure he doesn't come here again.'

'Thank you.' Jo sat down and poured herself some coffee. 'Perhaps I'll go to the estate agents in Saint Gilles this afternoon – see what they say.'

'That would be une bonne idée.' He finished his coffee quickly and got up to go. 'Excusez-moi, but my wife is waiting for me.'

'Ah, yes. Thank you for coming, Jean-Yves. Oh, I nearly forgot. I went to Fontevraud Abbey yesterday.'

His face lit up. 'C'est très tranquil, non?'

'Très,' she said, blushing. Although Jo understood quite a lot of French, she was nervous about speaking it. 'Do you know anything about,' she checked the note she'd scribbled in her diary, 'Count Raymond VII of Toulouse and his mother, Joan. She was a sister of Richard 'the Lion Heart', I believe.'

'A little,' Jean-Yves said, shrugging, 'but my wife knows more. I will ask her to visit, yes?'

'Yes, please,' she said. 'I'd love to meet her.'

After he'd gone, Jo went into the bedroom and opened the wardrobe door. Everything looked solid enough but she gave it a tap, like Monsieur Moreau had done, and around the iron fireplace too; but since she didn't know what she was listening for, she gave up. There were other things to get on with.

She took a large brown envelope out of her bag and tipped the contents onto the table. In addition to a key ring with two keys, there was a copy of Blanche's will and a smaller envelope with directions to the apartment scrawled on the outside in Blanche's spidery hand. Inside was a pretty card with butterflies on it.

'*Get on with your lives*', the card read, '*and I'll be watching over you. Don't mourn for me, I'm with my beloved Patrick. One last wish; I'd love my ashes to be interred in the garden of the apartment in France, next to the grave of my beloved cat, Thomas, who died there shortly after we moved in.*'

At the time Jo'd thought the use of 'we' to be strange, but had put it down to Blanche being unwell when she wrote the card.

'It's marked with a cross so you should be able to find it. No need for ceremony, just yourselves, please. I don't want anyone else seeing the last of me!'

Jo sighed and picked up the keyring. The larger key was a spare for the front door, but the other was a mystery. It was small and of the type that might fit a padlock. Blanche wouldn't have bothered putting it in the envelope if it was of no use; but Jo'd been unable to find anything in the apartment that it fitted. She went through to the kitchen and looked down into the garden. It was enclosed by high walls on three sides but their hard lines were softened by twines of clematis and honeysuckle. Typical for Blanche, the three central pear trees were full of bird-feeders, but very atypical for her was the small wooden cross in the left hand corner of the plot where the letter said 'my beloved cat, Thomas'. If Blanche had loved a cat here, it was a far cry from her feelings about cats back at home – on account of the way they chased her birds. Had it really belonged to Patrick?

Jo unlocked the door and walked down the metal staircase that doubled as a fire-escape. The heady scent of rose met her and when she got to the bottom of the stairs, she saw that the back wall of the building was almost entirely hidden by a yellow rambling rose. Most of the blooms had faded, but she pulled at one of those that lingered and breathed in the exquisite fragrance.

Dew persisted where the grass was still in the shade, and as she made her way over to the little cross, Jo made a mental note to find out who looked after the garden. There were no windows which directly overlooked this spot, except those of the upstairs apartment. Blanche had wanted this to be done privately, and so it would be. She'd do it tonight so there was no risk of Monsieur Moreau poking his nose in.

When Jo got back upstairs there was another knock at the front door and when she opened it, she found a woman in her late forties, with neatly styled grey hair and a ready smile. The woman picked up Jo's hand and shook it in hers.

'Welcome, welcome,' she said. 'I've been longing to meet Blanche's niece. I'm Rebecca, Jean-Yves' wife, and I've heard such a lot about you.'

But I've heard nothing at all about you, Jo thought, ruefully. ' How lovely to meet you, I'd like to thank you, and your husband,' she said, 'for looking after the apartment for us so well.'

'It's been a pleasure. Have you been able to find everything? I'm sorry I wasn't here when you arrived. I was visiting my mother.' Rebecca rolled her eyes. 'Maman grows very forgetful. Sometimes she doesn't even know who I am.'

‘Oh dear. Does she have dementia?’

‘Yes, sadly. The doctor says it won’t be long before we have to find somewhere else for her to live, but she loves her home.

‘Ah, Madame. I’m sorry.’

‘Thank you. Call me Rebecca, please?’

‘Is Rebecca a French name?’ Jo asked.

‘When it’s accented, yes, but I was born in England. I lived there until I was five, and then Maman met my French step-father – so we came to France.’

‘Can I offer you something to drink? I have coffee and some black tea that I brought with me. Do you like tea in the English style? Or would you prefer wine?’

Rebecca laughed. ‘I’ve never acquired the French capacity for wine and I’d love a cup of tea. Jean-Yves can’t understand why we all make such a fuss about it, but then he’s a coffee drinker, of course.’

It was lovely to sit at the table together, drinking tea and watching the river . There was so much Jo wanted to ask about Blanche and Patrick, but she knew she needed to be careful. Perhaps it would be better if their secret went go to the grave with them.

‘So then,’ she said, ‘Jean-Yves tells me you know about Joan, the sister of Richard the Lion Heart, and her son Raymond of Toulouse?’

‘Yes, did you go to Fontevraud?’ Rebecca put down her cup. ‘What did you think? I love those effigies in the nave. Joan was the daughter of Henri the second of England and Aliénor of Aquitaine; she grew up at Fontevraud with her brother, John.’ Rebecca laughed. ‘Listen, I could bore you with this all day. How long are you staying?’

‘I only came over because Jean-Yves contacted me about Monsieur Moreau.’ Jo couldn’t help frowning as she thought of him. ‘But, now I’ve been here…’ She looked around. ‘I never want to leave.’

‘That’s exactly what Blanche used to say,’ Rebecca said. ‘They were so close the two of them, weren’t they? So much in love. Always called each other darling. Patrick was the perfect gentleman and he told me one day that Blanche was the love of his life.’

Jo swallowed the lump that had suddenly appeared in her throat. This was the confirmation of her suspicions. Blanche and Patrick must have been having an affair. No wonder she never wanted to leave here. How hard it must have been for them to go back to their normal lives.

‘So, tell me,’ Jo said, hoping to avoid what could easily become dangerous territory, ‘what happened to Joan? There's no memorial for her at Fontevraud.’

‘Well,’ Rebecca said, ‘Joan had an exciting life before she even reached Toulouse. She’d been the wife of the King of Sicily, and was imprisoned when he died, but then she was rescued by her brother Richard who was on his way to Jerusalem. Joan became great friends with his wife, Berengaria – which is more than *he* did by all accounts. He hardly spent any time with her and, selfishly, didn't manage to leave an heir when he died.'

'How on Earth do you know all this?' Jo asked.

'It might be because I teach history at the local lycée,' Rebecca said, 'which is why you really shouldn't let me bore you to death!'

Jo shook her head, liking Rebecca. 'No chance of that. I'd always thought that medieval women sat at home sewing and waiting for their men to return from killing people.'

'Yes, well you'll probably find that such ideas belong more to the *romances* of the time, written by men, of course. Joan was as feisty as her mother Aliénor. Later on, when Joan was married to the Count of Toulouse, she thought nothing of trying to put down a rebellion in his absence but unfortunately she was betrayed and badly injured. She didn't know who she could trust and she went to find Richard – the brother who had always helped her – but unfortunately he'd died before she reached him.'

'Oh, no. So what did she do?'

'What most of us would probably do under such circumstances, I suppose. She went to find her mother. Aliénor had just nursed Richard until he died of septicaemia,' Rebecca continued. 'He was her favourite and she was devastated when he died. Then her daughter arrived, pregnant and fatally wounded. Joan managed to live long enough to call her baby Richard, but the didn't survive.' Rebecca took a sip of tea and grimaced. 'I've let it go cold after all.' She looked at her watch. 'Jean-Yves will laugh at me when I get back – I said I wouldn't be long! I'm sorry, Jo, I hope I haven't bored you?'

'Not at all,' Jo said, truthfully. 'I'm fascinated. Will you tell me what happened to her son, Raymond?'

'Ah,' Rebecca grinned. 'If you get me started on Raimondet, I'll be here until it gets dark. How about another day? Why not come to us for dinner, would you like that? Tomorrow evening – say seven thirty?'

'Yes please, that would be lovely,' Jo said, immediately looking forward to it – dinner with such a pleasant couple and the chance to find out what had happened to the 'knight without a body' on the wall of the Abbey – the young Count Raymond VI of Toulouse.

CHAPTER 50

Sept 1209
Pontigny Abbey, Burgundy

Matthieu knew he wasn't the first cleric to find refuge at Pontigny Abbey, and he wouldn't be the last. There was something about the soaring arches and luminous stone that soothed troubled souls. The architecture was simple but magnificent, and situated as it was, surrounded by undulating farmland and well managed woods, it provided a marvellous testament to the abundance made possible when man co-operated with man – in the service of God.

The Abbey was run by Cistercian monks and their technical expertise was astounding. Matthieu had strolled through gardens filled with fountains that created innumerable rainbows in their wake, and the continuous creak of the water mill reassured everyone that there would be plenty of flour ready for bread-making each morning.

A part of Mattieu's soul had been released by simply being here, but another part was sorely troubled. The news from the south was that Simon of Montfort had moved his army from Carcassonne to the Count of Foix's territory at Pamiers and had been welcomed by the Abbot of Saint-Antonin's. What that meant for the people of Pamiers, Matthieu could only guess, but his recent experiences of the crusade gave him little hope. How he wished he could know that Joana and Guillem were safe. It was hard not to fear the worst and he prayed that God would protect not only them but Raimondet also – the boy's face regularly appeared to him in dreams – and he was always drowning.

A cough to his right reminded Matthieu that he was taking part in the office of Terce and his eyes slid down the page to that day's designated reading from *2 Corinthians*. He translated as he read.'*Be ye not unequally yoked together with unbelievers: for what fellowship hath righteousness with unrighteousness? And what communion hath light with darkness...*'

Count Raimon could have done well to ponder that.

The cough came from a man who wore the robes of a Cistercian monk, but carried the aura of elsewhere. Whereas the regular monks habituated themselves to the choir stalls – perhaps smuggling in a small cushion for a painful back, or a folded blanket under the seat to keep out the cold – this man knelt tall and aloof, but brought to his prayers such fervour and concentration, that the very air around him seemed stilled.

*

Matthieu had just finished his midday meal when he was summoned to the Abbot's study.

'Come in, come in, Matthieu,' the Abbot said, waving him to sit.

To Matthieu's surprise, the man who had coughed was in there too, sitting comfortably upon a high-backed chair.

The Abbot's milky skin and closely cropped white hair suggested that he had spent most of his life in a library, away from the sun, but the twinkle in his eyes marked him out as far from dull. His desk was neatly arrayed with quill and ink, and a casket containing his seal of office. As Matthieu took his seat, the Abbot's secretary bustled in with a parchment.

'Thank you,' the Abbot said. 'This is a letter from Arnald-Amalric, Matthieu. I'll read it to you.'

Matthieu felt a prickle of alarm at the mention of the Legate's name and held his breath.

'My dear brother Abbot, greetings etc., etc.,' the Abbot said, rather irreverently. Matthieu looked at the other monk, but saw only a slight smile around his mouth. 'Ah, here we are – highly commend Matthieu of Poitiers to you as a true son of the Church, lately in the service of Count Raimon of Toulouse but expelled by that notorious heretic on account of Matthieu's loyalty to the Church, etc., etc. What it all comes down to, Matthieu,' the Abbot said, putting down the parchment, 'is that Stephen here has a job for you. How would you like to go to Paris, to the College of Theology?'

Matthieu felt so dizzy that he had to grip the arms of his chair and he looked uncertainly between both men. Were they mocking him? The tall man sighed and stretched out his legs.

'It's like this, Matthieu,' he said, speaking slowly with a strong a strong English accent. 'I was a Master of Theology at Paris until the Pope called me to Rome, and now I am elected to the Archbishopric of England; but King John has refused to allow me into his country.' He spread his hands. 'Until recently a countryman of yours, Godfroi of Poitiers, was helping me to organise my writings in Paris but he has become a Master himself and has studies of his own to pursue. I may have to go to England at a moment's notice, so cannot return to it myself. What I need is someone to carry on with my work in Paris. Will you help me?'

Matthieu stared so long at the man he now realised was Stephen Langton, the exiled Archbishop of Canterbury, that he thought the man's image would be forever engraved upon his mind. His first impulse was to move to kiss the Archbishop's ring, but since no hand was forthcoming, he stuttered out his answer.

'Surely, Your Grace must have many more fitting scribes that you can call upon?'

'None of them personally recommended to me by the head of the Cistercian order himself,' Stephen said, smiling kindly. 'You may recall that this order has given sanctuary to not only myself but the great Saint Thomas Becket before me, and I would like to show my gratitude. I admire a man who has a strong faith, Matthieu, someone not afraid to stand up for his beliefs – whatever it costs him and from what Arnald-Amalric says, you sound like such a man.'

*

Stephen asked Matthieu if he would like to take a stroll in the gardens. It was a pleasantly warm afternoon, with just enough breeze to freshen the air and they passed by pear trees so abundantly loaded with fruit that the monks had placed wooden supports beneath the boughs to bear the weight. Stephen twisted off a couple of the fruits and they carried on, munching through the sweet, juicy flesh.

Matthieu flexed his shoulders, feeling some of the knots of the last weeks beginning to release.

'Have you any hope of the situation changing in England?' he asked.

Stephen shook his head. 'John has been excommunicated, that's the last I heard. Have you ever met him?'

'Once or twice.'

'He's quite different from his brothers, isn't he? They were all men of action. John is deeper and broods; he never forgets for a minute that, until Richard's death, he was the youngest and relatively unimportant son. A start like that in life often brings out the tyrant in a man I've found.'

'And yet God has seen fit to have him crowned king?'

'Yes, God works in mysterious ways, does he not?'

They reached an open space and Stephen lay down on the ground, stretching out his long limbs.

'What I don't understand,' Matthieu said, 'is why God has called you to such an important post and then not allowed you to take it up.'

Stephen smiled. 'If that's the only thing you don't understand about God, Matthieu, then you're doing well. I didn't ask to become the Archbishop of Canterbury. That was the Pope's decision, and now I'm neither one thing nor another because John won't let me into the country. Is that what God wanted for me, to leave my studies and become a wanderer with no purpose?' he hesitated. 'I sense a great anger in you my friend.'

Matthieu swallowed. He too had become a wanderer with no purpose, and everything he once held dear had been taken from him.

I'm more perplexed than angry,' he said. 'I haven't lived a faultless life, but I always tried to do God's will. Only instead of rewarding that effort, He has tried me sorely at every turn. It's as if God mocks me for my weaknesses.'

Stephen looked directly at him. 'Are you talking about a woman?'

Matthieu coloured and turned away. 'Is it that obvious?'

'Ah, Matthieu,' Stephen said, putting his hands behind his head and gazing up into the cloudless sky, 'Saint Paul told us to flee temptation. I think it's a very good idea.'

'You have suffered too?'

'God doesn't promise that we will never be tempted, Matthieu, but He does promise to be with us in the midst of it. And each time we can choose either to know Him, or to turn our backs on Him; but every time we stray, He doesn't say, 'right, I've had enough of you, you're on you're own now' – like we would. No, he keeps on coming back, time after time. Until, eventually, we make the right choice.'

Matthieu looked up into the vastness of the sky and felt sweat trickling down his back. He hadn't made the right choice, not yet. Even though he was as far away from Joana as he had ever been, his body still ached for her.

CHAPTER 51

3rd October 1539
Hampton Court, England

'I found them in a reliquary,' Johanna said.

The King looked at her sharply. 'A reliquary? Whose reliquary?'

She bit her lip. 'Saint Thomas Becket, sire.'

'That impostor!' The King's shook his head impatiently. 'No, I meant... where did you get the reliquary?'

'Ah.' She hesitated. If she told him, it would seal Abbot Whiting's fate, of that she was sure; but then she reminded herself that if she didn't, Matthew would suffer instead. 'It was something my companion had been told to take to France.'

'Johanna...' A flicker of pain crossed the King's face as he stood up and the fingers of his right hand closed gently around her neck, almost caressingly – but Johanna was not deceived. She had seen him strike even Cromwell – and knew that he would snap *her* neck in two, should the fancy take him.

He picked up and cradled the largest diamond in his other hand and raised it to the light of the candles. 'By whom, Johanna?'

The pressure increased gently but inexorably until Johanna found she was struggling to breathe.

'It was his Abbot, Majesty.'

The King took his hand away. 'You were travelling with a monk?'

'No, Majesty.' Her legs were shaking so badly now that it was all she could do to keep upright. 'Matthew has taken no vows. He's an innocent party to all this.'

'Innocent, eh?' The King gave an impatient sigh. 'Johanna!' She practically jumped out of her skin. 'Which abbey did these come from!'

Johanna looked down at her trembling hands and could not prevent herself taking a small step backwards. 'From Glastonbury, sire.'

The King grasped her upper arm so tightly that she cried out. 'What did you just say?'

'G-glastonbury, sire.'

He let her go of her then and cupped the diamond in both of his hands, looking at it as though it were a phantom that might disappear any moment.

'Could it really be?' he said, wonderingly. 'Could it?'

His hands shook too now.

'The Star of Bethlehem, Johanna,' he breathed, all of his attention absorbed by the jewel. 'Said to have been brought to Glastonbury by Jesus himself. And I had thought it only legend.' His eyes betrayed his excitement. 'God save you, Johanna, for bringing this to me. I will find out the truth of why those knaves were trying to keep it away from me, you can be sure of that.'

He sat down again and pulled her back onto his knee then replaced the large diamond with the others on a table beside them.

'It was especially brave of you to come here, seeing how things stood between us.' His hand kneaded the flesh at her waist as he spoke. 'Do you know how long I have sought that diamond? And those evil monks have kept it hid from me. Pray tell us, what would Jesus want with a diamond, they said?' His face was earnest, almost pleading. 'You would not believe how they defile themselves, Johanna. Some of the things that come to pass in those so-called religious houses, I could not possibly speak of to a maid. And they store up treasure for themselves on Earth, make no mistake about that, even though they know the Lord forbade it; but what need have *they* of jewels, Johanna? They are not kings. It is *We* who must look magnificent in front of our people – it is expected. Priests do not need to go about wearing jewels.'

He picked up the large diamond again and Johanna looked at it too. Could it really havc bclonged to Jesus? Is that why it radiated such calm? Could she have unknowingly carried something that precious at her breast?

'They think nothing of stealing beautiful jewels like this from their King,' Henry continued, his megrim obviously completely forgotten. 'Well, let me tell you. I shall have a new crown fashioned for these diamonds, and the Star of Bethlehem will be at the fore.' He tilted her chin so that she was forced to look directly at him. 'And I'll tell the smiths to use the jewels from my old crown to make a new one for-' He stopped. 'I am to be married again, Johanna.'

So that's what everyone wasn't telling her. Henry had managed to find someone willing to marry him after all. Johanna's heart went out to the unfortunate bride, whoever she was.

'May I offer you my congratulations, Majesty?'

'Will she forgive me, do you think?'

Johanna was perplexed. Who did he mean?

'In my heart I still yearn for her, you know, sweet little Jane. But, you see, the country must have another heir. One boy simply isn't enough.'

'I'm sure she would be glad for you,' Johanna murmured. 'Queen Jane always had your welfare uppermost in her heart.'

Tears shone in his eyes and, appalled, Johanna looked around for something to dry them. She couldn't offer him the screwed up bit of linen she had in her sleeve...

'She did, didn't she,' he said, hoarsely. 'Ah, God, why did she have to die?'

Just then, Johanna spotted an edge of lace at the King's own sleeve, and pulled on it.

'Here now, Majesty,' she said, pushing the splendidly embroidered handkerchief into his hand. 'I'm sure Jane and all of Heaven is right glad for you in this match. It isn't good for a king to be without a queen. Everyone knows that.'

Henry took the handkerchief. 'And I'm sorry, Johanna. It's just that you remind me so much of her. Selfless. Look how you brought these to me, to your *King*, with no thought for yourself...'

Johanna bit her lip. Could he be losing his wits? The old Henry would have never assumed that. The old Henry knew that everyone demanded something of him, sooner or later.

After a while, he picked up the diamonds again. 'I must offer you something in exchange,' he said, looking down at her shabby gown. 'What would you have?'

This was the chance she had been waiting for – but it had come too soon and the information about the diamond had set her reeling. What had she done? If the largest diamond had really belonged to Jesus, then no wonder the Abbot had been willing to put their lives at risk and been prepared to go to the Tower himself, rather than allow it to fall into the King's hands. What evil had she done in her ignorance?

'F-for myself, I wish nothing, except your happiness, Majesty,' she stuttered.

'Nonsense,' the King said, smiling indulgently. 'I know you seek something, that's why you came.'

Johanna squirmed, wishing she didn't have to have this conversation whilst she was sitting on his knee. 'It seems but a small matter, now I know the provenance of what I carried.'

'Everyone seeks something of me, Johanna,' he sighed. 'It's something I have got used to. Is it this monk you wish to save?'

'If it pleases Your Majesty,' Johanna said, wondering if she should remind him that Matthew wasn't yet a monk, 'I swear he knew nothing about the diamonds, sire.'

'God's wounds,' the King said. 'What knaves these churchmen are! To use two children for such a task! And where is this Matthew you speak of?'

She took a deep breath. 'I fear he is in the Tower, Majesty.'

'The Tower, eh?' The King sounded serious enough, but something made her wonder if he was actually laughing at her. 'And you swear he's innocent, knew nothing about the diamonds?'

'No, Majesty.'

'Why were you with him, Johanna?'

She braced herself. 'When I made the mistake of leaving court, I had nowhere to go. My uncle and my family would not have me back, on account of my displeasing Your Majesty; so I went to the Priory at Amesbury. Now Your Majesty has taken a firm hand with establishments such as those, rooting out the corruption that I could see for myself had become part of their very foundation, and was soon to close.' She peered at him, to see how she was doing. 'I was on my way to Fontevraud Abbey, the place where I grew up, in France.'

The King smiled at the mention of Fontevraud. 'Some of my ancestors are buried in that Abbey, did you know?'

'Yes, Majesty,' Johanna said. 'The tombs of the second Henry and his son Richard are wondrous to behold.'

'So I'm told,' he said. 'You know, of course, that those lands were once part of my kingdom.' A faraway look came into the King's eye. 'It is my dream to win them back for England. But,' he gave himself a little shake, 'you were going to tell me how you came to be with this monk.'

'I met him at Weymouth,' Johanna said, sighing inwardly. If the King persisted in thinking of Matthew as a monk, it would go badly for them. 'He told me he was a novice at Glastonbury Abbey and was travelling abroad to complete his novitiate. We decided to take ship together, for safety, but before we left England he was arrested and left a package behind with me. I had no choice but to go on without him but there was a storm whilst we were at sea and the package broke open. It was then I could see that it contained a reliquary, with those diamonds concealed within it-'

'God's blood!' The King pushed her off his knee and stood up. 'It's the treachery of these churchmen that astounds me, Johanna! They seek to hide what is mine but are not brave enough to do the job themselves, and put young lives in danger. I tell you, Johanna, they are not fit to care for souls, truly they are not.'

And yet, she wondered sadly, are you – now that you call yourself the Head of the Church of England?

'Come to me tomorrow,' Henry said, 'and we shall walk in the gardens. Tonight, I shall speak to Baron Cromwell and find out what has happened to this friend of yours. Have no fear of that.'

CHAPTER 52

September
Saint Gilles de Loire, France

As evening came on, Jo picked up what she needed – a trowel, brought specially from home for the purpose, a sharp knife to cut the turf, a torch, kneeling pad, garden gloves, Blanche's ashes in their plastic pot and Blanche's prayer book. Feeling strangely breathless, Jo placed everything into two carrier bags and climbed down the iron staircase outside. It was quiet and warm, and there was just enough daylight left to complete her task. She walked over to the little wooden cross, pulled on the gloves and flopped her kneeler onto the grass.

The thought of inadvertently digging into the remains of a dead cat bothered her, so she cut into the grass well to the side of the cross, slicing away at the roots underneath so that she soon had a square flap of turf. Once she put that back over the hole and watered it, everything would look as before – just what Blanche had wanted. Right time to dig. Jo put the soil carefully into one of the empty bags and when the hole was almost big enough to take the pot of ashes, her trowel had hit something hard. Jo looked into the hole she saw the gleam of metal. Dammit! It was probably the box the cat was buried in. Jo looked at the cross. It was far away enough. How big had the cat been? For a brief moment she toyed with just emptying the ashes into the hole, minus their pot, but she'd promised a dignified end for Blanche's remains and dignified was what she would have.

Ten minutes later, Jo was still knocking against hard surface and she realised that she was digging out a sizeable metal box. As she cleared away the soil, she saw a padlock on one side and her mind flicked to the second key Blanche had left in the envelope. Could it possibly be for this? Jo shook her head. Why would Blanche leave a key for a box with a dead cat in it?

She looked at her watch. It was nearly ten o' clock and her back was aching. Jo sat back on her heels and stretched. Back up the metal steps, she retrieved the key and a couple more plastic bags. What would Jean-Yves or Rebecca think if they saw her digging in the garden so late at night? She could hardly tell them she was paying her last respects to the cat.

The key turned in the padlock with ease, as if someone had oiled the lock well before the box was buried, but Jo still couldn't open the lid until she'd dug it out further. This was a job for a spade not a trowel, she mused, but she couldn't stop now. Tomorrow she'd look for a garden centre because it would be impossible to cover up this size of hole with only that little square of turf. Perhaps she could say she'd planted a tree or a rose bush in honour of Blanche's memory.

When she started on a fourth carrier bag, all four edges of the box were visible in the light of her torch. She pulled at the lid. Nothing. With a sinking heart Jo realised that she was going to have to dig the box out completely. Sighing, she gouged at the soil, levering and sweating until she could at last lift out the whole thing, and then she collapsed on the grass, panting.

At least the box itself wasn't particularly heavy. Not a fat cat then, she thought wryly. To Jo's surprise she felt nervous as she lifted the lid. Why, when she dealt with death and dying all the time and dead bodies held no fears for her? But when an owl hooted overhead, she withdrew into her neck like a frightened turtle.

Jo shone her torch inside. Bubble wrap. Tons of the stuff, and underneath a supermarket carrier bag holding something oblong – another box with the cat's remains? Jo lifted the bag and sniffed. It smelled of earth and wood, but nothing else. Glad to be wearing gardening gloves, she stripped off the first bag and found another inside, and another – it was like a macabre game of pass-the-parcel. Five carrier bags later, she was finally holding a drawstring cotton bag and an envelope, with Blanche's writing, sealed inside a clear plastic bag. Jo squinted at it. This writing was more legible than that on the envelope upstairs and must have been written some time ago. Quickly, she tidied up as much as she could, hiding the bags of soil out of sight and dropping the metal box into the bin. Then she gathered the rest up and went back into the apartment, dumping everything inside the kitchen door.

What was the object in the bag and what secrets would she find in the letter? Was this where Mat learned that his true parents were really Blanche and Patrick – like happened in books? Jo spread newspaper out on the floor and exchanged her gardening gloves for Marigolds. The kitchen wasn't perhaps the best place to look at cat remains, but she was beginning to be sure there'd never been a cat in the first place. Blanche had left quite a few surprises since her death, but no one could have disliked cats more than she did.

Which to open first? Jo's fingers strayed to the cotton bag. It was simply styled, like an old-fashioned pump bag, and she loosened the neck so that she could peer inside. All that she could see was more plastic wrapping. Impatiently she peeled this away too and then caught her lip as she saw the unmistakeable glint of gold underneath.

Jo found herself holding a wooden casket stunningly decorated with gold and blue enamel. It was about a hand-span wide, half as high again and about a half a hand in depth and there were scenes on each side – men in armour carrying swords, one of them was having his head chopped off. Wait a minute, she breathed deeply, that man wasn't wearing armour. In fact, *he* looked like a priest. Her breath escaped slowly. Could this be Thomas Becket? She looked more closely. He'd been murdered in Canterbury cathedral – in fact, it was Blanche who'd told her the story.

Jo sat back, stunned. Was that why Blanche had called the 'cat' *Thomas?* Hardly daring to breathe now, she lifted the lid of the casket, and then nearly dropped the whole thing onto the floor. It was filled to the brim with pearls, rubies, emeralds, diamonds – all glinting in fabulous settings of gold: not what she had expected at all.

Shaking, Jo placed the casket on the floor and reached for the letter in the plastic bag.

'My dear Mat and Jo, If you are reading this now, you will finally know of my 'secret'. I am sorry to have to deceive you both for all those years but I'm sure you'll understand why it was necessary. I have never loved anyone as much as I loved Patrick, with the exception of you two of course, and the time we spent together here was some of the happiest of my life.

Shortly after we bought this apartment, a part of the bedroom wall collapsed. It was a frightening experience, as you can imagine, but it was when we found the reliquary. Our best guess is that it might have been stolen from an abbey during the French Revolution and then hidden inside the chimney.

Due to the sensational nature of what we had found, I'm afraid we had to keep its existence secret to protect our relationship – although we were thrilled to be sharing our home with such a great saint!

I did sell some of the jewellery, to help put things right in the apartment, but otherwise we left everything untouched. I am hoping that you'll be able to do what we could not – return Saint Thomas to his home in Canterbury Cathedral. And as for the jewellery? Well, that's up to you!'

Jo let the letter fall onto the kitchen table and shook her head in bewilderment. How hard it must have been for them, but how exciting too. A secret lover and a secret hide-away in France. And neither she nor Mat had ever suspected!

Jo bent to the casket and began to lift out the jewels one by one. Underneath, she found a much faded purple velvet pouch and tipped its contents onto her palm: a cockle-shell sized piece of yellow bone that looked like it might have been part of a skull, and a tattered piece of linen with a long lock of dark hair falling out of it. Could these really be actual bits of Thomas Becket? Surely his hair hadn't been that long, even before he had a tonsure? Jo suppressed a shiver and wondered what did one do in the presence of a saint's relic – kiss it, bow down to it? She tried to remember how long it was since Thomas Beckett had died – more than eight hundred years! Better slip it back into the pouch. She didn't want it to crumble before her eyes.

What was she to do now? Sweat was trickling down her back and she desperately wanted a shower but first she had to find somewhere safe to hide this.

As she looked around the apartment it suddenly came to her – could this have been why Monsieur Moreau had done all that tapping when he came to look round? Could he somehow have found out about the reliquary? Her eyes strayed to her mobile phone on the kitchen table. Mat would be asleep now but she would have to ring him first thing in the morning and ask him what she should do.

But how was she going to tell him that his adored aunt and his spiritual mentor had not only been lovers, but had been hiding the reliquary of a famous saint?

CHAPTER 53

May 1215
Paris

Matthieu took her letter to the window of his study and read it using the last rays of daylight. His mother was unwell and asking for him. He pursed his lips. If his mother was asking for him, then things must be very bad. She had sent no word at all to him since the Count cast him out.

The letter was from Joana and slowly Matthieu traced the letters of her strong, flowing script. He had taught her this himself, little knowing how much her writing would come to mean for him. Even now, when he hadn't seen her for over five years, the thought of her could still send a shaft of longing straight through his heart.

He turned around and placed the letter on his desk. Stephen had finally been allowed to take up his See in Canterbury and was even now manoeuvring John of England into signing a charter protecting the liberties of the Church and his vassals. Matthieu looked at the fine books arrayed on Stephen's shelves and the piles of parchments on his desk. Most of Stephen's writings were there somewhere, along with the notes Matthieu himself had taken during his lectures.

He ran his fingers over the smooth curve of his tonsure, seeking reassurance, and picked up his seal from his desk. Two months ago he himself had been dignified with the title of Master of Theology; something that still had the semblance of a dream.

Darkness was falling and roosting birds filled the air, circulating in waves around the towers of Notre Dame. Matthieu lit a candle and bent to Joana's letter.

'My dear brother. I hope to find you well and know that life is kinder to you than it is to us in the south. Since the great losses of Toulousan lives at Muret, Count Raimon has decided to go again to petition the Pope; so I believe it would be safe for you to come to Toulouse to see your mother.'

He closed his eyes, remembering the vision he had had in the courtyard of the Château Narbonnais, of the youth and flower of Toulouse lying, dying on a battlefield. Muret had been such a battle: Monfort the victor and King Pedro of Aragon slain. Tears ran slowly down Matthieu's face at the thought of that great king and defender of the Church being slain by those supposedly doing God's will.

'Guillem has reached almost eleven summers. He is in the service of the Count of Foix and I can hardly bear life without him, but I cannot

hold him back-'

Another stab of longing – Guillem and Raimondet were growing into men and Matthieu had seen none of it.

'*Montfort has decreed that no southern woman may take a southern lord as husband – all must marry a northerner. Recruits to the convents have increased by five hundred fold, as you can well imagine.*'

Montfort was attempting to stamp both his authority in the south – but at what price? His hold there was tenuous at best, and increasingly depended on outright brutality. At least Raimondet was safe in England, and would in all probability have had wish met to be taught by the great William Marshall; but when he returned? Matthieu shook his head. There was hardly anything left for him to inherit.

'*As always, I send my love and prayers for you and hope that, if you come to see your mother, you will not forget me. Yours ever, Joana.*'

Matthieu sighed. Forget her? Nothing was less likely than that.

CHAPTER 54

3rd October 1539
Hampton Court, England

Cromwell's eyes narrowed as Johanna and the King's emerged from his chamber. Peter Mewtas looked hopefully towards a stack of rolled parchments.

'Peter,' the King said, 'find Johanna a room for tonight. And bring her to me in the morning.'

'Yes, Majesty,' Mewtas said, hiding his dismay. 'Come with me, Lady Johanna.' He managed to push the parchments into Cromwell's hands as he passed.

Outside the King's rooms, Mewtas stroked his beard thoughtfully. 'Where would you like to be?' he said.

'Might I stay with Lord Lisle?' Johanna ventured, but Mewtas shook his head. 'Anne Basset has gone to stay with her kinsfolk the Denny's today and there are no other women at court now.' He tapped his front teeth. 'Follow me.'

When she realised where he was taking her, she faltered.

'I-I can't stay in the Queen's suite,' she said.

'Why not? It's only for one night,' he said, impatiently.

'But, there's no one else there at all.'

Only echoing rooms and memories of Jane's last day on Earth. No, she did not wish to go there.

'Well, you'll have to stay in one of the apartments around Base Court.'

'Yes,' she said. It was a little below her station, but in the circumstances she could hardly mind that.

*

Tucked up in a hastily warmed bed hung about with heavy silk, Joanna replayed her conversation with the King over and over in her mind and looked at it from every possible angle – whilst her heart pounded fiercely in her chest. So much depended upon Henry's goodwill. Would he keep his promise and speak to Cromwell? Or was she being hopelessly naive to hope that, now the King was actually in possession of the diamonds, he would do anything more than thank her as he had?

She groaned as she thought about the largest diamond, the one he had named the Bethlehem Star. Could it be possible that such a thing had belonged to Jesus, a man who kept no roof over his head and ate with sinners? It was said that Joseph of Arimathea had visited Glastonbury, and that the bones of the fabled King Arthur were buried there. But she had heard nought said of a famous diamond and there was no mention of Jesus owning them in the Bible; gold, frankincense and myrrh – yes, but diamonds? No.

Ah, Henry – he had cast off his first Queen Catherine and the Pope, and was now forced to look everywhere for signs of his righteousness. The Boleyn had turned out to be, by all accounts, a faithless shrew and dearest Jane had died. Would Henry now see the justification of his actions in God's provenance of bringing him the diamond?

She wriggled to get comfortable and thumped the feather bolster until the lumps dispersed. Could she have misjudged him? Had his entreaties to her after Jane's death been motivated by grief and not simply by lust? He hadn't made any demands upon her today, just been embarrassingly pleased that she'd brought the diamonds to him – her *King*. What must it be like to never know if you were loved for yourself rather than because you were the king?

She pulled the bed covers higher, tucking them in under her chin, and tried to remember some of the lullabies her nurse had sung to her as a babe. Tears welled up and trickled down her cheeks. It was unbearably sad that in this world no one was ever really loved for themselves, but only for what they were worth to another. The natural state of being was loneliness – unless one could look to God. She wondered how it would feel to raise a child, not as grand ladies like her mother had done – giving it up to a wet nurse – but to suckle, and grow close to it? As a nun, motherhood was something she would never know, but it was a sacrifice she was more than willing to make – if it meant she would not suffer the same fate as Jane.

But what if your husband was Matthew? a little voice said in her head. She smiled and wrapped her arms about her body. It was pleasant to imagine being in the arms of someone as handsome as Matthew, but the simple truth was that he was so far below her station in life that it would never be possible for them to make a life together – even if he were not serious about living the religious life. So why was she going to such lengths to save him?

She traced her lips with a finger, wondering how it would feel to be kissed, and then shook herself. How sinful her thoughts were. Why was she not praying for Matthew's safety?

Johanna climbed out of bed and knelt on the cold floor. In truth, it had been hard to pray since she'd found the evidence of their superior's betrayal in the diamonds, but she must not give up on God on account of human weakness.

But do I really need, she asked herself in growing bewilderment, to lock myself away from the world in order to love and serve God, when He is always and everywhere with me?

Before any answer could come, there was a loud knocking at the outer door of her suite and she heard the maid get up to answer.

'Is my Lady Johanna asleep?' she heard a man say, and with a start realised that it was Cromwell come to visit her.

'Yes, my lord,' Alice answered.

There was a pause. 'Then I'd like you to wake her.'

Johanna's stomach churned. Had he come to take her to some awful place? With shaking hands, she pulled on her robe.

'Baron Cromwell is here to see you, my lady,' the maid said, coming into the bedroom. 'I'm very sorry, but he says it's most urgent.'

Johanna found the Baron seated on a stool in the small anteroom where the maid had slept. she looked at him carefully, trying to judge his mood. He wore a velvet cap and travelling cloak, so he was definitely on his way somewhere...

She shivered and clasped her hands to stop them trembling, but he waited calmly, his fingers laced. She noticed his rings, many more than he had used to wear and that his chin now spilled a little over the collar of his shirt. Times were obviously good for Thomas Cromwell.

When he saw her he stood up and took off his hat. 'Lady Johanna,' he began. 'I am sorry to wake you.'

'Has there been an accident?' she said. 'Some emergency?'

'Accident, no,' he said, 'and I don't think this is quite an emergency; but I do need to speak to you.'

'Could it not have waited until morning?' she asked, lifting her chin a fraction, and trying not to sound afraid of him. 'I'm very tired, and the King wishes to walk with me in the morning.'

'So he does,' Cromwell said, smoothly. 'But he also wishes me to find this monk of yours. I'm on my way up to London now, as you can see.'

Johanna bit her lip at the term monk. The Baron was a very precise man, he had to be to keep up with the Kings mercurial changes of heart, and would have used that word deliberately, to try an irritate her, set her off-guard.

'Really? So late at night?' she said.

'I thought I'd pay you a visit before I set off. Perhaps get some details that will help me to find him.'

'Of course.' She could hardly believe her luck. He hadn't come to arrest her after all. 'Will you sit, Baron?' She turned to the maid, 'I need to dress and then you may sleep in my bed.'

When she had put on a kirtle under her robe and the maid, whose name was Alice, had taken herself off to bed, Johanna sat down with Cromwell.

'It's good of you to help me,' she said. 'I'm terribly worried about my friend Matthew. He was arrested, but he's innocent, you see.'

The Baron's dark eyes regarded her unblinkingly and for a moment she felt as if he were uncovering, secret by secret, all that was hidden inside her head and trying to decide which best to use against her. Despite her fear, Johanna felt an insane desire to snigger; Cromwell had just the right nose for his job – long, sloping, and ending in a snout!

'My lady, if your friend is innocent then you have no need to fear,' the Baron said. 'Now, tell me, where exactly was this Matthew when he was arrested?'

'We were waiting to sail to France,' Johanna said, knowing his assurance was an outright lie.

'Sailing?' Cromwell frowned. 'From which port?

'Er, not a port, exactly.' She dare not be too specific on account of Gerald. 'We were at a fishing village in Devon.'

'Devon?' Cromwell's eyebrows rose. 'I thought you were a novice at Amesbury priory. Surely there was somewhere nearer?'

Johanna tensed, knowing that Cromwell had little sympathy for those choosing the monastic life. 'Indeed. We were departing from Devon because we had been ordered by our superiors to take a reliquary of Thomas Becket to France.' She could feel sweat starting on her back. 'It's well known that the King's agents have been stopping people at the ports – to prevent valuables from the monasteries being taken abroad.'

He nodded. 'Which was exactly what you were doing, as it turns out. His Majesty has showed me the diamonds.'

'Yes.' She slid her palms together. 'But at that time we knew nothing of their existence.'

'Didn't you find them in the reliquary?' Cromwell said.

'Only after Matthew had been arrested. There was a storm as I was sailing to France. Everything in the cabin was flung about. The reliquary broke open.'

He eyed her sceptically.

'I'm telling you the truth, Baron,' she said. 'But for that I would never have looked inside of the reliquary.'

Cromwell stood up and took off his cloak. So, this was not going to be a short interview, then. 'So, when Matthew was arrested, where exactly were you and this reliquary?'

'I-' She hesitated, horribly aware that if she got this wrong, she could incriminate them both. 'I was on the ship, Matthew had yet to board. I had taken the reliquary with me.'

'I see,' Cromwell said, 'or rather I don't. Didn't you tell the King that *Matthew* had been asked to take the reliquary from Glastonbury to France?'

'Yes, but I was carrying it for him because he was bringing the bags.'

'*Bringing the bags*?' Cromwell's eyebrows lifted. 'How domestic.'

Sweat now trickled down her spine even though the room was cooling. 'We were travelling together so as not to attract attention – I told the King that.'

'Ah, so you did, and you were on the ship, with the reliquary, when Matthew was arrested. Why didn't you say something at the time, plead his innocence?'

'The captain wouldn't let me. He didn't want to be implicated. He set sail and there was nothing I could do.'

Cromwell sucked air in through his teeth. 'So you had the reliquary and you were on your way to France. Surely, Lady Johanna, you had what you wanted, so why come back? You knew the King was angry with you.'

Johanna paused, searching for the right words. 'When I saw those diamonds – I realised we'd actually been tricked into smuggling something away that rightly belonged to the King. I didn't think His Majesty would be bothered about the reliquary going, especially as he does not esteem the saint, but I know what the penalty is for concealing valuables from him-'

'Not pleasant,' Cromwell nodded. 'So you came back to save Matthew, even though you knew you would have to speak to the King on his behalf? Weren't you worried that Henry would refuse to see you?'

'Of course. But as you can see, His Majesty is well pleased to see me, on account of the diamonds and my honesty in bringing them to him.'

'Yes,' Cromwell sighed. 'Lucky for you, the King is partial to diamonds – and the company of a pretty woman. And yet there's no shortage of high-born women anxious to please him at the moment – so what, Lady Johanna...,' he stood and took her chin in his fingers, turning her head this way and that, 'is so remarkable about you, I wonder?'

She dare not pull away; so much depended upon his help her but she was taken aback by his presumption.

'I have no idea,' she said, 'but it's kind of you to call me pretty, Baron. In truth I think I am nothing special.'

'Hm.' Cromwell sat down again and regarded her as though she were a horse he'd like to buy.

'Have I given you enough information to find Matthew?' she asked.

'I think so,' he said, steepling his fingers and putting the tips to his lips. 'I'll see what I can do when I'm back in London.'

'I would be most grateful,' she said.

'I'm sure,' he said, replacing his hat, and then standing up to pull on his cloak. 'Sleep well, Lady Johanna, you must look your best tomorrow for your walk with the King. You know His Majesty is recently betrothed?'

He said it carelessly, as if an aside, but Johanna recognised what he was about.

'I do,' she said. 'He told me himself. Why do you ask?'

'Just making sure,' he said, with a thin smile, 'that you've no plans to marry him yourself.'

'Baron Cromwell!' Johanna straightened her back. 'I am committed to the life of a nun. My only marriage will be to God.'

'Of course, of course' Cromwell said, now barely concealing his amusement. 'Forgive me, but that's a pity – is all I can say.'

*

Cromwell's Rooms
Hampton Court

'Lord Lisle confirms that the Lady Johanna Grenfell brought the diamonds with her. He is not sure how many, but says she found them in a reliquary. I feel she is obviously the novice who was sent from Amesbury, and her 'friend' Matthew must be the monk from Glastonbury.'

Cromwell put down his quill and leaned back to yawn. The Prioress of Amesbury and the Abbot of Glastonbury must have been working together to get those diamonds out of the reach of the King. He pursed his lips. In his experience, 'working together' would be the very least of it. Why these people even bothered taking an oath of celibacy was beyond him.

Both novices were safely in the net, but which place had the diamonds come from? And why hadn't the girl been apprehended with the monk when they were travelling together? How had she managed to get away? He'd have words with someone about that. It would have saved a lot of trouble just now. God's blood! Henry was an amorous old fool. Couldn't he see the girl was no more interested in him this time than she'd been before?

'His Majesty has instructed me to look into the arrest of one novice monk named Matthew, who was apprehended at 'a port' whilst attempting to take four large diamonds hidden in a reliquary of the impostor saint, Thomas Becket, to France. The novice's companion, Lady Johanna Grenfell states that this Matthew had no knowledge of the diamonds.'

He didn't believe her, but then he wasn't about to antagonise her by telling her that. There had been a worrying look on the King's face when he was telling him all this. A look Cromwell didn't like. It was the one that said, I've been talking to someone far above your social standing, Crum. Someone a base born chap like you would never understand; but someone, by the way, I'd rather like to take to bed.

Well, that wasn't a problem. He didn't care one way or another who the King bedded, just as long as it didn't endanger the security of the country.

*

When she returned to her bedroom, Alice was fast asleep, one arm flung above her head, and her body lying diagonally across the mattress. Johanna shook her. She felt mean doing it but it was what the girl would expect. Alice woke with a start and climbed swiftly out of bed.

'Thank you, my lady,' she said, pulling her wrap around her and walking through to the other room. 'Let's hope no one else disturbs us tonight.'

She curled up in the warm space left by Alice, and willed her heart to slow down. She had not given a good account of herself to Cromwell, she knew that, but then he had not pressed her very much. He seemed more concerned that she didn't seek to marry the King!

Her stomach grumbled and she shifted about. It didn't look as though she was going to get any sleep tonight. Thank God and all his saints the King had kept his word and asked Cromwell to look for Matthew. Now all she could do was pray that when he was found, Cromwell would give the order to release him; but she had to admit to herself that there was no good reason why he should. She and Matthew were nothing. Two less novices in this world – and who would care?

It seemed such a short time later that Alice came to wake her. Her mouth was parched and her limbs grown stiff with tension. The maid had brought hot posset, and she drank it down, savouring the ginger and ale.

'Will you eat something, my lady?' Alice asked, but she shook her head. Even the mention of food had sent her sick.

There was a new gown and kirtle laid out for her over a cupboard.

'I've sent your other clothes to the laundress,' Alice said, anxiously. 'I hope you don't mind?'

'No, of course not,' she said. 'Thank you, Alice. I've done a lot of travelling lately. Who may I thank for these?'

'It was the Baron, my lady. He said to make sure you had everything you needed.'

Johanna sluiced herself over a pretty bowl with a jug of warm water, and tried to hide her surprise at the baron's thoughtfulness. Alice handed her some linen towels for her to dry herself and then she held out her arms for her chemise and allowed Alice to dress her in the finely brocaded kirtle and red silk gown. She didn't ask to whom they had belonged, for it was probably someone who had died, but allowed Alice to patiently comb the knots out of her hair.

'Shall I see if I can find you a hood, my lady, for your walk with the King? I heard you was going to be a nun, so I don't expect you have any of your own?'

'Thank you, Alice,' she said. 'I should like that.'

When Alice went off to find the hood, she quickly checked her purse. All she had in the world were a few silver coins and the opal ring. At this rate, she would be walking back to France. Taking a sudden fancy, she tried on the ring. It fitted her third finger and she admired it there, wondering who the 'Catharine' was that it had belonged to. She kept it on for it looked well there, and made her seem less poor.

Alice returned with a lovely, red silk French hood, its edges piped with contrasting dark red velvet.

'Oh, it's wonderful,' she said. 'Where did you get it?'

Alice tapped the side of her head knowingly. 'I've lived here a while, my lady.'

After she'd finished dressing, Alice gave her a satisfied grin and pointed to the mirror on the wall. To Johanna's surprise, the mirror was made of glass and faithfully showed her reflection. What she saw in its depths made her gasp. All the fat had gone from her cheeks, and the bones stood out there now, echoing the curves of her collar bones. Her green eyes regarded herself coolly, but she saw in them a steadfastness and maturity that she hadn't possessed before.

'Some rouge?' Alice asked, but Johanna shook her head. There was only so far she was prepared to go.

There was a tap on the door and Peter Mewtas stood on the threshold, holding a fabulous sable-lined cloak.

'Lady Johanna,' he said. 'The King awaits you.'

CHAPTER 55

September
Saint Gilles de Loire, France

'Mat? It's Jo. Can I speak to you?'

She watched the slow flow of the Loire out of her window, willing it to calm her down. Her hand was shaking and she had to sit down. How long had it been since they last spoke?

'Hi, Jo,' Mat said. 'It's good to hear from you. Are you in France? Is there something wrong? I meant to ring you but I've been working non-stop since I got here. Just give me a minute.'

She heard the background noise fade.

'That's better. I've found an empty room so we should get some peace for a while. How are you?'

'I'm OK,' she said. Of course she did. What else did people say to each other, even if they met in a doctor's waiting room? 'Er, Mat?'

'Yes?'

'There's something I need to tell you and it's complicated.'

'OK, fire away.'

'Well,' Jo shifted uncomfortably because she still hadn't decided how much to tell him, 'I found something in the garden here and I don't know what to do with it. Is there any chance you could come to Saint Gilles?'

Silence.

'You've found something, in the garden? You didn't dig up the cat whilst you were burying Blanche's ashes, did you?'

'No,' Jo said. Blanche's ashes were still in the urn on the kitchen floor. 'There never was a cat, Mat.'

'No cat? So what did you find?'

'I think it's something to do with Thomas Becket.'

More silence.

'At least that's what I'm guessing it is, Mat, a reliquary – if that's the right name, but there's more.'

He let out a low whistle. 'How can there be more than a reliquary of Thomas Becket? Are we talking bits of the True Cross here?'

She thought that might be a joke but didn't really understand it. 'I had a look inside. There's a lot of jewellery.'

'Well, that can't have belonged to Becket.' There was another long silence and Jo desperately tried to imagine what he was thinking. 'And Blanche hardly ever wore jewellery, or at least not that I remember. Did you find what ever it is when you were burying her ashes?'

'Yes. I found a metal box and that was in it.' She hesitated. 'One of the keys she left us in that envelope fitted the padlock on the box.'

'I don't believe this: jewellery, *and* a reliquary. What on Earth was she doing with them, and why had she buried them in the garden – of all places? If she'd let me know, I would have suggested she give it to Canterbury Cathedral.'

'It's really hard to explain all this on the phone,' Jo said, losing her nerve. How *could* she tell him that his aunt and mentor had been lovers, and that was why they couldn't tell anyone about the reliquary? 'Is there *any* chance you could come here, Mat?'

A long pause.

'Hello?' she said.

'It's all right. I'm still here. I was thinking. I can't drop everything and come over to France right now. It's impossible. How did you get on with the guy who wants to buy the place?'

'Not very well,' she said, miserably. Why couldn't he just agree to come? Why did she have to face all this on her own?

'Isn't he offering a decent price?'

'No. It's nothing like that. I don't really like him very much.'

'You don't like him? But what's that got to do with selling the place?'

'He's horrible, Mat. I can't bear to think of leaving Blanche's ashes here and letting someone like him buy the apartment.'

Another long pause and then a sigh.

'You'll have to go to the police with what you've found, you know.'

'I can't.' If he didn't say he was coming soon, she was going to cut him off.

'Why not?'

'I-I.' She couldn't find the words. 'Look, I don't really want to tell you over the phone.'

There were sounds in the background and Mat's voice became muffled. 'I'm sorry, Jo. Someone just came in. What were you saying?'

She took a deep breath. 'I was saying, I don't really want to talk to you about it over the phone.'

'Yes, I heard that, but I can't come now, Jo-'

'Fine. I'll deal with it myself.'

'Wait! I wasn't saying I won't come, but I'll have to talk to the Bishop.'

Of course he would. Being a priest gave him less freedom than an army recruit.

'All right,' she said. 'But send me a text to let me know, will you?'

'Yes. Soon as I can. Bye, Jo. Take care.'

She hit the disconnect button and threw the phone across the room. When would she learn? There was no point in relying on him. He wasn't his own master. She'd have to deal with this herself.

*

By the time the wood pigeons had started their mournful call the following morning, Jo had barely slept. All night she'd been trying to decide what to do about the relic, Monsieur Moreau and Mat. She'd found a hiding place for the casket late last night, having been sorely tempted to throw it into the bin and have done with it.

As she wandered into the kitchen to put on the kettle, Jo looked at Blanche's ashes. Couldn't you have made life any more difficult for me, she thought ruefully. You were supposed to be my friend.

Of course, she could have simply hidden the reliquary in her car, driven back to England with it and dumped it on the doorstep of Canterbury Cathedral to let *them* sort it all out; but ferry passengers were searched sometimes, it would just be her luck, and she *had* found the casket on French soil – which probably meant it belonged to France...

And then there was still the matter of Blanche's ashes. Jo was determined not to leave them here if they were going to sell the apartment to Monsieur Moreau – *whatever* he was prepared to offer.

As for Mat... well, he'd left her to deal with the selling of this apartment as though it were nothing to do with him, and when she'd rung him for help, he still hadn't come. Jo clattered the teaspoon she was holding into the sink. Damn him!

*

Usually, a trip to a garden centre filled Jo with enthusiasm, a chance to wander amongst plants, some familiar, some new, and to explore avenues of gadgets, maybe even grab a 'bargain' plant that needed nursing back to health. Her garden at home was full of afflicted specimens that the nurse in her hadn't been able to resist. Today, however, she found it hard to concentrate and nearly every plant looked like it needed rescuing on account of the heat. Eventually she chose a plum tree for the hole in the garden and a potted cyclamen to take as a gift to Jean-Yves and Rebecca that night.

Back at the apartment, Jo took the tree and the urn of ashes down into the garden. She watered the plum and then left it to soak whilst she surveyed the hole. It was already big enough, which was a bonus because she didn't relish the thought of doing any more digging, so she sprinkled in some bonemeal and then picked up the urn. If she put it in there, she would never be able to sell this apartment to Moreau. Well, so be it.

Quietly she knelt and lowered the urn. Tears were streaming down her face.

'Goodbye, Blanche,' she whispered. 'I hope you're happy wherever you are. I'm sorry it didn't work out for you and Patrick, but I hope you're with him now. Don't worry about the reliquary, I'll sort it out somehow.'

She took Blanche's prayer book out of her pocket and opened it at random. *'O, angel of God, my guardian dear, to whom God's love commits me here. Ever this day be at my side, to light and guard, to rule and guide. Amen.'*

Not bad, for a novice, she thought as she shook the plum out of its pot and placed it into the hole, pushing in extra soil from the carrier bags and firming everything down with her heel. Snuffling as she worked, she made sure that the 'Thomas' cross was still standing straight in its corner. Before she left, she would have to find out who cared for the garden and ask them to keep up with watering until the plum got established.

CHAPTER 56

June 1215
Pamiers, Languedoc

'You may not harbour this sin,' the priest said, giving Joana a hostile look. 'You were raised a Christian, have lived all your life as a Christian. Why behave otherwise now?'

Joana locked her fingers and stared into her lap, trying not to shiver. She wouldn't answer his stupid questions if she could help it, but interrogations such as this were becoming commonplace in the South and many *had* spoken, fearing for their children or their livelihoods. As Aimeric's wife, Joana had thought herself immune. Until now.

'I order you,' the priest said, his voice rising, 'to tell me what you were doing, yesterday, in the house of Fabrissa of Durfort when the well known heretic, Arnald of Fanjeaux, was visiting!'

When had she not been in Fabrissa's house? They were friends; as close as she and Catharine had been, if not closer – had brought up their children together, laughed and cried together. Fabrissa was the only other person who knew the secret of Guillem's real father.

'I know nothing of Arnald of Fanjeaux,' Joana said. 'And Fabrissa is not a heretic.'

'Oh, come now!' Father Robert had a jolly face, almost kindly eyes, and a prodigious appetite for sex – in fact, Pamiers was full of his bastards. 'I have seen for myself,' he said, 'all those so-called 'Goodmen' visiting her household; Pamiers folk sneaking in, thinking themselves unobserved, to listen to that doctrine of demons! Don't tell me you didn't notice any of them whilst you were there?'

Even though it was summer outside, the room in the bowels of the church felt icy and sapped her energy.

'No, I didn't, ' she said.

Father Robert let out an exasperated sigh. 'You might think your husband an important man, but that won't save you, or his lands if you're found guilty of protecting heretics. He'll lose everything. Spare him that, at least. The Pope has made his intentions clear, we are to root out the heretics that multiply like vermin around us. *Why* won't you help me?'

Joana fought to hide her distaste. The Pope had allowed Simon of Montfort to perpetrate crime after crime, without lifting a hand. Monfort's men raped Guirada, the kindly Lady of Lavaur, and then threw her into a well to die. Montfort ordered the prisoners he captured at Bram to have their eyes gouged out and their noses cut off. Monfort thought nothing of torturing and enslaving even those to whom no taint of heresy could be attached, and regarded suffering impassively. Montfort repeatedly had the vineyards torn up and the crops spoiled. Montfort was the victor at Muret. Joana shuddered. That was when the madness truly arrived. If a king like Pedro of Aragon, who had faithfully served God and the Church by driving the infidel out of his country, could be struck down by the crusaders – what hope was there for any of them? The only thing she could thank God for now, was that Guillem was still too young to fight.

'Father, I am God's faithful servant,' she said quietly, 'and if I see anything of concern at Fabrissa's house, then I shall make haste to tell you. Does that satisfy you?'

The priest's eyes narrowed, but Joana ignored him and got up from her chair, willing her hands not to tremble. She smoothed down her robe, glad she had worn a simple one of homespun wool, and faced him directly. 'If that's all, I'll go now.'

He raised his hand, but only to make the Sign of the Cross before her. 'May God bless you and bring you everything you deserve,' he said, turning away abruptly.

How this man irked her! Before the crusade, he had treated her with the deference due to her position, counting himself lucky to be able to do so. Now the randy little cockerel had become a man to be feared. She would need to watch herself.

Outside the church, Agnes her maid, was waiting.

'Look happy,' Joana hissed, 'and not as though I've scarce got away with my life.'

They walked across the market square to where Joana's horse and trap was tethered. She climbed onto the seat beside Agnes, mustering as much dignity and calmness as she could. Many eyes watched, and calculated. Had she told all, or kept her silence?

When they reached her manor, one of the farm hands came running to meet them.

'Good lady!' he panted. 'Come quickly!'

Joana's heart turned over. 'What is it?' she asked.

'My Lord Aimeric's collapsed in the barn. He's asking for you, Mistress.'

Aimeric was lying amongst the straw, with a hand clasped against his chest. His eyes were closed and his breath was shallow, ragged. Pink spittle bubbled out of his dusky lips.

'Aimeric! Speak to me.' Joana took his hand and he grasped at her, but that was all he could do. He could not speak. 'Agnes, bring hot water and the powder we keep for pain,' Joana ordered, 'and, hurry, bring some blankets and a cloth!'

Aimeric clutched even more tightly at her hand as his back arched in a violent spasm and then subsided.

'Aimeric! No!' Joana shook him, slapped him, pinched his cheeks, shook him again, clawed at him, blew in his eyes. The farm hand tried to pull her away but she beat him off roughly.

'Don't hinder me!' she screamed. 'Aimeric, don't leave me! Not now!'

But as Aimeric's body relaxed and his eyes slid open, she could see there was no sight in them.

'Is he – is he dead, my lady?' Agnes stuttered, returning with the powders and blankets.

'No!' Joana shouted. 'He can't be dead. Dear God, they'll make me marry some French bastard, if he is, but I won't have it. I won't marry against my will ever again. I won't! Oh, Aimeric, come back to me, please!'

CHAPTER 57

4th October 1539
Hampton Court, England

'Good morning, my dear,' the King said, as Johanna joined him at the foot of the privy stairs.

The air was fresh, rowdy, and whipped up the ends of their cloaks. Johanna pulled the sables closer, feeling an exquisite warmth and softness that she had never, ever, thought to experience.

'Are you cold?' he asked, his pudgy face creased with concern. 'Would you prefer to go back inside?'

She looked up at the high brick walls of Hampton Court and shook her head. Already she felt better, just from being outside. Gallantly, the King took her hand and placed it on the crook of his elbow. Peter Mewtas gave a sly smile and Johanna knew the reason for it. Not many people were allowed to touch the King's Majesty.

'Did you sleep well?' he asked, and Johanna fixed a smile upon her face.

'Yes, thank you, Majesty.' It would serve no purpose to tell him that she had barely slept five minutes together. He liked people to be happy around him, and avoided those who came pleading their woes. 'I hope you did too?'

Rather absent mindedly, the King's other hand covered hers. 'Not so well, I'm afraid, Sweeting.' He gave her a little look.

'I'm sorry to hear that, Majesty. Did you have a bad dream?'

The King's face lit up. 'Funny you should ask me that, Johanna,' he said, steering her through the box-bordered beds that were devoid of flowers this late in the year. They were heading towards a tall, tightly-clipped yew hedge with an arch in the middle, and as they passed under it Johanna's nerves tightened. There was a pavilion not far off, one in which Queen Jane had found some enjoyment whilst she sat out the tedious days of her pregnancy.

'It's a dream I've had before,' the King was saying. 'I've asked many people what the meaning of it is, but none has been able to explain it. Perhaps you might know, Johanna? Maybe you'll be able to fathom what it's about?'

'If it pleases you, Majesty,' she said. 'Then I should be honoured to make an attempt.'

She wondered how long this one was going to be. Sometimes he'd bored Jane for as long as an hour with describing his nocturnal imaginings.

As they reached the pavilion, Johanna could see servants moving about inside and, when they approached, one looked up and called to his colleagues. The door opened and four liveried Yeomen came out to make a guard for them to walk through.

Inside, a fire had been lit in the grate and there was the spicy smell of mulled wine.

'Thank you, boys,' the King said.

He allowed one of them to take his cloak and Johanna looked shyly at him now he was revealed. The King was robed in a doublet of grey satin, quite simply styled to cover his girth, but the cloak which had covered it was lined with ermine

'That will be all,' the King said, and the Yeomen left via the rear door.

Now they were alone, or at least as alone as the King would ever be, for a Yeoman would be listening intently at the door. Two lavishly decorated chairs had been set before the fire and it was there they sat, side by side.

'It starts,' the King said, settling himself back, 'with a swan.' Unconsciously he puffed out his already huge chest as he poured mulled wine into a golden goblet for her. 'And the swan is trying to swim, but something holds it back, as though its foot is caught in river weed, or something.' He screwed up his eyes, trying to remember. 'I'm standing on the bank, watching it, knowing that it's my duty to rescue it, but something is holding *me* back, too.'

Johanna sighed, inwardly. No wonder no one had dared tell him what the dream meant. The swan was a symbol of grace and *commitment,* and swans paired for life – surely he knew that? But, she reasoned, nibbling at honeyed-wafer, meaning was often obvious to all except the dreamer. The King droned on for a while longer, and what with the fire and the warmth of the spicy wine, Johanna was almost asleep when he finally came to an end and looked at her expectantly.

Brutally she pinched the tender skin on the inside of her wrist to wake herself up. How could she have even thought of dozing when so much was at stake?

'So, what do you think?' he asked.

What indeed? She cast around in her mind for inspiration, praying as she did; and when it came to her, she almost wanted to cry. She'd seen a swan once, lying dead by the side of the Thames. Although it had wonderfully pure white feathers, the skin underneath, she noticed, was black and coarse.

Boldly Johanna held out her goblet and Henry filled it up for her, then waited, turned towards her, only half sitting upon his chair.

'I think…' she said. Strangely, she was almost enjoying herself now. 'I think... you have no need to worry, Majesty,' she finished, solemnly.

A frown flitted across his face. 'How can you say that, Johanna. Weren't you listening? I've been having this dream for months, nay, years even.'

I can believe that, she thought. Probably ever since you walked away from Queen Catherine, and never looked back.

'Of course you have,' she said, 'and that's why I know you have no need to worry. Have you ever thought on the colour of a swan's skin, Majesty?'

'A swan's skin?' The King wrinkled his brow so much that she wanted to laugh. 'Now that you come to mention it, I'm not sure I have – or, wait a minute... is it black?'

'Yes,' she said. 'So a swan is white and pure on top...'

'And black underneath...! So all those swans I dream about are really those who deceive me, who want to lure me into the river to save them, as it were...' The King clasped his fist tightly in his other palm, 'and then when I put myself at risk to help them, they fly away, or worse still-' he turned to her, 'turn on me and try to drown me. Oh, Johanna, Johanna... there was I, thinking that the swans had been sent to warn me, when really they were telling me that I'm right not to jump in. Do you think that's it?'

She nodded, pleased with herself. This was why he had seemed to trust her in the first place, and in fairness she had always *tried* to tell him the truth.

'My Lady Johanna!' he said, theatrically, standing up awkwardly and sweeping a bow before her. 'Ask of me what you will, for I am at your command.'

'Your Majesty is too kind,' Johanna said, laughing. 'I could ask for nothing more.'

'Are you sure?' He pulled her up towards him. 'Would you like me to speak to your uncle for you? I know your family has been displeased with you, on my account, but they'll be relieved to know we're friends again.'

She thought quickly. 'That would please me greatly, Majesty,' she said, surprised to find that it actually would, even though as soon as her uncle knew she was back in favour with the King, his demands would not be far behind, 'and I'm glad we're friends again. I've missed Your Majesty's wit.'

He laughed. 'No wit, Johanna, I'm afraid,' he said. 'Just an old boar. I wish I could still go to it at the tilt yard – it used to keep me sharp.'

'I hear Your Majesty was the greatest jouster of all,' she said, giving him a shy look. 'No one could best you.'

'That was true,' he said, 'although Suffolk and Norris tried their hardest, you know. They never went easy on me, just because I was their King.'

She found that hard to believe, but kept smiling all the same.

'Do you remember,' he said, squeezing her hands between his, 'when I took it upon myself to be a stag, running for my life in the gardens here, and all my gentlemen were hunters? None of them could catch me. Or that time when we had the masque at Christmas, and even Jane could not guess who courted her?'

He lapsed then, the saddest look upon his face and she felt her heart go out to him.

'I miss her, you know, Johanna. She was a good wife; thought only of me and what was best for me. It's wonderful for a king to have someone like her at his side. Good for his soul.'

'I know, Majesty,' she said, 'and she was always kind to us, too, her ladies.'

'And my children,' he nodded. 'She made much of the Lady Mary and the Lady Elizabeth.'

Johanna waited, hardly daring to draw breath for she saw a suspicious shine in his eyes, as though a tear might fall.

'I pray nightly for the repose of her soul, Majesty,' she said, and was relieved when he brightened.

'You do?' he said. 'And so do I. I pray for... my other ladies, too. I care for them all, you know, even though there are those who think I don't. But they have no idea of what it means to be a king, or to have my responsibilities.' He gave a self-conscious laugh. 'They don't have a Cromwell coming up to them, every time they get a moment to themselves saying, 'Majesty, forgive me, but...' And it's always bad news, Johanna. Always bad news. Now I think my advisers cast lots between themselves – who shall it be next to bring me bad news?'

'Majesty-' He was still holding her hands, but he released them and placed a finger upon her lips.

'Not just now. I want to kiss you, Johanna, for you look so pretty this morning; the fresh air has done you good.'

Very gently he pressed his lips to hers, moving tenderly so that her mouth parted and, with a groan, his arms came around her waist.

'God's breath, Johanna, you send me reeling. Come to me tonight, my love, keep me company. Will you do that?'

She felt a sweep of colour come rushing up her cheeks and down into her neck.

'Ah, look now,' the King said, pulling back, 'I've embarrassed you. I'm sorry, my love, forgive me. I knew you were not much minded to take a man, but I had forgotten it – your lips enticed me so much,' he laughed ruefully, 'and I am, I'm afraid, very much a man. I could not resist you.'

'I'm sorry, Majesty,' Johanna said, her eyes downcast in what she hoped was a suitably abashed way.

The King led her towards the chairs and once again she caught a whiff of putrefaction coming from his leg. 'And yet, Johanna,' he said, his head a little to one side, 'I think you might not have minded my kiss *too* much?'

Johanna lowered her eyes, confused. It was true, her heart *had* traitorously quickened in response.

'Come now,' he said. 'Let us have some more wine together, and sit like a brother and sister might. We can tell each other stories,' he continued, picking up the pitcher of wine. 'How does that sound? Shall I go first?'

*

Later, the King announced that he could not put off any longer his 'Affairs of State', and sent for Peter Mewtas to escort her back to her rooms.

'How are you, Johanna?' Peter asked as they walked together through the gardens. 'It looks as if you're back in favour with the King.'

'I'm in good health, thank you,' Johanna said, ignoring the comment. 'How's life in the Privy Chamber?'

'Rather boring, I must say,' he said, with a little laugh. 'The King hasn't been himself since Queen Jane died, as you can imagine. Do you see a change in him?'

'A little,' she lied. She wasn't about to jeopardise herself by criticising the King.

'Mm. Well, I'm glad he's agreed to this Cleves betrothal. He needs a queen by his side.'

And he'd better look after this one, she thought, but then chided herself. 'Will the new Queen be arriving soon?' she asked, but Peter shook his head.

'The ambassadors have only just returned to Cleves and then they have to escort the Princess here. I can't see her arriving much before Christmas, even if the sea's calm enough. My lord Lisle is preparing himself for a long stay by his important guest in Calais, if the weather conditions are rough.'

'Is his Lordship still here?'

'No, he left for Dover today.'

'Oh, dear. I wanted to thank him.'

'You could write him a letter,' Peter suggested. 'I will give you the paper. So, what are your plans now?'

It was a good question. 'The King is going to speak to my uncle for me.'

Peter nodded. 'He has been pestering me to speak to the King on his behalf.'

Johanna felt almost guilty for a moment. 'Apart from that, I'm at the

King's mercy. This time, I'll wait until he says I may go.'

'A wise decision,' Peter said.

*

Alice had made everything tidy in Johanna's chamber, and there was a fire lit in the grate. Her bed beckoned, even though it was only mid-morning, and Johanna soon shrugged off her fine clothes and was sliding between the creamy linen sheets. She had no idea where Alice was, but the girl was likely to return soon. In the meantime... she was exhausted.

Austin Friars
London

An urgent communication in cypher had arrived from France and Cromwell took it upstairs to his study. It was from a woman he kept as a spy in the French court which was, she had written, presently residing at Amboise.

'*1st October. A man arrested late last night was suspected of being an English spy but claimed to be a priest on his way to the Abbey of Fontevraud. Revealed nothing under torture and is now dead.*'

Cromwell sat back and scratched his head. Suddenly, an awful lot of people were on their way to this Abbey of Fontevraud. As far as he knew, he had sent no spies to that area recently, so it was likely the man had been telling the truth and *was* a priest. So why was he arrested? The French were still in thrall to the Bishop of Rome and unlikely to torture a priest to death – that is unless he had something they wanted very badly – or he hadn't been able to give them something they felt *they* had a right to...

CHAPTER 58

September
Saint Gilles de Loire, France

Jo decided to wear a sleeveless cotton dress and to put up her hair for the evening with Jean-Yves and his wife. The dress was cream and draped flatteringly, but above all it was cool. As she finished clasping up her hair, Jo realised that she felt happier than she'd done all day. The prospect of some friendly company was cheering in itself, but she was also looking forward to learning more about Raymond of Toulouse. In fact, any distraction was more than welcome at the moment.

Jean-Yves met her at the front door of his home and his face broke into a broad grin as he took her hand and brought it to his lips.

'Bonsoir, Mademoiselle.'

He took the cyclamen from her with an appreciative look, and led her through to Rebecca who was in the kitchen. She gave Jo a kiss on both cheeks before urging her to take a seat at the table.

'Some wine?' Jean-Yves asked.

'Yes, please,' Jo said, thinking it would be a good way to help her relax.

She sipped the excellent Burgundy whilst looking curiously around the dining room of number twenty one. It was simply furnished, a sofa bed, an oak table, and an antique dresser sporting blue and white china. In the centre of the table was a vase of yellow roses.

'Jean-Yves,' she said, 'I've been meaning to ask. Who looks after the garden at the back? I planted a plum tree there today, in memory of Blanche, and I wanted to make sure someone could water it when I'm gone. Blanche loved her garden back home,' she said, wistfully, 'especially watching the birds feed.'

Jean-Yves smiled and pointed towards his wife. 'Your gardener is in there.'

'Ah, Rebecca!' Jo got to her feet. 'Thank you so much. The garden's lovely. If I'd known, I'd have asked you first before putting in the tree. Sorry.'

'Don't worry,' Rebecca said, carrying a large earthenware pot to the table. 'It's your garden, and I think a memorial to Blanche is a lovely idea. I'll remember to water it, don't worry, and I'll think of her whenever I see it – especially when the plums arrive.'

After a delicious supper of cassoulet, cooked especially for Jo, with cheese to follow, the conversation drifted around to the Plantagenets, as she had hoped it would.

'Funny you should have picked on Raimondet – that was his nick-name, by-the-way,' Rebecca explained, '– especially since there's only his feet left on that wall. Why him?'

'I don't know,' Jo said. 'It just seemed rather sad that the others had effigies but he and his mother are almost forgotten.'

Rebecca nodded. 'Mind you, they were a rather ill-fated pair.'

'Oh? What happened?' Jo asked.

'Well, his mother died after giving birth to his brother and I suppose you could say, the medieval Church happened to Raimondet,' Rebecca said, re-filling her glass. 'Have you heard of the Cathar crusade in the Languedoc region of France – although that region wasn't technically part of France at that time?'

Jo shook her head. 'I thought the crusades were in the Holy Land?'

'Not all of them. The Pope sent an army into the Languedoc because there were a lot of heretics there – or at least what he considered to be heretics. *They* considered themselves to be true the Christians. Not a happy state of affairs, as you can imagine.'

'Was Raimondet a heretic?' Jo asked.

'Not as far as we know, but a lot of his subjects were Cathars or had sympathies with those who were. His father, Raimond VI, tried for years to appease the Pope but either wouldn't, or couldn't, persecute the heretics in his lands because they were so interwoven with his people – especially his nobles. Raimondet was only young boy when the crusade started, but as he got older, he began to fight back.'

'So it went on for quite a while, then, this crusade?'

'Yes, unfortunately it was also the beginning of the Inquisition and I think it was about a hundred years before the last Cathar was burned at the stake.'

Jo winced. 'It was so barbaric back then, wasn't it? What was the point in burning people at the stake?'

'Ah, well,' Rebecca said, 'in those days, spending eternity in Hell was a distinct possibility if you didn't do what God told you. That's why the Church was desperate to wipe out any beliefs that put people at risk of ending up there. They chose burning at the stake as a way of warning others what they were likely to suffer.'

'So they really believed that was what God wanted?'

'Yes,' Rebecca shrugged. 'It was the medieval mind, I'm afraid.'

Jo sat a while. She was still angry with the Catholic Church for not letting her be with Mat, wasn't that part of the 'medieval mind' too?

'So how did Raimondet, as you call him, fight back?' she asked.

'Ah,' Rebecca said, lighting up, 'that was an exciting bit. Remember he was Richard 'Coeur de Lyon's' nephew and he managed to win a notable victory at a place called Beaucaire – the town where he was born. To be frank, I think he was a much better soldier than his father ever could have been, if not quite as cunning.'

'And did he manage to defeat the crusaders?' Jo asked, wondering why she suddenly cared so much.

'Yes, and no. The fighting dragged on and on and became increasingly bloody. Many atrocities were committed, by both sides.'

'Even by the crusaders?'

Rebecca gave her an amused look. 'You sound surprised?'

'Well,' Jo looked down, perhaps she did sound naive, 'I thought they were supposed to be fighting for God?'

'Yes, they were, but when Simon of Montfort became the leader of the crusade, he decided it was a good opportunity to carve a new dynasty for himself – out of the Count of Toulouse's lands.'

'And he managed?'

'No.' Rebecca held up the bottle of wine.

'Yes, please.' Jo said. She was enjoying this: good food, excellent wine, and good company. 'So what happened?'

'As I said, it dragged on for years and eventually, Monfort was killed. The older Raimond died officially excommunicate,' Rebecca said, suddenly looking very sad. 'He was listening to the Mass outside one of the churches in Toulouse, because he wasn't allowed to go in, and had a seizure. Raimondet was never allowed to bury him.'

'Gracious. The Pope must really have hated him, then?'

'The Papal Legates thought Count Raymond was in league with the devil.'

'Because he wouldn't persecute the heretics?'

'And because he didn't have much respect for churchmen.'

'Ah.' Jo pondered this. So much for good, Christian men!

'There's more to tell,' Rebecca said, 'but I think I should make coffee before we get onto that. Do you want some?'

'I'll make it,' Jean-Yves said, smiling. 'You ladies can carry on with your history lesson.'

They went to sit on the sofa and Rebecca took Jo's hand.

'It's lovely having you here. Are you really sure you want to sell the apartment?'

'No,' Jo said, 'but it's not up to me. I'll speak to Blanche's nephew again and tell him how lovely everything is. If he only came here, I'm sure he'd feel the same as I do.'

' Why didn't he come this time?' Rebecca asked.

'He's a Catholic priest,' Jo said, trying to stop the blush rising in her cheeks, 'and he's in Rome at the moment; so he wasn't able to come with me.'

‘Ah, yes,’ Rebecca said, nodding. ‘Blanche told me about him a while ago.’

It was no use, Jo’s cheeks continued to flame and she realised that Rebecca was looking at her with undisguised curiosity. Time for an escape to the bathroom! When she returned, Jean-Yves had brought in the coffee, and although Rebecca gave her a concerned look as she handed her a cup, she said nothing.

‘Do you mind carrying on?’ Jo said. ‘I’m fascinated.’

Rebecca laughed. ‘It’s not often I get to bore our guests like this, but if you insist! Where was I?’ She thought for a moment. ‘Ah, yes, I know. I was about to tell you what happened when the King of France became involved in the crusade. Pope Innocent had been wanting him to get involved for quite a while-’

‘Pope *Innocent*?’ Jo said, registering the name. ‘What a name for *that* Pope!’

‘Yes, well…’ Rebecca shrugged. ‘They were different days and their ideas of right and wrong were coloured by their understanding. Innocent tried to call a halt to the crusade but he was persuaded not to by the Legates. He died in 1216 and was replaced by Honorious the third.’

‘How do you remember all of this?’ Rebecca asked, settling back comfortably. She was now sitting between a delicious cup of coffee to her left and a glass of excellent red wine to her right.

‘I must confess, it’s one of my favourite periods of history,’ Rebecca said. ‘And just remember, you were the one who asked for all this!’

‘I did, I did,’ Jo said. ‘Please keep going.’

Rebecca smiled, ‘Philippe Augustus, the French King, had tried hard to keep himself and his son, Louis, out of the crusade; but when Simon of Montfort was killed outside the walls of Toulouse – they say it was a woman who sent the fatal rock at him, you know, from one of those catapult type things – and the Raimonds were back in charge, the Pope put more pressure on Philippe and, eventually, Louis was allowed to sally forth and take part in a massacre or two. Everything dragged on for so long and, as usual, it was the ordinary people who suffered most. They couldn’t plant their crops, and their vines were repeatedly pulled up by the crusaders. Toulouse had been one of the most prosperous cities of its age, but it became impoverished.’

‘So, how did it all end?’ Jo asked, now feeling even more sorry for the young Raimondet.

‘Well, as I told you,’ Rebecca said, ‘Simon of Montfort died and his son took over; but the son didn’t have his father’s tenacity and gave up everything his father had captured to Philippe, then wiped his hands of the matter. The Church sent the Inquisition into the south to carry on where the crusaders had left off, but Raimondet never really co-operated with them, any more than his father had done.

'Then Blanche of Castile, who was by the way another Plantagenet grandchild of Eleanor of Aquitaine, became Regent of France when Philippe's son, her husband, died at only thirty-nine. She was on the side of the Church and even though Raimondet was her cousin, she had quite a surprise in store for him.'

'What did she do?' Jo asked, and was surprised when Rebecca laughed. 'What is it?'

Rebecca pointed to her husband who had fallen asleep in his chair. Jo blushed furiously. 'I'm sorry, I didn't realise it was so late!'

'Don't worry, I could talk about this all day and all night, given half a chance,' Rebecca said. 'But perhaps, another night?'

Jo smiled. 'You must come to me, I'd love to give you both dinner, to thank you for all you've done.'

'It's no trouble,' Rebecca said. 'We were both truly fond of your aunt and uncle.'

Oh dear, Jo thought miserably, as the weight of what was facing her upstairs suddenly returned. Jean-Yves and Rebecca had no idea that Blanche and Patrick had been far from the happy couple they seemed to be.

'Perhaps when her nephew arrives?' Rebecca said. 'We've been longing to meet him too.'

'That's a good idea,' Jo said, wondering if that would ever happen. 'I'll let you now as soon as I've spoken to him again.'

*

That night Jo couldn't sleep and eventually took a blanket from her bed and went outside to sit in the garden. The air was heavy with the scent of honeysuckle and there was a vast array of stars overhead, twinkling in their ineffably distant way. Looking up made her feel a very small part of a very large universe, crammed with mystery. And was 'God' somewhere in all that? Was he part of it or just looking down on it? She shook her head. These kind of questions were too big for her, she'd never understand how people like Mat and Blanche could be so sure about it all.

She thought about Joana of Toulouse and her mother, Eleanor of Aquitaine, women of a distant age whose passion lived on in their stories; they plotted and planned, had adventures, bore disappointment and tragedy – much like people today, really. And yet... she thought of all those heretics who had been *burned alive* on the orders of the Church... perhaps some things were different now, thankfully.

CHAPTER 59

July 1215
Abbey of Lespinnasse, Nr. Toulouse

Blanche lay silently in her bed with the white linen sheets tucked in around her and the shutters closed against the sun. In the corridor outside, Matthieu could hear the quietly shuffling feet as the nuns went about their business.

'Matthieu,' Blanche croaked, her voice thin and reedy. She held out a hand covered in age spots and he took it in his.

'Maman.'

'I'm so glad you came.'

He bent to kiss the crêpey skin of her cheek. Her face was heavily lined but there was more peace in it than he remembered. 'How are you?'

'Dying,' she said, candidly. 'What did you think?'

'I had hoped otherwise,' he said, sitting by her bed. 'I'm sorry not to have been here sooner.'

'And I'm sorry I never wrote to you.' She reached up to stroke his cheek. 'Can you forgive an old woman?'

'Of course.' He kissed and smoothed her hand. 'I'm here now.'

'I've missed you,' Blanche said, looking hungrily at him. 'You were a fool, Matthieu, to cross the Count, but I forgive you.'

'I didn't mean to cross him, Maman.'

'I realise that. For a long time, I was very angry with you.' She looked off into the distance. 'Difficult days, but not many more of those for me, I hope.' She winced. 'Help me to sit up.' He slid his arm under the bones of her shoulders and raised her from the bed. 'That's better, I can see you properly now.' He pulled the pillows up to support her and Blanche lay back against them. 'He betrothed you to the wrong woman, didn't he?'

'What?' Matthieu only just managed to stop his mouth falling open.

'Papa, he betrothed you to Catharine and it should have been Joana.'

'Maman-'

'Hush,' Blanche said. 'It's too late now, but I'm sorry. Maybe I'd have had a grandson by now.'

Matthieu bit his lip, should he tell her?

'Aimeric's dead, you know,' she said.

'What?' Matthieu's mind reeled. 'When?'

'Two weeks ago, maybe more. The days are all one to me.' Her thin shoulders rose in a shrug and she coughed. 'Go and see her, as soon as I'm dead.'

‘Maman, don’t talk like that!’

‘Oh, don’t pretend it’s not going to happen, Matthieu. I know I’m dying.’ She pointed to a small wooden box underneath the window. ‘Bring it to me,’ she said.

Matthieu lifted the box into his arms. ‘It’s beautiful,’ he said, admiring the deep brown swirls in the grain. ‘Where did you get it?’

‘The Countess gave it to me. It’s made of olive wood and was a wedding gift from Count Raimon.’ She paused to cough again, her frail body rocking. ‘He could be nice to her when he wanted,’ she said, ‘and I suppose he loved her well enough, in his own way. Take a look inside.’

Matthieu lifted the lid and saw a casket inside, about a hand span wide, the same in height and perhaps half a hand in depth. It was gold in colour and enamelled with a lustrous blue substance.

His eyes widened. ‘Is this Limoges enamel?’

Blanche nodded. ‘Yes. *That* wasn’t a present from the Count; it was hers before she met him. She brought that with her when she came from Sicily. Oh, she was so very sick on the voyage there, Matthieu...’

Matthieu nodded absently and lifted up the casket. He had heard the story many times before of how, when she was a girl, the Countess had left England to marry the King of Sicily and been sea-sick the whole way.

What he saw pictured in the enamelling almost made him drop the casket.

‘T-Thomas Becket?’ he said. ‘Am I holding a relic of the Blessed Thomas?’

‘Of course,’ Blanche sighed. ‘The Countess never forgave her father for causing his death, you know, no matter how much he denied it. Mind you, Becket wasn’t much of a saint to her – was he? He could have spared the terrible end she had.’

Matthieu lowered his eyes; the guilt and helplessness he’d felt after the Countess’ death had never left him, but he couldn’t lay blame with the Saint for her end.

‘She gave it to me for safe-keeping,’ Blanche continued. ‘I would have left it for the nuns here, but when I heard you were working for the Archbishop of Canterbury-’ She broke off for a prolonged bout of coughing and then lay back, exhausted. Matthieu went to hold her hand again, but she pushed him away, pointing to the reliquary.

‘Open it,’ she croaked.

Matthieu lifted the lid of the casket and found inside a purple velvet pouch.

‘She cut the material for it from the King of Sicily’s robe, after he died,’ Blanche said. ‘She was the Queen of Sicily before she married Count Raimon. I suppose I’ve told you that before?’

Matthieu barely heard his mother. All of his attention was on the pouch as he lifted it out of the casket and loosened the golden cord that held it closed. Dropping to his knees, he made the Sign of the Cross and tipped onto his palm a yellowy fragment of bone, about the size of a cockle-shell. From its curve, it could have been a part of the martyr's skull and suddenly Matthieu found it hard to breathe. A loud whooshing sound filled his ears and his vision clouded so that he he needed to put out his hand to steady himself.

'Matthieu,' Blanche said, her voice barely rising above a whisper, 'please take Saint Thomas back to Canterbury.'

When Matthieu's vision cleared he saw that his mother lay at peace, a faint smile upon her lips. He bent to kiss her forehead and laid his cheek against hers.

'Thank you, Maman,' he said. 'Thank you for everything.'

*

The following day Matthieu took the road to Pamiers, avoiding Toulouse. Although most of the south was now under Montfort's control, in practice, a man with a tonsured head was not a popular sight – so he kept his hood up as much as possible and spoke little to those he passed. When he arrived at Joana's farm he saw the doors to the barn stood open and the door of the house was splintered and broken. Hens stepped freely in and out of the manor and a cockerel stood in the upstairs window, looking down at him.

Matthieu ventured closer, ears alert to any sound, his hand hovering over the hilt of his sword. No dogs came out, so he checked the barn first and surprised a clutch of hens off their nests in the straw. Two piglets lay dead near the door, their thin, fly-blown flanks almost touching in the middle. He covered his nose and moved towards the house.

Joana's pretty hallway was littered with chicken dung, and the house was empty, stripped of all its furnishings. Whatever had happened, the place was empty. He searched everywhere for some clue, but apart from a patch of freshly dug earth, there was nothing.

Puzzled and worried, he sought out the church of Saint-Antonin and lit a candle as he knelt before the statue of the Madonna and Child.

'Please, God, let her be safe.'

The clink of keys disturbed him, and Matthieu looked up to see a man wearing a tonsure and clerical robes striding past.

'Excuse me,' he said, getting to his feet. 'Are you the priest here?'

The man stopped. 'Who wants to know?' he asked.

'Matthieu of Poitiers, Master of Theology at the University of Paris. Good day to you, Father.'

'And, good day to you too.' The priest was clearly suspicious. 'I'm Father Robert. What can I do for you?'

'I'm looking for someone, Father,' Matthieu said, his eyes skimming the man's ample girth and pleasant, but ruddy face. 'The widow of Aimeric of Pamiers. Do you know where I might find her?'

The priest's high colour faded. 'May I ask why you have cause to be looking for her? And why you're travelling alone, for that matter?'

'The Lady Joana is my sister-in-law,' Matthieu said, suddenly feeling very tired. He had ridden over sixty miles since yesterday morning. 'I've just come from my mother's funeral at Lespinnasse and thought to call on her. I travel alone, Father,' he said, moving his cloak aside so that the priest could see the sword at his hip, 'because I was a knight before I was a cleric.'

Father Robert looked nervously at Matthieu's sword.

'These are terrible times,' he said, 'and I'm afraid my news for you is not good.'

Matthieu nodded and tiny, icy hands plucked at his neck.'Tell me,' he said.

The priest looked around. 'You'd better come with me,' he said. 'Waiting another little while will not affect what I have to tell you.'

The priest led Matthieu to the side of church where a door gave onto a sunny courtyard. A dovecote sat in the middle, and snowy birds perched in the alcoves. Beneath it lay a trio of 'sleeping' cats, their ears swivelling with every movement of the birds. Matthieu sighed. It was a stark reminder that however hard he might try to soar above evil, it would always lurk below, awaiting his fall with abundant, malevolent patience.

Father Robert pushed open a door at the far side of the yard and ushered Matthieu into a stone-flagged room. In it was a table with several stools around it, and a flagon of ale rested on the well-scrubbed surface.

'Hélis!' the priest called. 'We have a visitor. Where are you?'

A young, dark-haired woman came into the room. She had smooth, almond coloured skin and moved with exceptional grace, except that about her waist she wore a blood-stained apron.

'What do you want?' she said.

'Some food for our visitor,' Father Robert said, nodding towards Matthieu. 'He's come a long way and I have unpleasant news for him.'

Hélis looked boldly at Matthieu. 'Will you be wanting a bed for the night?' she asked.

Was it his imagination, or was there an invitation in those dark brown eyes?

'Er, no.' He shook his head. 'Just a drink will do.'

Hélis walked away, pulling off her apron.

'Lovely girl,' Father Robert said, watching herdepart through the door. 'Don't know what I'd do without her. Take a seat.' He pulled a wooden stool out from under the table.

Hélis came back with bread, olives and a hunk of cheese. She placed them on the table and then took two earthenware goblets and plates from a shelf by the window.

'Help yourselves,' she said, placing the goblets and plates on the table. 'I'll be in the barn, if you want me.'

'Have you ever lived in these parts?' Father Robert said, taking a hunk of the bread.

'I was once tutor to the son of the Count of Toulouse,' Matthieu said.

'You were?' Father Robert looked at him in surprise. 'How long ago was that?'

'Nearly six years. I haven't seen Raimondet in all that time. His father rejected me on account of my loyalty to the Church.'

'Ah,' Father Robert nodded, 'so now you teach in Paris. How did you come by that?'

'It's a long story,' Matthieu said, picking up a wedge of what he knew to be locally made ewes' cheese and savouring its sharp tang. 'When I left the south, I was not without friends. One of them commended me to the service of Stephen Langton, the future Archbishop of Canterbury. The rest happened after that.'

'Mm, you're an important visitor indeed,' Father Robert said, spearing an olive with the knife he took from his belt. 'Which makes what I have to tell you even more difficult. When did you last see your sister-in-law?'

'Before I left the south.'

'And what would you say was her state of mind and faith then?' the priest asked, watching Matthieu closely.

The icy hands were now crawling crabwise down Matthieu's spine. 'She was in good health, as far as I remember, and her faith was not in question.'

'You know her husband is dead?'

'My mother told me. Did it happen about a month ago?'

'About that.'

Why doesn't he get on with whatever he has to tell me? Matthieu thought. 'Has anything happened to Joana, Father?'

'That's what I'm struggling to tell you,' the priest said. 'I fear she has joined the heretics.'

'Joana would never do that!' Matthieu hoped the panic didn't show on his face.

Father Robert shrugged. 'Prior to her husband's death, I had cause to question her about her association with some well-known heretics hereabouts. She chose not to confide in me, and at the time I had no reason to doubt her further. Later, I heard her husband had died and customarily she would have contacted me to arrange his burial, would you not agree?'

Matthieu nodded, and was barely able to stop himself from grabbing the fat priest by the neck of his cassock and shaking the rest of the story out of him.

'I went to her manor, as you would expect, to offer my condolences; but it was deserted.'

'What had happened to Aimeric's body?'

'I have no idea. Perhaps she arranged burial for him herself?'

'In un-consecrated ground?' Matthieu thought of the patch of freshly dug earth.

'Exactly.' Father Robert pushed back his chair and scratched at his nose. 'I made enquiries, of course, and was told by one of her heretic 'friends' that the Lady Joana would wish to marry a northern baron no more than she would wish to marry the devil himself – and was taking charge of her own destiny from now on.' He raised his eyebrows. 'Have you ever heard of such a thing?'

Matthieu smiled inwardly. Only once.

'So, have you tried to find her?' he asked. 'The shock of her husband's death may have unhinged her mind. When I got to their manor, it looked as if the house had been looted.'

'Her servants claim she told them to take everything.'

'And the broken door?'

Father Robert mopped his face. 'I'm afraid I caused that when I had the place searched for heretics. They often make use of abandoned buildings – like the vermin they are.'

Matthieu let out a frustrated sigh. The man was obviously lazy and dishonest but probably no worse than many of the priests hereabouts. 'So you let a recently bereaved parishioner disappear, and you can't tell me what has happened to her?'

'Not exactly,' the priest said, slowly. 'I fear she may have gone to Montségur.'

'Montségur?'

'It's in the foothills of the Pyrenees. All the heretics are making their way there, but its out of my jurisdiction. Esclarmonde, sister of the Count of Foix, had it fortified when she heard the crusade was coming. What happens to your sister-in-law and to her manor now is in the hands of the authorities at Carcassonne.'

'But what about her son!' Matthieu said. 'That manor belongs to him. I believe he's in the service of the Count of Foix.'

'Yes.' The priest got to his feet. 'My feelings about the Count of Foix are probably best left unsaid, but my heart indeed goes out to her son, as it does to all the other innocents whose parents have taken leave of their senses and joined the heretics. Do you have any idea what it's like to be a priest here – with filthy heretics multiplying under your feet every time you turn around? It's a blow for me to know that I have lost another soul, but it is a blow beyond measure for her family because by becoming a heretic, the Lady Joana has not only denied her husband a decent burial, but has disinherited her son.'

CHAPTER 60

October 4th 1539
Hampton Court, England

When Johanna woke, candles were lit and she realised it was dark outside. She struggled to her feet in a panic. What was happening to Matthew? In her dream she'd seen him in terrible pain, on the rack, pleading for help. It was less than a day since Cromwell had left for London, not enough time to authorise the use of torture, surely? She knelt by her bed and prayed, reminding God that Matthew was His faithful servant and only wished to do His will – *so please, please help him*!

'My lady?'

Alice had come into the room on her silent maid's feet.

'What is it?' Johanna said, wiping at her tears.

'There is a message from Baron Cromwell, my lady.'

Johanna rocked on her knees. 'Yes?'

'Sir John Clements came here to tell it to you, but I said you was asleep,'

'You did what?' Johanna was aghast. 'Why didn't you wake me?'

'I'm sorry, my lady, truly I am,' Alice said. 'It was just he said it wasn't urgent. I'm sorry if I've done wrong.'

Johanna saw the fear in Alice's eyes and strove to control herself. Even here, she reminded herself, servants could expect to be beaten.

'I'm sorry,' she said, putting a hand to her head. 'I'm just rather worried about someone.' She sat down unsteadily. 'Please find Sir John and inform him that I'm ready to see him now.'

'But you ain't dressed, my lady!' Alice squeaked.

Johanna stifled a groan. How had she managed all that time in the convent without someone to dress her?

'Very well,' she said, knowing that Alice would likely gossip about her in the servants quarters if she insisted on dressing herself, 'but then make haste as fast as you can, please.'

*

Johanna walked restlessly around her rooms. *Please don't let anything awful have happened to Matthew.* What if he was dead? Her heart thudded. No, he can't be. God wouldn't allow it... but He *had* allowed men like Thomas More and Bishop Fisher to be beheaded. Good men, faithful servants... and all those saints...

She blanched. Better not to think about this right now.

At last, Alice returned.

What did he say?' Johanna asked.

'He said,' Alice took a breath, 'that the King would like you to sup with him tonight, and that tomorrow, Baron Cromwell would like you to go to London because they're having difficulty finding this person you've asked him to find.'

Johanna sucked in her breath and her nerves stretched taut, as if she were on the rack herself. Why couldn't they find Matthew?

'Are you sure the Baron hasn't asked me togo tonight?' she said, regretting the words instantly when she saw the look on Alice's face.

'And not dine with the King? Whatever are you thinking of, my lady?'

'Of course not,' Johanna said, quickly. 'I'm to sup with the King. That's wonderful, of course it is. I'm delighted to be asked to sup with the King, of course I am.'

'And will my lady require another gown for tonight?' Alice said, her face composed.

'Another gown? Do you *have* another one?'

'Of course I do!' the girl said, now grinning again. 'Just give me a while.'

*

'Johanna,' the King said, looking up with relief as she entered, 'thank God you're here. That's enough for now, gentlemen.'

He swept the parchments before him into an untidy pile and pushed them towards Thomas Heneage.

'Come and sit with your King,' he said to her, patting the stool beside him, 'and tell me how you are.'

Johanna did as he bid and surreptitiously looked about herself. Heneage, Sir John Clement, and four of the Privy Chamber servants were in there, all watching her as she took the seat next to the King.

'I'm very well, Majesty,' Johanna said, putting as much merriment into her face and voice as she could muster, and thankful that tonight she had given in to Alice and allowed the girl to brush some rouge into her cheeks.

'That's good, my sweet,' the King said, leaning indulgently towards her. 'I hope you're being well looked after?'

His gaze slid appreciatively to the low neckline of her gown where it skimmed the rise of her breasts. It was exquisite, fashioned of tawny silk over a kirtle of sage green silk that had been embroidered all over with golden leaves. Alice had found a pair of matching sleeves and pulled tufts of the kirtle through the slits, in what she said was now a very fashionable manner. Johanna regretted having nothing to wear about her neck, but the opal looked well on her finger, and Alice had rubbed and combed at her hair till it fell in gleaming waves down her back.

'You look exceptionally beautiful tonight, my sweet,' the King whispered. 'So much so that my heart feels moved to write you a poem.' He turned to Heneage. 'Bring me a quill and some parchment, Henny. I am minded to write the lady a poem.'

Whilst the King scratched his laborious script upon the parchment, Johanna screamed inside with hurry. What was happening to Matthew? Why was she here smiling and fawning when he could be suffering terrible torments?

Sir John Clement came up to them and it was all Johanna could do not to demand of him there and then that he give her his message. Sir John was a well-built man in his early thirties, with just a hint of grey in his neat black hair and beard. Johanna recognised him as one of those who had held the canopy over the little Prince Edward at his baptism, and knew he was distant cousin of Queen Jane's. Altogether he was rather typical of the men the King liked to surround himself with – young, charming, witty and excellent sportsmen.

'Did my lady receive my message?' Sir John enquired, standing deferentially a little way off.

'Ah, yes, Sir John, I did,' Johanna said, 'but there was little detail. Can you tell me more?'

'I had given the substance of it to your maid,' he said.

'But she told me only that you had-'

'Sshh!' the King said. 'I can't concentrate. What rhymes with pity, John?'

'Er, ditty?' Sir John said, surprised.

Johanna stifled a gasp as the King's hand connected sharply with the courtier's head and sent him reeling.

'Do you mock me, sir?' Henry shouted, deep red suffusing his cheeks. 'Am I a child to be given such an obvious rhyme?'

Johanna's mouth ran dry.

'Forgive me, Majesty,' Sir John said, nursing his jaw. 'I spoke without thinking.'

'Yes, you did. And you keep doing that, John. I'll have you remember that better than you have lost their heads who have mocked me. I will not have it, do you hear?'

'Yes, sire, forgive me, sire.' Sir John bowed before the King, who glared at him, before turning to Johanna with a twinkle in his eyes.

'Now, my sweet,' he said. 'Tell me, what do you think rhymes with pity?'

Fear made Johanna nearly dumb but she managed to stutter: 'Witty? City? Majesty?'

To her unutterable relief, the King's face broke into a grin.

'That's much better!' He bent again to his parchment. 'Your heart is taken, You offer me no pity, And thus for your love, I offer up the city, Of my heart.' He took her hand, the one with the opal, and kissed it. 'A pretty ring, my sweet, was it a present from another of your love-sick swains?'

'No, Majesty,' she said. Was he testing her? 'If I *was* ever minded towards a swain, then you should be the first I longed for.'

The King smiled. 'Do you hear that, John? The Lady Johanna knows how to keep a man guessing, even me.'

Sir John laughed, but in addition to the large red hand print on the side of his face, there was now a faint puzzle between his brows. Johanna could almost guess his thoughts: *so what is her relationship with this monk she seeks?* When she couldn't stop the colour racing into her face, she thought she saw him nod, ever so slightly.

'Why, Johanna,' the King said, highly amused, 'I do believe you're blushing. Perhaps you're not as cold to me as you seem?'

Fortunately, Heneage then came to inform them that the food was ready and Johanna was soon, unbelievably, seated next to the King, under the fabulous canopy of state, in the Privy Chamber. Hardly able to manage a mouthful from any of the platters of rich meat, she watched the King load his dish with everything and eat heartily, chattering all the while to the courtiers around him – none of whom had yet sat down to eat.

'Are you ill, Johanna?' the King asked, noticing how little she was eating.

She knew he had a horror of illness and hurried to reassure him.

'No, Majesty,' she said, smiling as bravely as she could. 'My stomach and I are simply overawed, that's all.'

'Hah!' He put a great arm tenderly across her shoulders. 'Come now, sweeting, have some wine and relax, and we shall dance later. My court has been sad too long, but now I have a betrothal to celebrate. Perhaps it is the time to cast off our glum humour – would that be fitting, do you think, Johanna? Would Jane mind, do you think?'

Dumbstruck that he should even ask her such a question, Johanna stared straight ahead, blinking against her tears. Instead of waiting for her answer, the King suddenly clapped his hands and commanded the minstrels to take up their instruments.

'A little music to accompany us, to soothe the senses, don't you think?'

After that, Johanna forced herself to eat a little and to smile as much as possible. The King downed goblet after goblet of rich Burgundy wine, and once he had finished eating, led her out to dance. The King was known as an excellent dancer, but tonight his steps shuffled on account of his leg, and Johanna silently blessed Lady Lisle for making sure that she could acquit herself well enough upon the dance floor, for his infirmity not to attract too much attention.

At long last, the King decided to sit down and was soon engrossed in a game of dice. This was her chance to speak to Sir John.

'May I enquire, Sir John,' she said, as soon as seemed polite, 'about your message for me today?'

'You may,' he said, draining the dregs from his goblet of wine. 'I was in London this morning, Lady Johanna, and a messenger arrived at my house from Baron Cromwell. I believe he knew I was on my way back to court today.' Sir John paused, and Johanna had to restrain herself from tapping his arm and saying, '*and?*' 'The Baron wishes you to join him in London tomorrow. He's struggling to find this Matthew that you seek.' Here he paused and looked at her carefully. 'How much of this does the King know?'

'Everything,' she said.

Sir John's eyebrows rose.

'If Cromwell doesn't know where my friend is, then who will?' She felt like adding: does the man not know who he has in his own jails?

Sir John's eyes darkened. 'Be careful, Lady Johanna. Baron Cromwell knows *everything*. I should remember that if I were you. If you value your neck?'

God's wounds. Who would want to live at this court?

'Forgive me,' she said, lowering her eyes. 'Did the Baron mention how I should get to London?'

'He did,' Sir John said, now watching her with a faintly sarcastic twist to his mouth. 'I am to escort you there.'

'Ah,' she said, unable to stop her face from falling.

'Lady Johanna, surely you can see that the King is smitten with you – at least for the moment?' Sir John whispered. 'Have a care not to seek this Matthew too determinedly, or you may find the one man who can help you turned against you through pique.'

Johanna nodded, absorbing the wisdom of what he said. 'Thank you, Sir John,' she said. 'I will try to heed your words, but I fear for Matthew. None of what has happened is his fault. That's what makes me want to hurry, not-' She broke off, reddening again.

'Your feelings for him,' Sir John finished for her. 'For your sake, my lady, I hope you mean that.'

Not waiting for an answer, he started to move away, so that she had to call him back.

'Sir John?'

'Yes, Lady Johanna?'

'Will you be so good as to inform His Majesty of our plans for tomorrow? And tell me where I am to meet you?'

'Don't you want to tell him for yourself?'

She paused, horrified at the thought.

He looked pleased, and not a little relieved. ‘Good. You’re obviously not as foolish as I’d thought.’

Johanna coloured furiously at this.

‘Just make sure you’re up and ready by six ‘o’ clock tomorrow,’ he continued. ‘I’ll send a messenger for you.’

She watched him make his way over to the King and bend down to speak into his ear, as though the episode with the poem had never happened. The King looked over and pouted, then beckoned Johanna to him.

‘I was hoping to take you hawking with me in the morning, sweeting,’ he said, ‘but it seems you have a prior engagement with my man Cromwell, and on a Sunday, too? Does that man never stop working?’

‘I’m sorry, Majesty,’ she said, paradoxically disappointed. Hawking was her favourite sport. ‘I should have liked that very much. Perhaps when I return?’

‘Perhaps,’ the King sighed. He led her a little way off, to a window seat where they had some privacy. ‘Johanna,’ he said, taking her hand, ‘I have to confess that I’ve been keeping you here, selfishly, for my own amusement; but I have your good name to think of. I shall send word to your family tonight, and afterwards you can lodge with them, but only if you promise to come back and see me often?’

‘If it pleases Your Majesty,’ Johanna said, bowing her head submissively. Her uncle would furious if he found out she had elicited the King’s aid to find such an unimportant person as a novice monk.

‘Well then, my sweet…’ Henry took her hand and placed kisses into her palm. ‘Are you sure I cannot persuade you to stay here a while longer with me tonight?’ he said, his eyes dark and compelling. Johanna felt that if she allowed herself to be drawn into them, he would devour her utterly.

‘Your Majesty is too kind,’ she stuttered, ‘but I fear I have to make an early start, and so I should retire to an early bed.’

‘Ah, Johanna, Johanna,’ the King said, withdrawing a little, and then laughing. ‘When you look at me like that, I can hardly resist you. But, wait a moment.’ He retrieved his poem from Heneage. ‘Sweet dreams,’ he said, pressing the parchment into her hand and kissing her briefly on the mouth. ‘Until we meet again.’

Austin friars
London

Cromwell picked the top parchment off the pile relating to the reliquary affair, as he now called it. He’d enquired why the girl was not arrested along with the monk and been given a lot of excuses. When they’d apprehended the monk at Weymouth they said he had managed to escape by jumping out of a second-storey window – which is why they thought the woman wasn't with him.

Cromwell grinned to himself. Well, she obviously *had* been with the him and he found the thought of the Lady Johanna jumping out of a second-storey window rather exciting; that and the fact she'd managed to make her own way back to England from France, and now had Henry hooked around her little finger.

Cromwell tapped his thumb nail against his teeth, trying to piece it all together. If the diamonds had been intended for the French King – an inducement from the utterly shameless English clergy who declared themselves for Henry, but made plans with his enemies to overthrow him – then there would likely have been someone to meet the young novices in France. And when no one arrived?

He sat back, lost in the ramifications. Well, they would have had to look elsewhere along the coast, alert their spies... Cromwell gave an exasperated sigh. He really *should* have asked her what became of that reliquary – that was an oversight on his part. She didn't have it with her now, he was sure of that – the maid at Hampton Court had searched her belongings, such as they were, thoroughly. No, there must have been another accomplice – perhaps that 'priest' who'd been tortured? Was that how it had gone? The poor sod ended up with the reliquary, but no diamonds and fell foul of the French?

Oh dear, oh dear. Strictly, he ought to go to the King with all this, but then Henry would be livid and, actually, he needed to keep him in a good mood until the Cleves marriage was finalised. It was inconceivable that the Lady Johanna would have innocently given the diamonds to Henry if she'd suspected they were part of a conspiracy to supplant him: so for now Cromwell would keep his own counsel. That way was good for England, and it was also good for Cromwell.

CHAPTER 62

September
Saint Gilles de Loire, France

The following day, Jo returned to Fontevraud Abbey, to enjoy its cool, airy presence and peaceful surroundings. Wandering about the gardens and cloister, and then finally sitting down for a cold *limonade,* she felt she could breathe more deeply. It was wonderful. No secret why so many influential women had chosen to 'take the veil' here. She pulled at a shoot of lavender, brushing it through the palm of her hand. Memories filtered back to her, a day in the sun with her mother, sitting out in the garden at home, sewing dried lavender into linen bags. How she wished her mother could have lived a while longer...

Jo wandered back into the church and drew close to the effigies again. They were as coldly inscrutable today as they had been before, but this time she lingered beside Eleanor, who was lying with an open book in her hands. The book was a symbol that she wasn't just a queen, wife and mother, but a person in her own right – someone with a *brain.* Well, she had certainly had had that all right.

Jo moved on to look at what remained of the mural of Raimondet. Not only had the poor man lost his inheritance, but most of his body too, for only his legs and feet remained on the wall that separated the nave from the choir. Was that why she felt drawn to him – because she felt the Church had robbed her too, of a future she wanted but couldn't have because God came first?

She shook her head. Sheer fantasy. How could she be robbed of something she'd never had?

CHAPTER 62

Late July 1215
The Ariege valley, Languedoc

Matthieu wound his way up the Ariège valley towards Foix. The road was pockmarked and rutted from cart wheels, and no one had the time or energy to mend it, so it seemed – or maybe it was because the Count of Foix had been away so much lately on account of the Crusade. Whilst he rode, Matthieu's thoughts alternated between his mother and Joana. How often he had failed those who loved him, and yet the truly unexpected thing was that they should still love him at all. Both were lost to him now, his mother through death and Joana – well, he had been the one to start the chain of events that had left her living here, amongst so many heretics.

In Paris, he had met many who were named 'heretic' but with whom he had secretly found sympathy. Not long after his arrival there, he remembered seeing the followers of a dead theologian named Amalric of Bene being burned before the gates of Paris. Amalric had been a proponent of the now banned teachings of Aristotle – teachings which Matthieu privately esteemed, and longed to bring into wider circulation.

Distance had lent its perspective to the Crusade in the south, and now it was obvious to Matthieu that however misguided the people of the south had been, they had only turned towards the heretics because they had not been well served by their own Catholic clergy. Priests like Father Robert, he mused, by a combination of ignorance and sloth were denying their parishioners any knowledge of the true gifts of God. *Faith by itself, without works, is dead.*

The Château of Foix rose before him on a rocky outcrop, its square towers as belligerent as its seigneur, and Matthieu guided his horse through the travellers and townspeople, his hood pulled down, his right hand fingering his crucifix.

When he reached the gates of the Château, he was stopped by a guard holding a well-sharpened pikestaff in his hand.

'I'm looking for Guillem of Pamiers,' Matthieu said. 'He's a young lad of about twelve summers.'

'And who wants him?' The guard chewed noisily on a strip of dried meat.

Matthieu pushed back his hood. 'His uncle.'

The man's eyes widened at the sight of Matthieu's tonsure and he looked around quickly.

'His mother is my sister-in-law,' Matthieu continued.

'Well, she's not here,' the guard said.

'I know,' Matthieu said, patiently. 'But I'd like to see my nephew. Tell him, Matthieu of Poitiers would like to see him. I've come from Paris.'

The guard lowered his eyebrows. 'That's a long way to come to see a youngster. What do you want with him?'

Matthieu bit back his irritation. 'My mother died recently at Lespinasse, and whilst I was visiting her, I heard about the death of my brother-in-law, Sir Aimeric of Pamiers. I was told by the priest that the child's mother had disappeared, so I came to find Guillem.' 'Hm.' The guard swallowed his mouthful and then spat on the ground. 'You better wait here.'

Matthieu had almost given up hope when a dark-haired, dark-skinned woman came out of the gates and said that her name was Fabrissa. She asked again what he wanted, and when Matthieu tried to explain, she seemed to have some idea of who he was – especially when he said he'd come from Lespinasse.

'Joana said you might come,' the woman nodded. 'We used to be neighbours, she and I. Come with me. My husband is a soldier here,' she explained. 'You can talk to him.'

Fabrissa led Matthieu through the narrow, crowded streets of the Château, to the inner walls where there was a wooden staircase up to the parapet. There she led him to the smaller of the towers and knocked at a stout, iron studded door with a wooden peep-hole. As it slid back, an eye appeared, and then the door opened.

Inside was a battered wooden table with two sets of booted feet resting upon it. Around the walls, armour and weapons hung, oiled and ready for use. Two other soldiers were rolling dice, but an older, stern faced man sat apart and watched Matthieu with interest.

'This is my husband, Isarn,' Fabrissa said.

Isarn stood up and held out his hand. 'Come next door, it's more private.'

Matthieu followed Isarn and Fabrissa into a small but spotlessly kept bedroom with a seating area of two chairs and a table to the side. Isarn must be a well respected soldier, Matthieu thought, to command so much space inside this cramped tower.

'Sit down.' Isarn indicated one of the chairs, and sat in the other himself.

Matthieu did as he was bid, wondering what further bad news he was going to have to bear, for their expressions were grim. Fabrissa fetched a jug to the table.

'Some wine?'

'Yes, please.' Matthieu's throat was parched.

She poured for them and then rummaged around on a shelf for some cheese and bread. Fabrissa had said he was expected. Did that mean Joana wanted him to know she was alive? Most likely this woman was a heretic too. Strange to say, Matthieu felt none of his earlier repulsion at the thought.

The woman placed two cups of wine on the table with a bowl of olives and the bread and cheese. Matthieu drank deeply and dipped his bread into the fragrant oil.

'What can you tell me?'he asked

Isarn sighed. 'How much do you know about Guillem?'

Matthieu shrugged. 'When she last wrote to me, Joana said that he was in the service of the Count of Foix.'

'And do you know why our Count was so keen to have him here?' Isarn asked, looking keenly at Matthieu.

Because he thought Guillem was one of his bastards? Matthieu shook his head.

'Our Count was – very kind to your sister in law,' Fabrissa said, slowly, earning a frown from her husband. 'And now she's gone, he treats Guillem as his own. Do you understand what I am saying?'

Only too clearly, Matthieu thought, dismally. In truth he had never dared to ask Joana about her relationship with the Count of Foix, and she had seemed so sure that Guillem was his. Yet could he really believe her, when the lad was here? He looked at the ground. They must not see his shame, lest they think it on Joana's account.

'The priest in Pamiers told me she'd gone to Montségur,' he said. 'Has she become one of the heretics?

A quick look passed between man and wife.

'It's all right,' he said, tiredly. 'I'm not here to question you, I merely wanted to see my nephew.'

Isarn got to his feet. 'We'd like to help you is the truth, and you look like a good man to me, but since this Crusade began there's been little love of churchmen and their like around here. My advice would be to leave the lad alone. He's happy and has a good future ahead of him with our Count. What is there to gain by you meeting him, except to make him question his loyalties?'

Isarn's words stung, but Matthieu had to admit there was truth in what he said. Whilst he didn't welcome the thought of his son being brought up by the Count of Foix, what better could he himself offer? The life of a novice monk? *The wages of sin is death,* he thought. Foix had won.

'Is there anyone who could take a message to Joana?' he asked.

Isarn's eyes hardened. 'Whatever folk say,' he said, stiffly. 'Our Count permits no truck with heretics.'

'Of course.' Matthieu stood up, a terrible weariness settling upon him. 'I thank both of you for your hospitality, and wish you a good day. May God's blessings go with you.'

The brooding towers of Foix mocked him as he rode away. Matthieu kept his hood up, speaking little to anyone, his mind set on the only place that he could even be sure of a welcome now – the Bishop's palace in Toulouse.

*

Joana stood up, the final words of her prayer still echoing in her mind. '*Grant us to know what Thou knowest and to love what Thou dost love; for we are not of this world and this world is not of us.*'

She stretched her limbs. It would soon be light and she was to travel with Roger to Fanjeaux. Thank God she was feeling better than she had of late. Travelling had become dangerous for the 'Goodmen and women' since the Crusade arrived, and they had to spend more time sleeping in the forests than they had done in the past – which meant they suffered more from agues and chills. She belted up her robe and threw on her long dark-blue cloak, just as a knock came at the door of her hut. Roger stood outside, his face barely readable in the early light.

'Are you ready?' he whispered and she nodded.

Together they walked down the steep slope before the stronghold of Montségur, to where their horses were tethered and waiting. Joana looked back up the hill, already missing the security of the huts that crowded about the rock, their roofs jutting out into nothingness. She heard the faint jingle of cattle bells in the distance as she mounted her horse and surprised a rabbit from its breakfast as they both cantered away. Long streaks of apricot dawn were beginning in the east, and the air in Joana's nostrils was cleanly scented with pine. Since joining the Good Christians, she now knew that being in the world was both a source of great joy and great sorrow.

Roger taught her whilst they travelled. He was much older than she and wore the silver buckled girdle of an elder. He'd been born at Gaja, not far from Fanjeaux, and his wife had long since died. He received the Consolamentum not long after Esclarmonde and Phillippa of Foix, from their bishop, Guilhabert of Castres, and was now one of the best teachers and healers the Good Christians had.

'Are you making progress?' Roger asked.

Joana knew to what he referred. It had been a constant thorn in her side ever since she'd learned the true nature of the world.

'A little,' she admitted.

She looked around, still conscious of the beauty that lay before her. But it was true that everything would one day pass away, that by its very impermanence could not be *real*. The 'lord of the world', Roger said, was not the true God. He was an imposter who attracted souls into matter – into prison in effect. She was urged to see herself as spirit trapped in matter, Roger told her, and must seek with all her heart to free herself – by prayer and meditation and avoiding the eating of flesh.

'But I still cannot see that all around me is evil.' Joana shook her head.

'The Church wastes all of its time teaching about the trials of Hell,' Roger said, 'and warns that if people do not follow their ways and sacraments they will descend into a pit of everlasting fire; but that is an illusion too. The only 'Hell' I know of is right here and now.'

'But how can you say that?' she protested. 'Surely the devil rejoices to hear you discount Hell, all the better to beguile the unwary.'

'Look,' Roger said. 'Look around you – everything corrupts, sooner or later – but there is no corruption with God. There is no up nor down, no good nor bad, no life nor death in God. Here on Earth we have opposites. Man struggles against man, not recognising that they both spring from the same source and that what angers him is merely the external appearance of one who *appears* to be different.'

Joana was quiet, digesting his words. Somewhere within her she recognised the truth of what he had said. She knew that the Good Christians viewed the Earth as Hell because it was where they were furthest from God – and said it was a battleground between good and evil.

'But how can evil create such beauty, Roger?' she said, as they reached a mountain waterfall. It cascaded from the top of a rocky chasm in a river of molten silver, and in the spray above hung a shimmering rainbow.

Roger smiled. 'Beauty is the underlying truth of everything, Joana. What you see around you is but the outer semblance of the inner harmony we all carry. The harmony of oneness, of God. Nothing can eradicate beauty because its essence is eternal and it is of the true nature of God.'

'But you told me that the world was evil because it wasn't created by God.'

'And so I did. But the self-styled 'lord of the world' can not create out of nothing because he is not God. Everything you see has God in it.'

Joana shook her head. It took a great deal of effort to try and understand what he was telling her. Sometimes, when she was meditating, clarity would come to her and she would understand a little more, but it had been slow progress.

A shout interrupted her thoughts and a man came running towards them dressed in the rough clothes of a farm worker.

'Good people,' he panted, performing a hasty bow, 'how fortunate to come upon you. My companion fell from a high rock and I cannot wake him.’

‘Where is he?’ Roger asked, nudging his horse forwards.

‘Behind me,’ the man said. ‘We were going fishing,’ he explained, ‘and he slipped off the path.’

Downstream they came to a bend above a deep part of the river. The farm worker ran to the edge and pointed to a ledge beneath.

‘He’s there. I can reach but not rouse him.’

Roger dismounted and followed the man down to his friend. Joana could see blood on the wounded man’s head and wondered if he had any chance of living. Lucky for him that they had been passing – she had seen Roger perform many feats of healing. One time he had amazed her by removing a barbed arrow from a man’s leg by first speaking soothing words to him until his eyes became unfocussed, and after that the man made no sound or protest when Roger cut into his flesh.

Roger knelt and carefully felt wounded man’s head. He looked up at Joana.

‘I need some salve,’ he said, ‘and a bandage.’

Obediently Joana retrieved them from Roger’s saddlebags, and then cautiously made her way down to the three men. Roger had his hands on the wounded man’s head and his eyes were closed. She knew he was asking for healing and pondered this anew. Why did he seek to heal people if he believed it was better for them not to be in a body? Surely he was preventing the man from doing that which he had said she must – to escape from the prison of matter? It was all so confusing but she would have to ask about it later, because now he needed her to help bandage the man’s head.

They used Roger’s cloak as a sling to lift the injured man off the ledge and back up to the path. Then they slung him over Roger’s mount until they reached the man’s village. By the time they arrived, he had begun to stir and after a bed had been found for him, managed to briefly open his eyes. A young woman pushed her way through the crowds standing around the bed, her mouth twisted with fear.

‘Will he live?’ she asked, before bowing to Roger.

Roger put his hand on the man’s forehead and waited for a few minutes. ‘He’s improving,’ he said, ‘but we’ll stay here tonight to make sure. If anything happens, we’ll be here.’

The woman burst into tears and an older woman came to comfort her. Soon food was laid out for them in a nearby house, simple fare but the best they had. Roger had done all he could to heal the man and that they only waited in case he was going to die, when he would administer the Consolamentum.

People gathered and Roger was asked to teach them. As always, he chose his words carefully and simplified what he had to say, and Joana listened as eagerly as the others. Why had the priests never taught like this? Why did they treat ordinary people as if they were inferior, instead of merely in need of instruction?

As evening came on, more people gathered as food was brought in. Still the questions came and Roger patiently answered every one, until the man's wife arrived. She was wearing a shy, relieved smile.

'He's improving, my lord,' she said, bowing before Roger.

'I am no one's lord,' Roger said. 'We are all the same here.'

Beds were found for them both. Joana slept in with the man's wife and her mother, and Roger in the house where they had eaten. As she went to sleep that night, Joana prayed for the injured man in the way she would have done before joining the Good Christians. There were so many mysteries in this new faith. Would she ever understand them all?

CHAPTER 63

October 5th 1539
London

For Johanna, the journey to London could not pass quickly enough. She rode beside Sir John and kept up conversation with him, but really she would rather have been silent so that she could pray. He himself was in a very good mood. He wore an ostrich plume in his velvet cap, and told her stories of his life in order to make her laugh – except that she didn't feel much like laughing. All she wanted to do was find Matthew.

Sir John had told her they were meeting Cromwell at the Tower and Joana could not help worrying at the sound of the name of it; but it was a reasonable thing to do, she told herself, the obvious place to start looking and she must not read too much into it. But what if Henry, despite all his fine words, had not forgiven her and she was riding into a trap? He was certainly capable of it. Look at how he'd treated Anne Boleyn.

*

Keys rattled in the door and Matthew's stomach turned over. What time was it? He glanced briefly at the grille but it was the same grey outside.

'Get up,' Mark said, wrinkling his nose at the pail. 'God's breath! How can so little stink so much? You're to come with me, but you'd best empty that first.'

After the trip to the jakes, they took a different route out to the courtyard, with the chains at Matthew's wrists clinking as he walked. Blinking in the bright light, he saw before him the bulk of the White Tower and over to his left a chapel, but they turned right, towards some smart, half-timbered buildings that he assumed belonged to the Constable of the Tower.

Mark rapped upon an oak studded door and it was opened for them by an elderly warden. He showed them to the open doorway of a room with two large, glazed windows that overlooked the courtyard. Inside was clean rush matting and the delightful, sharp scent of strewing herbs. The walls were lined with linen-fold wainscotting and to the centre wall was a great stone fireplace, filled with a glowing fire.

A swarthy, thick-set man in his mid fifties sat at a well-polished desk facing towards the window.

'God's wounds, Mark, what a state he's in,' the man said, eyeing Matthew.

He himself wore clothes that were somewhat at odds with his countenance: a neat black doublet of very good quality and a fine lawn shirt that was delicately embroidered at the neck and cuffs. 'Fetch him something clean to wear, for God's sake. He can't sit on Sir William's furniture like that.'

Mark hastened away and the man continued his appraisal, clearly in no hurry himself. He tapped his coarse fingers on the desk and Matthew was intrigued. His clothes were those of a well-to-do gentleman, but his body would have been more suited to being a prize fighter; and there were pale scars on the back of his hands and wrists, the sort a man might get when he is burned by hot metal. Matthew felt his guts spasm. Could this be Baron Cromwell, the son of a Putney blacksmith?

'May I have the honour of knowing your name, sir?' he said, surprising himself by his boldness.

A smile split the thin lips. 'You may,' the man said, 'but then you might wish you hadn't. I'm Thomas Cromwell.'

Ah! Matthew's heart tumbled. So he was right, which meant the Constable had requested the use of tortures beyond the limits otherwise permitted. He swallowed hard on a throat gone dry.

'G-good day to you, sir,' he managed to stutter.

Cromwell looked almost sympathetic. 'What are you doing here, Matthew? All you wanted do was to become a monk, or so I'm told, and now you're under investigation for treason and theft from the King.'

Matthew had expected the second, but not the first. 'Treason, sir?' he said, all but submerged by a wave of terror. 'Why do you say that? There must be some mistake. I'm not a monk, I'm a married man. I was travelling with my wife. We were going to visit her family in France because her mother's ill. That's the honest truth, sir.'

'Matthew, Matthew,' Cromwell said, 'do I look like a stupid man? You were carrying something out of this country, were you not? Something you knew His Majesty wanted, and you were ordered, were you not, to give it to his enemy, the King of France?'

Matthew's head jerked up. *Why would the King of France want Saint Thomas' reliquary?*

'Can you prove you're married?' Cromwell asked, throwing Matthew by changing the subject so quickly.

'I had a marriage licence, if that's what you mean, sir.'

'Really?' Cromwell sat back. 'A marriage licence, eh? And where would that be?'

He'd been crossing this river for days now and the ice had grown very thin. Please, God, now wouldn't be the time he fell in. 'The King's commissioners took it from me, sir.'

'Took it from you?' Cromwell looked delighted. '*Of course* they did.'

He motioned to his scribe, who sat at the opposite side of the desk.

'Edmund, send a messenger to Layton to ask him where that licence is.' He turned back to Matthew. 'So tell me, Matthew, *why* were you carrying your marriage licence on a trip to visit your in-laws? Surely they knew all ready that you were married?'

*

The Tower came into view as they reached Southwark. Johanna pulled her riding cloak closer about her and hid under its hood, so that she could neither see the decaying heads on London Bridge, nor the bawdy houses that clustered thereabouts.

They crossed the bridge and rode to the west gate of the Tower – through the archway which led to the inner wards, and there she had to dismount. A young warden waited for them, dressed in a dark-blue uniform. He guided them towards a tower that formed a part of the inner wall. Johanna caught her breath. If she walked in there, would she ever come out again?

*

Cromwell was now tapping his fingers impatiently on the arm of his chair whilst the scribe, who had hastily found a messenger and then returned to his position, finished scratching words onto parchment.

'Marriage licence, eh?' Cromwell said, looking directly at Matthew, and then he then fell silent and started to look out of the window.

Matthew followed his gaze and saw a young woman being escorted by the warder, Mark, and a man wearing a hat with an ostrich feather. When he caught sight of her face, Matthew tried desperately not to react, but it was too late.

*

Sir John took Johanna's arm and gave her a reassuring smile as they walked up the steps into the tower. She felt squeezed because the young warder was very close to her and she couldn't move away because Sir John was close by her other side. Panic seized her. She was being arrested!

'Sir John,' she said, fighting to stay calm, 'where are you taking me?'

'To meet Baron Cromwell, I thought you knew that,' he said.

'But, it feels like you're arresting me.'

'Don't be silly,' he said. 'You've heard too many rumours, that's all.'

But his eyes did not meet hers and he grasped her arm a little more firmly. She wanted to be sick.

'Take me back outside again, please,' she urged. 'I don't like it here.'

'Lady Johanna,' Sir John said, quietening his voice so that only she could hear. 'Hush this nonsense! You're behaving like a convicted criminal. For the sake of the Virgin, look calm, please!'

The warder went before them, guiding them to the second floor and Johanna followed on knees almost too wobbly to walk. He led them to an oak door which opened onto a sparsely furnished room and then left.

Johanna immediately crossed the bare floor to the narrow window in the curved wall and looked outside. She saw the young warder striding briskly towards some smart buildings to her right and he seemed to be carrying a bundle of clothes. Were they for Matthew? Had they found him after all?

She clenched her fists. What kind of fool was she? Nothing with Baron Cromwell was that easy.

*

'Anybody you know?' Cromwell asked.

Matthew shook his head. If only he wasn't so tired. If only his brain was working properly.

'Are you sure?' Cromwell leaned forward. 'Only it looked to me like you recognised her.'

'No.' Matthew hung his head and blinked back his tears. He had failed. If Johanna was here, then all was lost.

'Take him away,' Cromwell said, as Mark arrived with the clothes. 'And bring him back when his memory's better.'

Mark pushed Matthew before him. Anger burned in his breast but it was all he could do to drag one foot in front of the other. Why was she here? What had happened to the reliquary? Why had God abandoned them like this?

'Easy now,' Mark said, noticing Matthew's curled fists. 'I can do more damage to you than you ever can to me. Did you recognise her, then?'

Matthew didn't reply. If he had tried so much as to raised a hand to Mark, the other warders would have been on him in seconds.

*

Unconsciously, Johanna's fingers traced the indentations in the cold stone to the side of the window until she stood back to look. It was a man's name and a date. Had he been a prisoner here? Was she, even now, standing in a prison?

'Sir John,' she said, her heart pounding. 'I'd like to go outside, *please*.'

'Later, I've said we'll wait for the Baron here.' He sat down on a wooden stool and attempted to warm his hands before the meagre fire. 'Might as well make ourselves comfortable,' he said, pointing to a second stool.

'I don't like it in here,' Johanna said. Her panic now threatening to choke her. 'Take me outside, please...'

He came and stood by her at the window. 'We won't be here for long, I'm sure. Come and sit down.'

Her hands shook as she followed him. 'Are you married, Sir John?' she said, vainly attempting to distract the thoughts which all but overwhelmed her.

'Unfortunately not,' he replied. 'Unless you count to the King. It's with him that I spend all my time.'

Johanna nodded. 'Do you mind?'

'Not at all. Nothing else in the realm comes anywhere near to being with the King at court. Don't you agree?'

'Not really.'

He studied her with a frown. 'Tell me, Lady Johanna,' he said. 'Did you really want to become a nun, or were you just running away?'

It was a good question; one to which Johanna thought she had known the answer, until recently. But she couldn't tell him that. Not now.

'No, I really wanted to become a nun, Sir John, and I still do – although with no convents left in the country...'

'Yes, I see,' he said. 'Not easy that. Have you ever given any thought to marriage instead?'

Inspite of her fear, Johanna looked up sharply. 'I have,' she said, but she couldn't stop her eyes slipping away from his, towards the window. Matthew might be out there. So close... 'But I know I should hate it.'

'Really?' He gave a bark of laughter. 'And how did you come to that momentous conclusion, may I ask, when you're still so young?'

'Plenty of women have, and rued the day. I wanted to do something useful with my life, to study and give praise to God.'

'So, becoming a married woman and a mother is not useful, is that it?'

She thought he might be mocking her – but what did she care? Let him think what he wanted.

Cromwell kept them waiting a long time. Sir John grew agitated and walked about the room, examining the names carved into the walls. She could not have borne to do that, but she felt them anyway, calling out to her, begging for help. At one point the voices grew so loud that she put her hands to her ears, forgetting they were coming from inside her head. In the end she pulled her Rosary beads from her bag and started to whisper the prayers, counting the beads off one by one. Every time she said the word, *Jesus*, she bowed her head, and when she had finished, she saw Sir John scowling.

'Don't let Cromwell see you doing that, for goodness sake, will you?'

She put the beads back into her bag. 'Can you tell me, Sir John, what is so wrong about praying to the Mother of God?'

He shook his head and walked away from her, giving her no answer. Finally, they heard the quick sound of footsteps and Baron Cromwell pushed open the door. Johanna clasped her trembling hands in her lap.

'Good morning to you both,' Cromwell said, his expression brisk. Behind him trailed a scribe carrying parchments. 'My apologies for keeping you waiting. I had sent for some information and had to wait for it to arrive. Sir John...'

'Yes?'

'Could I have a little time alone with the Lady Johanna? There are matters we need to discuss, of a... delicate nature.'

Sir John looked surprised and at first she thought he was going to refuse. 'Very well,' he said. 'How long do you need?'

'Not long,' Cromwell replied. 'There's a warder downstairs. Tell him to direct you to Sir William's apartments.'

After Sir John had gone, Cromwell came to sit beside Johanna.

'I'm so glad you're here,' he said.

She inclined her head. 'Have you found Matthew for me, Baron?'

'Alas, I'm afraid that I thought I had,' he said, 'but it seems the Matthew we have here is married; and of course, you told me to look for someone who was a novice monk.'

Johanna struggled to swallow. Had Matthew stuck to his story to protect the Abbot, thinking her safe in France?

'That *is* a shame,' she said. 'Are you sure this person is not unwell in some way, a blow to his head, perhaps, something that made him forget who he is?'

She saw appreciation in his eyes as Cromwell nodded slowly.

'Yes, it may be possible,' he conceded, 'although he seemed quite lucid when I spoke to him, just now.'

'Just now?' Johanna frowned – the wily toad. 'Did he see me arrive?'

'Yes.' Cromwell watched her closely. 'But he denied knowing you, unfortunately.'

Johanna laced her fingers tightly, sure now that they were talking about the same Matthew. Cromwell had let him see her walking across the courtyard, so that he would think she'd been arrested. That was why she'd been so closely guarded when she arrived. What a cruel trick, and she had played into their hands.

'May I see this man anyway? Just to be sure?'

'Perhaps,' Cromwell said, looking faintly amused. 'Maybe tomorrow, if we haven't found anyone nearer to your description by then.'

Tomorrow sounded a very long way away.

'Um, Lady Johanna,' Cromwell continued, 'do you perchance know the family name of this Matthew you seek?'

'I don't believe I do,' Johanna said. 'As I told the King, we were only together by chance.'

'By chance, eh?' Cromwell stood up and went over to the window. Warily, Johanna watched his broad, heavy back as he leaned against the wall. 'Would you leave us, Edmund?' he said, turning to his scribe.

Edmund obediently put his quills and ink away and left the room, closing the door behind him. Cromwell put his hand into the front of his robe.

'I have here a marriage licence. Would you care to look at it?' He unfurled it in front of her, and Johanna pretended to read as though she'd never seen it before. 'As you can see it names one Matthew Manners, occupation woodcutter, and one Johanna Grenfell, seamstress. Quite a coincidence, wouldn't you say?'

Johanna's mind screamed danger at her and she was at a loss for what to say. She scanned Cromwell's face. He was grinning broadly at her.

'Come, come now,' he said, sitting down beside her again. 'There's no need to look like that. His Majesty has cheered up beyond measure since you arrived – believe me – which means I've cheered up, too. Don't underestimate your importance to me, Lady Johanna.'

'Tell me what you want from me, Baron,' she said, now completely unable to hide her distress.

'Want?' He shuffled to get more comfortable. 'Nothing much, really, but I would like you to tell me something.'

She stiffened.

'Nothing difficult, I assure you,' he said, re-scrolling the licence. 'Just tell me what the relationship is between you and this Matthew you seek.' He tapped the scroll onto the palm of his open hand.

'There isn't one,' she said, dully. 'We're acquaintances, that's all, Baron. You must believe me.'

'So this licence is nothing to do with either of you? Made without your knowledge so that you could smuggle a reliquary out of the country? In which case I can throw it onto the fire-' He jerked his arm forwards, watching her, and then drew back. 'Good. You obviously have no objection to me doing that,' he said, 'which tells me a lot.'

'Thank you,' Johanna said. 'As you can see, it means nothing to me.'

'Clearly not. Well then,' Cromwell said, 'where do we go from here?'

'What do you mean?' she said.

'Only that now we have some clarity on your relationship with the monk,' Cromwell's grey eyes challenged hers, 'can you tell me what your intentions are with regard to the King?'

'My intentions?' she stuttered. 'I-I don't have any, except for giving him those diamonds, of course – and I had hoped for his forgiveness...'

'Of course,' Cromwell said. 'So tell me; are you really going to walk away from here and sail to France, as soon as I find Matthew for you?'

'Yes,' she said.

He got to his feet. 'How if I were to propose something that would be of help to us *both*?'

Johanna said nothing, but looked at him through her lashes.

'Something that would enable this Matthew of yours to go free, to France or wherever he chooses?'

Surprise robbed her of breath. She had not expected anything so reasonable. 'I should like that very much, Baron,' Johanna said, 'but what condition would you hold for yourself?' Her heart was pounding fast now, spurred on by hope and fear.

Cromwell sat down and shuffled his stool nearer to the fire. He held up the licence. 'Can you imagine what His Majesty would say, if I showed this to him; or to your uncle for that matter?'

Johanna blanched. Henry would be livid and her uncle would disown her forever.

'So what I'm suggesting is that we come to some... arrangement.' He mimed throwing it into the fire again.

'Baron Cromwell,' Johanna sighed, 'let's not waste any more time. Just tell me what you want me to do.'

'That's better,' he said, beaming at her.

The strain of the last few weeks was becoming unbearable. All she really wanted to do was to sleep for a very long time.

'Very well,' he said, 'in essence it's simple. I want you to keep the King happy until his new bride arrives from Cleves.'

'Is that all?' Johanna said, incredulously. 'And for that you will release Matthew *and* destroy the licence?'

'Yes,' Cromwell said.

She stared at him. 'What are you not saying, Baron?'

'Nothing much. You keep the King happy, *whatever* that takes, which keeps the country happy, and me happy, and then you've earned your reward. When the Princess of Cleves arrives, you can go where you will, and I will destroy the licence.'

Johanna closed her eyes. Now she understood. It was all in that little word '*whatever*'.

*

Matthew tried to get comfortable but the ticks from the mattress pestered him mercilessly with their biting and itching; and all the while he worried about the Abbot and Johanna. What was happening to them, how much pressure were they under? Cromwell's sardonic face taunted him in the darkness and he could find no escape, not even in prayer.

Hell's teeth! If he still had his knife...

Groaning, Matthew turned over. What had his life been so far except nineteen years of wasted opportunity? God forgive him for betraying Johanna to Cromwell, but he had been dumb-founded when he saw her, as well they knew he would be. Ah, *why* was she here?

He thought of her luminous eyes and soft, white hands, and how she'd been with him in his heart, even when he'd thought her very far away. Angrily, he forced himself to think. There must be some way out of this. God could not have deserted them.

*

Cromwell sent Johanna to his house at Austin Friars, in the north of the city. She was astonished at the size of the place: an imposing three storey frontage with huge oriel windows overlooking the street, two further wings behind and a large, graceful garden which backed onto the priory of Austin Friars. No doubt which loyal palace servant was going to benefit most from the dissolution of *that* particular priory.

Johanna was greeted pleasantly enough on her arrival, as Cromwell's servants were well used to people arriving at any time of day or night and expecting a bed. She was taken to a room on the first floor, overlooking the garden, given a generous supply of candles, wine and food, and then left alone.

She walked to the window and stared out of it. Here ended her dream of a life lived on her own terms. She shook her head. In truth, it was a marvel that she had managed to maintain the illusion as long as she had. Inevitably her uncle would arrive and then the recriminations would begin. He would demand to know everything about her relationship with the King – how Henry looked at her, what he said, how much he was in love with her, and what she'd done to keep his interest. Especially that. Then her uncle would make sure she was in all the right places to meet the King, flirt with him, entertain him and, yes, bed him – if that helped advance her uncle's cause.

Johanna took a deep breath and pounded her fists on her thighs, screaming noiselessly. Why did life have to be like this, why?

*

'You! Come with me.'

This was a different warder, one Matthew hadn't seen before and he gaped at the man, whilst trying to shield his eyes from the light of the lantern.

'What time is it?' he asked.

'Never mind what time is it? Get up!' The warden's heavy boot connected with a sharp *crack* against Matthew's ribcage and he doubled up in pain.

'Get up!' the warden shouted. 'Or I'll string you up!'

Matthew dragged himself into a standing position and held one arm around his chest. The pain made him dizzy, especially when he took a breath.

'Follow me.'

The warder walked so quickly that it was all Matthew could do to keep up. He was in too much pain to even wonder where they were going – so it was a surprise when they reached the bulky White Tower which sat in the centre of the courtyard. Bleakly, Matthew wondered if this was where the dungeons were to be found and if, finally, this was where he would be put upon the rack.

When the warder made not for the stairs going down, but those going up, hope flared briefly in Matthew's breast; but that only added to his pain as he strove for breath, trying to keep pace with the man in front. At last they stopped before a door where two warders stood guard outside.

Matthew looked around frantically as the door opened and he was pushed inside – window, fireplace, desk, three men – no rack. He fell to the floor.

'Dear God on Earth, what have you done to him?' Cromwell said.

'The idle swine refused to get up, sir,' the warder said. 'I had to help him with my foot.'

Cromwell's face swum before Matthew's eyes. 'Let's have a look, lad,' he said, trying to lift Matthew's arm away from his side.

Matthew stifled a cry as Cromwell's searching fingers reached the sore place on his ribcage.

'Feels like a couple of ribs gone, you clod-head.' Cromwell said. 'How am I supposed to talk to him when he's like this?'

'Sorry, sir,' the warder said, staring straight ahead, 'only you did ask me to bring him here as soon as possible.'

'Go away,' Cromwell said, 'and ask Sir William to send his surgeon.'

'Might I be able to do something?'

Matthew's heart missed a beat at the sound of Abbot Whiting's blessed voice; but he pretended ignorance and carried on attempting to get up.

'Steady now,' Cromwell said. 'Wait until I've had someone to look at your chest.'

'Baron Cromwell,' Abbot Whiting said, 'I really must protest at such inhuman treatment of a young man. May I know his crime?'

Cromwell let out a humourless laugh. 'Nay, Richard, I was rather hoping you'd be able to tell me that.'

'Really?'

Matthew wondered if the Abbot truly did not recognise him.

'Yes!' Cromwell said. 'That is if you care a jot for him, or his welfare.'

'A name would suffice,' the Abbot said, 'or should I know that as well?'

'For goodness sake.' Cromwell stood up. 'He's Matthew Manners, son of Abraham Manners, woodcutter, lately a novice at Glastonbury Abbey, where I believe *you* were the abbot?'

Abbot Whiting was silent for a moment. 'Then I do know him,' he said, quietly, his voice filled with pain. 'May I ask why he's here?'

'Yes, you may; but better still, search your memory, Richard, because *you all ready know*.'

They were interrupted by the surgeon who came in and knelt on the floor beside Matthew, causing him to cry out in agony when he started to feel along the broken ribs.

'Some opium?' the surgeon said, removing Matthew's shirt and then winding a linen bandage around his chest. 'The lad looks very thin. How about some pottage as well?'

Cromwell hesitated. 'Leave the opium with me. He can have it when I've finished, and as much pottage as he can hold – if he tells me all I want to know.'

The surgeon nodded and finished bandaging. 'That should do it.' He rummaged in his bag, placed a small phial on the desk and left as quickly as he'd arrived.

'Are you ready to sit up now?' Cromwell asked, and Matthew managed to nod, for despite his pain he desperately wanted to see the Abbot.

The Abbot's white beard and tonsured head looked more unkempt than usual, and there were deep lines of strain about his mouth, but apart from that, he seemed uninjured.

'Right,' Cromwell said, taking a seat at the desk. 'Start writing Edmund.'

'Do you realise, Baron,' Abbot Whiting said, 'that this is Sunday and neither Matthew nor myself have been to Mass?'

'Mass,' Cromwell sighed. 'Add it to the list with the opium and pottage, Edmund.'

Abbot Whiting's lips tightened. 'I'm afraid I find no humour in this situation, Baron, even if you do.'

'Humour is always optional,' Cromwell shrugged. ' Now, can we start?'

'Very well,' the Abbot said. 'But first of all may I ask: Matthew, how are you feeling?'

Cromwell's fist slammed the desk. 'I could put both of you on the rack, right now, if I wanted to!' he growled. 'So, gentlemen, I suggest that you do not try my patience any further.'

Matthew trembled.

'Abbot,' Cromwell said, 'oblige me by explaining exactly why you tried to send Matthew to France, with a reliquary full of precious diamonds that were destined for the King of France's coffers!'

The Abbot's eyebrows shot up and he glanced quickly at Matthew. Cromwell adopted a martyred expression and Matthew's head reeled. Diamonds? What had they to do with the reliquary?

'Don't tell me,' Cromwell said. 'That's the first time either of you've heard of this?'

'Why, yes,' the Abbot said. 'What do you think I would be doing with diamonds in the first place?'

'Hiding them from the King?' Cromwell said. 'He's not best pleased with you, Richard. He says one of them is the 'Star of Bethlehem' and that he's been asking you about it for years. Apparently it was brought to England by Jesus himself?'

'I shall tell you,' the Abbot said, 'exactly what I told the King when he asked me. What use had Jesus for the treasures of the Earth? *There is no such diamond.*'

Whilst they argued, Matthew tried to marshal his thoughts. If Cromwell was to be believed, and the reliquary had contained diamonds, who would have authorised that, and why? He must keep his wits about him, however hard that was, for all of this could merely be a false attempt to ensnare the Abbot.

'Matthew,' Cromwell said, 'why did the Abbot here give you the reliquary and ask you to take it to France?'

'He didn't ask me to take the reliquary to France,' Matthew said. 'Abbot Whiting was not at the Abbey when I was sent away.'

'I know that,' Cromwell said, irritably. 'But who did give the order, that's what I want to know?'

The Abbot folded his hands and Cromwell let out an exasperated sigh.

'Matthew,' he said. 'Who gave you that reliquary, and what did they tell you to do with it?'

Matthew looked quickly at the Abbot, who nodded sadly. 'Tell the Baron, Matthew. We must be honest in our dealings with His Majesty's... trusted men.'

Matthew opened his mouth and then closed it again, remembering Brother John's frightened face. If he did as the Abbot asked then not only had he failed in his mission to save the reliquary, and Johanna, but he was going to betray a man who had been kind to him at the Abbey. The pain in his ribs increased as his breathing quickened. He couldn't do it, no matter that the Abbot had told him to, the words just wouldn't come out.

'Please, Matthew,' the Abbot said. 'You're in enough pain as it is.' He bowed his head and appeared to be praying softly.

Matthew cast around the room for inspiration and then his body convulsed as a loud rapping sounded at the door.

'What now?' Cromwell said, scowling at his scribe. 'Whoever it is, send them away.'

Edmund went to the door and held a low, hurried conversation with the person outside, then returned carrying a letter and a package.

'These are for you, Baron,' he said, handing them over. 'Seems they've just arrived from Glastonbury.'

Austin Friars
London

The book had a secret cut out compartment inside which contained a folded letter, written in Thomas More's hand. Cromwell opened it and read, his hand stroking his chin. It was an exposition of More's arguments against the King assuming position as the Head of the new Church of England, and had obviously been sent to Abbot Whiting in response to his doubts about signing the Oath of Supremacy. It was well written: More's mind had been more agile than most, but the Abbot was a fool to have kept it.

It was enough to condemn the Abbot with or without the reliquary business. Glastonbury would be closed like the rest of them; but the sheer perfidy of it irritated Cromwell beyond belief. If he wasn't mistaken, by bringing the diamonds to Henry, the Lady Johanna had single-handedly foiled a plot to buy the favour of the French king – no doubt one begging him to invade England and solve all the Catholic clergy's problems.

But who was behind it, that was what he needed to know. Was it the Poles again? Those Plantagenet remnants? He had thought that beheading two of them and keeping the mother, the Countess of Salisbury, in the Tower would put that particular family off any further mischief, at least for the present. No, it was unlikely to be them again so soon – but if not, then who?

CHAPTER 64

September
Saint Gilles de Loire, France

The following morning, Jo took the reliquary from its hiding place into the lounge so she could take a proper look at the jewellery inside. She had no idea whether it was all genuine, but judging from the tone of her letter, Blanche had thought so. In fact, she'd sold some to pay for repairs on the apartment

The first thing Jo picked out was a heavy golden chain with a cross shaped pendant containing ten identical red stones. She watched it shine in the light steaming in through the window. Never in her life had she held something as potentially valuable as this, and there was something so unreal about the situation that she felt queasy. Jo dropped the cross back into the reliquary and picked up a delicate silver brooch, intricately studded with blue stones surrounding a centrally placed, heart shaped 'ruby'. She held it against her chest and laughed. If she was going to try on jewellery like this, she would need grander clothes than her pyjamas!

Next she pulled out a length of rosy pearls. Their beauty awed her and she looked helplessly into the casket at all the clasps, pins, earrings – what on Earth was she going to do with them? Finally, Jo picked up the faded velvet pouch.

Could there really be a 'bit' of Saint Thomas Becket in this? How did she know it wasn't just a bit of old sheep, used for the purpose? And yet, and yet. The queasy feeling came again and she closed her eyes. It was as if someone (Blanche or Saint Thomas?) was reaching through time, and taking hold of her hand.

After that, she resolved never to touch the reliquary again. First of all she'd had those funny feelings when she first saw the 'knight without a body' and now this. She'd be hearing voices soon.

She put everything back into the casket and sighed. When Blanche died, she'd managed to leave more questions than answers.

'Well, Blanche,' she said out-loud, wondering where on Earth she could find a place safe enough to keep this reliquary, 'you certainly know how to keep me guessing.'

*

When she let herself out of the front door to go shopping, Jo saw Jean-Yves and Rebecca loading bags into their car.

'Jo!' Rebecca said, coming over and kissing her cheeks. 'Bonjour! Are you going out, today?'

‘Only to the Intermarche,’ Jo said, trying not to look too nosily into their car. They were obviously going away for a while.

‘I was just coming to see you,’ Rebecca said. ‘We had a phone call this morning. My mother is in hospital.’ She loaded another bag into the boot. ‘She had a ‘stroke’, I believe you call it, and I don’t know how long we’ll be away, but Francine is looking after our cats. She lives at number fifteen and has a key, so there’s nothing for you to worry about. She knows about you and she’s very friendly. Give her a call sometime. I’m sure she’d be pleased.’

‘Thank you,’ Jo said, feeling a twist of trepidation. With them away, she would be on her own with Monsieur Moreau. ‘That’s very kind of you. I hope your mother gets better soon.’

‘Yes, so do I. Au revoir.’

They drove away and Jo waved after them, suddenly feeling very lonely. She hadn’t realised how much having the two of them downstairs meant to her. Anyway, she shook herself, perhaps she’d feel better when her fridge was full of lovely French goodies. As she walked into the centre of Saint Gilles, she admired the local church and made a mental note to visit it as soon as possible. She should also call into the estate agents, she thought, and ask them to do a valuation; but she quailed at the prospect. Conversations about selling houses were not found in the usual phrase books. Perhaps she’d wait until Rebecca came back, but that could be days, she scolded herself. Shouldn’t she do something about selling the apartment before then? Probably, she conceded, but the biggest problem was – she didn’t really want to sell it.

Confused, Jo sat on a sun-warmed bench and watched the town of Saint Gilles waking up. Her nose wrinkled at the distinct smell of diesel fumes as cars drove past her, and her eyes envied the long, brown legs of the women as they went about their daily business.

Was she really hanging on to the apartment because she still hoped there might be chance for her and Mat to do what Patrick and Blanche had done? Was that why she was reluctant to part with it? Jo took a deep breath. It was part of it, certainly; a hopeless, and not very honest part. But it was more than that. She genuinely liked the apartment, liked Rebecca and Jean-Yves, and liked Saint Gilles. Gazing around she saw housewives buying ‘Moules from Barfleur’ at the fishmonger’s, and the owner of a brasserie sweeping out his front terrace. A well-coiffeured woman emerged from the hairdresser’s and Jo silently admired her elegant clothes as she walked to her car.

At least she still had a week of her leave still to take, and keeping the reliquary secret for another week wasn’t going to be that difficult. In fact, there was a claw hammer and some nails in the bottom of one of the kitchen cupboards. She would hide it under one of the floorboards. There was bound to be a loose one somewhere, one that Monsieur Moreau hadn't managed to find – and then she would just forget about it for a while. In fact, she might even leave it there forever, she thought, especially if Mat couldn't be bothered to come over to help her sort it all out.

Once Jo arrived back at the apartment, she set off on her quest, tapping at the floorboards. Mostly she was disappointed. Jean-Yves' cousin had obviously done a good repair job, but in the bathroom she found a short wobbly section near the radiator. Half an hour later and she'd only managed to prise two of the nails out and was trying to lever the other two out by pulling on the plank. Why had she ever thought this would be easy? Fortunately, the space underneath was quite dry and would be a perfect hiding place for the reliquary, if only she could lever this bit up further… there!

She fetched the casket, now back in its multiple wrappings, and slid it beneath the floorboards. As she hammered in four new nails, Jo silently thanked her father for letting her help him around the house. Apart from a small, unavoidable splinter, there was nothing to suggest that the plank had recently been moved, and after a bit of tan coloured shoe polish, you'd have to look really closely to see it. Phew!

*

Hiding the reliquary – out of sight and out of mind – meant that Jo felt more relaxed than she had done for days, and she decided to get an early night; but predictably, as soon as she lay down, her thoughts strayed to Mat. She hadn't heard anything from him since that phone call. Whilst Blanche was ill, he'd been the most considerate of men, but since her death, all of that seemed to have evaporated.

She checked her watch. Eleven-thirty. So much for the early night. Frustrated, Jo got out of bed and heated some milk in the kitchen. What she needed was a way to banish him from her head completely. She saw what she thought she saw a flash of lightning outside the window and waited for the thunder, but none came. Strange. Jo opened the door and looked out. There wasn't even any rain. Pity, it would have helped the plum tree to get established. She took one last lungful of cool, night air and shut the door. At least she was feeling sleepy now. If only she could go to bed and not *think*…

A tinkling noise awoke her and her sleep fuddled brain tried to come up with an explanation, but the sound was somehow mixed up with her dream. Had there even been a noise? She listened. Nothing. Silence stretched into every corner of the apartment, even downstairs. Too bad Jean-Yves and Rebecca were away. Should she get up? Not yet. She listened again. Even though there was no sound, the apartment felt different – as if someone was there. She shivered.

A creak. Only one. The kitchen door. Oh, God! Jo turned to the bedside table for her phone, but it wasn't there. Why now, of all nights not to have brought it to bed? Where was it? She remembered checking the time when she left the supermarket. Had she left it in the car? She must run downstairs before whoever it was moved out of the kitchen. Could she do it?

Jo grabbed her rucksack and ran for the stairs. The kitchen door was the only thing standing between her and the intruder. He was bound to hear her, come after her. *Saint Thomas, save me*, she prayed, as her feet flew down the stairs so fast that she feared she would trip; but she dare not trip. Desperation made her fierce. If he came after her she would fight back; bite, scratch, knee him in the balls. Whatever it took. She would fight.

The front door was locked but she kept the key nearby, in case of fire. Jo scrabbled it into the lock. Footsteps now, on the landing above her. Sobbing, she turned the key and yanked the door open. She was barefoot and in her pyjamas but her car wasn't far away. Thank God she had the keys in her rucksack. Jo stopped. There was a strange car parked outside, with a man in it. An accomplice? The man was looking away from her and she could see him outlined by the street light. Instinctively she crouched down and felt her belly crunch against her ribs. It was hard to move, but he mustn't see her and she *must* get away.

Oh, God! He was getting out of the car. Where could she hide? There was nowhere.

'Jo?'

That couldn't be right, it was Mat's voice.

'Jo, I've been trying to ring you.'

'Mat?' What miracle had brought him here, now?

'What are you doing?'

'Mat! Call the police. There's a burglar in the house.'

'Arrêtez!'

Monsieur Moreau stood in the doorway of the apartment, illuminated by the street lamp; and he was pointing a gun at them.

'Donnez-le moi,' Mat said, holding out his hand.

'Mat!'

Moreau swung the barrel of the revolver towards her. 'What did you find?' he said.

'Give me the gun,' Mat said, putting himself between Jo and Moreau.

'Mat, don't!'

'Go on,' Mat said, his voice calm and level. 'Give me the gun or shoot me. I am a priest and behind me is a woman. Are you really that brave?' Mat suddenly lunged forwards and an explosion jolted Jo half out of her body. Splinters of wood flew past her face and Mat fell onto the floor with

Moreau on top of him.

'Mat! Oh, no!'

She tripped over something hard and landed painfully on her knee. It was the hedgehog boot scraper. She picked it up and ran towards them then brought it down with all her strength on Moreau's head. His hands went up and he let out a loud yowl, then he slumped backwards onto the ground.

'Mat, are you all right?'

'I think so.' He pulled himself up and looked at Moreau. 'What on Earth did you hit him with?'

She showed him the hedgehog and he shook his head in disbelief. When Moreau started to groan, Jo lifted the boot scraper again.

'For God's sake, Jo, don't! You'll kill him. Look, I've got the gun. Call the police.'

'Can I help?' A hastily-dressed woman in her late twenties was looking at them with wide, worried eyes. 'I'm Francine, a friend of Jean-Yves and Rebecca. Is someone injured?'

'Francine! Thank goodness,' Jo said. 'Rebecca told me about you. Can you call the police, please? That man broke into our apartment with a gun.'

'A gun!'

Mat briefly showed her the revolver and Francine pulled a mobile phone from her pocket then punched in three numbers. He took off his jacket and draped it around Jo's shoulders then pushed her towards his car, all the while watching Moreau.

'Shouldn't we do something, like put him on his side?' Jo said. 'He could choke like that.'

'Well, he shouldn't go around threatening people,' Mat said, his face taut. 'But I suppose you're right. Stay here, in case he's faking.'

Francine was still talking into her phone and Jo slid into the passenger seat of Mat's car, her teeth chattering with shock. She pulled the jacket closer about her and was comforted by the smell of him, but she was still horrified by the thought of what might have happened.

'The police are on their way,' Francine said, coming to stand by the car. 'I've asked them to send an ambulance, too. Is there anything I can get you? A drink?'

Jo shook her head. 'I couldn't trust myself not to be sick right now, but thank you. Would you like to sit in here, too?'

Francine opened the back door and got in. Together they watched Mat roll Monsieur Moreau onto his side.

'Who is that man?' Francine asked.

'His name is Moreau. I thought at first that he was a friend of Jean-Yves,' Jo said, 'but I don't think so. He said he wanted to buy the apartment, but I think he was looking for something. It's complicated.' She shook her head and felt dizzy. Francine's phone began to ring and she got out of the car again to answer it.

A siren sounded in the distance, coming louder, then the police arrived, barking questions and orders. Mat stood in the midst of everything, answering, pointing this way and that, speaking immaculate – as far as she could tell – French, and looking so confident that she didn't suspect anything worrying when a policeman came to open the door of the car.

'Pardonnez-moi, Mademoiselle. You will come with me to the Commissariat de Police? I must ask you some questions, yes?'

'Er, yes.' Jo got out of the car.

'Excusez-moi,' he said apologetically, taking what looked like a cable tie from his pocket and fastening it around her wrists.

'You're arresting me?' she said, alarmed. She looked around for Mat, but he was having his hands fastened too.

'Don't worry, Jo,' he called. 'It's just a precaution. I'll get everything sorted out as soon as I can.'

'Francine?' Jo looked around for the woman. 'Can you lock the door for me? The key's in the other side – and tell Rebecca where we've gone?'

Panic was beginning to overtake the shock. What if the police didn't believe her? She was a foreigner. Moreau was French. What if he died or was brain damaged? An ambulance was forcing its way into the small street and one of the policemen went to meet it. She sat in the police car and watched Moreau being moved into a sitting position. He was holding his head so at least he was conscious. That was a relief, she thought, and then felt pleased that he'd probably have a dreadful headache.

CHAPTER 65

Sunday 5th July 1220
Canterbury, England

Matthieu stood with his head bent, hands clasped in prayer. It was evening and candles flickered in the wall-sconces of the crypt. They waited in silence as four, especially-honoured monks began to slide the cover off the coffin. '*Who shall roll back the stone?*' Archbishop Stephen Langton was there, as was the Archbishop of Rheims and the papal legate, Pandulf, along with Prior Walter and many others whose names Matthieu had not had the time to learn.

The scraping of marble against marble ceased and everyone craned forwards to see what had been uncovered. Matthieu pushed forwards too, as keen as the rest to get his first glimpse of the Martyr's remains. Some saints were reputed to be so holy that even years in the grave did not corrupt their bodies; but as the monks attempted to lift up Thomas Becket's remains, they crumbled to dust, leaving only bones and scraps of fabric.

Archbishop Stephen laid the bones in a feretum with what remained of the skull in the centre and the rest in a pattern around it; but he left aside three wrist bones which Prior Walter placed into a soft leather pouch. They were destined to be given to the Pope and other worthy recipients, those who had helped Stephen make this occasion into an event that would be remembered in history.

All those present prostrated themselves on the floor and offered up devout prayers of thanks, and then the monks began to chant as they filed out of the crypt.

*

Two days later, the seventh of July, on a date to so auspicious that it made Matthieu's head spin, he found himself seated in the crowded nave of Canterbury cathedral. This was a leap year and a Jubilee year – and the tenth day of the seventh month after seven times seven years from the date of the Saint's martyrdom. Not to mention that it fell on a Tuesday – which was the day of the week on which the Saint had been born, the day he went into and returned from exile, and the day he became a martyr. And as if all of that were not amply sufficient to mark the date, it was also the anniversary of the burial of the king who had caused the Saint's death – the second King Henry.

The bells rang and Matthieu turned in his seat to see the young grandson of that King Henry, another grandson of Aliénor of Aquitaine, walk down the aisle, robed entirely in cloth of gold. He was wearing a newly fashioned crown for the crown he should have been wearing, the one that had belonged to the Kings of England, had disappeared along with the rest of the crown jewels and most of the English treasury when the boy's father, King John 'Lackland', had sunk aptly enough into that region of England they called 'The Wash'.

What a debacle that had been. Archbishop Stephen had been trying to mend the broken relationship between the King and his nobles by getting John to sign the Magna Charta, but John had appealed to the Pope and had Stephen sent into exile again. The nobles, fearing they had no one left to turn to, had invited the French King to invade, and the whole sorry affair had only been saved for England by the clear thinking of William Marshall. Matthieu shook his head. The Marshall had died last year and at his funeral, Stephen had named him 'the greatest knight who ever lived'. How much harder it was going to be for this third King Henry to rule, without the counsel of William Marshall.

Behind the young King walked the clergy: Archbishop Stephen the and Papal Legate Pandulf to the fore, faces solemn; and behind them, four grizzled noblemen carried a gold and gem-encrusted casket upon their shoulders. Into it had gone the Saint's remains from the crypt, and the reliquary that Matthieu had brought with him from Lespinasse.

He rubbed at the new, soft place on his finger. Before he had handed the reliquary to Stephen, he had put into it the emerald and opal rings that he and Catharine exchanged as marriage rings, and the lock of hair he had taken from Catharine's head before she was placed into her coffin. Matthieu sighed and involuntarily thought of Joana. She still wrote to him occasionally, and he still yearned for her as he read her letters – before burning them. A Master of Theology could not be found in possession of the letters of a heretic.

Saint Thomas' casket was placed on an altar that had been especially erected before the choir screens so that all in the church could see it. Stephen proceeded to say Mass, accompanied by Pandulf and the other archbishops. There were tears in Matthieu's eyes as he listened. Not only were they celebrating Saint Thomas' elevation from the lowness of the crypt to the place he deserved, but they were celebrating Stephen's triumph too. England had a new King and Rome a new Pope. The Magna Charta was in progress again and there was every confidence that Church and State would find a new accord after the long years of tyranny. In their new abode in the Trinity Chapel, Saint Thomas' relics were destined to become a beacon to the faithful, a light shining in the darkness. Truly, '*the lamp, brought forth from its hiding place, has been lifted by God onto the lampstand.*'

CHAPTER 66

6th October 1539
London

Johanna's eyes were still heavy from crying when she awoke. She swung her legs out of bed and sat on its edge, feeling lifeless. Oh, how much she didn't want to do this. If only she'd left Matthew to his fate she would have been safe now, in Fontevraud.

A jug of warm water and a bowl had been brought into her room, and the drapes were drawn back. She sluiced her hands and face and then rubbed her body all over with a linen towel. Neatly laid across a stool were her undergarments and chemise. Someone had managed to wash and dry these for her overnight and she picked them up, smelling the fresh scents of lemon and lavender. On the table by the window was a platter of bread and cheese, and a mug of small beer. She ate and drank gratefully and then rummaged around in her bag for the stick and dentifrice with which to clean her teeth.

'Would my lady like some help to dress?' a young maid said, coming into the room without knocking.

Johanna frowned. Was this discourtesy a reminder of the fact that she was more prisoner than guest?

'Yes, please,' she said, deciding to be friendly. It would be pleasant to have someone to chat to, especially as she might learn something useful.

'Do you have a comb for me, my lady?' the girl said, looking around the surfaces of the room.

'Wait a moment, it's in my bag still.'

Johanna took out her comb and the ribbon she'd bought in Calais, and the girl, whose name was Phyllis, helped her to put on the green silk again. Johanna noticed, with a mixture of pleasure and embarrassment, that overnight the hem had been cleaned and patched and a contrasting velvet trimming applied to the cuffs to hide the frayed edges. Phyllis gently tugged at the knots in Johanna's hair and then fixed the ribbon.

'Is Baron Cromwell at home?' she asked.

'No, my lady,' Phyllis said.

She digested this. 'Phyllis, do you know if anyone else came to stay last night?'

'I'm not aware of anyone, my lady,' she said, 'but I can ask if you wish?'

'No, that's all right,' Johanna said, trying not to feel too disappointed. Cromwell would quite obviously make her wait before releasing Matthew.

‘Will my lady be wanting to walk in the garden, today?’

She nodded.

‘Very well, I’ll fetch a wrap for you. Steward thinks there might be snow – but I hope not.’

‘Where’s my travelling robe?’ Johanna asked, her eyes searching the room.

‘It’s being cleaned, my lady. The Baron has sent out for more things for you and he said we was to make sure everything you had was presentable, in case you had to go to Windsor. It must be wonderful,’ Phyllis went on, ‘to actually *meet* the King. What’s he like, my lady?’

Johanna took a moment to answer, conscious that everything she said would be reported back to the Baron. ‘He’s tall,’ she said, ‘and handsome; kind and gentle in his speech, especially to women.’

‘He sounds wonderful,’ Phyllis said, making an adjustment to the ribbon. ‘You never know, one day I might see him, too – if I’m lucky.’

‘Perhaps,’ Johanna said, realising the girl knew nothing of the King’s forthcoming marriage. There would be ample opportunity to see him then, as he paraded his Queen through the streets of London.

She spent a pleasant half an hour walking around Cromwell’s garden and then came to sit in a sheltered spot, pondering with trepidation what the future held. *To do whatever it took to keep the King happy*. Johanna shivered. She was to play the part of a whore, then, and Heaven alone knew how far she wold have to take that role, how far maidenly modesty would protect her. She prayed for the Princess of Cleves to arrive with all speed, whilst pitying the fate of that young woman. To lie with Henry, bloated and vile smelling as he was now...

And what had become of her resolve to take her vows and become a nun? All she knew was that at one time she’d been absolutely certain, but somehow she had allowed Matthew’s plight to divert her, and now? Sir John’s questions about marriage had re-awakened feelings she’d long thought dead, especially those about becoming a mother. In truth, being a wife would depend upon who the husband was, but having children? She thought of how much she had loved her little brothers – when they were still allowed to speak to her. Johanna hung her head. How could she even thing like this, when her immortal soul was about to be damned by being forced to lie with the King? And, she thought, would any man even want her, once the King had done with her?

The wind picked up, swirling away what few leaves were left in the garden. In the sky, the clouds turned a deep opaque grey. Perhaps Cromwell’s steward had been right about snow. She shivered. How long would it be before her uncle arrived? Probably just as soon as he’d re-ingratiated himself fully with the King.

In her bedroom, Johanna took out her Rosary, and keeping a keen ear out for footsteps, started to pray. She could still reach up for sweet consolation from Heaven and ask for forgiveness. After all, her sin was to be committed for a higher good, wasn't it?

Johanna ate a solitary dinner and then walked again in the garden, noticing the sting of ice in the air. By nightfall she was back in her room, with Phyllis helping her to undress. Other than the girl, she had barely caught more than a glimpse of anyone else in the household; but at least she'd had time to rest, and her muscles no longer ached with fatigue. After praying the '*Memorare*', Johanna lay down upon the bed and slid into a restless sleep.

*

'My lady, my lady!' Phyllis called, drawing back the bed-hangings. 'Get up, get up do. The Baron has sent for you to attend the King at Windsor!'

'What time is it?' Johanna protested. 'Surely he doesn't want me there so soon? It's before dawn.' She sat up.

'Those are my instructions, my lady – to wake you and get you ready as soon as possible.'

Johanna crawled out of bed. 'All right, I'm coming,' she said, stretching, and then she stopped. 'Whose are those?' She pointed to the blue velvet gown and silk kirtle which were draped over a chair.

'Yours, my lady,' Phyllis said, barely able to conceal her excitement. 'Aren't they wonderful?'

Johanna stroked the gold embroidery on the kirtle, but said nothing, not wanting to appear too overawed. Phyllis lifted the velvet gown. The pile of the fabric was cut in an intricately scrolled pattern which matched exactly over the whole of the skirt which was split up the front, where it would reveal the kirtle. Cromwell must have found an excellent seamstress, and persuaded her and her staff to work all night to have these ready so soon. The sleeves were in matching velvet and lined with white satin, turned back with grey jennet. Johanna stroked the sleek fur. Once, she would have thought herself the luckiest woman on Earth to wear something this grand.

After she had completed her toilet, Phyllis helped her on with the garments, and then stood back to admire.

'My goodness!' she said, making the final touches to a dainty, velvet clad French hood. 'You look wonderful. The prettiest Lady I've ever seen. And that's not all,' Phyllis went on, excitedly, 'there's a carriage waiting to take you to the river, my lady, as soon as you're ready.'

Johanna bumped and jolted her way to the Thames, where Cromwell's wherry was waiting for her, and travelled upriver to Windsor Castle. Cromwell came out to greet her, and after enquiries about her health and other insincerities, led her to the King's watching chamber, where he left her. Johanna looked at the shelves of the enormous oak buffet, that almost filled one wall, and marvelled at the amount of silver and gilt plate that it held. Along the other wall hung enormous tapestries of Greek myths, and dotted about the room stood splendidly liveried Yeomen. They watched her covertly and Johanna cursed Cromwell. Why had he left her here, with no escort or maid to give her respectability?

An age ticked by and Johanna drifted to the row of windows that overlooked the inner court. From this height she could see the palace servants going about their business, meeting, greeting, quarrelling, carrying-

'Lady Johanna!'

She turned to see Sir John Clements making his way towards her.

'Sir John...' Johanna gave a little curtsey, pleased at least to see a familiar face, and he responded with a bow and a kiss upon her hand.

'You look magnificent,' he whispered. 'Just wait till His Majesty sees you. Things must be looking up, Johanna, if you can afford to go out hawking dressed like that.'

Hawking? In this beautiful new gown? Johanna hastily re-arranged her face, trying not to let her dismay show.

'Here he comes,' Sir John said, as the door to the Privy Chamber swung open. The King emerged, surrounded by his gentlemen, and Cromwell.

'Johanna!' the King boomed, a great smile breaking across his ruddy face. 'We're about to go hawking, will you come?'

'If it pleases Your Majesty,' Johanna said, dropping into a deep curtsey before him. 'I should be delighted to accompany you.'

She noticed that Cromwell was looking well pleased and was holding a tightly scrolled parchment from which hung a large, red seal.

The King held out his arm. 'Come along, my dear,' he said. 'This is a day to celebrate. My marriage treaty is signed and the ambassadors have left for Calais. God speed them on their way.'

It was a jovial party that streamed out into Windsor Park. Johanna rode beside the King, a hooded sparrowhawk upon her gloved fist. Silver bells tinkled about its feet and an enormous pearl nodded on the top of its hooded head. The King carried a gyrfalcon; its hood was embellished with golden embroidery, and from his glove swung tassels of gold and silver.

Spaniels ran ahead of them, in an excited pack, to flush out the ducks from the undergrowth by the river; whilst the falconers beat the water and banged their drums. The birds erupted, panicking, from their nests, and the King let loose his falcon. It flew straight and deadly towards one of the ducks, bringing it to ground in its talons.

Henry laughed. 'Did you see that? No hesitation. What do you think of my Blanchepenny, Johanna?'

'She's magnificent, Your Majesty,' Johanna said, hardly able to breathe, for her sparrowhawk had sighted a young grey heron.

The heron tried to escape but it was no match for the hawk who fastened her claws onto its back and clung on even though the heron weaved madly and stabbed its beak viciously behind. The Sparrowhawk clung on, oblivious to her own safety, and wrestled the heron to the ground. To Johanna's relief she saw a greyhound streak out to retrieve it, with a falconer not far behind.

'Quite a fight that,' Henry said, quietly.

She turned to him, aghast at the jealousy in his tone, but there was merriment on his face.

'I can see I'll have to bring you hawking more often, my love.'

The whole of that day was spent at Windsor, and Johanna smiled, laughed and employed every artifice she could think of to keep the King in a good mood – and it worked! He kept her by him all the time, asked her opinion of this and that, kissed her hand and watched her with the pathetic look of a love-sick swain. Inwardly Johanna dreaded where this might be leading as time drew on; but that evening, she twirled sedately in his arms with the atmosphere light and jovial, she realised that she was enjoying herself.

Life in the convent had provided her with the security she badly needed at the time, and with no shocks or surprises in its orderly day. It had given her a refuge for emotions that she barely recognised in herself and even less understood, but now in the King's company she found that she had rediscovered a love for life *itself,* that she no longer wished to shut herself away, but to *live*.

'Are you happy, my love?' the King said, later, when they were standing in his bedchamber, sipping Malmsey wine from goblets of solid gold.

'Yes, Majesty. I am,' she said. 'It's been a wonderful day.' She was losing track of how much wine she'd drunk and her head was beginning to spin.

'I'm glad you've enjoyed it, Johanna,' he said, picking up and dwarfing her hand in his. 'I could not take my eyes off you today, you looked so ... *radiant.*'

'Your Majesty is very kind-'

'Not kind, Johanna,' he said, 'truthful.'

She felt the heat rise in her neck.

'How sweetly you blush! Such perfection.' He put his lips to the fluttering pulse at her neck. 'Do you miss your old life at Amesbury?'

'Life in a convent can hardly compare with the splendour of your court, Majesty,' Johanna said, shivering involuntarily as his lips explored lower.

‘Truly?’ Henry drew back to look at her. ‘Shall I take that as encouragement, or have I merely enticed you with tawdry revels?’

‘No, Majesty,’ Johanna said, shaking her head as his kisses reached the low-cut neckline of her gown. ‘How could anything Your Majesty does be described so?’

‘True, true,’ he said. ‘Well, Johanna-.’

He straightened up and kissed her full on the mouth, his lips urging hers to part. The wine had made her bold, and for a time Johanna allowed herself to be kissed, but when he thrust his tongue into her mouth, she couldn’t help but stiffen.

‘What ails, dear heart?’ he said, pulling away. ‘Do I frighten you still? I forget you’re such a gentle maid.’ He sighed. ‘Never fear, I will not force you, Johanna.’ He passed his hand down the back of his head. ‘Forgive me, sweeting, do.’

The King sat down on his Chair of State and indicated the chair next to it for herself.

‘Your Majesty is a true knight,’ Johanna said, fighting to regain her breath. Thank God she had not offended him.

‘And I am your bounden love, my lady,’ Henry said, perking up. ‘Give me a task, so that I may win your love.’

Johanna pretended to think, a trembling finger pressed to her lips. ‘Do you see that far mountain, Sir Knight?’ She pointed over his head towards the window.

Henry nodded, following the direction of her finger, playing the game even though it was dark.

‘Upon it lives a dragon of evil repute, and it is foretold that only the greatest knight that ever lived can slay it.’

The King stood up and took his sword from a nearby table. He put his right arm dramatically across his chest and bowed to her. ‘Then I accept the task gladly, my lady, for only God knows who is the greatest knight, but in your service, I would gladly lose my life.’

Johanna breathed a sigh of relief and sent up heart-felt prayers of gratitude.

‘Well said, brave sir!’ She took the opal from her finger and gave it to him. ‘Accept this token of my affection, fair knight. You may carry it with you on your quest.’

CHAPTER 67

September
Saint Gilles de Loire, France

Jo pulled back the curtains and cast a quick look at her reflection in the mirror. There were dark circles under her eyes, courtesy of being at the police station for most of the night, and she looked ghastly. Typical. Just when she was looking her best, Mat was actually here and asleep in the sitting room...

She gazed through the open doorway at his tousled hair and broad bare shoulders. How she longed to kiss the softest part of his neck, slide her body against the warmth of him, make the world stop and never start again. But, she sighed, it would probably be more useful if she got on with breakfast.

The police would be back soon because they'd said they wanted to see the reliquary. This time she'd let *them* take the floorboards up. At least that part of events was out of her hands now. No more wondering what to do with it.

Water gurgled through the coffee maker and Jo looked in the cupboard for croissants. Dammit, why not go for fresh ones? The boulangerie was only up the road. She'd bring back some fresh bread, too.

A strong breeze blew off the Loire as she stepped out of the house, and the air held an unexpected chill. Jo looked at the splintered door jamb and shook her head. Unbelievable. Monsieur Moreau had turned out to be even more unpleasant than she first thought. What would have happened to her if Mat hadn't been there? It didn't bear thinking about.

The smell of autumn saddened her and leaves drifted past on the breeze, landing in the river. It would be time for her to go home soon, if the French authorities let her.

When she entered the boulangerie, the conversation halted and curious eyes surveyed her.

'Bonjour, Mademoiselle,' the owner said. 'Comment-allez vous?'

'Fatiguée,' Jo said, blushing. This had been a mistake. Everyone was looking at her. 'Deux croissants et un pain, s'il vous plait,' she said, looking anywhere but at the other customers.

'Excusez-moi, Mademoiselle,' one of the women said, touching her on the arm. 'We are sorry to hear of your trouble.'

'Merci, Madame,' Jo said, her eyes blurring with tears.

The other women nodded too, and gave her sympathetic smiles.

'C'est combien?' she asked, turning back to the counter.

'Gratis. Bonne journée, Mademoiselle.'

'Gratis?' They were all being so nice to her. 'Merci, Madame. Vous etês très gentille.'

Jo left the shop followed by more smiles and nods, and made her way back to the apartment. Along the river she spotted a couple lazily paddling a canoe, and their voices carried to her on the breeze. She waved, and they waved back. Suddenly, the sun slid out from behind the clouds.

Mat was up when she got back, dressed in jeans and a polo shirt. She wished he was wearing his collar, however ridiculous that might seem around the apartment. Without it, he looked too normal – like someone she might just mistake for a much-desired partner.

'How long have you been up?' he said, yawning, but watching her carefully. 'I helped myself to coffee. Are you having some?'

'Er, yes,' she said, putting the croissants to warm and searching for some apricot jam in the fridge. 'I was pretty tired when I woke up but, as you can see, I've been to the boulangerie. They were talking about us when I arrived, Mat, I'm sure of that, but then they were so nice and the owner gave us these for free.' She sat down at the table and tears streamed down her cheeks. 'I'm sorry. It's all been such a shock.'

Mat stood behind her. He put his hands on her shoulders and the warmth of them seeped through her clothing. 'Not least of all you cracking Moreau over the head with a cast-iron hedgehog. Where on Earth did you find that? I always had you down as a gentle, caring soul...'

Jo leaned back against his body and he didn't withdraw. 'Blanche had one at Station Row, too, don't you remember? It was outside the back door so she could scrape her boots before coming in from the garden.'

'Now you come to mention it, I suppose I do.' Mat's fingers began to knead her shoulders and she could feel herself responding.

'You know I don't believe in God, or saints, or any of it?' Jo said, trying distract herself. If he knew what an effect he was having, he would have stopped right away.

'Ye-es?' he said.

'Well, yesterday when I was frightened out of my wits, I prayed to anyone who would listen: God, Saint Thomas, you name it. I asked them all for help.'

'And you *were* helped, of course. I turned up.'

She sighed. 'Of course. How can you can say that? How can you be so sure?'

'I wouldn't be doing the job I'm doing, if I wasn't,' Mat said. 'Want my handkerchief?'

'Yes, please,' she snuffled. 'Oh, no, Mat! Help!'

'What now?' His hands flew away from her as she leaped from the seat.

'The croissants are burning!'

*

'Mat,' Jo said.

'Um?' he said, exaggeratedly licking jam off his fingers. 'That was delicious.'

'Yeah, right,' she said. 'Burned croissants do it for me too. But listen, there's something I have to tell you before the police arrive.'

'OK.' Mat looked straight at her. 'Is this what you were *not* talking to me about on the phone the other day? Should I brace myself?'

His eyes flicked briefly to her belly and Jo stopped, appalled. Was that what he thought she was going to say? How could he?

'Blanche wasn't the only person to live here,' Jo continued, almost too hurt to speak.

'I assume we're not talking about the cat?'

'No, we're not talking about the bloody cat!' Jo took a deep breath. 'I mean, when I got here, Jean-Yves said he was sorry to hear about the death of my aunt. I could understand him getting mixed up about that, but then he said her death had come so soon after *my uncle*.'

Mat blinked at her until the light dawned and then his face crumpled. Jo wished she could take back what she'd just told him.

'Did he say what this 'uncle's' name was by any chance?' Mat asked.

'No, but I think we can both guess. Jean-Yves' wife, Rebecca, said they were a devoted couple and so in love. No wonder Blanche was always happy to go on holiday on her own. I had no idea.'

'Nor I.' The breath whistled out of him. 'I suppose it makes sense, it's just that...' He put his face into his hands and shook his head. 'It's just that I thought they were different. You know, that they loved each other but had decided not to take it any further – like we did. I looked up to him because of it.'

A strange feeling started in Jo's chest. 'Are you terribly disappointed?'

'No,' he said, tiredly. 'No, I'm not disappointed. He'll always be a wonderful example to me, for many reasons; it's just, it's just...' He couldn't go on. Jo tentatively laid her hand on his shoulder and he rubbed it with his cheek. 'It's just that I thought that if *they* could manage it then...' He sought her face. 'If they could manage it, then so could we.'

Her heart plummeted.

'Mat,' she said, 'do you have any idea what I've been through these last few months living without you? And you looked at my belly just then, for goodness sake! What did you think I'd been doing?'

She couldn't wait for an answer but turned and ran out of the apartment, down the back steps into the garden. What she saw brought her to her knees.

'Oh, no,' she groaned. The plum tree lay uprooted on the grass and Blanche's ashes were scattered everywhere.

'What is it?' Mat said, coming down the steps, his face completely white. 'Did Moreau do this?' He crouched down, uselessly sweeping at the ashes with his hands. 'How much longer before the police arrive do you think? I've got to tidy this up.'

'Don't, Mat,' she said. 'It's a crime scene. We need to leave it as it is.'

He turned away and she saw his shoulders shake.

'Mat...'

'Not just now,' he said, sounding completely broken. 'I'm sorry, Jo. I can't deal with anything else right now. Sorry.'

CHAPTER 68

12th April 1229
Paris

Raimondet – now the seventh Count of Toulouse and a strapping, ruggedly handsome man of thirty two – knelt before the splendid façade of Notre Dame, clad only in his shirt and breeches. The great barons and Churchmen of France sat in rows behind him, waiting for the spectacle to begin. To one side, his cousin, the Dowager Queen Blanche of Castile, sat beside her young son, King Louis IX of France, under a spreading canopy of gold.

It was almost twenty years since the lad's father had suffered this same indignity, Matthieu reflected, watching the young Count's muscles tighten as a different Papal Legate, Romano, brought his birch switch down upon them. Matthieu's eyes strayed to Queen Blanche, and he recalled that this was the granddaughter Aliènor of Aquitaine had crossed the Pyrenees in winter to find, to marry Louis VIII of France.

He studied Blanche's impassive face as the birch switch whistle through the air. Unfortunately for Raimondet, their mutual grandmother had chosen well. There was the same steel and fierce intelligence in this Queen's face as in Alienor's; but what would that amazing woman have thought of one grandchild ordering the scourging of another?

Matthieu drew in his breath. Raimondet had been forced into an agreement with Blanche, but would the new Treaty of Paris bring the south any lasting peace?

After the scourging, the young Count was led into Notre Dame and those watching began to disperse. Matthieu was filled with a familiar yearning – that he might one day see his own son. Joana had written that Guillem had been several times to Montségur, to try to persuade her to leave. Matthieu sighed – the boy obviously took after himself more than his mother, thanks be to God.

*

After much lobbying, Matthieu was finally allowed to see Raimondet. The young Count had a room of his own in the Louvre, with a window overlooking the Seine, a comfortable chair, and one spare for his visitor.

'Matthieu?' There was a look of genuine puzzlement on Raimondet's face. 'Is it you, or are my eyes deceiving me?'

Matthieu felt himself relax. He had feared outright rejection. 'No, your eyes see true, my lord. How are things with you?'

Raimondet's eyes travelled mockingly upwards towards Matthieu's tonsure.

'So you joined them, after all?'

'Yes,' Matthieu said. 'May I sit?'

'Yes, but first-' Raimondet stood up and clasped his old tutor in his arms. 'How are you, my friend?'

Tears sprang into Matthieu's eyes. He had not expected this. 'Getting older, as are we all. I was sorry to hear about your father.'

The young Count's eyes shadowed. 'They won't lift the excommunication so I can bury him. I suppose you knew that?'

'Sometimes,' Matthieu said, quietly, 'our Church is less forgiving than God.'

Raimondet gave him a sharp look. 'Be careful,' he said. 'You know I am now sworn to deliver heretics, *wherever* I find them?'

Matthieu smiled, sadly. 'If only your father had done so whilst he was still alive.'

'If only I'd been older,' Raimondet countered, his blue eyes challenging. 'Monfort most certainly would not have had so many victories.'

'How is your daughter?' Matthieu asked, hoping to change the subject.

Raimondet let out a frustrated sigh. 'She's to be married to Louis' brother. When I die, they'll take everything.'

Matthieu's heart twisted at the pain in Raimondet's voice.

'Anyway,' Raimondet walked across the room, stretching his back, 'I've done all I can for now, Matthieu, let's talk about something else. A kinsman of yours, Guillem of Pamiers, has come into my service recently. I believe he's your nephew.'

Matthieu's heart beat uncomfortably fast at the news. 'Is he with you?'

Raimondet shook his head. 'No, I dare not bring him here, on account of his mother being a heretic. I though they might light a bonfire under him. Did you know she was one of the heretics?'

'Is he well?' Matthieu said, ignoring the question.

'Well enough. Did you ever meet him when you lived in the south?'

'Only once, when he was a small boy.' Would he ever forget those eyes peeping from behind the maid's skirts? He had to ask, could not resist. 'Do you know where the mother is?'

'She's at Montségur, so I believe.'

'And? Will you report her to the tribunals?'

'I won't have any choice, will I, once I return?' Raimondet said, sulkily. 'That place is not even in my territory *and* it's on top of a sheer mountain – but I'm supposed to be responsible for whatever goes on there.'

Matthieu said nothing. Raimondet could drive all heretics out of the south in a few years, if he was so minded...

‘So you’d better hope she comes to her senses,’ Raimondet said. ‘Or I shall be the one sending her to the stake.’

*

According to the Treaty of Paris, Raimondet was to return to Toulouse and found a new School of Theology. Many of the teachers in Paris were eager to go with him to take up posts. In public, the founding of the new university would be to ‘*exalt the cedar tree of the Catholic faith where the thorny brush wood of heresy had spread like a forest*’. In private, Raimondet begged Matthieu to come with him, saying that he needed a friend during this influx of northern churchmen – especially since he’d been told to expect the company of Bishop Foulques!

*

‘No one could have worked harder or longer for the salvation of those miserable people,’ Foulques told Matthieu on the long ride back. ‘But do they remember? I think they would hang me as soon as listen to me now.’

Yes, they probably would, Matthieu thought, looking at the man who had been his good friend. All they will remember is that you betrayed them to Simon of Montfort – and they will remember *that* until the end of their lives.

A terrible sight greeted them as they reached Toulouse. Twenty years of strife had impoverished the cité. French troops had razed crops and uprooted the trees and vines for miles around; and pulled down the walls. Raimondet brought his horse to a halt, and wept.

Accommodation was somehow found for them all but the Consuls welcomed back their young Count with trepidation. For six months they had suffered outrage upon outrage. Matthieu saw the sparks of rebellion in their eyes. Had Blanche provoked too much resentment?

Matthieu was impatient to find his son. Every nobleman and churchman in Toulouse would be at Mass on Sunday, perhaps he’d be lucky enough to see him there? The ceremony took place in the Cathedral of Saint Étienne, and was presided over by the Legate and Foulques. Every seat was full, as if there were not a heretic in the whole of Toulouse.

After the service was over, Raimondet caught Matthieu’s eye and beckoned him aside.

‘I see you’ve moved back in with the serpent,’ he whispered.

‘Ssh, my lord.’ Matthieu spoke very quietly. ‘Better the devil you know...’

‘If you say so,’ Raimondet said. Although he was still a young man, intense weariness stared out from behind his eyes. ‘I feel as if I’ve brought a Hell full of devils back with me, Matthieu, not churchmen. They’ve started sniffing around already for heretics. I’m sure that Legate wants to make an example of someone whilst he’s here. Mark my words, it won't be long before you smell burning flesh.'

'He'll give them a chance to recant, first, my lord,' Matthieu said, wondering just who he was trying to reassure. 'He's only trying to save their souls.'

'But that's the problem, don't you see? *They* think they're giving up their souls to the devil if they recant, because that's what the Church is to them – the church of the devil. Pray for us, Matthieu.'

'I am praying, my lord, as must you-'

'Guillem!' The young Count called out to a young man with dark, wavy hair who was passing by with his companions. 'Come here, I have someone who wants to meet you!'

Matthieu's eyes roved hungrily over the face of his son – seeing in him the clear green eyes of Joana and the dark brown hair, so like his own. What a fine, straight man he had grown into – with little trace of the shyness he had shown as a boy.

'My lord!' Guillem bowed to his seigneur. 'It's good to see you back, sire. We were worried that they would never let you return. How are you?'

'Well enough,' Raimondet said, unconsciously flexing his back. 'Six months in the same room just about drove me insane. I intend to go riding every day from now on. Anyway, Guillem, I'd like you to meet your uncle, Matthieu of Poitiers.'

'My uncle? How's that, my lord?'

'My wife was your mother's sister,' Matthieu explained. 'I haven't seen you since you were a very young boy.'

'Did you come to visit us once?' Guillem asked, his broad brow creasing into a frown.

Matthieu nodded. 'When you were about four summers.'

'Yes, I remember,' Guillem said. 'You were one of the crusaders, weren't you?'

'Not exactly,' Matthieu said. 'I took no part in the fighting.'

'That's right,' Guillem said, smiling faintly. 'My mother must have been very fond of you, Matthieu. She cried for weeks after you'd gone.'

Raimondet gave Matthieu a searching look. 'Did she now?'

He couldn't help it, the heat rose in his cheeks and Matthieu looked at the ground, desperate not to give himself away.

'I think I'd better leave you two to catch up on family matters,' Raimondet said, barely suppressing a smirk. 'I'll go and make sure there are no heretics lurking around here.'

*

Matthieu and Guillem spent two wonderful months together in Toulouse. To Matthieu's delight, his son had a quick and agile mind and was always seeking to know more.

‘I have a thirst to learn, uncle,’ Guillem confessed one day as they rode together beside the banks of the Garonne. The air was cold, but not frosty, and both wore thick woollen cloaks, tightly belted at their waists. ‘It’s like a fire inside of me that will not be put out, until I sit in front of a book and lose myself.’

Matthieu nodded. ‘I once felt like that too, and since I became a scholar, I have had plenty of opportunity to read the most wonderful books. Have you heard of the works of Augustine and Aristotle?’

Guillem smiled eagerly. ‘I have heard of them, but never seen them.’

‘Well, why do you not put yourself forward for the new university?’ Matthieu asked.

‘I’m afraid they will not accept me, uncle, on account of my mother,’ Guillem said, candidly. ‘She’s with the heretics at Montségur. I’ve tried to persuade her to leave them but she says I don’t understand. Do you think you would have more influence over her?’

CHAPTER 69

October 1539
Hampton Court, England

'Lady Johanna?'

She leaped to her feet as she saw Cromwell making his way towards her.

'Baron,' she said, watching him intently, 'what news of Matthew?'

'He is well, decently housed, wants for nothing-'

'Except his liberty.'

Cromwell inclined his head. 'Except for his liberty. You might be able to see him soon,' he said, taking her aside, 'but I can't release him. Not yet.'

'And may I ask, why not?' she said, weary beyond measure. The day had started early, she had gone hunting with the King and then danced with him, and now she was standing around with the other courtiers, trying to look decorative, whilst Henry played at the card tables.

'I would have thought that was obvious.'

She frowned, twisting on her finger the fabulous pearl and ruby ring that the King had bestowed upon her last night. 'You mean to keep Matthew in the Tower until the new queen arrives?'

'I can think of worse places.'

Johanna took a long breath and fixed the smile back on her face. He'd said she could see Matthew. That was something.

'Very well. How will I get there?'

'We'll go tomorrow. His Majesty has plenty to occupy him here, I can assure you of that.'

*

She sat alone in the same room at the Tower where she'd waited with Sir John. The fire was lit in the grate but the room had even less cheer than on her first visit, and the voices from the walls still called out to her. She shook her head, trying to silence them, just as the door started to open. Cromwell stood outside. Was that Matthew with him? She stood up.

'Well then,' Cromwell said, smiling at her. 'Here he is.'

A bowed old man stepped into the room. There was a large bandage across his chest, his hair was matted and greasy and he was wearing a shirt that must have belonged to a much bigger man, for the sleeves hung down to his finger tips. Disappointment churned in her. This wasn't Matthew. Had all of her waiting been in vain?

'Lady Johanna.' Cromwell moved nearer, looking concerned – or was it merely mockery? 'Is this not the person you were looking for?'

When the man looked up, Jo's balance very nearly failed. They must have put him on the rack to reduce him so, she thought.

'Matthew?' she stepped towards him.

'Lady Johanna,' Matthew rasped, holding out his hands in supplication, 'forgive me.'

Johanna looked towards the Baron, who looked away.

'May I see Matthew alone?' she asked.

Cromwell clicked his tongue and shook his head. Anger flared in Johanna's breast and she could have easily run at him then, run at him and dashed out his brains with the poker from the fire, but what would it serve?

Matthew staggered forwards and would have fallen to the floor if she had not managed to help him towards the stool. He shook violently and silently she wrapped her arms around the bones of his body, hearing him moan as she touched the bulky dressing on his side. Bitterness flowed in her mouth.

'Oh, Matthew,' she said.

*

The King wore only a lawn chemise and breeches. They sat on the side of her bed and he stroked his hand down her thigh and leg, then hitched up her kirtle and petticoat until the tops of her stockings showed.

'Do you know, Johanna,' the King said, as he trailed a pudgy finger on the soft flesh of her inner thigh, 'how wondrous the skin of a woman is to a man?'

'No, Majesty,' she said, trying not to shudder.

He tugged at one of the garters, unfastening it, and bringing the frothy band to his mouth to kiss it before dropping it onto the floor.

Thus is a man flayed alive Johanna thought, inch by slow inch. Now the other garter was off and her stockings slid by themselves down her legs. She fought the urge to pull them back and run from the room. The effort made her tremble.

'Are you cold, my love?' the King asked, looking at her curiously.

'No, Majesty,' she lied. There was an obvious place that would be warmer. Warmer but not safer.

'You're trembling,' he said, lifting her chin and kissing her slowly. His breath was laced with wine and honey and he sucked at her, devouring-

'Feel me,' he said, taking hold of her hand and fumbling at his groin.

How strange it felt; warm, dry, hardish. No one could have been a Maid of Honour as long as Johanna had without learning, and hearing, what went on between the sheets – but this, this was *the King*. She swallowed and would have taken her hand away, but he held on to her.

'Don't be afraid, for I shan't hurt you,' he said. 'Clasp me so-'

He guided her hand more firmly around him. Anne Basset had whispered to Johanna, as they lay in the same bed in the outer room of Queen Jane's chamber, that in this way a woman could satisfy a man without bedding him; and she had also whispered of other, even more sinful ways that Johanna didn't want to think about just now. The King's breath escaped from his mouth in short gasps, and he lay back completely on the bed. His face contorted and his body made jerky movements, and Johanna thought he was about to have seizure. She tried to let go again, but he protested.

'No, NO! Don't let go! Ah!' Sticky wetness dribbled through her fingers. 'More, Johanna,' he gasped, 'harder!'

She took a deep breath and did as he asked.

The King's eyes were screwed closed, his lips had drawn back over his teeth as if he were in agony, and Johanna felt a giggle bubbling in her throat. Desperately she pumped at him, her hand cramping with fatigue, but still he moaned and hissed, turning his head from side to side and groaning loudly, patently enjoying himself; but looking anything but happy. In fact he looked quite ridiculous.

At last the King relaxed and took her hand away, an indulgent smile upon his face. She was surprised to see how much younger he looked.

'What a clever girl you are, Johanna,' he said. 'Are you all right, sweeting? Did I frighten you?'

'No, Majesty,' Johanna lied, thinking he could have frightened her a lot more. 'I'm only glad to have been able to please you.'

*

It was the third hour past noon. Cromwell sat to Johanna's left at the end of the long oak dining table. His nephew, Richard, had been there and also his son, Gregory, with Gregory's wife, Elizabeth, who had been both sister and Lady in Waiting to Queen Jane. Elizabeth was obviously very much in love with Gregory. They had four children between them already and, if Johanna wasn't mistaken, there was another on the way. She sighed. Elizabeth looked sleek and content, her hands resting gently on her belly – whenever she was not using them to touch her husband affectionately, that is.

But now they had all left and Johanna was alone with the Baron. He looked contented too, she thought, for his star rose and rose; but she'd lived in his house long enough to know that star was supported upon the long hours that he worked.

'How are things with the King?' Cromwell said, wiping his knife and stowing it in the pouch at his belt.

'Very well, I believe,' she said, not quite looking at him.

'Are you invited to the masque tonight?'

'I wasn't aware of it,' Johanna said.

'Really?' Cromwell frowned. 'I must find out why. Do you know?'

She shook her head. 'Except that the King thinks I should rest.'

'Rest?' She had all of his attention now, but it was directed at her belly. 'Are you with child?' He frowned again. 'There hasn't been enough time.'

'No, I'm not with child – the King's or anyone else's.' She glared at Cromwell, unwilling to tell him that she had pleaded an indisposition yesterday and that was why the King had asked her to rest. She was, in truth, exhausted. Even with a painful leg, the King kept a busy schedule and had wanted her with him nearly every day.

'You're not slipping out of favour are you?' Cromwell said.

'I don't think so, but then, one can never be sure of His Majesty's moods – as you well know.'

His dark brows came together, and Johanna glimpsed the turbulence beneath the calm exterior. How long had *he* played this game of keeping the King happy? For her it had been only a matter of weeks; for him it had been years.

'No matter,' he said, subjecting her to that look again, as if she were horse flesh. 'He seems happy enough just now.'

Johanna relaxed a fraction. 'May I see Matthew again?'

'It depends,' he said.

'On what?'

'On nothing that I can tell you about right now.'

Frustrated, she stared at him, trying to read behind the carefully bland expression; but men who wore their secrets openly upon their faces never climbed to the heights that Thomas Cromwell had reached.

'And now if you'll excuse me,' he said, 'I have matters to attend to.'

*

Although he was still kept prisoner, Matthew had a much better room; a bed with blankets, and crucially, a window. It was a pleasant day outside and the bright autumn sunshine cast geometrical shadows around the Tower walls. Whenever he was not praying, Matthew stared out of that window, watching the ebb and flow of the river and the life of the Tower. He delighted in the birds that daily landed upon the stone windowsill, and wished with all his heart that the window would open so he could leave them crumbs – but wishing for that was as impossible as wishing himself safely back at Glastonbury.

His one comfort was that the Abbot and Johanna had looked well when he saw them, but there had been no opportunity to speak to either, nor to find out what had become of the reliquary. Had it really contained diamonds? If so, he feared for the Abbot. But why would Abbot Whiting have conspired to give diamonds to the King of France? Unless there was something sacred about them that he would not trust the King with, now he had broken from Rome.

Matthew stiffened as he heard the turning of the lock, and slowly turned to face whatever was coming.

'Follow me,' Mark said, his voice strangely gentle.

Outside the room loomed two more warders. They all marched him briskly down the stairs and out into the courtyard. The ravens hopped away as they walked towards the White Tower. Matthew's breath was catching in a half sob his throat. Was this where he would finally be put on the rack? Had that time come?

Inside the White Tower, Matthew went *down* the stairs for the first time, into the basement. It was dimly lit, but no darker than Matthew's thoughts, and his body trembled as he walked along the damp corridor. He was pushed into a windowless room with a brightly burning brazier, and it was there he saw the rack – the thick wheels and ropes blatantly advertising its purpose. His legs gave way and the warders dragged him onto a chair then snapped manacles about his wrists. Mark pointed to an iron hook high up on a cross bar.

'That's where they'll hang you first,' he said, 'until your arms have pulled out of their sockets and you scream till your throat gives up.' His face came nearer, lip curling contemptuously. 'Don't think you can get out of it by fainting,' he said, pointing to three buckets of water on the floor. 'One of those will bring you round, soon enough. And then, if you still haven't told us what we want to know, it'll be the rack for you. No one survives *that* without singing. Do you hear me – *no one*!'

Matthew's eyes refused to focus. Although he desperately wanted to appear unafraid, he could only stare blankly at the fuzzy outline of Mark.

'Right, that's enough,' Mark said. 'Take him upstairs. Baron Cromwell wants to speak to him.'

*

They left Matthew alone in the same room where he'd met Johanna, empty now of everything except the dust that swirled in a single shaft of sunlight. He tried to pray, but even his thoughts stuttered. How would he hold out if they put him on the rack?

'Good morning,' Cromwell said, pleasantly, as he came into the room followed by his scribe carrying a couple of stools.

Mark came too, pulling along a desk.

'Put it here,' Cromwell said, 'and fetch something to light that fire. It's freezing.'

Mark looked doubtfully at Matthew, but Cromwell laughed. 'Off you go. I can cope.'

The Baron sat down on one of the stools and his scribe on the other. Matthew supported himself against the wall and prayed for courage. Wearing manacles embarrassed him. They took away his humanity, made him vulnerable.

Cromwell seemed in no hurry. He waited until Mark had made up the fire in the grate and fanned it into life, and then sent him away again to fetch beer and food. Matthew's stomach turned over. He'd been trying to eat but it was as if his stomach had forgotten its purpose.

'How are you?' Cromwell asked, looking up at him from the desk.

Matthew was so afraid that his voice would betray him that he merely nodded. Mark came in with the food.

'We need another stool,' Cromwell said.

Glowering, Mark turned and left the room again.

When everything was ready, and Matthew was seated, and Mark had been sent to wait with the other warders outside, Cromwell offered him a mug of beer and some cheese, but Matthew shook his head.

'Come on, you look like you need it, lad,' Cromwell said. 'Try a bit.'

Matthew took the mug and the cheese, but sipped and nibbled slowly, his stomach roiling. Cromwell sighed and looked at the fire, then drew his fur lined cloak closer about him.

'Right then, as we haven't got all day, we'd better get started. Edmund?'

The scribe, who had just finished sharpening his quills and setting out his ink, nodded.

'Matthew,' Cromwell said, pulling a note towards himself and studying it. 'I want you to tell me why were you were sent to France with a reliquary containing diamonds.'

Matthew shook his head. 'I'm sorry, Baron, but I wasn't.'

'What do you mean, you weren't?' Cromwell looked up. 'Didn't you ever look inside?'

'Never.'

'So you didn't see any diamonds?'

'No.'

Cromwell drummed his fingers on the desk. 'So, where were you asked to take this reliquary?'

Matthew hesitated. It was pointless denying it. 'To an abbey in France.'

'And then?'

'I don't know. That's all I was asked to do.'

'Nothing more?'

'No,' he said.

'Were you expected to return or to stay there?'

'I don't know.'

'God's wounds,' Cromwell said. 'Sent out of the country, your life put at risk, and no instructions about what you were to do when you got there?'

Matthew said nothing.

'What do you know of His Majesty's reforms?' Cromwell said.

It was unexpected, and Matthew stammered as he tried to answer. He knew it was a test of whether the Abbot had carried out the new rules at Glastonbury, and was nearly impossible to answer because, despite all the noise and decrees, it still wasn't clear to Matthew exactly what the King had had in mind when he declared himself to be the Supreme Head of the Church of England.

'Hm,' Cromwell said, when he finished his halting reply. 'Did you ever hear Abbot Whiting speak about the Pope?'

'No, Baron, not after the reforms.'

'Never?'

'Never.' He shook his head to emphasis the point.

'Did he ever dedicate a Mass to the Pope?' Cromwell said, leaning forward. 'Or wish him well, or direct any of you to pray for his health?'

'No, Baron.'

'What about the King? Did you ever hear the Abbot speak about the King?'

'Yes, Baron.' Matthew was sweating now, even though the fire had barely started to heat up the room.

'And what did you hear?'

It was hard to remember, he was so frightened. 'We prayed often for His Majesty's health, and wished him a long and happy life as the Head of the Church.'

'Of course you did,' Cromwell nodded, his lips thinning. 'What about the King's marriage to Anne Boleyn, did you hear anything said about that?'

'No, Baron.'

'Or anyone speculating upon how long the King should live, or his health?'

'No, Baron.'

Cromwell gave a frustrated sigh and pushed back his chair with a loud scraping sound. 'Can you tell me why, then,' he stood up and leaned over to check his scribe's notes, 'you've just said that you prayed often – for His Majesty's health and wished him a long life?'

Matthew shook so much he could only stammer. 'F-forgive me, Baron, I may have used the wrong words, but I'm sure, I was never meant to have anything other than the King's good at heart.'

'And yet, you were asked to take a reliquary out of the country containing diamonds that *belonged* to him. Was that having his good at heart?'

'It seemed to be all done in a hurry, Baron.' It was the only answer he could give.

‘In a hurry?’

He nodded.

‘So much of a hurry that someone had time to write a marriage licence for you and arrange for you to meet your ‘wife’ at Weymouth?’

‘I-I’m not sure,’ Matthew said, his hands clenched tight together.

‘You’re not sure.’ Cromwell’s eyes were hard. ‘So tell me who it was who gave you this?’ He stalked towards Matthew and held the marriage licence under his nose.

Matthew swallowed. ‘I’m sorry, Baron, it was all such a rush, and a long time ago. I’m afraid I can’t remember.’

‘You can’t remember!’ Cromwell’s voice rose. ‘So you probably can’t remember whether the Abbot spoke well of the King or otherwise, can you? Or whether you prayed everyday instead for the health of the *Pope*?’

‘No, no,’ Matthew said. ‘I can remember that.’

‘Matthew,’ Cromwell clamped his hand roughly around Matthew’s chin and turned his face up to look at him, ‘do you know how many tools I have at my disposal to *help* you with your memory?’

It was impossible to move his head, so Matthew let his eyes slide away from the cruelty he saw in the other’s face. *Forgive them father, for they know not what they do.* He could feel words forming on his tongue, desperate words that wanted to flood out to save – what? His skin?

The realisation came so quickly that Matthew slumped forwards. His body was dispensable, but his beliefs were not. He forgave Cromwell, forgave the King – and Abbot Whiting.

Cromwell shook his head.

‘We’re done here, Edmund,’ he said. The Baron walked back to his desk with a thin smile upon his face. ‘You’ll be released later today,’ he said to Matthew, and walked from the room.

Austin Friars
London.

Cromwell chewed a knuckle of chicken and tried to make up his mind. It was obvious that neither Johanna nor Matthew had known anything about the diamonds before they set off. After all, the girl had brought them straight to Henry when she found them, *and* put her own cousin in jeopardy by letting him carry on without them in the reliquary; but he wished he could say the same for the Abbot of Glastonbury.

He tossed the chicken bone into the fire. Right now, he’d like to burn quite a few churchmen, but Henry wouldn’t let him. He was still in thrall to the old ways, whatever he said, and though the abbots and bishops had signed the Oath of Supremacy and paid lip service to it, in their hearts they’d *never* change. Which meant there would always be plots like this –

threatening to undermine the country every time he turned his back.

Of course he blamed Reginald Pole. Every Pole he'd been able to lay hands on had been rounded up the last time they conspired to replace Henry, and they'd either lost their lofty Plantagenet heads, or were safely locked up in the Tower; but Reginald Pole was still on the Continent, pretending to be a cardinal – despite being no more suited to the role than Cromwell himself – and stirring up trouble. It was even rumoured that the Spanish ambassador had Pole in mind as a suitable husband for the Princess Mary. What a cosy Catholic family that would make!

*

'There's a young gentleman here for you, Lady Johanna,' Phyllis said, coming into the garden. 'The Baron says you may see him, but only for a short while. Where shall I put him?'

Johanna looked around, her heart thudding. 'I don't know. Is there anywhere private here?'

'There's the Ladies' Parlour upstairs, I suppose,' Phyllis said. 'Nobody goes in there much.'

'Do you know his name?' Johanna asked, trying to keep her hope under control – but it couldn't be anyone else, could it?

'Steward said it was a Master Manners. Do you know him?'

'Yes,' she said, keeping her relief as hidden as possible. 'I believe I do.'

Phyllis went on in front with a duster 'to check that all was well', and when Johanna was finally allowed into the Ladies' Parlour, she thought it a sad little room. Cromwell's wife and daughter had died many years ago, of the sweating sickness, and even though there were tapestries upon the walls and a bowl of fragrant herbs, the seats showed no signs of ever having been sat upon and the air smelled stale.

'Shall I bring him to you now, my lady?'

'Yes, please,' Johanna said, and sat down on one of the velvet chairs, clasping her hands; then she stood up and walked around the room, feigning interest in the tapestries. If only she would be allowed to see him alone, even for a few minutes!

'Here he is, my lady,' Phyllis said, opening the door again. 'I've asked Steward to send some refreshments up for you.'

Johanna hardly dared to look, because Matthew had appeared so wretched the last time she saw him; but although the strain of his captivity showed plainly on his face, at least he was cleanly dressed and groomed.

'How are you?' she said, moving towards him, her hands outstretched; but she was not allowed to touch him because one of the servants came in then with a tray of food, and stood beside Matthew, his arms folded rigidly across his body.

'Well enough,' Matthew said, his eyes searching hers eagerly. 'And you?'

'Well enough,' she said.

*

They had barely had time to sit down together before Cromwell came hurrying into the room.

'You may leave us,' he said to the serving man, and then sat down. 'And?'

'And, what?' Johanna said, puzzled.

'No thanks, a remembrance in your will? Matthew is here, just as you asked.'

'For that I thank you, Baron,' she said, trying to sound sincere; for in truth she *was* grateful.

'You can see that he is in good health and well cared for?'

Cromwell was watching her keenly.

'Indeed,' she said, putting on a smile. 'Perhaps later, when you've finished with us, we may be allowed a little time alone?'

'Perhaps,' Cromwell said, absently. 'But there's something I have to ask you both first, if I may?'

'What is it?' she said.

'Tell me,' Cromwell said, 'do either of you know a Gerald Grenfell?'

She tried not to show it.

'I thought so,' he said. 'In fact, am I right in thinking he was your cousin, Lady Johanna?'

She wished he'd just tell her, rather than stringing out her nerves like this.

'A distant cousin,' she said.

'Of yourself and Lady Lisle, I believe?' Cromwell said, one eyebrow raised.

She said nothing.

'Come now,' he said. 'It's not like you, Lady Johanna, to be so quiet.'

Johanna risked a look at Matthew. His pose was rigid.

Cromwell's mouth twisted.

'Very well,' he said. 'I'm afraid I have to tell you that your cousin is dead, Lady Johanna. His body was found in France. He had, it appears, been tortured to death.'

She felt the blood leaving first her face and then her body. She pitched forwards, her vision dark.

'Put her head between her knees,' she heard Cromwell telling Matthew somewhere in the distance. 'That usually does the trick.'

*

When Johanna finally recovered enough to speak, she was lying on deep cushions in the Ladies' Parlour and Matthew was sitting at the far side of the room with his head in his hands.

‘Baron,’ she said, ‘can you think why someone should have done such a terrible thing to Gerald? He was a priest, as you probably know, and a good man. I cannot think of any reason why this should have happened to him.’

‘Can you not, Lady Johanna?’ Cromwell said, his eyes sharp. ‘May I ask when you last saw your cousin?’

When he saw that she wasn’t going to answer, Cromwell got to his feet.

‘For the love of God,’ he shouted. He looked around at Matthew. ‘Can’t either of you see what has happened? Once you took the diamonds out of the reliquary, Lady Johanna, did you not spare a thought what might happen to Gerald when he arrived without them?’

Johanna held a hand across her mouth, determined not to be sick. Someone, other than the Abbess of Fontevraud, must had been expecting those diamonds, and tortured poor Gerald to death on account of them.

‘Do you have any idea of the import of this matter?’ Cromwell asked. ‘If I were you, I would not try my patience any further.’ He came over and shook Johanna roughly. ‘When was the last time you saw your cousin?’

‘I cannot think, Baron,’ she pleaded. ‘Not when you are shouting at me, so.’

‘But I can,’ Matthew said, speaking for the first time. His face had gone very white. ‘The Lady Johanna knows nothing of this but when Abbot Whiting first sent me to get the reliquary from Canterbury, there was someone else with him in the crypt at Glastonbury. It is possible that man might have something to do with the diamonds.’

‘In the crypt at Glastonbury?’ Cromwell’s eyes were feral. ‘Did you recognise him?’

Matthew shook his head.

‘Can you describe him?’

‘It was a long time ago.’

‘Not that long,’ Cromwell said. ‘It would be worth the remembering.’

Matthew took his time. He was trembling inside but he knew that somehow he had to protect Johanna. When he mentioned that the man had a moustache that pointed downwards like the fingers of a clock, Cromwell could barely contain his excitement.

‘Would you remember this man again?’ he asked.

‘I don’t know,’ Matthew said. ‘It was dark in the crypt and he didn’t speak to me.’

‘But you could try?’

For some reason, Cromwell didn’t wait for Matthew to answer but chased out of the room, leaving them alone at last.

‘Lady Johanna,’ Matthew said, his face creased with concern, ‘*why* are you here?’

She had expected him to be pleased to see her, but all that was upon his quickly-aged face was concern. Her voice came out in a whisper.

'I couldn't leave you, Matthew, especially not when I found the diamonds. I realised we'd been tricked. '

'Why put yourself in all this danger for me?' he said, his shoulders drooping. 'All that sustained me was the thought that you and Saint Thomas would be safe at Fontevraud.'

'Matthew...' Johanna's voice shook and tears tumbled out of her eyes.

He came to kneel before her and took her hands in his. 'What did you tell them about me?'

'That you knew nothing about the diamonds.'

'The diamonds.' He sighed heavily. 'How can jewels be worth more than our lives? So you gave them to the King in exchange for my freedom?'

She nodded.

'And, what else?'

She couldn't look at him. Her shame was complete. She had thought to save him, but found that he didn't want to be saved.

'Oh, Lady Johanna,' he said. 'You have freed me, but lost yourself.'

*

Well, well, well. Could Gardiner, the slimy toad, have made a fatal mistake at last? Of all the people in England, Bishop Gardiner was the biggest thorn in Cromwell's side. He dashed off a letter to enquire about the Bishop of Winchester's movements for the next few days and then ordered his steward to open the barrel of Burgundy that Lord Lisle had sent him only last week. Lisle knew his wines, there was no doubt about that.

Only then did Cromwell remember Johanna and Matthew. He'd left someone listening at the door of course. Let them enjoy their 'tender reunion' because they wouldn't be seeing much of each other from now on. And if he could get the lad to identify Gardiner? Well then, he'd promise to let him go...

*

'There's still time for an honest man like you, Matthew,' Cromwell said, as they sat in the barge.

'Oh?' Matthew said. 'To do what?'

'To save your Abbot.'

Matthew studied Cromwell's thuggish features. If he were not one of God's creatures, it would be hard to bear him.

'I take it he has already been condemned?' Matthew said.

Cromwell's olive-grey eyes widened regretfully. 'There were valuables secreted all over the Abbey, Matthew, and treasonous writings in his study. That alone is enough to cause him to swing – without the matter of the diamonds.'

'Ah, the diamonds.'

'Yes, the diamonds. A little present for King Francis, if I'm not mistaken – and a sort of invitation.'

'To do what?'

Matthew didn't like where this conversation was going, but in truth, he'd already gone there himself last night whilst he was trying to sleep. Someone, either in Canterbury or Glastonbury, had put those diamonds into the reliquary and planned for them to be taken to France. If what Cromwell said was true, they were part of a plot to replace the English King with a more Catholic monarch. Ice ran in his veins.

'Someone was hoping to persuade the French to take over this country, Matthew.' Cromwell said. 'That's just about the highest treason I can think of. I know you have a lot of faith in abbots and bishops, but from where I stand they're just as selfish and vain as the next man. If you remember that the King, *our* King, has been anointed by God, then why would anyone seek to replace him with a king of *their own choosing*, when I'm every day assured by churchmen that they only wish to do the will of God?'

Matthew couldn't answer. Anger churned in his breast; Johanna's life had been ruined, Gerald had met a dreadful end. Must more people be sacrificed?

'Why are you offering me the opportunity to save the Abbot, if you've already made up your mind about him?' he asked, finally.

'Because,' Cromwell said, pursing his lips, 'if you recognise the man who was in the crypt with you that day, and tell me truthfully – which I'm sure you will, being the God-fearing man that I know you are, Matthew – then you and the Lady Johanna will be free to leave. And the Abbot will become a key witness to treason. If he's helpful, I may be able to show him some leniency – perhaps persuade the King to have him beheaded rather than...

Matthew winced. He was well aware of the grisly fate of traitors. 'And what will become of the man I recognise?'

There was no answer, Cromwell's jaw had clenched tight.

*

Johanna looked tiredly down over the balcony of the King's private Pew in the Chapel Royal at Hampton Court. The congregation had been in their seats for at least half an hour, but as yet, there was no sign of the King. The Celebrant had been arranging things on the altar and talking with the choir master, but now he looked up irritably to where she was sitting. Johanna took in a sharp breath. There was only one man in England who would dare to publicly express his irritation with the King, one man whose influence and spy network could rival that of Cromwell:

Johanna shuddered. The moustache on Bishop Stephen Gardiner's long, serious face, had ends which pointed downwards, like the hands of a clock. Dear God, please don't let him be the man Matthew had seen in the crypt at Glastonbury that day, she prayed. Gardiner was Cromwell's greatest foe, and the Baron would spare *no one* to bring him down. If he was implicated in this plot, she and Matthew would never see the light of day again.

*

Liveried men helped them to shore as the barge glided to a halt. Beyond the landing stage, Matthew saw a grand palace built of costly red brick, with numerous, individually decorated chimneys. How many fireplaces must there be in such a building?

When they walked through the entrance gates into an echoing courtyard, Matthew was amazed to see everyone tiptoeing around and speaking in hushed tones. Cromwell grinned.

'It's nearly time for Mass. The King likes a bit of hush whilst he's worshipping.'

Matthew's heart leaped painfully. How long it had been since he was last allowed to attend the Mass? How long since his only worry was incurring the Novice Master's anger because he'd been delayed feeding the chickens?

They passed under an arch and almost immediately took the stairs to the left, eventually arriving in a hall so grand that Matthew could merely gaze in awe at the floor to ceiling tapestries. Gold and silver threads glittered in the streaming sunlight and the characters on the hangings were so beautifully drawn and coloured they looked as if they might come to life at any moment.

Cromwell spared him no time with such marvels but passed on quickly through other splendidly arrayed galleries until Matthew was ushered into a small room, the front of which ended in a balcony.

*

Johanna scanned the congregation below her anxiously. Cromwell would know that Gardiner was going to say Mass here today. It would be an ideal opportunity for him to bring Matthew along, perhaps have him waiting outside, so that he could see Bishop Gardiner leaving? In which case, there may well be still time to warn him. Her heart thumped against her ribs as she stood up to leave, but as she opened the door at the rear of the Pew, she saw the King standing there, resplendent in green velvet and with a heavy collar of gold hung about his shoulders.

'Johanna!' he said, jovially. 'Where are you going, sweeting? The Mass is about to start, is it not?'

'Yes, Majesty,' she said, wondering what she should say. If she said she was ill, he would send her into quarantine somewhere until he was sure she wouldn't affect him. 'I was concerned about you, Majesty,' she said, 'when you did not appear. But it seems you are quite well?'

'Very well, sweeting,' he said. 'Now, come, let us sit down or the good Bishop will never be able to start his service.'

*

The first thing Matthew noticed was the colour of the ceiling beyond – a wondrous blue, filled with golden stars. Moving forwards he found himself looking down on a sumptuously decorated chapel and a congregation waiting to start Mass. Immediately he dropped to his knees.

'We're in the Queen's pew,' Cromwell whispered, coming to kneel very close to Matthew. 'Don't get too comfortable. We haven't time to stay. Have a look at the man on the altar.'

Matthew looked out over the rail and yearned to be there too, on the altar, faithfully serving God. He recognised the man immediately, even though he was now attired in the robes of a Bishop celebrating Mass. Cromwell's breath came quickly.

'That man has a moustache that points like the hands of a clock, does he not?' he said.

'Yes,' Matthew replied, taking a deep breath. 'But I'm afraid he doesn't look anything like the man I remember.'

CHAPTER 70

September
Fontevraud Abbey

They stood together in the nave of the Abbey, Mat's arm draped casually about her shoulders.

'So these are the famous Plantagenet effigies,' he said. 'Kind of spooky, aren't they? Do you think they're a good likeness?'

'Who knows,' she shrugged, missing the warmth of his arm as he took it away to get a closer look.

Her attention was already moving over to the wall, to the disembodied-knight's feet.

'Your Church disinherited him, you know,' she said, pointing.

'Somebody didn't care too much about what he looked like, either, did they?' Mat said, surveying the almost empty wall.

'And they refused to bury his father.'

'Who did?'

'The Church. He was excommunicated.'

'Ah. Difficult that.'

'They thought he was a heretic.'

'This is the father we're talking about?'

'Yes, and they persecuted the son until there was hardly anything left of his inheritance. When he died, everything went to the King of France.'

'Who was? Do you know?'

'Louis IX.'

'Ah, *Saint* Louis.' Mat nodded. 'He built a wonderful chapel in Paris. It's called Sainte-Chapelle. Have you seen it? He built it to house the Crown of Thorns apparently. I've been there – and it's spectacular.'

'More relics.' She shuffled her feet. They were not her favourite subject at the moment.

'Up there with the best.'

Jo looked down at the guide book in her hands. 'Mat, when we get home, will you explain what it was about the Cathars' beliefs that upset the Catholic Church so much?'

'If I can,' he said. 'Although I don't know much about what they believed.'

*

They sat together on the sofa, close but not touching. The police had requested that they stay in Saint Gilles until the investigations were completed, which didn't seem likely to be any time soon, and they'd been together in the apartment for a week already. Jo's nerves were frayed to breaking point by having Mat so near, but not being able to touch him.

The situation was so complex. Not only was there the attempt on their lives by Monsieur Moreau, but there was also the finding of a potential national treasure and the fact that Blanche and Patrick had found the reliquary but not reported it.

So,' Mat said, leaning back, 'the Cathars. Tell me what you know about them.'

'Well,' she said, wishing she could just curl up next to him, 'they lived mainly in the Languedoc region, although I believe there were other groups, mostly in Italy and the Balkans. And they were successful, so much so that the Pope ended up having to send a crusade against them.'

'Yes, I think I've heard of it,' Mat said.

'When that didn't work, they started the Inquisition.'

'Yes, I knew it hadn't started in Spain, despite what people usually think. And the Cathar beliefs were, what?'

She saw him half-close his eyes as he prepared to concentrate on what she would say. How she loved him in that moment.

'It's really difficult to say. What I've been able to find out mostly comes from people who were opposed to them – like the Inquisitors. According to them, the Cathars believed in two gods-'

'Two gods?' Mat opened his eyes in surprise 'Well, there's your answer for a start.'

'Yes, but they didn't worship them both. Only the good one. They thought the bad one had come about through ' the fall' and he was the one who made the Earth. They didn't call themselves Cathars either, Mat, they believed that they were the *true* Christians – and lived as Jesus had meant them to.'

His mouth turned down, ruefully. 'As have many people over the ages. The Church has come in for a lot of criticism for having too much wealth etc – not all of it unjust, I have to admit.'

'So, could they have been right, do you think? Is that why the Old Testament's so full of 'God' smiting enemies and being wrathful, because he was an evil god?'

Mat shook his head. 'There's only one God, Jo. That I know with the whole of my being.'

She marvelled at his sincerity. His relationship with God was so *personal*. 'But didn't Christians believe that God is a Trinity – you know, Father, Son and Holy Spirit?'

'Careful,' he said, wagging his finger, 'if you're going to start talking about the Trinity and don't get the wording exactly right, I might have to light a bonfire under you.'

'What?' Shc searched his face.

'Just joking.' He breathed out a long sigh. 'Do you know, having to preach on Trinity Sunday always brings me out in a sweat because the concept is so difficult,' he admitted. 'Yes, God is a Trinity, but he's not divisible, Jo. It's a paradox we just have to live with. '*For now we see through a glass, darkly; but then face to face: now I know in part; but then shall I know even as also I am known.*' It's from 1 Corinthians.'

'Is that Saint Paul?' she asked, pleased to sound knowledgeable for once. 'The Cathars liked him – or at least some of his stuff.'

'That's interesting. So, tell me more of what they believed.'

'Well, because they believed that the evil god had created the Earth – they believed he had created the Catholic church, too.'

'Of course.' Mat was nodding as she talked. 'Their beliefs are a form of Dualism whose roots go way, way back – further back than Jesus in fact. But what you're actually describing is ditheism – gods in opposition.' He shook his head. 'What's always been a struggle, Jo, is to understand why, if our God is a good God, is there so much suffering in the world?'

'And do you have an answer?'

'Not an easy one. In the end, it has to come down to faith, I'm afraid, and the fact that we can't see the bigger picture. But try telling that to someone whose child has just been murdered.'

She nodded. 'When I look around the world, I know horrible things happen, but I can't actually see the Earth as *evil*, especially not nature. Plants do die, and they have diseases, and natural things like storms batter crops until they're useless – droughts and fire can cause devastation on a grand scale. If you look at the Universe, suns and planets are born and die, in fact everything is in a state of flux, but *we* expect *our* lives to be different because we think we're special.'

Mat's hand crept along the back of the sofa until it was touching her. 'And then we blame God. This is a big subject, Jo, and I'm hungry. Do you mind if we carry on over dinner?'

Her breath caught in her throat. Slowly his head came towards her and their lips met. Fire ignited instantly and he pulled her on to his knee, his arms tight around her. Oh, how she wanted him! The kiss deepened and she gave herself up to it, hardly daring to breathe. Would he reject her, push her away when he realised what he was doing? As his hands slid up her shirt towards her breasts, the phone in his pocket suddenly started to ring. Damn it, why now! She pulled away wanting to howl, scream, throw herself at the walls.

'I'd better answer it,' he said, shakily, 'it might be the police.'

Jo walked into the bathroom, her head drumming with frustration and tears. Reaching up, she turned on the shower. Better make it a cold one. Twenty minutes later, she emerged from the bathroom to find Mat standing in the sitting room with his bags packed.

'That was the Bishop,' he said. 'I'm really sorry, Jo, but the British press are on their way down here. Apparently they've heard there might be some juicy scandal. He thinks they've only just found out about Patrick and Blanche. I can't be here when they arrive. I have to find somewhere in Saint Gilles.'

Had she ever felt so miserable in all of her life?

'All right,' she said. What else could she say? She felt so foolish now, an evil temptress trying to lead him astray.

'Come here,' he said, pulling her into his arms. 'Don't look at me like that. It breaks my heart.' He stroked her hair and kissed her again, hard and long. 'Have you any idea how much I love you?' he said, raggedly. 'I know I've no right to say that because I can't offer you anything and I know it makes you angry but God help me, Jo, it's true. I told the Bishop, you know.'

'Oh?' She pulled back to look at him.

'I went to see him after the last time I was with you, and told him we were in love.'

'What did he say?' she said, her chest tight.

'He asked me to think about it, of course, and take some time. Then he asked me if I wanted to go to Rome.'

'And you said yes...' So much was obvious.

He ran a hand through his hair. 'I thought I should at least take his advice, Jo. After all, that's what I asked him for, and...' he sighed heavily. 'I needed to give myself some time.'

'And have you...' She struggled to voice the next words. 'Have you had enough time?'

His arms tightened. 'I thought so, until I saw Moreau waving that gun at you.'

'So that was going to be the end of it?' How could he be still holding her in his arms and tell her that? 'You'd have protected anyone,' she said, tears spilling down her face. 'I know you would.'

'Yes, but that wasn't what I meant.' He took out his handkerchief and gently wiped her face. 'If he'd killed you, I wouldn't have wanted to go on living. I knew that then. The rest of my life suddenly emptied of meaning and,' his eyebrows rose, 'that's a huge sin, Jo.' His hands trailed down her back, moulding her to him. 'It's not about how attracted to you I am – although Heaven knows I am.' He pushed closer to prove it to her, and despite herself, she had to smile. 'It's about how much I love you. I'm not just talking about here and now.' His voice dropped to a whisper. 'I'm talking about eternity, Jo. If I give into this temptation, which is *sooo* strong right now, to rush you into that bed and rip your clothes off-'

'Mat!' she giggled.

'Then I'm not really loving you – not in the way you deserve. All I've actually done is satisfied my lust. And I want more for us than that, Jo. So much more.'

CHAPTER 71

June 1243
Paris

'*Most esteemed uncle*'...

Matthieu angled the letter nearer to the candle so that he could read Guillem's writing. He had been expecting this letter, dreading it even, ever since he heard the news that some Inquisitors had been murdered at Avignonet by '*faidits*' from Montségur.

'*You will, perhaps have heard of the terrible events that took place here at the end of last May*'...

Matthieu closed his eyes and the years peeled away. Brother Stephen panting into the refectory at Saint Gilles, his normally cheery face contorted with fear as he rushed to tell them that Pierre of Castelnau had been stabbed by one of Count Raimon's men, and was on the point of death. The murder of the Pope's Legate had precipitated the crusade in the South. What calamity would this episode of butchery provoke?

'*The murder took place in the house of Raimon of Alfaro, the bailiff of Avignonet. As you may remember, Alfaro is married to the Count's half-sister. The Inquisitors William Arnald and Stephen of Saint-Thibery, along with numerous others of their entourage, were hacked to death in their beds. Raimon of Alfaro had welcomed the men into his home but then, it is said, he sent for the faidits from Montségur. The Inquisitors' records all were taken. Rumour has it that they contained evidence against someone very important, mayhap even the Count.*'

'Mayhap even the Count'. Matthieu put down the letter. So it continued, the unholy allegiance between the Counts of Toulouse and the heretics. He dropped his head into his hands. The Pope had sent Dominican Inquisitors to root out the last of the heretics in the South; and now families were forced to testify against each other, neighbour against neighbour, old enemies saw it as a means of settling scores. Children were finding themselves destitute because their parents had been sent on lengthy pilgrimages, or thrown in jail. Matthieu's stomach roiled – and it was all done in the name of God.

'*Kind Uncle, I appeal to you as to one who has the listening ears of the Church. I know you have encouraged me, often, to come to you in Paris and for that hand of friendship, ever held out, I thank you most humbly.*'

Many times he had urged Guillem to come to Paris, but the answer had always been the same – '*I need to protect my mother*'. But just how did he hope to do that, especially if Raimondet was encouraging the heretic, as his father had?

'But now I must ask you to come south again, for I fear that Montségur will become the next destination for the Inquisitors. I beg of you, as your kinsman, to come to Toulouse with all haste, and to journey with me to that place to which the heretics cling with their last breath.'

Matthieu looked at his hand, it was trembling. How many years was it since he had last seen her?

CHAPTER 72

January 1542
London

Johanna held out the shirt so that she could see how the pattern was progressing. It was made of the finest linen she'd been able to find, and the embroidered leaves and citrus fruits on its collar and cuffs were cheery and neat. She sat with her ladies in her newly decorated solar, and their conversation had been bright, if a little forced, all morning. Putting a hand to her back, she massaged her spine.

'Are you all right?' Anne Basset said. 'Are you laced too tight?'

'A little,' Johanna said, and Anne put down the spaniel she'd been cuddling and came to help her loosen her bodice.

It was lovely to have Anne here, even if only for a short while. Too much had happened, too much affecting them both, and it was comforting to be together, well away from Henry's court...

She noticed that Anne was crying.

'Ladies,' she said, softly. 'Leave us, please.'

After they had gone, Johanna patted the cushion next to her.

'What is it, dear heart?' she said, taking the other's cold hands in hers.

Anne could not speak, and Johanna pulled her into her arms. In truth, she felt close to tears herself.

'It's just that she's so young,' Anne sobbed. 'One minute as happy as a child, and the next...'

'Hush,' Johanna said, in a whisper, afraid to speak openly even in her own homes.

Catharine Howard, Henry's fifth queen, had been found guilty of adultery. Francis Dereham and Tom Culpeper's heads were already decorating London bridge, and Jane Rochford, Anne Boleyn's vicious sister-in-law, ho had been accused of allowing the men into the new Queen's bedroom – was now in the Tower, raving and apparently out of her wits.

'Has he asked for you again?'

'Yes,' Anne said, 'the letter came for me this morning.'

'Oh, Anne.'

Johanna's heart went out to her friend. Anne had been lodging with her ever since Catharine Howard's ladies had been dismissed. She could not go home to her family for they had been thrown into disarray by the arrest and imprisonment of Lord Lisle, nearly two years ago – as if Arthur Plantagenet would ever have betrayed his nephew, the King!

‘I’ll have to go,’ Anne said, ‘for the sake of the Lord my step-father. I have to do all I can to persuade the King to pardon him.’ She twisted her handkerchief. ‘You know there’s no evidence against him, Johanna?’

Johanna nodded.

‘I think the King may have forgotten him,’ Anne continued, ‘since all his trouble with his queens.’

‘I’m sure he’ll be released soon, Anne,’ Johanna said. ‘At least, that’s what Sir John told me.’

Anne looked up at her. ‘You said nothing?’

‘I didn’t want to raise your hopes. I know how hard these last years have been for you.’

‘The King is turned into a monster,’ Anne hissed, her face blotchy. ‘I cannot bear to let him touch me again, Johanna.’

‘Hush,’ Johanna said, again, looking around nervously, even though she knew the room was empty.

‘But it’s true,’ Anne persisted. ‘Oh, Johanna, you don’t know how lucky you are to be here, safe with Sir John.’

*

Right up until the Princess of Cleves arrived, Cromwell had refused to let Matthew go – even though the Abbot of Glastonbury’s head had long since been impaled upon the gates of his Abbey.

And when Henry set eyes upon the Princess of Cleves and said he would not have her, the whole court was thrown into turmoil.

‘She’s frigid’, one said, ‘the King is impotent with her’.

Poor Queen Anne even threw off her dowdy German fashions and adopted the French hood, but still he was repulsed by her, and none could understand why. It was painful even to sit in her presence, so frightened were they for her future. The King had executed a woman he claimed to love above all others. What fate would befall a woman he so obviously despised?

*

Johanna had been sitting in the solar at Whitehall, when Sir John came in, sporting his usual cheery smile. Not a few of the ladies sat straighter and checked that their gowns showed them to best advantage, for he was wearing a very fine mauve silk doublet decorated with bands of purple velvet, and his white lawn shirt had the very latest frills at neck and wrists. He looked so dashing and handsome that, for a moment, Johanna failed to pay him any attention, convinced that he would have come for Anne, or one of the other fashionable young ladies at court: but it turned out that he had come for her, to escort her into the grounds.

‘Will you be comfortable there, Lady Johanna?’ Sir John asked, finding her a pleasant place to sit upon a stone bench, next to a little pool and fountain.

'Yes, thank you, Sir John,' she replied, both curious and nervous at the same time.

'Lady Johanna,' he began, clearing his throat. He did sound a little husky and she asked him if he was well.

'Quite well,' he said. 'Just a little hoarse from shouting for Thomas Culpeper's success in the Lists. We gentlemen of the Privy Chamber look out for each other.'

Johanna looked him fully in the face, searching for what he was about.

'Yes. I've heard he's an excellent horseman,' she said, forcing her smile to disguise the fact that she abhorred Thomas Culpeper, a man who thought nothing of the rape and murder of commoners.

'Lady Johanna-' Sir John coughed again.

'Yes, Sir John?' Her feeling of apprehension grew by the minute. Was this something to do with Matthew? Is that why he'd come?

'There's something I feel you should know.' He looked over his shoulder and she realised he was very nervous. 'Do you remember I escorted you once, to visit your friend in the Tower?'

Johanna nodded, feigning composure, but her heart had started thumping wildly. She was furious with Cromwell for not releasing Matthew as he promised, and all she had been given by way of an excuse was that 'there was still the matter of treason' to take into account. Neither the King nor Cromwell were the slightest bit interested in her pleas now, because the King's dislike of the Princess of Cleeves was nothing short of a constitutional disaster.

'I know you were hoping to have him set free and that Baron Crom- excuse me Lord Cromwell-'

She nodded to cover his mistake. Cromwell had risen even further and was now made the Earl of Essex – a peer of the realm at last.

'- had told you that Matthew would be released when the new Queen arrived?'

'Yes…' Johanna hid her fists in the folds of her gown.

'Well, I have to tell you my lady, that the gentleman in question is long gone. Months ago, in fact. I confirmed that myself when I was visiting Lord Lisle in the Tower.'

The shock reverberated within her. Matthew gone. Long gone? And she had not been allowed to say goodbye? Sir John put out his hand to comfort her and it was all she could do not to push it away, but she forced herself to swallow her pride and outrage.

'Thank you, Sir John,' she said, 'for telling me.'

'What will you do now?' he asked, watching a dove take flight, as if he had no real interest in her answer.

'Do?' she said.

'Yes. Are you still planning to become a nun? Will you go to France?'

‘I-’ She had no idea. All of her thoughts had been of holding on until Matthew was released, and now she was thrown into confusion. If he had gone, where had he gone, and how? Was he even alive?

‘Would you consider marrying me?’ Sir John said, setting off another avalanche of emotions. ‘I know I’m a poor match for the daughter of an earl, but I have the King’s friendship and can offer you much.’

‘Sir John?’ Johanna had been far too stunned by the news of Matthew to take in what he was saying.

‘Am I so much worse a suitor than your poor monk friend?’ he said, looking abashed. ‘I know you do not really regard me, but I had thought…’ He trailed off, and by a supreme effort Johanna managed to bring her scattered wits together.

‘Sir John, are you really asking me to marry you?’ she said, and when he nodded: ‘But how could you want *me*?’

‘Want you?’ he said, nonplussed. ‘How can you ask me that when every man at court is in love with you?’

*

Checking the nursery was the last thing she did, every night without fail – when she was allowed to be at home. Little Henry lay on his back, his blonde hair tousled and his face angelic in sleep. Beside him lay little Blanche, her breath escaping in sweet short ‘pops’ from between her perfect lips. How could she have ever thought she didn’t want children?

Smiling, Johanna tiptoed out. In her bedchamber she let her maid undress her and help her into her bedshift. Whilst her hair was combed out and rubbed with linen towels, she marvelled anew at her fortune. To have a husband as good and as loyal as Sir John, was truly fortunate. She smiled at her reflection whilst she dried her face and hands, then scrubbed at her teeth. Whilst the maid was drawing a warming pan over the bed, Johanna slipped on a robe and knocked briefly at the door to his bedchamber. He would not be long, for even though they had been married nearly two years, he was still attentive. She knelt to pray and soon heard him come in to the room and kneel beside her.

Sir John read from his prayer book, whilst Johanna recited the forbidden Rosary inside her head; five decades, and a different Mystery every night. Tonight she was starting on the Glorious Mysteries, the first being ‘The Resurrection’, and as she prayed, she felt her hopes resurrecting too. When she finally came to the last ‘Glory Be’, she added, as she had done every night since she last saw him, a prayer for Matthew’s safety.

CHAPTER 73

November
Station View, Wesley Village, Yorkshire

Jo sat alone in her sitting room, her lap top on the table before her. The reliquary and jewels were still suspended in legal limbo in France, but at least she and Mat had been allowed to return; although they would probably have to go back for the trial. Mat had gone straight to Rome, but she had stayed on for a few days, mainly to rebury Blanche's ashes and say goodbye to Jean-Yves and Rebecca.

She pressed the 'on' button and her lap-tap whirred into life. Her head throbbed from crying and her eyes were so swollen that she could barely see the screen, but she was determined. She couldn't put herself through this forever. Why couldn't she just meet someone who could reciprocate her love? It couldn't be that difficult.

She shook herself. The women she had learned about at Fontevraud Abbey, Joan Plantagenet and Eleanor of Aquitaine, their lives had been ones of dependence upon and obedience to men – and even though they had shown themselves to be spirited, they had paid dearly for it. Well, this was a different age, for goodness sake, one where women had just as many opportunities as men to fulfil their lives. *She* had a choice – a painful one perhaps – but it was *her* choice, none the less. She could wait patiently for any scraps of time that Mat might throw her way, or... she could find someone else.

Johanna opened up the Internet.

'I am... a woman, *seeking a...* man, *between the ages of...* twenty eight and forty.'

That ought to do it. She put in the rest of her details and was about to press enter when her phone started to ring. It was Mat.

'Hello,' she said.

'Jo, it's me. How are you?'

'Oh, you know...' She bit her lip. It wouldn't do to tell him how much she was missing him.

'I hope I haven't caught you in the middle of anything important it's just that...' As he hesitated, her smile twisted. If only he knew! 'They've called a Synod of the Bishops. Do you remember all those Italian women who said they were in love with priests and wrote to the Pope?'

Of course she did. Their pain was her own.

'Well, he's hoping for a reconciliation with the Orthodox Church, and celibacy is one of the stumbling blocks. *They* allow their priests to marry, do you see? I told you, didn't I, that priestly celibacy wasn't actual Church doctrine, just Canon Law? And because of that it can be changed. Jo? Are you still there?'

Was she? Could she bear to climb back on this roller-coaster again?

'I am,' she said. 'Carry on.'

'Well,' his voice hesitated, 'that's it, really. They're going to call a Synod and I know there's a lot of bishops out there who've been speaking to their parishioners. It's coming, Jo, it's got to.'

'But what about...' she said. 'What about your vows, and everything? You told me that when you became a priest, you felt that you'd married God. Changing the rules isn't going to make any difference that that, Mat. Is it?'

There was a long silence and she wished she hadn't said anything, just gone along with him. Dammit! But that *was* what he'd said.

'I know this might sound strange to you,' he said, quietly, 'and I don't want to keep quoting the Bible... but do you know the story of Abraham and Isaac?'

She thought for a bit and realised she probably did, but said, 'No, go on. Tell me.'

'God asked Abraham to sacrifice his only son, Isaac, so Abraham took his son onto a mountain and was prepared to slaughter him because God asked him to.'

'I don't think Social Services would accept that as justification,' she said, determined to inject a little humour. He sounded so serious, so passionate. In truth, she felt a little scared of what he might say next.

'Different days, Jo. But the point is, Abraham was willing to make that sacrifice because he trusted God to know best; though when it actually came to it, God sent an angel and told him not to do it. He let him off the hook.'

'Right...' She really wished she knew where this was going.

'So if God wants me to be celibate, Jo, then that's a sacrifice I'm willing to make. But if the Pope changes the rules, then God has a hand in that, too, don't you see? If they change, then I'm off the hook' – so to speak. Jo, loving you hasn't made the slightest bit of difference to my love for God. It's not like I can only love one of you properly. This is the answer, Jo – except, I hardly dare think about it – in case it doesn't happen.'

Jo sat quietly, the phone still in her hand and the dating site winking at her on her lap-top, but her thoughts were miles away. Could she, dare she, allow herself to hope again?

'Speak to me, Jo,' Mat said. 'Tell me what you think. What I really need to know now, more than anything, is... are you prepared to wait for me?'

CHAPTER 74

The Château of Montségur
March 1244

Joana squinted out over the stone parapet to the roofs of the houses below. They were clustered together tightly, clinging to the rock of the mountain: an eyrie for the faithful. She could see Matthieu and Guillem waiting further down the hill, of course, near to the palisade of stakes and pales. They had come to save her now the siege was nearly over. To save her from herself; as if the last thirty years of her life had been a mere aberration to be shrugged aside now it was time for her to die.

Guillem stood taller than Matthieu by a head, his dark, wavy hair contrasting vividly with the sparse silver tonsure of his father. They were haranguing Berengar, and it was clear that he was going to let them in. The Goodmen and women, who had been trapped inside for over nine months, had managed to buy for themselves two weeks before this final, absolute surrender. In those two weeks, all who wished to had received the *Consolamentum*. Others were leaving. They had been promised a full pardon if they recanted their beliefs, even those who had taken part in the murders at Avignonet; but for those who chose to stay, the faggots were already being heaped inside the palisade.

Matthieu must have bribed someone to get this far, Joana thought, as she angled her face up to the sun. Inside she felt as light as the air that gusted around her; but then they'd had so little to eat. Everything had been shared out and given to those who were leaving: wax, paper, grain, oil, salt, pepper. There wouldn't be anything left for the 'victors' to rejoice over. Everything of true value, mainly books, had gone over the walls one dark night some time ago. Bertrand Marty had seen to that. She looked down into the courtyard. There was a celebration taking place there, not of Easter's and its commemoration of new life coming into the world, but of severing of the ties that bound them to a life which was really a death.

Bertrand Marty had given the *Consolamentum* to the *faidits* who had murdered the Inquisitors at Avignonet, even though he had strongly counselled against them going. No good ever came of evil, he had said, and so it proved, for now the Goodmen and women were driven from their last refuge. And who would hold the Truth now, when they were all gone?

She swayed back as she saw Guillem looking up towards the battlements, not wanting him to see her yet. She was not ready quite yet, to meet him and his father. His father! Matthieu had filled her dreams, sleeping and waking for so many years, and he had given her away to save his soul, had denied his *love* for her to save his soul, had even turned his back on their son – to save his soul.

Aimeric's death had been the start of her awakening. Whilst she sat beside his poor, dead, bloated body all that night and most of the next day, Beatrice had thought her grief-stricken, and pleaded with her to call the priest, brought tasty morsels of food in an attempt to awaken her appetite, and generally did everything she could to help – but far from being grief-stricken, Joana was having an epiphany. As the candles spluttered their way to their roots, she had asked the questions over and over again until her head rang with the lack of answers. For as long as she could remember, she'd lived her life at another's pleasure. Why would God create humans only to watch them suffer – even his Son?

But still no answers came, and at last she realised that there could be no answer; not in anything she'd been brought up to believe. And if she couldn't get answers through her faith, what good was it? What good was anything: Church, state, marriage – except to bind humans so they had no choice?

For a long time she'd wondered what to do, but in the end it had been easy. Guillem would lose the manor, but Foix would take care of him – she'd earned him that at least. All she could hope was that one day Guillem would follow where she was going, and learn that what was needed was not land or possessions, but freedom and Truth.

She had gone to Fabrissa, and from her it had been a steady journey to the slopes of Montségur; but it was a journey she would never regret. Now she understood why happiness was never a possibility in this world, where everything was subject to disease and decay. But Spirit never decayed. Spirit was eternal. The only purpose in coming to Earth was to liberate others from the illusion of matter that corrupted, attracted, and enslaved. Detachment was the only protection from that illusion, the only way for a soul to be free to find its way back to Heaven.

The soldier who had been talking to Matthieu and Guillem turned around and came up towards to the main gate. She heard his booted feet on the stairs inside the walls, his steps tense and quick. His name was Berengar, and Joana had known him since he was a young boy because he was Aimeric's nephew. Thus it had gone in the South – kin turned against kin.

'Goodlady, your son and brother-in-law are asking for you,' he said, his eyes gentle, but his face was ingrained with worry and dirt. 'They want you to go with them to Toulouse. Won't you consider it?'

Joana took a deep breath and clasped her hands. 'Tell, them no. You know why.'

'But they don't believe me, Goodlady. You have to speak to them yourself.'

Panic took hold of her then, making it hard to breathe. If she saw them, touched them, spoke with them, the old ties would reach for her across the years, renewing the very bonds she had worked so hard to loosen.

'My mind is made up, Berengar,' she said, steadying herself against the wall. 'In some ways, death cannot come quickly enough.'

The stairs to the ground floor were steep and she took her time. Her bones ached from living so long on this draughty mountain and the hand that clutched the rail beside her looked suddenly old and wrinkled. Most of her teeth had long since fallen out, along with her hair. Joana gripped the rail fiercely. What would Matthieu think of her? Would he find any trace of her? Would he pity her the loss of her beauty?

How easily the mind played its old tricks, she thought. She would ask for this to be their last gift to her – letting her go. If only they could understand that what she needed was not help to live, but to die. Please God they would be gone away before she went into the fire.

She reached the last step. They were only feet away from her – her son and her lover. Berengar opened the gate.

CHAPTER 75

Pontigny Abbey, Burgundy

Matthew placed the candle on the table before him and knelt by the side of his bed. His room was almost devoid of furnishings: just a table, a wooden cot and a place to kneel. He slept in his habit, as did all the monks, so that they would always be ready for prayer.

As he picked up his Rosary beads, he composed his thoughts and let the silence of the Abbey enter his body. He had been at Pontigny for many years now. The longing for Glastonbury had faded, slowly at first, but now almost completely – along with all his other fears and yearnings. Tonight he was going to pray the Sorrowful Mysteries – from the Agony in the Garden to the Crucifixion – God's supreme sacrifice for man. All Matthew had ever wanted to do was to thank God for that sacrifice, and to offer his life in return.

When he came to the last 'Glory Be', he added, as he had done every night since he last saw them, a prayer for the Abbot – that peace be granted to his soul – and a prayer for Johanna – that God would forgive what she had done for his sake.

CHAPTER 76

The following year? Or so...
Saint Bernadette's Catholic church, Wesley Village, Yorkshire

With the words, '*take this ring as a sign of my love and fidelity, in the Name of the Father, and of the Son, and of the Holy Spirit,*' Mat slid a shiny golden band onto Jo's ring finger.

They were married! At long last! When the Nuptial Mass was over, Father Stephen invited Mat to kiss Jo, but to her dismay, he simply picked up her hand and brought it to his lips.

Then the panic really set in – although in truth it had been there ever since the day he'd asked her to marry him. She couldn't believe she'd put herself through all that instruction, sincerely undertaken to become a Catholic, and Mat still wasn't prepared to acknowledge his feelings for her in public.

Tears blinded her as they walked into the vestry to sign the register. She felt like turning and running away without him; but Mat was one of the first Catholic priests to be allowed to marry under the new rules, and there were at least half a dozen newspaper cameramen waiting outside.

What had she done? Was she going to be his wife in name only, an unnecessary appendage for a Catholic priest who'd managed fine without her so far? Perhaps he'd been celibate so long that he'd always feel embarrassed being with her, and never behave like a normal, loving man when they were near a church.

Mat gave her a keen look and Jo blinked furiously. If she wasn't careful, she was going to have her pre-wedding make-over smeared all over her face.

'What's the matter?' he whispered.

But she couldn't answer. Something large and unswallowable had stuck in her throat.

'Jo?'

'Stop looking at me!'

'Stop looking at you?' His mouth dropped open. 'I can't take my eyes off you. I'm the proudest man in the world today, you look so lovely.' He bit on his lower lip. 'Wait a minute.'

He pulled a white handkerchief out of his trouser pocket, sat Jo down with it in front of the register, and went to speak to Father Stephen and the witnesses who had gathered in the room.

'Please,' she heard him saying. 'I just need a bit of time with my wife. Can you go back into the church, just for a while?'

They all shuffled out, and Jo started to feel ridiculous.

'Please tell me what's wrong,' Mat said, coming to sit beside her. 'This is the happiest day of my life, but the woman I love is crying. Are you regretting marrying me already? Should we have waited a bit longer? I know it's been stressful...'

But all Jo could do was dab underneath her eyes to stop mascara running down her cheeks. Mat's face had folded in on itself. She'd never seen him look so haggard. Tentatively, he drew his forefinger down her cheek and brushed away her tears.

'Do you know something?' he said. 'I never believed this day could, or would, ever happen to me. All I want is what's good for you, and if you've changed your mind about marrying me, then I'll try to understand. I don't want you to have to do anything that makes you this unhappy – not ever.'

By now she could no longer stop the tears and they cascaded down her face.

'You did-didn't kiss me,' she sobbed.

'When?' he said, frowning.

'J-just then, in the church.'

'You mean... when I kissed your hand?'

'Y-yes...'

'And that upset you?' He was incredulous and got to his feet. 'Do you know something, I think you're right. Perhaps we should quit now.'

'What?' She looked up at him. Was he really going to give her up so easily?

' I thought kissing your hand like that was being gallant – like a knight in shining armour. I'm sorry Jo, perhaps this isn't a good idea after all. I'm not going to be much good at being a husband if I can get something that simple, so wrong.'

'I thought you were too embarrassed to kiss me properly.'

He stared at her, then dragged her from her seat and up into his arms.

'Mat, stop it,' she said, but he carried her back into the Church.

'Ladies and gentlemen, reverend fathers.' Mat looked from the perplexed congregation to the priests on the altar. 'I'd just like to do something again. Apparently I didn't get it right, the first time.'

Mat bent his head to kiss her, and suddenly a wonderful warmth filled Jo's body. As the sounds of the congregation cheering and clapping faded into the background, she finally, irrevocably, knew that everything was going to be all right.

'*Thank you Saint Thomas,*' she found herself thinking. '*Thank you for everything.*'

Glossary

Braies: men's underpants, usually made of linen.
Caparison: an ornamental covering for horses featuring the owner's heraldic devices.
Cité: city.
Codiniac: quince marmalade.
Consolamentum: unique sacrament of the Cathars.
Cross of Toulouse: the device on the coat of arms of the family of St. Gilles, Counts of Toulouse in the Middle Ages.
Crown (money): in Tudor times there were twelve pennies in a shilling, five shillings in a crown and four crowns in a pound. A typical labourer would earn 5-10 pounds per year.
Crucifix: an image of Jesus on a cross as distinct from a bare cross.
Destrier: a war horse.
Faidits: when the crusade in the Languedoc dispossessed members of the local nobility, some of them became outlaws and waged a guerilla style war against the invaders.
Gambeson: a padded jacket worn either alone and many layered, as armour, or underneath chain mail or plate armour.
Genet: a cat like nocturnal mammal. Member of the civet family.
Hauberk: a knee-length tunic or coat consisting of chain mail.
Jakes: the toilet.
Kirtle: woman's garment worn over the chemise or smock, and under the gown of a wealthy person.
The Lauragais: an area reaching from the south east of Toulouse, down towards the north west of Carcassonne.
The **Lists**: an area enclosed for a jousting contest.
Lute: stringed instrument, perhaps like an early guitar.
Manchet: bread made with white flour. Expensive.
Megrim: a migraine headache.
Mesnie: the household knights.
Moules: Mussels
Outremer: French for "overseas", was a general name given to the Crusader States established after the First Crusade.

Palfrey: a riding horse.
Posset: hot drink of milk curdled with wine or ale, often spiced.
Pottage: literally the contents of a pot. Usually a form of soup or porridge.
Quintain: used as training for jousting, where the competitor on horseback attempts to strike an object with his lance or other weapon. The object was usually a dummy person holding a shield and mounted on one arm of a swivel with sometimes a bag of sand on the other. If the dummy was struck true, the swivel would rotate quickly and the sand bag would knock the competitor off his horse, if he didn't get away quickly enough.
The **Song of Roland**: a heroic poem based on the Battle of Roncevaux in 778, during the reign of Charlemagne. It is the oldest surviving major work of French literature.
Shawms: an ancestor of the oboe. turned from a single piece of wood, and terminated in a flared bell somewhat like that of a trumpet. Came to Britain with the crusaders.
Virginals: keyboard instrument of harpsichord family.

Author's note:

The idea for writing this novel came to me whilst going to sleep one night after a visit to Glastonbury Abbey and the Tor. I had come across the story of how Richard Whiting, the last Abbot of Glastonbury had gone to his death, and wondered, as have many others, if he was guarding something from Henry VIII.

I also had a strong impression of a rather sweaty crusader knight whose name was Godfroi of Poitiers. Googling this name the following morning revealed that there had been a theologian of this name at the school of Theology in Paris in the 13th Century, far too early to be anything to do with Richard Whiting and definitely not a sweaty crusader. Further searching came up with a Geoffroi of Poitiers who was also alive in the 13th Century and had been, according to the 'Song of the Cathar Wars' by Janet Shirley, a tutor to the young Count of Toulouse at the time of the Cathar crusade. As spelling was rather fluid in those days, I decided to go with him, but changed his name to one that would translate better through time.

Weaving these people together has been great fun. I apologise in advance for any historical inaccuracies. If you find any, please let me know and I will make the changes accordingly.

If you enjoy the book, please leave me a review on Amazon and also let me have your email address so that I can let you know when my next book is available.

Its title is Kingfisher Silk (A Tale of Two Women), and it is set in the Tudor era after Henry VIII's death. It tells the story of those stormy years from the points of view of a very wealthy and a very ordinary woman, whose lives become entwined during the most remarkable of circumstances.

My email address is clarkemary60 at gmail dot com

24173089R00223

Printed in Poland
by Amazon Fulfillment
Poland Sp. z o.o., Wrocław